HIS LIPS WERE LIKE A COOL FIRE ROAMING OVER HER SKIN

Now, Mary. You are ready. You know the words, pull them from my mind and I will see you as you want to be seen.

Words rose in Mary's mind, vibrating between them intense and exciting, as the weight of pleasure pressed closer.

. . . and I will ride her thighs' white horses.

Now he was insatiable, devouring her with a perfect knowledge of her every want and need. And after five bouts of lovemaking, he turned to her once more, moving his mouth down to her right nipple.

Again? You are mine, Mary. Do you need me again?

And again Mary's lover lay on top of her, penetrating her with deep, steady strokes. She could feel all his violence and mystery surging within her, sweeping her up in a liquid dance of exquisite pleasure that was more than human. . . .

THE SELKIE

More Bestsellers from SIGNET

(0451)

- [ ] **TAR BABY** by Toni Morrison. (122240—$3.95)*
- [ ] **SONG OF SOLOMON** by Toni Morrison. (114469—$2.50)*
- [ ] **KINFLICKS** by Lisa Alther. (119851—$3.95)
- [ ] **ORIGINAL SINS** by Lisa Alther. (114485—$3.95)
- [ ] **THE BARFORTH WOMEN** by Brenda Jagger. (122275—$3.95)†
- [ ] **NIGHT SANCTUARY** by Monique Van Vooren. (120558—$3.95)*
- [ ] **HEADING WEST** by Doris Betts. (119134—$3.50)*
- [ ] **HEART CHANGE** by Lois Fried. (119169—$2.95)*
- [ ] **LOVELIFE** by Judith Searle. (118227—$2.95)*
- [ ] **SINS** by Judith Gould. (118596—$3.95)*
- [ ] **A WOMAN OF FORTUNE** by Will Holt. (111052—$3.50)*
- [ ] **WOMEN'S WORK** by Anne Tolstoi Wallach. (116100—$3.95)
- [ ] **ENTANGLED** by Paul Jason and Jeffrey Sager. (122267—$3.50)*
- [ ] **THE MEDUSA SYNDROME** by Ron Cutler. (120574—$2.95)*

*Prices slightly higher in Canada
†Not available in Canada

THE SELKIE

CHARLES SHEFFIELD
&
DAVID BISCHOFF

A SIGNET BOOK
NEW AMERICAN LIBRARY
TIMES MIRROR

PUBLISHER'S NOTE

This novel is a work of fiction. Names, characters, places, and incidents are either the product of the author's imagination or are used fictitiously, and any resemblance to actual persons, living or dead, events, or locales is entirely coincidental.

TO

PENNY WILSON

AND

RICHARD HUTTON

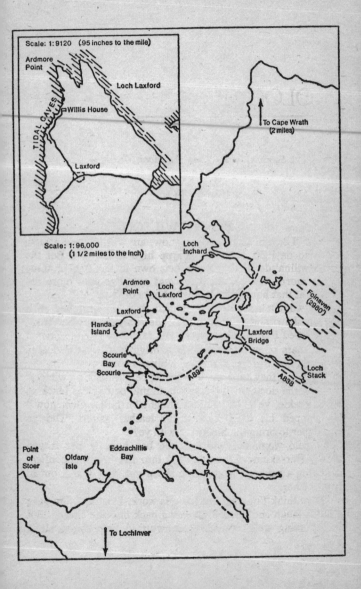

Scale: 1:9120 (95 inches to the mile)

Ardmore
Point

Loch Laxford

Willis House

TIDAL CAVES

Laxford

To Cape Wrath
(2 miles)

Scale: 1:96,000
(1 1/2 miles to the inch)

Loch
Inchard

Ardmore
Point

Loch
Laxford

Foinaven
(2980')

Laxford

Handa
Island

Laxford
Bridge

Scourie
Bay

Scourie

A894

A838

Loch
Stack

Point
of
Stoer

Oldany
Isle

Eddrachillis
Bay

To Lochinver

PROLOGUE

Some moment when the moon was blood,
Then surely I was born.

Scotland, 1786.

"You see, ye cannot tell it to the babies," said Dr. Murchison. "Leave it to me or you, now, an' we'd choose a birth in broad daylight, with the sun up high in the sky. But the babes willna' do it, they have their own ideas. Two or three in the morn, that's when they want out. I've seen more delivered at that hour than in all the hours of daylight."

The woman next to him nodded, her head muffled with woolen shawl and bonnet against the sharp November frost. She seemed too tired to speak. The face beneath the bonnet was a mass of wrinkles around a bright pair of faded blue eyes, and her expression showed a bitter stoicism.

"Aye, an' they take no mind if it be summer or winter," went on the doctor. "Summer moonshine or frost as black as Auld Reekie, ye'll find these midnight birthings. Och, now." He slapped his hand against his leather gaiter. "Did ye remember to bring the birthwort with ye?"

The old woman delved into the bag beneath her frayed shawl. Her skinny hand emerged into the bright moonlight clutching a package wrapped in sheep gut. She held it out in front of her.

"D'ye think I'm a novice for this work, Doctor?" She gave a harsh laugh and ducked her hand back into the shawl. "But I'm thinking we'll not need birthwort to help things along

1

tonight. Annie Macveagh will have no trouble that way, not with the haunches on that lassie."

"Then I should be home in ma bed." The doctor sounded as good humored as ever as the trap bucked and quivered its way along the coast road. "So why did you drag me out, Maggie, if we're not looking to see a breech baby?"

"Annie's a Macveagh, ye know that." The old woman's voice rejected his good humor. "An' she's in childbed, with no sign of a father. Ye know what that means."

"Ah, Maggie." The doctor sighed and shook the reins. "There we go again, the old wives' tales. The old nonsense. I'm tellin' you, Annie Macveagh'll give birth to a fine, healthy bastard—an' as for the father, it could be any rantipole tinker between here and Lochinver."

The old woman sat bolt upright, her mouth pinched to a stubborn line. She shook her head.

"My father saw it, with his own eyes. Forty years back, a year after the Rebellion, when a' the poor lads were comin' back from Culloden. That time it was Janie Macveagh, heavy with a young 'un, waitin' by the church but wouldna' go inside. An' then the birth . . ."

"And who told you that?" said Murchison. He held firmly to his cheerful tone. "Your father wasn't one for talking."

She turned to face him, her mouth and sharp chin clear in the moonlight. "He wasn't one for talking. But he saw it, an' I heard it from his own lips."

Her voice was shaking.

"Ah, but that was right after the Rebellion, Maggie, an' a terrible bad time for every man." Murchison's tone was mild. An upset midwife was the wrong choice for any delivery.

They drove on in silence toward the lonely house near the head of the cliff. Big and sturdily built, it was braced by turrets at each end looking westward to the sea. From the parapets on a fine day, a keen eye might see clear across the channel of the Minch to catch the faint gray green line of Lewis Island and the Hebrides forty miles to the west.

As they approached the house a dark figure moved from the moon-shadowed front and advanced toward them. Murchison handed down the reins and swung stiffly off the wooden seat.

"We are in good time? She has not delivered?" His voice was more formal than it had been in the carriage—he had

2

few secrets from Maggie Robson. They had shared too many midnight rides, sad and happy.

"Aye. In time." Robert Macveagh without another word led the horse away to the back of the house.

"Come on," said Maggie. "He's reliable, but ye'll get no small talk out of Robbie."

The oak door, stiff on its hinges, resisted her efforts. Murchison moved to her side and leaned against the wood. It creaked reluctantly open. The staircase, worn and uncarpeted, ascended directly from the entrance hall. The ground floor was deserted, lit by a single oil lamp at the foot of the stairs.

"Not here," said Maggie. "She'll be on up, in the big bedroom."

She led the way, one thin hand on the banister and the other clutching her old leather case with its supply of dressings and potions. Dr. Murchison followed her cautiously into the darkness. As he reached the top of the stairs he heard Robert Macveagh enter the house through the kitchen door. He stood until the other man came into the entrance hall.

"Wait here, Robbie. There's things as'll need doing later."

"I'll be here."

Macveagh watched as Murchison went on up into the big bedroom. *Now all was in the hands of God.* He bent his head and mumbled a prayer. That was how Beth had been lost, in a birth twenty years ago.

Who was the father? He'd done all a good parent could, beating Annie until she was black and blue and he feared for the life inside her. She said not a word. She wore the bruises on her arms and shoulders proudly to the village, making her shame his shame. And still no one could tell whose child she carried.

Macveagh looked up. There were muted voices above, the creaking of floorboards. How long would this vigil be? No matter, it could never be as long as months that had come before it. Robbie was no stranger to waiting. He sat motionless, staring into the red heart of the burning peat fire.

In the bedroom another hearty fire glowed, filling the room with a smoky and ruddy light. After the clear chill of the November night the air felt damp, heavy, as though the oxygen had been bled away from it. Maggie had loosened her

3

scarf and walked to the side of the bed that stood against the far wall. She placed her hand on Annie Macveagh's cheek.

"Ye'll be fine, my lass." Her voice was gentle. "The waters havna' broken yet, have they?"

Annie shook her head. She was fair haired, with a smooth forehead and a creamy, unblemished complexion. Her neck showed well muscled and graceful as she lay, knees raised and legs straggled wide. Her shapely, powerful arms lay clear of the rough wool blanket and showed big hands curled into tight fists on the cover. As Dr. Murchison walked forward and lifted the blanket she made a weak attempt to close her legs and cover herself with her hands. Maggie moved to her side.

"Lie soft. The Doctor's not lookin' at ye that way—he's seen ten thousand like ye." She took the girl's hand. "Wait for the cramp, an' push with it."

At the midwife's soothing tone, Annie lay back and let her hands fall to her sides. Murchison placed a practiced hand on her swollen belly, measuring the pelvic arch with his eye. He nodded to Maggie and smiled down at his patient.

"Ye'll be fine, Annie. Has the baby been kicking hard tonight?"

"Aye, an' last night." The girl winced with the pain of another contraction. "He's been restless, 'tis the full moon." She smiled. "I can't wait to see an' hold him."

"Him or her, Annie."

"No, 'tis a boy." Her face glowed with happiness. "I can feel that inside of me like a promise."

Murchison nodded, familiar with a mother's proclamation. He bent to pick up his case of instruments from the bedside.

"We'll have no need of these, Maggie. Things couldn't be better. You see to her, an' I'll be off downstairs and make sure we've hot water."

"Aye." The midwife was suddenly more relaxed. "Now it's women's work. Go on down an' enjoy a dram with Robbie."

As Murchison carried his instruments from the room, Maggie lifted the blanket again from Annie's body. It was good to see *those* gone. They were necessary for difficult births, she knew that, but every woman carried a dread of the curettes, the scalpels, and the terrible wooden forceps. She settled herself by the bedside.

Murchison found the silent form of Robbie in the chimney

4

corner, hands cupped around a full glass. Robbie nodded at the request for hot water, placed his glass on the mantelpiece, and walked through to the kitchen. His thoughts were hidden behind that dark, iron face. If he had worries over his daughter's confinement, there would be no sharing of them with strangers.

Fifteen minutes after the water had been carried up there was a faint, piping cry from above. Murchison lifted his glass to the other man.

"Here's to the first grandchild."

Macveagh shook his head. "God grant 'tis a wee girl," he said at last. "An' grant that Annie is all right. I'll drink with ye to that."

While Macveagh stared into the fire and the doctor tossed back his dram, there was a creak at the head of the stairs. Maggie Robson stood there, her face a pale blur in the darkness.

"Dr. Murchison." Her voice came down to them like stone, flat and lifeless. "Come up now. An' bring the instruments with ye."

Murchison put his glass on the table and went up the stairs two at a time. Maggie had opened the big window that looked out onto the sea, and a faint, aromatic breeze rippled the light curtain. Murchison wrinkled his nose, trying to identify the unfamiliar smell. It was a musky fragrance mixed with salt and seaweed. He moved to the bedside.

Annie lay amid the rumpled blankets, a small form huddled against her breast. Already it was at her teat, blindly seeking milk. Murchison moved closer.

"What's happening, Maggie? The babe can't be feeding already . . ."

The old woman's eyes were wild. "I had hoped . . . I prayed that father was wrong, that we wouldn't find . . ."

As Murchison leaned forward, his instrument bag fell heavily to the floor. The room was silent except for the sucking of small lips on Annie's heavy teat.

When the thump sounded, Robbie Macveagh turned his dark head and looked up. There was a heavy clatter of footsteps above his head. He heard the sob of anguish from his daughter, a startled curse from the doctor, and a damp rip-

5

ping sound. Then there was silence. He closed his eyes and leaned his head against the wooden chair back.

Murchison's footsteps were on the stairs. He came to the back room and stood there, instrument case in hand. In the firelight his face was pasty and granular, all color drained from it. He put one hand on the door jamb to steady himself.

"I'm sorry, Robbie Macveagh. I had to—it was no use. 'Twas a stillborn." His voice had reverted to the strong accent of his childhood. "We couldna' help the baby . . . an' Annie's all right, she'll be all right . . ."

"Was it a lassie, Doctor? If it'd been a lassie . . ."

Murchison shook his head. He walked forward, poured a full glass of whisky and drained it in one gulp. Macveagh's gaze fixed on the cuff of the doctor's right sleeve. It was wet with a dark-red stain that was spreading slowly up the heavy cloth. Murchison put down his glass and turned quickly to the door.

"Maggie will be done up there in a minute. Go and comfort your daughter. I'll arrange for the burial in the morning, over in Laxford."

Macveagh followed him as he blundered out of the house. The night wind carried that strange scent into the house, the musky perfume with its underlying hint of aromatic oils.

"An' the burial, Doctor? In consecrated ground, will it be, for the little 'un?"

"Hush now, Robbie." The voice came from behind him. Maggie Robson stood there, leather case in one hand and a blood-stained bundle in the other. "Don't bother the doctor. I'll do all I can for the burial—as for a stillborn. Ye go on up an' see Annie. I'll be on by in the morning."

She walked past him. Unlike Murchison, she seemed to have gained in strength and stature in the past hour. She patted Robbie Macveagh on the shoulder.

"Take a dram on up with ye. Mebbe Annie can use it, an' ye can for sure. Get inside with ye."

She closed the door. Robbie stood for a full minute, silent. Head down, he at last began to climb the stairs to his daughter's bedroom.

Scotland, 1976.

He laughed, and laid down the pen.

6

Finished, by God! There were details to be filled in, and everything had to be organized, but that would be easy.

Patrick Knowlton stood up from the desk. *Finished.* Over the past year, he had seen a seed of a suspicion and an interest in old legends swell (to his own amazement) to something that would knock modern science back on its heels. He had taken it, the chaos of bits and pieces of facts and legends in the Scottish Northwest, and structured a tightly logical whole. And he could prove it!

Knowlton poured another whisky. Forget that he'd have a hangover at the meeting tomorrow. Looking at sites for a nuclear power plant was nothing now. He went back to his desk and pulled the notes and papers to a tidier pile. Then everything went back into the wardrobe, beside the heap of old magazines and Sunday supplements, the only legacy from the previous occupant of the old house.

Two minutes more and he was on his way, with a promise to bring back a couple of pints for the housekeeper—little enough to repay her for the endless store of local legends she had passed on to him. Her brain seemed to be a complete store for the collective unconscious of Laxford; the cliffs, the tidal caves, and the dour Scottish setting.

"Evening, Mr. Knowlton."

The voice came as he was about to turn the ignition key in the blue Mini—one of the few perks that JosCo had provided him. He jerked nervously to look out of the open window, at the same time feeling behind him under the seat for the tire jack.

"God, you startled me there." His voice was quivering in spite of his attempts at control. "What are you doing here at this hour?"

The man beside the car was young, pleasant-featured and strongly built. He wore a leather jacket and tight jeans.

"I was working round the side," he said. "I stayed late to fix that window sash. I was wondering if you might be going to the village?—save me a walk."

"Hop in." Knowlton unlocked the left-side door. "I'm going to the Over The Water."

"Me too. Meeting a couple of youth hostelers from your part of the country—from Bristol. Would you like to meet 'em? I've been wondering what to do, there's two girls and I

7

don't see how I could take one of them for a stroll without the other."

"Let me see them first." Patrick Knowlton wasn't the man to remove an unattractive woman to leave the field clear for somebody else. He released the hand brake and headed down the lane toward the village.

"All right. Don't blame you, but they're both beauties—looking for fun, too."

That's what I need tonight.

"I'll be glad to see somebody from down South. The women here are all locked up too tight."

"There's ways." His companion grinned. "I was down on the beach this morning with Maggie Doan. There's a nice one for you."

"Margaret Doan?" Knowlton leaned back, relaxing. "I'm surprised by that."

"Well, it wasn't the way I'd hoped. We found this dead thing on the beach, it put her right off. I thought mebbe it was a walrus. You ever see a walrus?"

Patrick Knowlton took his foot off the accelerator. "Yeah. I didn't think walruses . . ."

"Well, I don't *know* it was a walrus. But it was all oozy and smelly."

"Where was this?"

"On the beach." He pointed out of the car to the right. "Just past here, where the road comes close to the cliff."

"Do you think you could find it again? I'd like to take a look before the tide washes it away. You know, my job here—the Ministry likes us to keep an eye on the animal life."

"*Now?* What about Elsie and Janice? They won't wait forever."

"But they'll wait a few minutes, won't they?" Knowlton stopped the car.

"Sure." A sniff of wounded pride. "But the other lads'll be after 'em."

"Five minutes. That's all it'll take." Knowlton rummaged in the back seat for the Leica with the flash attachment. "There's a path down, right?"

"Aye." They climbed out of the car. "Christ, it's cold here." The young man pulled out a hip flask and unscrewed the top. "Here's a quick one."

8

Knowlton took the flask and swigged at it. *Have to be careful.* No good to be half-pissed when he took the pictures. "Think we'll see it from the cliff?"

"Maybe. There's not much of a moon. Let's take a look."

He led the way to the top of the cliff. Knowlton followed, a little uneasy. He didn't like these cliffs, or the beach beneath, but for a picture (or maybe even a body sample—the ultimate proof!) it would be worth it.

He put the strap of the camera around his neck to leave his hands free. Past a last clump of heather the edge of the cliff became pure rock, coated with moss and lichen. There was a faint mist on the shore, and the sea damp drove the night's cold deeper into his body. He knelt at the cliff edge and craned his neck. There was nothing but stone, sand, water, and faint swirls of tide-borne phosphorescence.

"Are you sure it was around here?"

"Yes. Keep looking. But the more I think of it, the more I'm sure it must have been a walrus."

"Why do you say that?"

He was not sure he heard the reply. Perhaps it was imagined, a voice conjured from the night wind and the breakers far below. *"Because, Mr. Knowlton,"* it said, *"we do not die."*

There was a sudden violent force at his back. He scrabbled for a hold on the edge, failed to find one, and fell forward. He seemed to drop forever. A jutting outcrop tore his jacket and broke his arm, spinning him over in the air. He felt the pain, the rush of cold sea air. Before he could scream he had impacted with terrible violence against the steep cliff face. He bounced, tumbled down and down, unable to believe the jolts of agony. He had lost consciousness before he reached the stony beach.

He awoke with the taste of blood and brine in his mouth and the chill of the sea on his face. As he opened his eyes he saw a wave retreating from him, like the pseudopod of some great, gray beast. He gasped out water and tried to move. Bone edges grated in his legs, and he gasped again. New agonies swirled through him from broken ribs.

He set his teeth and tried to turn, away from the sea. The tide was rising, lapping higher up the beach.

A fool. He'd been an absolute fool. The moment that the evidence was in his hands he should have fled, that same hour. Back inland, as far as he could go, away from this

9

shore and back to London. Now it was too late. He made another attempt to pull himself around, to begin the crawl up the beach, but he could not master the pain.

"Here, Mr. Knowlton." Someone was there beside him. "Drink this. It will make things easier."

His head was lifted. The top of a flask jammed into his mouth, past his teeth. He swallowed and swallowed, unable to breathe. The fiery fumes of the whiskey filled his mind, dimming the pain of broken bones. When the flask was removed he lay flat on the sand, coughing feebly.

"And now let's move you to a comfortable position," said the voice beside him.

There was a sharper agony as he was picked up and dragged, legs trailing, along the beach. He was lifted, then wedged sharply between two rocks. They squeezed his broken ribs, pushing the ends together. He lay, head down, until another wave broke over him. It tugged harshly at his legs. As it retreated he forced his head up, gasping and spluttering. He blinked his eyes, feeling the salt water and the sand under his eyelids.

The next wave was coming.

He was a dead man. He willed himself dead, now, away from the cold and the pain. His body would not comply. He began to weep.

When he lifted his head again he saw a vague figure in front of him, walking out into the sea. A watery nimbus of phosphorescence swarmed about its outline. In the faint light of the moon, its skin seemed to shine with a silvery white coat.

Knowlton watched until the form had disappeared into the moving waters. Then he let his head fall forward again to the sand. He was well below high-water mark, and the tide would rise for another two hours.

When the next wave came he resolved that he would not lift his head. He would breathe the cold northern waters and end it at once.

If he could. Even in his pain, he knew that some small part of him would fight for air, would make him struggle past all reason. He would lift his head against the agony of broken bones, again and again, until he could not strain high enough to get his nose and mouth above the water. Then, at last, he would have the blessed agony of release.

CHAPTER 1

"The Shiant or 'Charmed' Isles which lie in the Minch, the channel dividing the Outer Hebrides from the mainland, are surrounded by turbulent seas churned by storm kelpies known as the Blue Men of the Minch. Their glossy blue figures and grey, bearded faces bob in the waves between the Shiant Isles and Lewis, a tideway called in Gaelic 'Sruth nam Fear Gorma'—Stream of the Blue Men. There they attack any vessel whose skipper cannot answer their riddles. Afraid of being lured to their doom in the blue men's undersea caves, the Hebridean fishermen avoid the stream."

—*Folklore Myths and Legends of Britain*

Manhattan, 1979.

Propped outside the rusty railing of the old brownstone, Mary skimmed through the letter. Don's staccato scrawl made it hard work. A thorough read would have to wait until she was on the subway—and if she didn't leave now she'd *never* make that luncheon appointment on time.

She hurried to the station and down the worn steps. The fall day was unseasonably warm, as though Manhattan was reluctant to surrender its stored summer heat. By the time the train screeched up to the platform, Mary was holding her sweater in one hand and Don's letter and the battered manila folder in the other. She regretted the woolen dress—and why had she brought the sweater? Manhattan was a city of small choices, and she generally managed to make the wrong ones.

11

As the train lurched into motion she opened Don's letter again, ignoring the admiring look from the bearded man opposite her. He looked ready to start a conversation, but she wouldn't raise her eyes. She knew the probabilities. About one man in ten was strongly attracted by her large-framed figure and pale complexion. One in fifty would find her fascinating to pursue regardless of her interest, and for one in two hundred the feeling would be mutual. She had already noted the portfolio he was carrying under his arm, and she could imagine the line he would take. Sculptor in the Village, just the model he needed for his next piece . . . would she be interested? Then the admiring sighs, the enthusiastic sketch, the suggestion that it should be a nude study. . . .

She fixed her attention firmly on Don's letter.

Well, sweetie, don't hold your breath but it looks as though that hundred-to-one shot may come off. Remember what I said about Lord Jericho? He sold me on the project, now I think he's going to sell the people at the Electricity Board. We had the "best-and-final offers" session for bidding the day before yesterday, and Jericho went in to talk to all the stuffed shirts. He's not their type at all—even I can tell his accent's different from theirs —but when he came out he was grinning all over his face.

I'm beginning to get the feel for Jericho now. "Don't bet against *him* in a poker game," Roger Wilson told me a couple of days ago. "Or you'll lose your arse and hat."

I believe it.

Last time I talked to you on the phone we were still sweating over the changes to our bid. That was bad, not what I expected England to be like at all. Three days shut up in that shitty hotel near Hampton Court, with no ice and Crusades-style plumbing.

We finished up at two o'clock Wednesday morning, and before I could catch my breath Roger Wilson had me out of the hotel and in a cab heading for Kings Cross Station. We caught the first train to Edinburgh. Lord Jericho had pulled a string somewhere, and we were getting a private tour of Dounreay. You won't find that on a map; it's a nuclear installation up at the very top right hand corner of Scotland. Hell to get there, too, even with a good car—the roads sort of fade away north of Inverness.

The trip was mostly a blur, dozing in a first-class compartment. I nearly lost Roger when he got out to look for a newspaper at Doncaster Station, but he jumped back on board at the last second. He didn't turn a hair, said he wanted to see yesterday's racing results. Farther up north we slowed down and nearly stopped, and

I saw a man leaning on a fence by the tracks, looking in at us. I looked right back at him, and I thought, "There's one to show Mary." He seemed to prove your ideas about inbreeding, he had a big pudding face, a flat cap, and a vacant look. He didn't seem to be doing anything but chewing on a stalk of grass. I pointed him out to Roger, and he laughed to bust a gut.

"That's the stationmaster, Don," he said. "His paper qualifications are probably better than mine."

It isn't true, but you'll have to get used to that style of talk over here. Roger's highly qualified, but its like an inverse snobbishness, where we would boast about our high quality training the English like you to think they did it all by pure genius.

Edinburgh was our last stop, and we—

Mary, subconsciously cued by the word "stop," looked up. Fifty-third Street! She skipped out through the closing doors, hustled up the steps and out on the street. Her long strides cut a quick path through the luncheon crowds. A frowning youth handing out color pamphlets for a massage parlor almost made her pause—she was tempted to take one, just to see his expression. It was one of the city's harmless pleasures, perplexing street people.

No time for that right now. She crossed Third Avenue against the light, risking an accident and displaying her newly won New York indifference to a cabbie's shouted curse. The stone and steel towers and faceless crowds would crush you flat if you let 'em. Defiance meant dignity and self-respect.

She opened the stained oak door to the restaurant. Paul Revere's was Ellie's choice because of its large portions of meat, though as often as not she finished up ordering a chef's salad.

Where was she anyway?

"Mary! Over here." A voice called from a shadowed corner. Already the Maître d' was nodding curtly, gesturing Mary to her place so he could go back for the next customer.

The inside of the restaurant was pleasantly cool. Mary flopped her sweater over the back of the spare chair and sat down opposite Ellie.

"Sorry I'm late. I missed my stop."

"No problem, I just got here. The late Ms. Willis? Let me introduce the dead Ms. Durning."

"Bad morning?" Mary placed the manila folder on the table in front of her.

13

"Just awful. Remember I told you about *Dreamland*? We had an editorial meeting, and the shit finally hit the fan. They yanked the graphics—that's an extra month right there, if we're *lucky* and everything else hits on schedule. Blocker was foaming." Ellie picked up her wine and took a healthy gulp. "Who'd be an editor? *Publishers Weekly* says the paperback market's going soft, but I think it's the heads of the publishers."

"Last year was good." Mary felt obliged to provide the ritual optimism. "It's not fair to compare this year with last—there had to be a falloff."

"Tell that to Blocker. He expects sales to rocket on to infinity. Oh, shit, who cares? I do my best, good year or bad. Let him do the worrying, that's what he's paid for." She leaned over and tapped the folder. "Is that *The Blackstone Legacy*? Let's have a look."

She held the typed page close to the candle. "*She had to choose the castle or the man . . . and one of them wanted to kill her!* Not bad. It'll do. I read it again, and by the end I wished one of them *would* kill her. But this is OK; these books are a sure thing; they always do well."

"Could I do something else? Anything, westerns, thrillers, you name it. I'm a bit tired of Gothics." Mary leaned back as her glass of white wine arrived. The hidden light above the table shone on her pale hair.

"Problems, Mary?" Ellie was looking at her shrewdly. "What's wrong, Don again? I thought he was off across the Atlantic solving the European energy crisis."

Mary pulled Don's letter from her folder. "I'm halfway through this; it came this morning. Nothing bad so far, but I'm dreading every paragraph. Want to read over my shoulder?"

Ellie nodded. Her waspish expression had disappeared. If Mary had a friend in New York, it had to be Ellie Durning. Funny how a woman who worked so hard at the no-nonsense, hard-as-nails image could be so steady and sympathetic when it was needed.

Mary passed the first two pages across the table.

A nice drive, but they say its hell when the bad weather comes a month or two from now. We got to Dounreay late Wednesday night. I was tired out and went straight to bed. Thursday was

14

meetings all day, doing reactor core calculations. If we get the Laxford job I'll be able to use a lot of that, it's a thousand megawatt station.

About three in the afternoon we piled back in the car and set off for Laxford. We took the north road, and it was dark by four. In mid-December it must be dark almost the whole damn time. We're only a few degrees south of the Arctic Circle here, like being up the north end of Labrador. The trip was a pain. Roger fell asleep (he's about the best eater and sleeper I've ever met), and the driver's the model of a taciturn Scot. Six words from him, and he thinks he's treated you to a speech.

"Nice day," he said when we stopped for petrol. It was drizzling, but he meant it. God knows what he would describe as bad weather. I tried some light conversation on him, and it went down like a lead balloon. Roger warned me not to try jokes when I told him about it.

"Don't look for a sense of humor in a Highland Scot," he said. "It's not consistent with the climate or the history."

I thought he was joking, but on Friday noon it began to drizzle again, and there's no forecast for it stopping. Gloomy country. You'll love it here, you and your rain-poems. And it's freezing cold, just the way you like it. There has to be a lot of truth in what Roger says about the effects of climate on temperament.

Somehow or other the word seems to have got around in Laxford that we're here for something connected with a new power plant. That's supposed to be a big secret even down in London, with the final choice of site not made yet. But the locals have got hold of the rumors. We were down in the pub last night, relaxing a bit, and the landlord came over to buy us one on the house and sound us out.

Remember my Uncle Bill? That's the landlord, Hamish Macveagh. He has the same bald head and big red nose, and he's got that alert look, like a bantam rooster. His pub's called the Over The Water, and it has something to do with Bonnie Prince Charlie. He explained all that to me, and I still don't understand it.

Anyway, after a lot of hemming and hawing he finally asked us what we were doing in Laxford.

We'd been briefed by Lord Jericho before we left London, because he thought we might get questions. Roger trotted out the party line. We're consultants to the Department of Environment, checking the patterns of pollution that come up the coast of Scotland with the Gulf Stream and affect the west coast fishing. He said it all very well (he's a damned good liar), and Hamish Macveagh stood there and nodded his head politely.

"Aye, there's pollution offshore, no doot of that," he said when Roger had finished. "Mind you, it might be a good deal worse if

15

there were a big nuclear (he pronounced it noo-ker-leer) power station up on yon headland."

Dead silence.

It's a good thing Roger was there, or I might have put my foot in it. He just stared at Macveagh as though that were an interesting new thought; then he said, "Don't talk like that, man. They have enough trouble at Environment with this part of the country, just from the oil drilling and the tourists. We get letters all the time about the changes in migrant bird life."

That shut Macveagh up, even if it didn't really satisfy him. I noticed he was watching us for the rest of the night, even when he was serving other customers. Afterward I asked Roger where he learned to lie so well. He says it's part of the private school education over here; if you can't lie fast and smooth you get wiped out in the first few months. We'd had a long day, so we left the bar before closing time.

Ellie laid down the page as the waitress appeared at their table. She stared at Mary for a moment, rubbed at her unruly dark hair, and picked up the menu.

"Well?" said Mary, as soon as they had ordered and the waitress had gone.

"Unsettling." Ellie shrugged and lit a cigarette, holding it in delicate tobacco-stained fingers that trembled just a little. Talk was usually her shield, her defense against a tough business that had provided two husbands and twenty affairs in eight years. Now she seemed reluctant to talk. Mary sensed that another readjustment in the Mary-Ellie relationship was taking place.

When they had first met, four years earlier, Mary had just moved with Don from Iowa. At a party, thrown by one of Don's engineering cronies to celebrate a job in California working on earthquake-proof building design, they had been delighted to find each other. Here was another person who would rather talk about books than stress-strain relations and moments of I beams. She and Ellie had found a quiet corner, and Mary's education had begun. A major in English at a Midwestern school had no relevance to New York publishing.

Ellie had been retrieved by her disgruntled date, three hours later. He was an off-Broadway actor with literary pretensions who hoped that Ellie would buy his novel in return for his affections. Ellie had told Mary that she had read the book, and the trade-off wasn't worth it.

16

"Not even Casanova would be enough to justify inflicting that piece of garbage on the public," she said, as she was dragged off to dinner. "I'll tell him the bad news tonight. Here's my card—call me tomorrow and we'll have lunch."

As simple as that. At the first lunch, Ellie had unloaded four book manuscripts and asked her to read them.

"Fifteen dollars each for a careful read-through and a one-page summary of how bad it is. Interested?"

"Well, sure. But I've never published a word of my own. All my stories have been rejected by the publishers."

"You don't need to play the fiddle like Heifetz to know that the guy next door sounds like a cat on the roof." Ellie pushed the box of manuscripts across the table. "Here. Don't lose them, that's all I ask. Some authors don't keep a copy, and they play hell when we even spill coffee on their masterpiece."

"How bad are these? Do you think they'll be good enough to buy?"

"Mary, dear, that's what *you're* going to tell *me*. I don't have too much hope, you've got the real slushpile there. But who knows? Perhaps you've got *The Thorn Birds* in that heap. Give it a try."

Mary had moved gradually from slushpile reader to cover-copy writer. Their relationship had matured, even somehow surviving Ellie's brief affair with Don when Mary had moved out on him after a messy domestic quarrel. Now Mary was relying more on Ellie's evaluation of Don's letter than on her own premonitions. It was as though they were looking at a literary work together, Mary giving an opinion but Ellie having the final say.

"So what do you think of it?" she said at last.

Ellie gave her a quick look from dark, long-lashed eyes and put down her bread stick. She placed her elbows on the table and cupped her chin in her hands. "All right. Let's be honest. Reading between the lines, Don hasn't cured his problem. He's making that English job sound like a big opportunity, instead of a last hope. And there's one comment in there that ought to make you a lot madder than it did me."

"About me liking Scotland because it's cold, and the relation between climate and temperament? I wondered if I was reading something in that wasn't there."

17

"It's there. And he's drinking again, no doubt of that. Do they know his history over there?"

"God, Ellie, I hope not. It's sure as hell not on his resume, and the official reason he left TAMS was medical."

"Yeah. But when somebody leaves Ammann and Whitney, and Parsons, and Bechtel, and TAMS, all for medical reasons, he'd better have a good explanation ready as to why he's not dead." She leaned over and patted Mary's hand. "Sorry. That's the sort of crack I ought to keep for the office. I like Don, you know that. He's in a tough situation. If they don't know he's had a problem they'll be putting him into setups where he has to drink to be sociable."

"That's what I'm afraid of. I wonder if I'm part of his problem. Do you think we need a marriage counselor or something? I'm not the sexiest woman in Manhattan. It's terrible to say this, Ellie, but I don't even miss it."

"That's just as well, with Don three thousand miles away." Ellie suddenly put down her fork. "Look, by the sound of it you'll be on your way over to Scotland in a couple more weeks. I've got a suggestion for you."

"About Don?"

"No. This is something that might stop you brooding over him. You've read enough romantic suspense stories to know the plot by heart. North of Scotland, romantic setting, lonely American girl, mysterious strangers, scary old house. Can't you see it? So write me a book while you're there. I was going to ask for letters but this would be better."

Mary bit her lip. She lowered her wine glass and shook her head. "It sounds a marvelous opportunity. But you've read my stuff. Remember what you said about it?"

"No story? God, you've got the story handed to you. Invent a few scary things to happen to the heroine, but mainly write about *yourself*. What are you?"

"I'm an oversized, big-footed Amazon."

"Bullshit. Play it up. You're Junoesque, divinely formed and fair, the unfulfilled Diana. Did you read Moorcock's *Gloriana* yet? That's you."

"You make it sound too easy. You could do it, but I don't know if I could. Of course, I'd love to try."

"So do it." Ellie caught the waitress's eye and made a scribbling motion in the air with her right hand. "Think how nice it'll be to read something where the author knows how to spell and punctuate. Let's talk plot tomorrow. I have to get out of here. I've still got one ass to kick and one ass to kiss before five o'clock tonight. And don't get too worried about Don. You'll be able to keep an eye on him soon enough. Can I see the last page of his letter?"

In ten more minutes we'll be going out to dinner to a place south of here. Macveagh's food at the inn isn't bad, but Roger wants to go somewhere better to celebrate.

You noticed that last word? Lord Jericho just called from London. We're getting the contract, the whole ten yards of it, design and implement. Better start packing your bag because they want me to stay at least through Phase One—that means a year up here. I can't call you about this until next Tuesday, when the official word is supposed to come out. When you make a call from here, I think the whole village sits at the Post Office extension and listens to everything you say.

I'll keep an eye open for a place for us to rent near Laxford. The main JosCo offices will probably be in Lochinver, but I won't be there more than a couple of times a month. I've already seen one prospect for us to live in. It's an old house up on the headland, and it's empty now. It looks run-down, but it's solidly built. Roger thinks it's about three hundred years old. It's made of gray stone, and it has real turrets on each end like a miniature castle. I walked round it and took a look inside, and the foundations seem to be in good shape with no signs of damp. Roger says we could probably get a one-year lease for less than a hundred a month (pounds, not dollars). Prices here are a pleasant surprise after London.

I have to go now. I'll call you as soon as I can, and we'll make plans to get you here. Rush, rush, rush (but round here it's usually to fit in with the pub's licensing hours). Wish you were here, I miss you terribly.

All my love, Don.

Mary had lingered in the restaurant after Ellie left, rereading the last part of Don's letter. As she walked slowly back to the apartment she tried to straighten out her own ideas.

Did she really want to go to Scotland? Put aside for a moment the biggest question: how hard was she willing to work to patch up a marriage that seemed to be heading for a classical breakdown? Start with the small things.

Her job. Ellie had talked of making her an assistant editor. But so what? Her old ideas of an editor coolly reading

19

manuscripts had gone out of the window as soon as she had visited Ellie's office. On a good day there was just time to read the mail. Most of it was interminable meetings. Reading was for weekends and evenings, with little bits fitted in on the subway.

Forget all that. What else did New York offer?

Ellie, of course. There'd be nothing in Scotland like Ellie's takeoffs of the high and mighty of the publishing world. And the city itself was a plus, no matter how Don put it down in his letters.

She went a couple of blocks out of her way so she could stop at Third Avenue Records. The new Kinks album looked promising. She bought it, then on impulse added a progressive New Wave album by Ultravox. Don and Ellie would laugh at her for that, but they were in with the untouchables, the Over Thirties. Mary liked to point out the width of the gulf between her twenty-seven years and their antiquity. But where would she ever find new albums in Laxford? By the sound of it, nowhere. England was a small country; she ought to be able to get to London sometimes for shopping and concerts.

She picked up her pace through the rush-hour crush. That was another plus for the city. It was street music, rumbling engines, honking horns, portable tape recorders blatting out a disco beat. Even the screaming fire sirens blended in with the rest. New York was noise city, impossible for somebody with frayed nerves. But she loved it. When she had gone home for a week's vacation to her old home in Dubuque she hadn't known what was missing there. It had taken her return to the city to prove that she thrived in the middle of this frantic mess. There would be so much silence in the Highlands. She imagined endless expanses of heather and mist.

At the corner of Fifty-ninth Street she paused and looked about her.

There was no decision to make, not really. She would not leave Don. If the contract was signed, and if he was committed to a year in Scotland, she'd be there with him. Any other possibility would just fade away when she got down to real decision making.

As she looked out across Central Park she realized that she and Don had stood there together in that first winter in Manhattan, when everything was going right for them. It had

20

been freezing cold, with stars over the park and piercing bright lights from the surrounding buildings. It had been a magic time.

Mary quickened her pace. With a five-hour time difference it would already be almost ten at night in Laxford. She didn't want to miss a possible phone call from Don.

CHAPTER 2

The rock structure around Laxford possesses peculiarities not found elsewhere on the Scottish mainland,
but well-known in the Outer Hebrides. The granite is
exposed, grey in color and coarse in grain. It has
broken down in places to the individual rock crystals,
resulting in a degenerate form called 'rotten granite.'
Along the sea coast, the action of the waves has
steadily removed this and has scooped out a great
series of tidal caves, extending in from the west coast
to form a complex, interconnected labyrinth of caverns, of unknown extent.

The sea caves have acquired a certain fame in
Sutherland County, as the home of 'The Sleepers', a
legendary tribe of mermen. The area is shunned by
local fishermen. The visitor is advised to shun the
tidal caves for a quite different reason—they have
never been explored or mapped, and the danger of
being caught in a tidal race inside the maze of caverns is considerable.

—WILLIAM PEARSON, *A Guide to the Highlands*

Laxford

Don Willis awoke little by little. Scraps of memory seemed
to float past, tugging him from a heavy sleep. He lay motionless, the woolen blanket soft on his chin. *Where was he?*

Slowly now, take it at its own pace . . .

Sunday: Last night there had been the long and expensive
dinner south of Ullapool. Back over the twisting road,

22

muffled in the back of the car, drowsing. No memory of coming back to the bedroom.

Another bang on the door. Was that what had started him back on the road to waking?

Another bang. The door sounded hollow.

Don ran his tongue experimentally over the inside of his teeth. The taste of booze was still there. Must have missed cleaning his teeth when he came up. Thick feeling. He opened his eyes a little bit and squinted over at the window. Light outside. *What the hell?* Early Sunday morning, no plans for the day—and somebody hammering on the door.

"What is it?"

"Got to get up." Roger's voice, full of energy. "You awake at last? I've been banging here for five minutes."

"I'm awake. What the hell's happening? It's hardly dawn yet."

"Eight o'clock. Sorry to drag you out, but I just had a call from old Jericho. He's on his way up here by helicopter, called a council-of-war for ten o'clock—he'd like to begin the design phase at once."

Don lay back. *Holy Mother of God.* A business meeting at ten on Sunday morning! What about that famous relaxed English attitude to work? Worse than New York.

"I'm getting up. Here, Roger, save my life. See if Hamish can make a pot of strong coffee instead of that bloody tea. I'll be down there in twenty minutes."

"Bacon and eggs?"

Don's stomach rolled over at the thought. "Christ, no. Bread or toast, and butter."

"Spot of whisky in your coffee?"

"Now you're talking." Don sat up and swung his legs out of bed. Gently, now. No rapid movements for a few minutes. "OK, Roger, I'm moving."

"Twenty minutes, then. I'll get Hamish to make some porridge for you—that's a good eye-opener."

Don walked over to the huge china wash basin and poured water into it from the heavy jug. He put one finger into it. Freezing.

All right now, here's the countdown. Five, four, three, two, one—zero. Lean forward, hands in and head down; scoop over the top of the head and back of neck—*now*.

Don gasped. The shock was so great he could feel his testicles move up, contracting close to his body. He forced himself to splash another double handful of water over his face, laving his eyes and forehead and under his chin.

After a few more seconds he felt for the rough towel hanging over a rail by the dresser and rubbed it vigorously over his head and neck. The worst was over, he knew that from experience. Now it was just a question of avoiding any attempt at thought until he had a couple of cups of black coffee inside him.

He opened the thick curtain. It was another gray October day, with a threat of more rain. No wonder it seemed like the middle of the night—and no wonder so many Scotsmen seemed happy to go and live in other parts of the world.

Don squeezed the tube of toothpaste directly into his mouth, chewing on it and working it around his teeth, then followed that with a mouthful of cold water before picking up his toothbrush. If it turned out that the house up on the cliff had no running hot water, that was going to be the first order of business when he and Mary talked of lease signing. On a day like this, it was a crime to make a man face work before he had spent ten minutes in a hot shower.

The helicopter flew in along Loch Laxford and made two circuits of the village before the pilot landed on the flat cliff top, a quarter of a mile north of Laxford.

Roger Wilson and Don walked slowly over to it, looking at the people who had come out of their houses as the unfamiliar whomp-whomp-whomp of the rotor blades first sounded through the village. A few children were heading toward the helicopter, but most of the villagers watched for a couple of minutes after it had landed, then went back indoors.

They passed the church, nodding to the minister standing outside it and receiving a disapproving glower in return.

"What's got into him?" Don turned for another look, and found that the frowning face was still watching their progress up the hill. "Is there some ritual greeting for a Scotts parson?"

Roger was wearing a tweed sports coat, apparently unaffected by the chilling damp that seemed to be rolling down on them from the hills to the east. He laughed. "Don't you have something over there called the Blue Laws, that stop the shops opening on Sunday? Well, here we have something a

24

lot stronger, it's called the Lord's Day Observance Society, and it's against *anything* happening on Sunday. Its most determined members live up here in the northern Highlands—and people like our friend back there are its strongest supporters. He'll be preaching a sermon in less than an hour, and he wants the attention on that, not on some godless machine flying in from the south."

Don shivered. He was wearing a short corduroy overcoat, but he was still a little hung over and the damp seemed to be seeping into his bones.

"I wouldn't enjoy sitting through a service in that church. Does it have any heat?"

Roger gave him a quick look from bright gray eyes. "You're serious, aren't you? Thought for a minute that had to be a joke—you'll not find heat in any church this old. It's considered conducive to sinful drowsiness and wicked thoughts. The same philosophy where I went to school—cold rooms, cold baths, toilet seats like blocks of ice, I can still feel 'em."

Don was about to point out that the toilet seats at the Over The Water were no better, but they were almost at the helicopter. He didn't want his third meeting with Lord Jericho to begin with a speech about lavatory fixtures.

Instead he said, "I thought we were supposed to lie low about all this until Tuesday? Won't the helicopter start everybody in the whole area talking?"

Lord Jericho was stepping down from the cabin and had caught Don's words. He straightened up, a man in his midfifties, heavily built, with a rosy complexion and a bald head surrounded by a neat monastic fringe of gray hair.

"It will that," he said. "We had people looking up at us all the way from Lairg. Can't be helped, we've got to move faster than I thought."

His voice was cheerful, with flat vowels and a way of speaking that made each syllable of long words of equal weight. Don's ear wasn't attuned to English accents, but Roger had told him that he was hearing a West Yorkshire voice, slightly modified by years spent in London.

"What is it, Joshua?" said Roger. "Is there a question on the contract still?"

"No." Jericho grinned. "Nowt as bad as that. We'll be signing with a fat incentive clause for early completion. A week

25

saved now'll be worth a mint in a few years. I learned it back in the forties, jobs get in trouble at the end because of time wasted at the front end. Come on, let's talk in the cabin."

He turned and led the way back inside. The interior had been designed as a working office, with file cabinets, telephone, tables, typewriters, desks, and dictaphone.

Don noticed a microwave oven and a refrigerator neatly tucked away in one corner, and a miniature bar set into one cabin wall. He turned and found that Lord Jericho was looking at him smugly.

"Not a bad little setup, right?"

"It's great." Don hesitated. Despite Lord Jericho's instruction to call him Joshua, it was difficult to do until he knew him better—felt like *lèse majesté*, or something. He wasn't used to dealing with lords, despite Roger's airy, "Joshua's only a life peer, you know—you're not dealing with one of the Plantagenets."

"Lord Jericho," went on Don at last, "do you mean that it's all right to release the news now about the station? I'd like to try and get a house lease up here as soon as I can, so I can get my wife over."

"Give her a call, the sooner she's here and looking after you, the more work you'll be able to get done. You can't operate as well out of a hotel, I know that." Jericho waved his arm around the helicopter's interior. "That's why I did all this. I can get a good night's sleep—there's a cot in the back—and still be where I want to every morning. Did you two get a look at the area this past couple of days?"

"Some." Roger Wilson looked at Don. "What's your evaluation, you're our siting expert?"

"Pretty good, but we'll have to look a lot closer at those tidal patterns round the caves. If there's much reservoir capacity in the caves themselves, we'll have to watch it when we calculate current flow and effluent temperatures—not an easy job." Don felt better. His head was clearer, and this was something he knew inside and out. Nobody could calculate tidal flow with complete accuracy, but he seemed to be able to improve the computed values with a sort of intuitive feel for the way the currents would work. "We'll have to do some on-site survey work, inside the caves. There has to be a fantastic tidal flow in there."

26

Jericho nodded and slipped off his heavy jacket. Don saw that his shirt sleeves were about two inches too short.

"Bloody ridiculous, isn't it?" said Jericho, following Don's look. "I bought a shirt factory last year, and they sent me twenty-four as a Christmas present. I told 'em the wrong arm length. There's twenty-three more of these buggers back home. I wear 'em to remind me not to guess at facts."

He sat down at the desk and pulled open a drawer. "Roger, we might be able to shorten the on-site stuff. Remember the work that Knowlton did?"

He turned to Don. "When we were first getting into this, oh, near three years back, I had another bloke come up here and do a first-cut at station siting. I've got his report back in the London office."

So he wasn't the first man in on this job! Don felt a sudden twinge of alarm. "I'd like to see that. And I'd like to spend some time with Knowlton, as soon as I can."

"Only one way I know of to do that, and it's not one you'd choose," said Jericho. He looked up at Don over the top of his glasses. "Do you drink much, Willis?"

So soon. Don felt sick, the coffee turning to bile inside him. "I take a drink now and again. Why do you ask?"

"You said you'd like to meet Knowlton, the chap I had up here. You'd have to do what he did. One night he got blotto, so drunk he didn't know what he was doing. He went out for a walk along the cliff and fell off it." Lord Jericho laughed grimly. "That was the end of him. I'll give you his report, but you'd have to arrange your own meeting."

Don sat down uninvited and tried to keep his expression calm. If Jericho was going to make jokes like that, he'd have to adjust to the style.

"He was renting that house you were looking at," said Roger. Neither he nor Lord Jericho seemed to have noticed Don's reaction. "You know, the one with the turrets up on the headland. That's why you ought to be able to get it cheap—they're a superstitious lot around here, and we might as well take advantage of it."

"I'll see what I can do later today." Don took a deep breath. "What's the plan, now? I was hoping to get Mary over at the end of next week, but if we're going on to do the survey I'll have to be up here for that."

"You'll have to be here, but I see no problem there—not

27

unless you have to meet her yourself down in London." Jericho turned to Roger. "I've got a job for you down there this week. Remember old Petherton?"

"Pethy-Wethy?" Roger was still standing up, leaning against the cabin wall. "No way I'd forget him, not after the hassle over licenses. I thought we'd done with him once the contract was approved?"

"Not quite." Jericho sniffed. "Now he's on a new tack—preservation of the Laxford local environment. He's afraid that we'll mess up the local flows of water with the station, enough to change the bird life."

"It will. He's still worried about the future of the great crested tit, eh? All right, I'll have a go at him." Roger turned to Don. "He won't talk much to Joshua, not after their last meeting."

"It's not that." Jericho laughed. "You're Rugby Union, I'm Rugby League, and he's sensitive to the difference."

Don was lost. He thought he had been following the conversation, more or less, but not any more.

Roger Wilson noticed his confusion. "That's our picturesque way of saying that Petherton thinks I'm a gentleman, and Joshua isn't."

"He's right, too, the silly old bugger," said Jericho amiably. "At least, he's right about me—I'm none too sure of you, Roger."

Down the hill, the church bell began to toll. It was a gloomy, brazen tone, ringing out across the loch and the sea to the west.

"Nearly eleven," said Jericho. "I'll have to be off in a few minutes, I've a lunch meeting in Lairg. Here's what I suggest. We'll fly the copter back up here tomorrow, with the report on the tides that Knowlton made. You'll fly back down with it to London, Roger, and meet there with Charles Petherton." He turned to Don. "If your missus can get over here by next weekend, why don't we have Roger meet her at Heathrow Airport, and we'll fly her up here for you?—better than a long train trip, and save you time, too. That'll give you a chance to lease a house, and get ready to move into it."

He stood up. "Any problem? Otherwise, I'll be off."

"What should we tell the locals?" asked Roger.

"Give 'em the truth. You can say you'd have lost your jobs if you'd talked earlier."

28

He shepherded them out of the cabin, and stood on the steps. It had started to rain, a fine, foggy drizzle, and the hills to the east were almost hidden. The church bell maintained its steady, somber tolling.

"Matins," said Jericho. He turned back into the cabin. "By gor, I've sat through some dull 'uns in my time. We had a vicar back in Bradford that'd run a sermon forty-five minutes eight Sundays out of ten."

He stood silent for a moment. The calling bell seemed to have carried him back through the years. For the first time, Don could see the awkward young man who lay behind today's successful and bustling exterior. Jericho had lifted himself by drive and talent from the worst of the industrial slums, up to a peerage. It was a rare moment when he allowed himself a look backward.

After a few seconds Jericho shook his head, as though he was clearing it of some disturbing noise.

"Get well clear." He shook his head again. "You don't want to be under the rotors when we take off. I'll see you in a couple of days, Roger." He paused again for a moment before sliding the cabin door shut. "Wilson and Willis, eh? People won't keep your names straight, but I think we've a good team here."

Don and Roger moved away from the helicopter, closer to the edge of the cliff. They watched as the rotors spun faster and the odd, unsteady but characteristic rise from the ground took place. The helicopter dipped, swayed, and turned, like a big insect searching for something on the ground, then it headed off to the west and was gone into the blurring drizzle.

"How do you argue with him, Roger?" Don was still looking after the vanished helicopter.

"With Joshua? I don't try it, unless I really care about it. Then he'll give in without another word. You'll get used to it, Don. He expects a lot from you, but he's the best boss I've ever had."

They had walked forward together to the edge of the cliff. Don looked down to the rocks and broken water beneath. It was almost sheer here.

He shivered inside. Had Knowlton fallen over at low or high tide? That made the difference between drowning, or smashing on the boulders. Not a good choice. He looked along up the hill, to the big house on the top. It was almost

29

invisible through the fog and rain, with just the nearer turret darker against the sky. If they were going to spend winter in the place, there'd have to be decent heating.

"Come on," said Roger. "If I've got to leave here tomorrow, we ought to do a good deal more talking. Do you have a picture of your wife with you? I've seen people wearing signs saying 'Mr. Smith' at London Airport, but I'd rather not be one of them."

Don shook his head. "I don't have a picture with me. Don't worry, you'll have no trouble recognizing her. Mary stands out in a crowd."

ARRIVING LONDON NINE O'CLOCK SUNDAY MORNING ON PANAM 102. TELL ROGER WILSON I WILL BE LOOKING FOR A MAN WEARING SIGN SAYING MISTER SMITH. DO YOU WANT ME TO BRING YOUR FUR HAT, YOU FORGOT IT WHEN YOU LEFT? LOOKING FORWARD TO SEEING HOUSE, IT SOUNDS MARVELOUS. ELLIE SENDS PLATONIC LOVE. CALL ME FRIDAY IF YOU GET A CHANCE, I TRIED TO GET YOU AT OVER THE WATER ALL DAY YESTERDAY, COULD NOT GET DECENT LINE. ALL MY LOVE, MARY. XXXXX AND MORE.

It had been a long week, a flurry of packing, passporting, telephoning about long-term storage of clothes and furniture. What had she forgotten to do? Mary ran over the list one more time, mentally crossing off the items that were either done or un-doable in the time she had left. As usual, she stuck at the final one: the diary. Where had she put her diary, the one written creation to show for her four years in Manhattan? She had kept it faithfully, scribbling her notes last thing at night and first thing in the morning. Now it was gone. She *must* have stuck it in with the other books that went air freight—that, or it was lost forever. She'd looked in every corner of the empty apartment. Damn. Woman, what did you do with it?

As she walked on through the park, Mary realized that it had been a long week for the city, too. While she had been scurrying to get ready, fall had quietly and firmly taken over from summer. There was a chill in the air, the leaves were showing an edge of brown, and for the first time in months it was possible to imagine winter in the city. The park was still full of struggling joggers and hand-holding lovers, but Mary imagined she could see a hidden urgency in them—"and summer's lease hath all too short a date,"—days beginning to squeeze down again, Solstice cometh.

She began to walk faster. There was nothing like leaving a place to make it seem full of hidden new meanings. Meanwhile, she had dawdled away the spare fifteen minutes that had persuaded her to come through Central Park instead of taking a bus.

As she came to the southern exit, she relaxed. Ellie wasn't sitting on the bench at Sixtieth Street, biting her fingernails and cursing. One nice thing about having an editor for a friend—no matter how late you were, you stood a fifty-fifty chance of being there first.

"Over here." Ellie's voice broke into her musing. She was sitting on the grass over near the wall, two brown paper bags beside her.

"Why the switch?" Mary walked over and bent to feel the ground.

"It's dry, I checked that." Ellie was wearing a heavy brown coat that looked like a shaggy hearth rug. She patted the grass next to her. "Go and take a look at the bench if you want to—it's got dog shit all round it. I think the canines are going to take over Manhattan. Are you all packed yet? I got you pastrami with mustard and a big pickle."

"More trouble at the office?" Mary had learned the symptoms. Rapid changes of subject equals nervousness equals problems with a man or with the job. She sat down and took the bag that Ellie held out to her.

"The usual. And a big lump of envy." Ellie hunched down inside her coat.

"You don't mean for *me*, do you?"

"Sure I do." Ellie crunched at a pickle and grimaced at the sour taste of it. "We had a session this morning about next season. Everybody was all gung ho, and I sat there thinking, we spread these schlocky fantasies around like *candy*. All these bodice rippers and Sidney Sheldons, for housewives with yelling kids dangling from their aprons—opiate for the masses. Then we give each other all this asshole talk about *literature*. That stuff's about as much literature as a comic book, it's just more pretentious. It's printed pablum."

"Well, look at *me*, Ellie. It's all right for you to talk about how bad the books are—but I'd love to get something of

31

mine published, and you know quite well there are thousands more like me. It's schlock to *you*, you see too much of it. Can you imagine what it's like to have a whole bunch of rejection slips, and know that means you're not even as good as the stuff you say is so awful?"

Mary was leaning back against the wall, her eyes half-closed. There was still enough heat in the sun to make a sheltered spot offer a brief illusion of summer—and from all that she had been reading, that wasn't going to be true once she got to Scotland. "If you publish schlock, what does that make me?" she went on, when Ellie showed no signs of answering.

"The lucky one. You'll be over there living a new life, and I'll still be churning out the same old crap here. *That's* what's getting to me, Mary, if you want to know the truth. I wish I were going, too. Here, see what I got for you."

Ellie scrabbled around in her handbag for a few seconds, taking things out of it.

"I swear to God, I'm going to throw everything in here *out* one day and start from scratch." Ellie sounded more cheerful, as an untidy heap of tissues, scribbled notes, lipsticks, nail polish, memo pads, tampons, hair clips, pens, and safety pins grew on the grass in front of her. "Damn it, I only bought it the day before yesterday, over at Bloomingdales, and now it's disappeared. Why do I carry all this *crap* with me? Here we go."

She took out a miniature bottle and handed it to Mary. "This caught my eye when I was looking for something to give Alice for her birthday. Didn't you say that you'll be staying in Laxford? Look on the bottom of the bottle."

Mary turned it over. The tiny perfume flask was shaped like a hunting horn and contained a cloudy green liquid. She peered at the small lettering engraved on the flat underside.

"An exotic fragrance from the Highlands of Scotland. Created on the shores of Loch Laxford," she read. "Ellie, how could you have this 'catch your eye'? You just about need a magnifying glass to see these words."

"Well, if you want the truth, I asked if there was such a thing as a Scottish perfume. I really wanted to get you a little going-away present."

"It's for me?" Mary turned it right side up. "Thanks ever so much, I didn't expect anything. What's it called? *Climax!* Ellie, that's *not* kind."

"I know." Ellie shrugged. "I'm not being a shithead, that's the *only* Scottish perfume they had. I have the impression that Scotland isn't the place for these delicate products—they go more for porridge and haggis. Anyway, I thought that maybe it was an omen—they're not too subtle these days, are they? Might as well call it 'orgasm' and have done with it. Try it, see how you like it."

Mary loosened the stopper and poised it over the back of her hand. "Expensive?"

"Mary!" Ellie shook her head. "You ought to know better than to ask a question like that. We in the publishing business disdain to talk about price."

Mary rubbed the stopper along the back of her hand, bent her head, and sniffed. She straightened up suddenly. There was a tight spasm of feeling in her belly, and the scene in the park seemed to contract at the edges, leaving her looking down a black-walled tunnel at the trees and rocks. She put her hands to the grass, steadying herself.

"Here, are you all right?" Ellie had heard a gasp as the contraction hit Mary deep in her belly.

"I—I guess so." Mary gave a shaky laugh. "I'll be OK. I shouldn't skip breakfast, I just felt faint for a second."

Even with Ellie, it didn't seem right to mention her erect nipples, pushing hard and urgently against her dress. She shivered, wondering what was happening to her.

Ellie had picked up the bottle where Mary had let it fall to the grass. She sniffed thoughtfully at the stopper and wrinkled her nose. "It's a strange perfume. Sort of makes me think of darkness and water—what's that musky smell in it? I can't decide if I like it or hate it. Makes me feel all shivery."

She re-stoppered the flash. "I hope *you* like it, Mary—you don't think it was this that made you feel faint, do you?"

"How could it?" Mary laughed again, trying this time to make it sound more relaxed and normal. "It would have to be powerful stuff—one sniff and I feel strange."

Ellie handed the bottle back to her. "I suppose not. Anyway, that would miss the whole point. A perfume is supposed to make the man you're with feel horny, it's not supposed to do anything to you. But it'd be just my luck, buy something that made *me* turn on and *him* turn off—you've got the story of my life, right there." She hesitated. "Mary, do you want to keep this? If not, I'd buy you something else for a present."

33

Mary took it and tucked it away in her bag. "I want it. Maybe the name they gave it isn't a piece of wishful thinking. I'll try it when I get to Scotland, and see what happens. Look, are you still sure you want to give me a ride out to Kennedy Airport? You'll waste your evening?"

"I'll enjoy it. You know me, Tuesday I'll work until eleven, but I'm damned if I'm going to work on Saturday night. I'll pick you up at about four; we'll have a quick run out there and a farewell drink." She looked at her watch. "We'd better eat something quick, I have an out-of-town biggie coming in at two. What do you hear from Don?"

Mary took a huge bite from her sandwich before she answered. She was suddenly hungry, ravenously hungry, as though she had been starved for days.

"Working his head off," she said with her mouth full. "Won't even be able to meet me in London. Roger Wilson, the man he's always talking about in his letters. Remember him? He's supposed to meet me at Heathrow."

Ellie was watching her eat, the strong muscles of her jaw clenching hard at each bite. "Mary, you've got to learn to eat more slowly. You're not still back on the farm, you know. You look like a starved lioness. Why can't Don break loose for a few hours and meet you himself?"

Mary shrugged. "Big White Chief says no, Don has to get some calculations done, and then he has to take them over for review to a place on the other side of the country—apparently it's an all-day trip there." She had finished her sandwich and was eyeing Ellie's. "Are you going to finish that?"

"Here." Ellie sighed and handed over a half-sandwich. "You're a big girl, I guess you need the nourishment. So you're going to be looked after by tall, fair, and handsome Roger, eh? Think Don's putting off seeing you?"

"Dunno. Why should he?"

"Well, if he's hitting the booze again . . ." Ellie stopped, shook her head.

Mary licked her lips and looked around hungrily. "I'm still feeling starved. Look, Don knows me too well to try that. He can't avoid me for more than a couple of days, and I always know when he's on it. Remember the signs? Even when he's cold sober, he'll be rubbing his hands and fidgeting. No, I really think it's work this time. Lord Jericho's put everybody on a bonus basis for an early completion, and they're all busting their tails to get things done quickly."

"But not friend Roger?" Ellie looked at her friend shrewdly. "You getting nervous?"

"A bit. I'll be away a long time—more than a year, Don says."

"Right." Ellie sighed and stood up, rubbing at her knees as she did so. "Shit, I think I'm getting old. Here you are, going off for wild romance across the ocean, and here's poor me, still splashing my way through the same old crap. Know what's waiting for me this weekend? An eight hundred page manuscript—the agent who brought it in says it's 'the Albanian *Gone With The Wind*.' How'd you like to trade places, you stay and I go?"

Mary had stood up too. She was almost six inches taller than Ellie, and she stood for a long moment looking down at the other woman. Her face was serious. "You're joking. But you know, I've got this feeling about Scotland. I know we've gone too far to change things, but I'm not keen on going." She shivered. "I've just got this strange feeling."

"No wonder. I'd have it myself if I'd just bolted down about a pound and a half of bread and meat. If there's justice in the world, Mary, you're about to experience the bane of the publishing business—violent indigestion." She began to walk toward the park exit. "Come on, back to the grindstone. Maybe you can walk it off."

Mary had picked up her bag and taken out the small flask of perfume. She looked at it again, weighing it in her hand, hesitating. Finally she put it back in the bag and hurried after Ellie.

CHAPTER 3

Where is your Place?
Here, with the Elders.
When will you take it?
After the Second Change, when work is done.
How will you earn it?
By labor among the Others; by holding the Secret; by
*   guarding the Place; by spreading the Seed.*
What will the End be?
Life for the People.
Who will face Death for it?
I will.
Swear.
I swear.
Drink.

"Good morning, ladies and gentlemen. We are now approaching the west coast of Ireland, about an hour and a half out from an on-time arrival at Heathrow."

The words of the pilot, distorted by the cabin speaker system, pulled Mary slowly from her dream. The thresh and roar of sea breakers merged into the deep murmur of aircraft engines. She sighed, moved uneasily in her seat, and opened her eyes.

"Our cabin attendants will shortly be serving breakfast," went on the voice. "Seat trays down, please, if you wish to eat."

On Mary's left, a passenger raised the window blind to show the first glimpse of a dark-blue dawn. The plane was

36

coming to life about her, seat lights going on and men and women moving along the aisles of the half-full Boeing 747.

What a dream! Mary had a sudden need to look down and check that she was fully clothed. Ellie would have had a field day with it. As the dream-reality slowly faded and lost focus, Mary was left with a languor that was more than simple fatigue.

She looked at her watch. Two-thirty, New York time. She reset it to seven-thirty, then unfastened her seat belt. Even for her, the seat was small and cramped. She watched a man who was at least eighty pounds overweight waddle past her, and wondered how he ever fitted into the limited space. Did he have to take two seats?

Rubbing her eyes, Mary stood up, stretched, and headed for the toilets at the rear of the plane. As she splashed tepid water onto her face and examined the dark bags under her eyes, the dream hit her again. She hadn't had one like it since she had been an adolescent.

She had been trapped, out on the edge of a cliff. Below her, the waves were breaking with a constant, deep boom (a sound, she realized, just like the engines of the 747). Three dark shapes were steadily advancing on her, blocking her way back from the cliff edge. In the twilight she peered at them, trying to see their forms more clearly. The sun, pale and feeble, gave just enough light for her to make out general outlines, without colors or clear edges.

Mary felt for her flashlight, the one that she always carried in the side pocket of her handbag. Where was it? She *had* to get a good look at the shapes. She could not find her bag, it must have fallen from her as she ran along the cliff. She still seemed to feel the weight of it on her shoulder.

They were only fifteen yards from her now. Their movement was graceful and sinuous, sliding easily over the short grass of the clifftop. The one in the middle was a little in front of the others. He moved with something cupped in his hands in front of him, as though he carried something small and delicate there. She looked behind her again. The water still broke steadily over the rocks, black and booming. Even in the poor light she could see the wave front quite clearly, see each drop of spume that flew from the breakers.

How could she protect herself? Mary realized to her horror that she was naked. Her skirt, blouse, bra, pants, and shoes

37

had vanished as she ran, and she could feel the damp night air on her skin and the tufts of grass cool beneath her bare feet.

She turned to the cliff edge. The fall to the water was a long one, but she knew she had to jump. Her feet would not respond to her command, would not move forward out from the cliff. They seemed stuck to the wiry grass. She tried to lean outward, to let her weight topple her over. Above the noise of the waves she could now hear a hoarse breathing, only inches from her. The skin of her bare back was pimpling into gooseflesh, waiting for the first touch.

She opened her mouth to scream. No sound came out as she was grasped firmly by the waist and moved back from the edge of the cliff, down onto the springy turf.

In the instant before her back touched the damp grass, she was overwhelmed by a new feeling. There was a fire in her veins that was no longer fear. It was a surging anticipation . . .

Mary splashed more cold water on her face and frowned at the mirror.

So what would Ellie say about this one? "And you, pet, are the one that told me you don't even miss it! I ought to charge you fifty dollars an hour to explain the meaning of *that* dream to you, but it would be taking your money for nothing. It's so obvious. You know, my shrink would scream with joy if I ever came up with anything as straightforward and textbook Freudian as that for him. All I ever bring him are nightmares of missed deadlines and run-ins with the bastard Blocker."

Mary dried her face on the paper towels, noting the faint final scent of *Climax*. It was certainly persistent stuff. She had applied it before she left for the airport—most perfumes would have faded away hours ago. The lingering after-smell was like pungent lavender.

By the time that they had landed and been through Immigration, Mary was back to normal except for an increasing fatigue. She collected her two cases, went through the green area for Customs, then stood looking at the sea of faces waiting for arriving passengers. There were many cardboard signs being held up, but no "Mister Smith" that she could see. She looked round her again.

"Mary Willis?" A fair-haired man fell into step beside her.

38

She looked at him in surprise. He was about her height, maybe half an inch taller. Good features were marred by a rough complexion that must have fought many youthful bouts with acne twenty years earlier. His gray eyes were lively, as though he was enjoying some private joke. She had scanned his face when she first came through Customs and had gone right past it. The image that she had formed from Don's letters was nothing like the man who was standing next to her.

"Are you Roger Wilson?"

"I'm afraid so." He had caught her surprised look. He smiled (very nice teeth). "Don't worry, it's a face that grows on you."

"How did you recognize me?"

"I could say it was from Don's glowing descriptions." Even his voice was not what she had imagined. "Winchester and Cambridge," Don had said, and that had made Mary think of another Englishman, a publisher who had come to Ellie's office to inquire about backlist titles. He claimed to have been educated at Eton and Oxford. Mary had expected that same sort of voice from Roger Wilson, the sort of nasal drawl that Ellie said afterwards sounded as though it had been filtered through a whalebone corset.

"Actually, it was a lot simpler than that." He spoke what Mary thought of as "neutral" English, with just a trace of a lisp that she found very engaging. "Don carries your picture in his wallet. He said he didn't have one, but I asked him to take a look and he found that he did after all. It's a cultural pattern, you see. American men always carry photographs of their wives and family, Germans carry pictures of their cars and mistresses, and Frenchmen carry little cards that tell you the best years for different wines."

His tone was light and humorous.

"And Englishmen?" said Mary, feeling a bit like a straight man. She had suppressed her liberated reaction and allowed Roger to take both her cases.

He gave her a quick sideways look from those bright gray eyes. "I'll tell you that when we know each other better. How tired are you feeling?"

"Not bad at all." It was true. The chilly morning air and the walk through the terminal had cleared her head. "I'll probably want to sleep on the train, but I guess there's lots of

39

time for that. Don said it was a long journey up to Laxford."

"It is. That's why I have another suggestion." They had walked through the tunnel connecting the air terminal to the London subway, and Roger was buying tickets. Mary looked at the unfamiliar coins that he was holding. She ought to cash some travelers' checks, or she would be dependent on Roger Wilson for everything.

"Here." He seemed to be telepathic. He was holding out an envelope of coins and paper money. "It's a care package from Don. He had to go over to Dounreay, and he won't be back at Laxford until tomorrow night. We can head up there by train, and then by car. It will take us all day, and we won't be there until about ten o'clock tonight, even if there are no rail slowdowns—they do most of the repair work on Sunday. Or"—he looked directly at Mary, eye to eye. She decided that he was certainly no taller than she, maybe even a fraction shorter in these heels—"or we can spend the day here in London, see some of the sights—I'm a marvelous tour guide, though I say it as shouldn't—stay over here tonight, and tomorrow morning Lord Jericho's helicopter will be back from Paris. We can run up to Laxford in it, and eat, drink, and be merry in comfort. It's only a six-hour trip."

"Well, if you put it *that* way." Mary smiled. "But I'd need somewhere to stay—and who pays for that helicopter ride?" (He was interested in her, she had no doubt about that, but it was a good idea to get the ground rules clear now—no "lots of spare room in my apartment" suggestions.)

Roger was looking hard at her. He seemed to have read the real meaning of her last remark. "The ride to Laxford's free, compliments of JosCo. Lord Jericho prefers to see things used and working—equipment and people. As for where you stay, there's a single room reserved for you, early arrival, at the London Embassy Hotel in Bayswater Road. That's on JosCo's account, too. All right?"

Mary smiled and nodded her unspoken apology.

Roger picked up her cases. "We'll take the Tube over to Holland Park and get you registered. Then you can grab a couple of hours sleep while I meet our senior nemesis from the Ministry—you'll hear all about Charles Petherton later. I should be able to get rid of him by midday. I'll pick you up

40

at the hotel, we'll grab a bite of lunch, and then see what's open in town and worth a visit. How does it sound?"

"It sounds marvelous." (He might not be the Saint-ly figure that she'd made up from Don's letters and Leslie Charteris's old stories, but Roger Wilson had his own—charm? No. Effectiveness.) "Do you mean I ever had a choice?"

By one o'clock the temperature had climbed to the mid-sixties. Roger had readily accepted Mary's suggestion that they walk over to the exhibition.

"You're probably here just in time for the last little bit of summer. It'd be a shame to waste it." He took a quick look down at her shoes as they stood in the hotel lobby. "Make sure you really want to walk, though. It's going to be a couple of miles, and there'll be lots more walking when we get inside."

"These are my walking shoes." Mary wasn't used to this degree of concern from her male companions. Most of them assumed she was big and strong enough to stand anything. "A couple of miles is nothing. I'm good for four or five times that in these shoes."

"And you're from New York? I thought it was one of America's sacred rules, never walk anywhere."

They started to walk along the north side of Bayswater Road, keeping in the late October sun before cutting through the park to Olympia.

"You're probably thinking of Los Angeles. If you want to get anywhere in a hurry in New York, it's best to walk." Mary noticed that Roger insisted on walking on the road side of the sidewalk—to keep his sword arm free, he had explained (with a perfectly straight face) when she asked him about it. He was still wearing the scruffy brown tweed jacket and gray flannels that he had met her in at the airport. Apparently Sunday meetings justified no suit, even when they were with senior officials from the Ministry. With his heavy brogues, and a corduroy cap stuffed randomly into a pocket of his coat, he didn't cut a very dashing figure. At least Mary felt at ease with her own heavy skirt and flat-heeled shoes. Anyway, it made Roger look an inch or two taller than she. It was a fact of life that half the men she met would be shorter than her five feet ten, but why should she have to pretend she liked that? How could someone her height, and a

41

hundred and forty pounds, lay claim to a sensitive and delicate soul? Thank heaven that Don was a couple of inches over six feet. An alarming thought, but would they ever have married if he'd been four inches shorter?

"Hold it." Roger grabbed her arm as she was about to step into the roadway. "If you're going to walk against the traffic light, it would help if you at least looked in the right direction. That bicycle would have had you there."

"Sorry, my mind was wandering." After a second or two Mary quietly disengaged herself from his firm grip. "I'll adapt. When I first arrived in New York from Iowa I had a dozen near misses in the first day. I expected the cars to stop for red lights."

(And Don had laughed when she jumped for her life. Why hadn't *he* taken her arm before she left the sidewalk?)

Mary felt a sudden irrational annoyance at Roger Wilson, then immediately recognized it as 'referred' irritation. Remember Ellie's final words. "You'll never get things sorted out with Don if you brood over the past annoyances." She smiled her thanks to Roger for his thoughtfulness as they crossed the street.

The Highland and Lowland Exhibition took her mind off her worries. It was a surprise to her. She had expected—what? Bagpipes and sporrans and porridge and haggis and claymores. And clan tartans everywhere. Instead, most of the exhibits were modern. There were industrial chemical plants, oil refinery equipment, electricity generators, nuclear reactors (was Don working on one like that? It was frighteningly complex), monstrous bulldozers and earth-moving machines, tiny computer micro-chips, and revolting artistic displays from the Edinburgh festival. It wasn't until they finally found the section on ancient Scotland that Mary's interest perked up.

"I didn't know there was a civilization in Scotland six thousand years ago," she said excitedly, bending over the display of red Highland gold. "All they ever taught us about in school was Egypt and Mesopotamia."

"Depends what you call a civilization." Roger was leaning elegantly against a pillar, smoking a horrible little cigar—the sort Ellie called Tampon Rejects. (But Don had been right in his letter. "They're so damned self-confident, as though everything will work out their way in the end.") "Don't forget what Sam Johnson said. According to him, there has *never*

42

been a civilization in Scotland. You know, 'the noblest prospect that a Scotchman ever sees is the high road that leads him to London.' Some of the Henge monuments are real enough, though. They have to be getting on for four thousand years old, and I think they were a sign of real civilization."

"What do you mean, *some* of the Henge monuments?" (Could it be that English engineers were interested in more than flow rates and material yield points? Or was this an unusual specimen of the group?)

Roger shrugged. "Old Sir Walter Scott has a lot to answer for. He convinced everybody that the Highlands are romantic, so there was this big wave of Scottish artistic interest. It got to the point where people were putting in their own henges. Did you know that there's a place in the Orkneys, at Stenness, where they thought an ancient set of stones had been ruined by vandals? Then they found the whole thing had been set up in Victorian times, by Sir Walter's admirers."

"And what about this one?" Mary was leaning over staring at an ancient stone, one that bore a faint tracing of a Gaelic inscription carved on its greenish surface.

"Where's it from? Sutherland County? Well, there are brochs there, I've seen them. But this stone looks a lot more recent, maybe a couple of hundred years old. What's the inscription say?"

They bent together over the neatly typed white card that was pinned below the exhibit.

"*From Cape Wrath to Lochinver,*" read Mary. "*Beware the monsters; from the air and the sea, from the depths they will rise; taking the young ones, using the women-folk. Man and yet not-Man, Cuckoos of the Minch, Lords of Samain's Eve, Bane of Macveagh, Kings of the Waters.*" She shook her head. "Well, all we need now is a translation of *that*. What's it supposed to mean?"

Roger was crouching low, reading the tiny handwritten comments on the bottom of the typed card. "I can get some of it. 'Lords of Samain's Eve' seems straightforward enough. You have Samain's Eve. Isn't it much bigger in the States than it is here?"

Mary shook her head. "I've never even heard of it."

"I'll bet you have, you know. Samain is All Saints Day,

43

November the first. Samain's Eve is October 31—better known maybe as Hallowe'en. Trick or treat, Mary?"

"Why doesn't it *say* that?" (Was it Mark Twain, "two countries, separated by a common language"?) "So Lords of Samain would be like Halowe'en witches, but they'd be men. What about the rest of it?" She bent close to him, heads together as they looked at the card. He smelled strange—fresh hay and shoe polish, and a little of the horrible cigar mixed in with it.

"I can't understand much more of it. If you really want to know, you should consult the translator. He's curator of the Scottish exhibits at The British Museum." Roger frowned. "I can see some of it. Cape Wrath to Lochinver is a piece of the northwest coast of Scotland—Laxford's smack in the middle of it. Cuckoos of the Minch? God only knows. The Minch is the channel between the northwest shore and the Outer Hebrides, but I've never heard of cuckoos up there."

"The Hebrides? And a cockoo? Wait a minute, I know it! I do." Mary put her hand to her head and stared frowning into her memory. " 'A voice so thrilling ne'er was heard / In springtime from the cuckoo-bird / Breaking the silence of the seas / Among the farthest Hebrides.' There. It's Wordsworth," she said triumphantly. "It's, let me see now, it's 'The Solitary Reaper.' "

"Very good." Roger straightened up and looked at her quizzically. "*Of course.* That would make everything clear. Wordsworth must be the cuckoo of the Minch, and this is part of his epitaph." He spoke so seriously that it took Mary a second or two to realize that he was joking.

"All right." She laughed. "I don't know what it means— maybe Wordsworth saw the same translation."

"Or something else." Roger's eyes were alight with interest. Suddenly, he and Mary had moved much closer. "Suppose we forget old Wordsworth and just think of the cuckoo. 'Using the women-folk', it says. Did you know that cuckoos never make nests? They lay eggs in another bird's nest, and when they hatch out the other bird looks after them. Maybe the Lords of Samain's Eve rape the Scottish women and have them bear their children—the original freeloaders."

"Of course." Mary deliberately mimicked Roger's voice, doing her best at a British accent. "That would make everything clear."

44

Roger was laughing, still very close to Mary. (Why couldn't she laugh like this with Don? Was it because he thought all this sort of thing was 'trivial'?) She laughed back at him, ignoring the people who were looking at them in surprise—there shouldn't be anything funny in an old inscription.

"Maybe we should take a look at something else," she said. "It's nearly five, and we haven't seen any of the Crafts section yet."

Roger turned back to the stone and its translation. "You go on there if you like, and we'll meet later. We've proved one thing, these translations may not be profound, but they're certainly obscure. I'll stay here awhile. Why don't we meet in the section on the chambered tombs? That's beyond Crafts. Say at quarter to six?"

Before she left, Mary took a last look at the inscribed stone, with its moss-grown and stained surface. Soon she would be living in a place where the Roman invasion was recent history. It made her usual view of antiques (anything over fifty years old) seem peculiar and naïve.

Roger watched her walk away, admiring the flow of her hips under the long skirt. Just his luck. She was exactly the kind of woman who excited him most, and she was married to Don. He saw the men she passed giving her secret glances. The combination, that tall full-bodied figure and the unblemished creamy complexion, usually only came from Scandinavia. How had she preserved that through her American upbringing? Don Willis didn't seem to know what he had in Mary.

Roger bent again over the inscription, his pulse rate higher and his breath coming a little faster. It looked like the same story, ignore the available ones and covet the unattainable. Maybe he should stay here with the old relics for a while and cool off. What was that, under the typed inscription?

He could decipher it, painfully slowly. It was some sort of ritual. *"Where is your place?" "Here with the Elders."* As Roger worked on through the faint penciled words, his mind came back to Mary. He forced his attention to the card. Joshua would stand for a lot from his employees, if they did their jobs, but eternal triangles were not acceptable.

What *did* the inscriptions mean? No one would chip something into solid stone unless they thought it was important.

Mary sat on the edge of the bed and wiggled her bare toes. No blisters, but a good deal of redness and chafing on heel and toe.

It was her own fault. After the first walk over to the exhibition she had pushed Roger along—first with "Let's walk to dinner"; and then, coming stuffed full and more than a little over-wined out of the restaurant on Charlotte Street, "It's not cold. Why don't we walk back and help our digestions?"

She had been proving a point. Americans walked, and don't let him forget it. It hadn't worked too well, because Roger had nodded agreeably each time and showed no signs of being foot-weary even when they arrived back at the hotel.

Mary looked at her watch. One o'clock. The walk back must have taken over an hour—including interruptions. It was a real case of *in vino veritas*, starting with her casual, "How's Don doing on this job?", then on to Roger's comment about Don taking to the pubs like a man born to it. A bit more fencing like that, and finally Roger had stopped as they walked along Oxford Street and swung to face her.

"Why don't you just ask me right out, Mary? I was the one who checked Don's references before he was hired for the job. Don't you think I called the places he worked in New York? I know all about Don's boozy habits—so does Joshua. But I'll tell you one other thing, something you don't seem to realize at all. Don's the best man in flow analysis I've ever seen. I heard it from the others that he worked for and I hear it from our people. He seems to *feel* the way that currents will flow. I've seen him write down all the flow rates in a complex connected system before we had the computer runs back. He's got some gift that I've not seen before. The tidal caves at Laxford are complicated. We need Don as much as he—and you—need this job."

His face was all thin lines in the poor street lighting, and she could not see his eyes. It was not necessary. He was telling her that she didn't trust her own husband.

That outburst had changed the mood. Before that, Roger had been an attentive and admiring male companion. Mary knew that a pass was coming, probably when he said good night to her. (It was a single room at the hotel, true enough—but it had a double bed in it.) She had been enjoying his attentions, looking forward to saying no in the nicest

46

possible way, when Roger's sudden defense of Don had put a new distance between them. After they reached the hotel there had been no more than a moment of hesitation, then a polite "See you at eight-thirty in the lobby." Roger had kissed her hand, but it was mock gallantry.

Sighing, Mary stood up and went over to the desk. She had taken a long, hot bath in a wonderful big tub and she had washed her hair. Now she felt boiled-lobster all over and squeaky clean. Don would have grabbed her in a minute if he'd been here. He loved her when she was "too clean for decency."

Mary sat at the desk and opened the center drawer. Hotel stationery wasn't ideal, too small and fancy, but it would have to do. She *must* buy a decent-sized notebook, maybe tomorrow morning before Roger got to the hotel. This would have to be copied into it when she got to Laxford.

She picked up a pencil. Now that something was *happening* in life, a diary mattered. How had she found something to write every day through the four years in New York? She looked at herself in the mirror—all pink and white, damp blond hair pulled severely back off her face—and wondered. When did today *begin?* After a few seconds, she began to write.

During the night the wind had veered from south to northeast. The new air carried cold from northern Europe and moisture from the North Sea. By the time that Roger reached the London Embassy Hotel a chilling downpour was well established. The slick road surface had filled with a Monday-morning traffic jam of empty-eyed commuters, heading slowly into the City.

The weather matched Roger's own mood as he wedged Mary's cases into the small trunk of the MG and headed out into the stream of cars. He felt terrible. He hadn't noticed it, but he must have drunk far too much at dinner. A churning stomach had wakened him well before dawn in his flat in Knightsbridge, and for a couple of hours he lay there in the darkness aghast at the way he had intruded his views into the Willis's marriage. Mary had seemed to invite it, but that was hardly sufficient reason. Analyzing his own reaction, he decided that it was a form of guilt. He had designs on Mary, so to compensate for that he was obliged to overreact in support of Don. Ridiculous, but not unprecedented. The trouble was, he had set up the pattern—now he was afraid that he'd be in for more of the same, all the way up to Laxford.

Mary's greeting outside the hotel seemed to confirm his fears. She was frozen faced and distant, hardly seeming to want to speak to him at all. There was no sign of yesterday's animation, the health and vitality that he found so attractive. They exchanged monosyllables until Mary suddenly grasped his arm as he halted for a traffic light in Maida Vale.

"Roger. Wait here."

"What are you going—"

She was out of the car and away across the pavement before he could finish the question. He pulled out of the stream of traffic and sat staring bleakly through the windshield at the rain-swept gray street. After a couple of minutes he switched off the engine and sat there numbly, swallowing bile and feeling more and more uncomfortable.

Ten unhappy minutes passed before Mary opened the passenger door and slipped back into the car. Her hair was soaked, and she was pale as fine porcelain.

"I'm sorry, Roger. I should have said something before we started, but I was afraid I'd make us late. I feel a lot better now. I think maybe it was those mussels we had for an appetizer. Do you think they might have been off?"

Roger stared at her. The garlicky mussel taste suddenly swept up on him again. He swallowed hard.

"Excuse me."

He was out of the car and off across the street. Ten minutes later he returned to find Mary explaining to a sympathetic and amused bobby that she'd be happy to move the car along, but she'd never driven on this side of the road before.

"You'll be all right to drive, sir?"

"I think so." Roger slipped the car into gear. "Hell of a way to start a Monday morning." He wiped his mouth with a blue handkerchief.

Mary managed a smile as the unflappable bobby waved them back into the traffic. "We're off to a good start. Will the helicopter wait for us?"

Roger sighed. "So long as we don't do it again. Did you have any breakfast?"

"No. Couldn't face the idea. Did you?"

"Not a bite. I'll tell you what I'm going to do. I'll stop at the next phone booth and call Matson—he's our pilot—and tell him we've been stuck in a traffic jam. Then I'll take you over to a place in Kilburn High Road that does a solid old-fashioned breakfast. We need to get something into our stomachs before we take off. Any objections?"

Mary belched loudly, then put her hand to her mouth. "Do I need to say anything after that?"

They both were laughing, though it hurt Roger's long-suffering stomach.

"One more thing," said Mary. "About last night. I'd like you to forget about it, if you can. I shouldn't have tried to get you to tell me what you thought of Don. You must have decided I'm an absolute asshole." She saw him wince. "Sorry. A real bounder, is that better?"

He lifted his left hand from the gear shift and crossed his fingers. "Pax, or kings, or whatever you say over there. I felt bad too—some of it must have been the mussels, but let's start over."

By the time they had finished breakfast, the morning rush was ending and the rain had slowed to a steady drizzle. Mary noticed their pilot give Roger a wink and a sceptical grin when she climbed out of the MG. So Roger had been late other mornings. She managed to resist the urge to talk about the traffic jam as Roger introduced her to Matson.

Visibility was bad after takeoff. It stayed poor most of the flight, so that Mary's patient window watching didn't pay off until they were into the Highlands and north of Fort William. Even then there was little to see, bare, broken peaks of gray and purple brown, with no signs of towns and villages.

"Not inland," said Roger, in reply to Mary's question. "Up here in the Highlands most of the people live out along the coast. There's not enough good soil to make good farming."

"But what about all those stories of the highlanders running over the glens? Where were they running?"

Matson had turned his head at that. "It's the kilt, miss," he said. "You try going around wivout your trousers, you'd move quick enough, I reckon."

After that, she could get no serious answers out of Roger, though he did regale her with all the old legends and horror stories that he had picked up in the exhibition.

"You'll like Laxford," he said cheerfully. "There's plenty

of gruesome tales up there. Ask Hamish about Sawney Bean as a fine example of Scots taste. Sawney lived in a cave with his wife and kids. They used to run down travelers, kill them, rob them, and eat 'em. People disappeared for years before they finally caught on and rooted the Beans out and executed them. Lots of good stuff like that in the Highlands—be great local color for your book."

"Oh. Please, don't talk about that." Mary looked anguished. "I don't want people to know about it until I get something written. It would be awful to talk about it and then find I couldn't do it."

"As the bishop said to the actress." But Roger had dropped the subject at once.

Their slow start had cost them almost two hours, and Roger was due for a late afternoon meeting over in Dounreay. He had just enough time after their landing on the cliffs outside Laxford to carry her bags to the Over The Water and introduce her to Hamish Macveagh.

"We'll be back tomorrow for the housewarming," he said. "I'll make sure Don doesn't go out on the tiles tonight."

Macveagh shook his head disapprovingly as Roger hurried away.

"All rush, and where's the end of it?" He picked up Mary's bags, grunting at their weight. "You're here to stay, missie, from the feel o' these."

He struggled into the Over The Water and dropped the bags at the door leading to the kitchen. Mary followed him slowly, looking around her before going on into the inn.

The Over The Water faced east and inland, toward the curving shore of Loch Laxford. It was built of dark, ancient stone, with irregular insets of mean, pinched windows that seemed as opaque as the walls. Small panes of green glass were crossed by a diamond-shaped lattice of gray lead strips. Doors and windows showed that the walls of the inn were almost two feet thick, massively formed from shaped blocks of solid stone. Mary walked back a few paces and looked at the upper story. Red brick chimneys, one at each end of the building, sent twin columns of pale brown smoke straight up into the still, foggy air. The late October afternoon seemed to be all grays and browns. In front of the door a parked motorcycle, bright red, made an incongruous splash of modern color.

Far away, behind the solid bulk of the inn, Mary fancied that she could hear a mutter of sea breakers on the coast. They were invisible beyond the edge of the cliff.

Hamish Macveagh had returned to the doorway and was looking back at Mary. He was short and wiry, with a shiny bald head and a big nose. Mary could hear him still panting with the effort of carrying her cases. She felt a moment of guilt—she probably outweighed him by forty pounds—that changed to a patient amusement when she saw his expression. She had seen it before from small men. He was staring at her in open admiration, what she thought of as Whymper taking the measure of the Matterhorn.

"My, but you're a fine, handsome lassie, Mrs. Willis." (There, she hadn't been imagining it.) His face was glowing red with pleasure or exertion. "I had no idea we would be getting such a beauty here in the village. Here, now, ye have to be feeling tired out after coming here all the way in that machine. Can I get you a wee drop of drink, now, just to settle your stomach?"

Mary followed him in. The main bar of the Over The Water was all dark, seasoned oak. In the big fireplace on her left, brick trimmed with black iron fittings, a big coal fire was burning orange red—the first coal fire she had seen since she was growing up in Iowa! She walked over to it and held out her hands, while Hamish Macveagh went to the bar. Behind the long, broad surface of dark wood sat a line of small oak casks. He held out a glass by one of the spigots and looked at her inquiringly. Mary shook her head.

"Not just now, Mr. Macveagh, unless maybe you have a cup of tea or coffee?"

He was smiling. "Not Mac-*vee*, miss, or you'll upset half the people in the village. Mac-*vay*, it is—ye'll just have to ignore the spelling. Mr. Willis had the same problem, wanted to call me Mac-vee-ag."

That sounded like Don. He had a tin ear for languages. Mary thought of her struggle to get him to pronounce Aunt Leonie Urquhart's name correctly.

"What I'd really like to do would be to get the keys of the house and go on over there. My husband won't be back until tomorrow night, and I'd like to have everything ready for him when he gets here."

"Aye." Hamish Macveagh looked at the glass he was holding for a moment, then half-filled it from one of the casks. He held the pale fluid up to the light, sniffed at it with pleasure, and drank it down.

He licked his lips. "It's the best malt in the west, Mrs. Willis, Lochinver Honey. Ye'll have to try a drop a bit later." He sniffed and pulled out a big dark-blue handkerchief to wipe his nose. "Now, regarding this house of yours. There, we've got a wee bit of a problem. Nothing serious, so don't be worrying about it, but Mr. Willis told us he wanted a spare set of keys, so you'd each have 'em. An' I thought ye'd be coming in here tomorrow. So when Mr. Campbell—he's the minister—told me he had to be goin' on down to Ullapool today, I told him it would be a big favor to us if he'd take the keys and have another set made. An' he took 'em, and now here we are with never a set to let you on in."

He saw Mary's disappointed expression and came out from behind the bar. "Now, it's not the problem you might be thinking. He'll be back here tonight. But it'll be late on, an' I don't expect ye'd want to be going on up the cliff and openin' up the house in the pitch dark, right? So it's best I'd say if ye spend the night here, at the Over The Water, and first thing in the morn we'll get Walter Campbell to come on over here with the keys, and take you to the house." He waved his hand. "If you're thinking of the expense, now, there'll not be any, because we keep one room all the time for people coming up here for JosCo—it's instructions from Laird Jericho, and he pays for all."

He nodded his head back to the door where Mary's cases were standing. "An' back in the kitchen we've the best bit of Scottish beef I've seen in a long while—ye'll never have tasted the like over in America. So what I suggest we do is, we have one of the lads carry your bags on up, an' if it's all in order wi' you we'll have tea for you in a few minutes, aye, an' home-baked scones an' heather honey to go with it. An' about six o'clock, we'll be ready to serve you dinner, so you'll have time for a bit of a rest and unpack your things before that."

Mary took a deep breath and smiled at him. So much for Don's letters about the taciturn Scots! If she didn't get a word in soon, Hamish Macveagh would have her whole life arranged for the next year.

"That all sounds good to me, so long as you're sure we can

52

get an early start tomorrow. Don told me that there's a bit of cleaning up to do on the house, and if you know him at all you'll have some idea what that could mean. I'm expecting we may find rubbish all over it."

Macveagh pursed his lips and shook his head slowly. "Mebbe, but I really doubt that. Mrs. Macdougal was cleaner there, when poor Mr. Knowlton was livin' in the big house." He paused for a moment, an uneasy look on his face. "Aye, well she is a very met-ic-ul-ous woman for the cleaning. We'll get ye there early enough, though, don't you be worryin' about that. Walter Campbell's not one to lie abed—he'll be up and about by six, and here by seven. So would you come on back wi' me, then, and we'll get you settled?"

He opened the door at the rear of the bar, and led Mary into a dark corridor. It never seemed to occur to him to swtich on any lights, though the afternoon was already sinking toward a gloomy twilight. As her eyes became used to the dark, Mary saw that the walls were covered with paintings—presumably of the many generations of innkeepers. They were a dour, bewhiskered group, with not a smile in the line. When had it emerged, the idea that everyone had to be smiling all the time in photographs? Probably when fast film was developed—no one could hold a fixed smile for hours. She thought of her passport photo. If Don saw that he would ask for a divorce.

Hamish Macveagh was patiently waiting for her by a small table at the foot of the staircase. As she came up to him he turned and shouted back along the corridor.

"Tommy! Cases, to the big bedroom. And now, miss"—he turned to Mary—"if you'd just sign in the book here for us. We'd not bother you with it, but I have to get the record to send off to JosCo. Just sign in here with your name, and we'll take care of the date and the address an' all that."

He handed Mary a pen with a much-chewed end. She bent over, with Hamish breathing a pleasant Scotch-scented breath down her neck (maybe she'd try the Lochinver Honey after all) and signed her full name. He looked on with interest.

"Thank ye, miss. Mary Vayson Willis, eh? Now that's interestin'. So where'd you be gettin' that name Vayson, your middle name there?"

"It's my maiden name." She saw that Hamish was looking blank. "In America, when a woman gets married she usually

53

keeps her old name and uses it as a middle name. You don't do that over here. Before I married, I was Mary Vayson."

"I thought so." Hamish was beaming. "I *thought* to myself, when I saw what a fine big juicy lass you are, I thought it then."

"Thought *what*, for heaven's sake?" (Hamish was looking at her as though she were some kind of prize vegetable he'd just found in his backyard.)

"Why, thought that you belonged around here. Ye see, miss, it's that name of yours, Vayson. Ye didn't know, then, that in Scotland 'Mac' means 'son'—so ye'd have like Macandrew meaning Andrew's son? An' when Scots people go on down south an' live in England, they often enough change it to the English form."

Mary frowned. "So that way, you mean that Vayson would be—"

"—the same as Macveagh." Hamish looked at her and shook his head. "Mary Macveagh, that's who you are. An' you know, I thought it, soon as I had a good look at you. She's the spitting image of a Macveagh, I said to myself. Now then, we'll have to drink on this a bit later, after ye get settled in your room. You come on down, soon as you like, an' we'll have tea an' have you meet people. I tell ye, you'll find that you're here among friends."

He turned and began to lead the way up the stairs. On the fourth step he halted and turned back. "Aye, an' I ought to say one other thing, Mary Macveagh. Welcome home."

CHAPTER 4

> Then there arose at her bed's feet
> Ane grumley guest . . .

Not much sleep on Saturday night, flying over from New York; then traipsing around London all day Sunday, showing off how well she could walk. She was dead tired. Don't forget the internal miseries of Sunday night, and the long trip up to Laxford. She *had* to be dead tired.

So why couldn't she get to sleep?

Mary went across to the chest of drawers, picked up the heavy stone jug, and poured a glass of water. She gulped it down, ice cold. As she walked over to the door to switch out the light, her arms and legs felt heavy and clumsy and weighed down with fatigue. Before going back to bed she stepped to the French window and opened it wide. The moon was high overhead. It threw a pool of light around her feet, leaving the room behind her dark. The chilly night breeze carried in the sound of far-off breakers, advancing slowly up the beach as the moon called them closer.

She shivered, turned, and hurried back to her bed. Pulling up the crisp sheet she snuggled down deep under the blue eiderdown and thick blankets. The warmth of her body still clung to the covers.

She couldn't blame the bed. That was fine—soft and deep and long enough for her to stretch out full length and flex bare toes against the clean sheets. She turned onto her right side, buried her face in the down pillow. The smell of mothballs carried her back home to Iowa, to Gran's old house.

Moths and constipation, those had been Gran's mortal ene-
mies. There were little slivers of camphor in the pockets of
every dress, and molasses and senna pod tea every night
when it couldn't be quietly poured away outside. Laxatives
were important for Gran, but no one had never noticed any
useful effect on the children.

Gran seemed ancient, a living fossil. She spoke about
Teddy Roosevelt and Woodrow Wilson on familiar terms. It
had come as a shock to meet those two names later, in
school, and find that they were not members of Gran's immediate family. They had been part of the house. They belonged
to Gran, just like the white-haired man with the curved
moustache who sat in the photo frame on top of the black piano, faded to brown and ivory by the aging paper. None of
them could remember Grampa, but they all knew him very
well.

The way he liked his eggs; the time he hurt his foot in the
mowing machine, when Gran had run a great distance—four
miles? five miles? it got more with each retelling—to bring
help from the town. The old medals in the writing desk were
Grampa's. They had looked at the fading purple and red and
yellow ribbons and imagined the deeds of valor that went
with their award. Grampa had been in the 'infantry' (she had
been confused by that word; it suggested a group of small
soldiers, the same size as the people in kindergarten class).
Gran said that Grampa should by rights have been in the
cavalry, he was a natural horseman who had been born too
late for his real war.

He had been over to *Europe*. When Gran talked of it to a
five-year-old, it was a place beyond the moon, the exotic and
sinister location that big children talked about in whispers.
Gran told about the trip; about the French that Grampa had
spoken when he came back (polly-vous, to Gran it was all
polly-vous); and about the way that he lifted her off her feet
when he came back home and carried her from Junction
Springs Station all the way to the house, lifting her up to
smell the mauve lilac that was just opened to bloom next to
Peabody's store, squeezing the breath right out of her. . . .

A banging door two floors below brought Mary sharply
back from the edge of sleep. Late leavers from the Over The
Water. She heard a loud laugh, gruff voices saying something
about "footba," the scuff of boots on gravel, and a roaring

56

belch. A car radio went on, with a loud rock beat. *Music, when soft voices die.* . . . Damn them all, didn't they know people were trying to get to sleep? Now she was right back to square one.

She took a long, deep breath and tried to relax completely. Overtired, that had to be the problem—physically and mentally. What was it the Arabs said? Your soul couldn't move from one place to another faster than a walking camel. She was still somewhere in mid-Atlantic. So think how poor old Grampa must have felt. He had been shipped to Europe straight off the farm. She had at least been exposed to English people in New York, so she knew London pretty well before she ever got there, well beyond the picture postcard and movie backdrop level.

But talking about England and being there were quite different.

Mary rubbed at her stomach through the piled bedclothes. She had a funny tingly feeling there, just as though she was going to catch a plane or a bus. How was it different here from the way she had imagined it? The food, of course, and lots of the smells. Funny thing. She was so sensitive to smells, and Don never gave them a thought—he hadn't even noticed that blocked drain in their first apartment, and she had gagged on it.

It had to be mostly the people, that's what culture shock was all about. There were plenty of other differences—the breakfast that Roger had ordered in Kilburn would have been banned by the AMA; so much fat, so much cholesterol, and so delicious—but that sort of thing was easy to adjust to. The way that people looked and spoke when they caught her accent, that was hard. Worse here than in London, they must be used to Americans in London. And yet she was a lot more at home here, even though the local speech in Laxford was a problem, with all its "ochs" and "achs."

"Don't you worry, miss," Hamish Macveagh had said when it was clear that she was missing half the things that had been spoken at supper. "Just you gi' it a few days an' tell people to say it over if ye don't catch on the first time. You'll get used to it quick. I'm telling ye, ye're a Macveagh, right?"

That was the way that he insisted on introducing her to people at the bar: "Mrs. Mary Macveagh Willis." Mary liked the sound of it. Dignified and comfortable. Laxford had its

57

points already, even before she saw their rented house. She had stuffed herself on Hamish's roast beef, with boiled potatoes and parsley, Brussels sprouts, and fluffy Yorkshire pudding. Those, and beef gravy made with flour and beef drippings, nearly thick enough to stand a spoon up in.

Hamish hadn't asked if she would like more. He assumed it. (A weight problem on the horizon unless she got away from the pub's style of cooking and eating). No dessert offered. Strong tea with milk and sugar finished the meal.

There had been five of them at supper; Hamish, Mary, two elderly women whose relationship to Hamish and to each other was still unclear, and Ronnie, a shy lad who was just developing his first traces of a beard. He was painfully self-conscious, blushing whenever Mary spoke to him or even looked at him. He had come from even farther north in Scotland, spending the winter months in Laxford while his mother and father were away doing something mysterious in the Shetland Isles. She had picked up that information a little bit at a time from Hamish and the two women. Ronnie had eaten everything in sight, but he kept his look down on his plate and didn't look up even when someone spoke to him directly.

"Right," said Hamish as she finished her last section of Yorkshire pudding. "Now ye've got a bit of a linin' on yer stomach, let's go into the bar for a minute. Dora and Lizzie will clear up in here for us. Mebbe we'll have Mr. Campbell in soon, and he'll have yer keys wi' him."

"The minister will come into the Over The Water?"

Hamish had grinned. "Aye. He does that. But don't get the wrong idea on it. He doesna' drink a drop hisself—he looks on in to make sure the rest of us all feel miserable. Ye'll see it. Watch the way he looks at the lads in there."

The main bar was a good deal more cheerful with the lights on and a dozen customers standing up by the counter or sitting over near the fireplace. Hamish shook his head when she asked him for a Scotch and soda.

"No need to say Scotch in here, Miss—that's the only sort ye'll get. An' with respect, Miss Mary, it's a crime to put fizzy in wi' good whisky. Will ye try it wi' plain water, good clear water from one o' the burns?"

He didn't fit the idea of the reserved Britisher at all well. She took the glass (at least a double Scotch in there) and

58

nodded her thanks. Hamish Macveagh had to be controlled, or he would be running her whole life in Laxford before she knew what was happening.

She raised her glass. "Cheers."

"Aye. *Slainte*." Hamish lifted his own glass. "An' here's to a long an' happy stay in Laxford."

The customers had been watching them closely, with open curiosity. Hamish turned to the group over by the fireplace. "This is Mrs. Mary Macveagh Willis, come back here after—how long away, miss?"

She felt her own blush starting—she was no better than young Ronnie. "I—er—I don't really know. I think my grandfather left England about seventy years ago."

"So he did now. And what was his name?"

"William Vayson. William Charles Vayson. But he went over to America from England, not from Scotland."

"Aye. That's the first step that's led many a good mon astray." Hamish winked at the regulars. "First England they go, then on farther afield. William Charles Vayson, eh?"

"There was a Willy Macveagh, lived on down a few miles east of here, back in Dad's time." The speaker was old, a thin man with a wispy beard and a heavy wooden walking stick. It was hard to imagine his father. "He went on south, wi' his brother. Never came on back up here, either one of 'em. Could be that'd be the lady's granddad—timing'd be about right, seventy years or so."

There was a nodding of heads. She felt that all eyes were on her, watching her as she drank her whisky, waiting for her to reply. Surely it was ridiculous, the idea that anybody could track a person back to a particular village, and a particular house—even the very family. But what had the local population been seventy years back? Maybe she was the ignorant one, maybe the old man knew a lot more than she did about all this.

"I don't know," she said at last, looking down into her empty glass. (That had gone down quickly; maybe she shouldn't blame Don too much for taking one too many when he was staying at the Over The Water). "My father's father died before I was born, so I never heard him talk any about his past, or where he came from. They didn't have much in the way of records back then, either. It *could* be the man you say, but who's to know."

59

"We could ask over in Lochinver," said Hamish. He took her glass and refilled it without asking. "We'll check there. I'm sure that ye'll be interested to know—"

She followed his look, wondering why he had suddenly stopped speaking. The man who stood in the doorway of the bar was staring at them intensely.

It was a figure from another century, from a time before her grandfather's. He was short and slight, dressed in a rusty black tight-fitting suit, with a thick waistcoat. His black shoes were heavy, and polished to a high shine. She was astonished to see that he wore actual gaiters, black buttoned ones of dull leather. The clerical collar around his neck was the only relief of lighter tone about his whole person. Even the buttons seemed dull, like lumps of hardened soot on his coat.

"I didn't think you'd be in quite this early, sir." Hamish finally broke the uncomfortable silence. "Good trip to Ullapool?"

The other man did not speak. Hamish at last turned to Mary. "Mrs. Willis, here's someone I know you've been waiting to meet. This is Walter Campbell, our minister in Laxford."

She was suddenly very conscious of the half-full glass of whisky that she was holding. She placed it on the bar counter and stepped forward, holding out her hand.

"I'm pleased to meet you, Mr. Campbell. I really appreciate what you did for us, having copies of the keys made like this."

He looked for a moment at her hand before he stepped forward and took it. He gave it a brief clasp with a hand that was thin and very warm, with tough work-roughened fingers.

As he lifted his gaze she saw for the first time had a close look at his face. A high forehead and strong pointed chin were framed by long, steel-gray hair that grew down well past his ears. His eyebrows, thick and bushy, were a few shades darker, above protruding gray eyes, intense and unblinking. She dropped her own look before the blind stare, past his wide, thin-lipped mouth. Walter Campbell's face was red and lumpy, a patchwork of moles and blemishes on the tough skin.

"It was nothing," he said at last. "Nothing at all." The minister's voice was surprisingly attractive, a deep soft burr with a hint of a stammer in it. "I am sure that you are keen

60

to move into your house, and get away from this"—he cast another long, probing look around the room—"this place here."

"Tomorrow morning, if I can." She was feeling a sudden sympathy for Hamish Macveagh. If Walter Campbell came in here every night and offered damnation to the customers it must be terrible for business. It wasn't fair to Hamish, trying to ruin his livelihood. She turned deliberately, picked up her glass, and drank from it before speaking again.

"If you happen to have the keys with you now, Mr. Campbell, I'll be happy to take them and go on over there first thing in the morning."

"But if he do that, miss," interrupted Hamish, "it's better if one of us goes on up wi' ye. There'll be things to turn on, and things to turn off, and it's a sight easier to show you than to tell you. If ye'll wait until mebbe ten o'clock, I can go on up wi' ye meself."

"I'd like to get there earlier than that." She hesitated. "You see, Don will be back tomorrow night, and I'd like to have everything ready for him, and I have no idea how much work it will be to get it in shape. I'd like to go on and start the cleaning—"

"I can help you on that, if you'll let me." Walter Campbell's speech was different from Hamish's, less guttural but still no easier to understand. He was standing up rigidly as though to attention, but still a few inches shorter than Mary. She was becoming more uncomfortable before that high-intensity stare.

"I did not think to bring your keys over here with me. Foolish, but I left them back at home with the rest of the materials that I brought from Ullapool. But I can be here, with the keys, at seven o'clock tomorrow morning."

"But that will be a lot of trouble for you!"

"Or earlier, if you wish." He did not seem to have noticed her reluctance to bring him over so early. "Also, I know the house very well where you will be staying. I can show you where everything is, how everything works."

"But it will take hours . . ." She stopped when she realized that it would take Hamish just as long. And Walter Campbell, unlike everyone else in Laxford, had his heaviest work day on Sunday and a lot of time to spare during the week. She nodded.

61

"Seven o'clock will be wonderful. I'll be waiting in the kitchen for you."

"Good. There are other things that I want to talk to you about."

Campbell nodded, turned his head, and took a long look around the room. When he looked again at Hamish Macveagh his expression was sad.

"No sign of Jack coming in this evening?"

Hamish shook his head. "He's away east today, pickin' up timber. Mebbe back tomorrow."

"Ah." The minister nodded. He looked wistfully over in the corner of the room at a small table, nodded again, and left without another word. As the heavy door swung to behind him there was a noticeable lightening in the atmosphere of the long room. Mary smiled at Hamish.

"Not much for conversation, eh?"

He grinned back. "Not with old Walter. You saw his big weakness there, the only thing he allows himself."

"I didn't see anything."

"That's 'cause Jack Woodward isna' here. Most nights the two of 'em sit over there and play cribbage. Thirty minutes is all the minister allows himself. You can see him sit there and struggle with himself when time's up. I've seen him sit there as long as three-quarters of an hour, and when he got up he looked as guilty as if he'd murdered his mother." Hamish sniffed at his glass. "So he wants to talk to you, does he? Are you Presbyterian?"

"No. I'm Lutheran, I suppose, and not much of that for these last few years." Mary laughed self-consciously. In four years in New York no new acquaintance had ever once asked her about her religion. "Do you think he wants to try and convert me?"

"Walter? Oh, he might, if ye gi' him a bit of a chance." Hamish shrugged and refilled his glass. "Conversion's not so much his style, though. If ye go by the way he *talks*, we'd still be burnin' people at the stake. He's a good man, but he does his good deeds on the quiet. There isn't a poor person round these parts who hasn't been given somethin' they need that Walter 'happened to run across' on his travels. He's wheedled things out of me that I hated to give him, then they show up in a crofter's cottage. The only thing I don't like is when he sits me down and talks about religion—though I'll

62

give him his due, he's more interestin' than most. An' he never tries to get me into the kirk. Thinks I'm too far gone, mebbe."

"But doesn't he have a bad effect on your business, coming in here and glowering at everybody with a drink?"

"You'd think so, wouldn't you? But it seems to work the other way round. There's not a body in here doesn't need another dram after Walter's been in hell-firing us. We'll all be in for a big shot of eternal damnation, and if that's so we might as well have a bit of fun afore we go. Can I fill ye up again?"

"No." She shook her head and put her hand over the top of the glass. "I've had more than I'm used to—I'm not much of a drinker and I have to get up early tomorrow. I think I'd best head off to bed now, it's been a long day."

"D'yer need an alarm clock? If you do, I'll see what we can find. I reckon ye'll be up long afore me, but Dora will fix you a good breakfast. She's a mornin' bird, can't bear to have her head on the sheet a minute after dawn. Ye'll find there's nothing better than Lochinver Honey to give you a good sleep at night."

That had been at eight-thirty. So much for Lochinver Honey. Now it must be close to eleven, and she didn't feel any closer to sleep than when she first lay down.

She wasn't uncomfortable. Quite the opposite, if anything. It had taken a while to understand why she felt so much at home in this room and this bed. She had finally caught on from the smell of the sheets, camphor and lavender. It was just as though she had been plumped back into childhood, with all the comforting old-fashioned smells and feelings. That must be why old places are so friendly. They carry us back to the way we felt when we were very young, when things were well-defined and safe and certain. This could have been a room in Gran's house.

What had the inside of Gran's front room looked like? She hadn't been there for fifteen years, but she should be able to recall it exactly. Start with the piano, the one that no one was ever allowed to play. Next to that there had been a blue settee, with an embroidered lace cloth along the back, pictures of dragons and butterflies in orange and yellow. And next to that?

Some sort of wooden chest, was it? Carved with curly patterns, like the leaves of one of the trees in the backyard.

It was becoming difficult to get a clear mental picture. The memory was clouding, beginning to overlay the image of this room. The striped wallpaper, was that here or there? And the dresser. No, that was Gran's, it had the little figure of the china shepherdess on top of it, the one that Gran said was brought back from Dresden. But the mirror could be either room, and the drapes over by the big window, with the light streaming in through them . . . the setting sun, or the cooler light of the moon . . .

. . . sheets, blankets, heavy eiderdown. Mary's body was warm beneath them. Her last thought was a faint touch of drowsy surprise. It had been a full day and more since she had applied any perfume. Back at the apartment, before she left for the airport, days ago. She seemed to sense it now about her, as though a trace of *Climax* still somehow clung to her skin, breathing off her warm flesh and hanging in the air above the bed. The touch of the night wind through the open window seemed to mingle with the perfume and fill the room around her with an elusive, languorous scent. . . .

Mary found herself awake again. It was sudden and complete, as though she had been splashed with cold water. She felt a few frightening moments of total disorientation in time and space.

Where was she? What time, what place?

Moonlight on the wall in front of her, broken into a pattern of diamond shapes. Cool air on her face, there was a definite draft from somewhere near. She heard the faint rustle of drapes, down past the end of the bed. Farther off, a hollow roaring sound, distant breakers. It brought a gradual awareness of where she was. She blinked sleepy eyes, turned her head, and looked over to the window. That was the source of the sea noises. It was still deep night outside, with only a pale wash of light from the moon, lower in the sky now, to mark the layout of the room.

Mary snuggled lower in the bed, pulling the covers high up to her eyes. It had happened before, but usually only when she had a good reason for nighttime unrest—worry, or fever, or loud and sudden outside noise. It had taken months to adapt to the nighttime alarms of Manhattan. Every passing fire truck had her awake in an instant.

This was different. Except for soothing sea murmurs, the silence about the inn was complete; not even the creaks and squeaks that earlier movements had drawn from the old timbers.

She felt a sudden longing for Don, stronger than she had felt since he left New York. If only he could come into the room and snuggle up to her, spoon-fashion, the way he used to when he came back late from a business meeting.

Where was he now? Stuck in some fusty hotel near Dounreay, thinking the same thoughts that she was having? One thing about this job, there was little danger that he'd find another woman on his travels.

She imagined his body behind her with the comforting rough tickle of his chest hair and the scratch of his chin against her shoulder. Then the gentle, persistent stroking of her breast and thighs, the way he would awaken her if she had already fallen asleep. That slow steady touch on her sleeping body had brought her closer to readiness than anything else. It made her feel that if she could only keep her mind submerged and let her body free she would achieve the orgasm that always eluded her.

Don had blamed himself at first. He was careful to rouse her before he entered her, and he drew out their lovemaking as long as she wished. It was no good. Something in her wakened mind held her back, blunting the sharp edge of her first responses. He kept trying, though she had despaired long ago.

If only he could come back from Dounreay tonight. Mary was astonished at her body's sudden response to that thought. Her nipples were swollen, standing out beneath the sensible cotton nightgown, and there was a surprising pulse of feeling from her vagina and clitoris, as though she had already been touched there.

She put her hand to her left breast, perplexed by her own excited state.

What was happening to her? It was ridiculous, to feel hornier when Don was not even here than she usually did when he was making love to her. She had to stop fantasizing and get some sleep. Tomorrow was one day that she didn't want to feel a wreck—not with work to do on the house. How

65

would Don feel if she told him she couldn't go for the real thing because she had worn herself out thinking about it?

Mary stretched, took a deep breath, and rolled over onto her back. She looked over to the window again, wondering how long it would be before the moon went down to leave the room in darkness.

Something was out there, peering in at her.

Outside the French window stood a shape, a form that interrupted the weak moonlight. Her scream caught in her throat. At first she thought that she was looking at a skull, a smooth round skull on top of a square, powerful body. Then she saw the heavy muscles along the jawline and the ears flat to the head.

The figure was quite motionless, peering in through the window. One hand was on the side of the open frame. The features of the face were in shadow, deepset eyes mere pools of darkness in a white background.

Mary closed her eyes tightly for a moment. Years ago, living in her bachelor apartment in college, there had been nights when she awoke convinced that someone was standing at the foot of her bed. It was a dark and indistinct figure, never quite visible, but the sense of someone present was strong and direct. She would lie silent, not daring to move, not daring even to cry out. With eyes shut tight she waited hopelessly for it to make its advance.

Nothing had ever happened. Surely this had to be the same thing, imagination working overtime. She counted to ten, then forced herself to open her eyes again and sit up.

Afraid of what she would see there she looked again at the window. The shape was gone, vanished into the moonlight. The thin side drapes were moving and billowing in a sudden breeze. That must have created the illusion, some trick of light that had made a phantom from the shadow of the curtains.

She pushed back the covers, pulled down the nightgown that had somehow ridden up above her waist, and swung her feet to the floor. The linoleum was a shock of cold to her bare soles. It added the final touch to bring her all the way to wakefulness, to tell her that now at any rate she was not dreaming. She was conscious again of her distended breasts and sensitized genitals. Conscious of them, and amazed. How could sexual excitement survive the fear that she had just

66

felt? When worry, fear or fatigue hit her, any interest in or thought about sex was usually the first thing to disappear. Barefoot, she padded across the smooth floor and took hold of the handle that would close the French window.

The balcony outside was a small one, no more than four or five feet deep. Beyond the dark iron railing she could see the thicket of windswept trees that stood to the west of the inn. She looked beyond them to where, farther off, the moonlight glinted off the breakers below, a faint tracery of spilled salt on a dark blanket. The moon was low on the western horizon, dipping toward the sea.

Mary bent lower. Her eye had caught something closer to hand. From the window where she stood, leading over the edge of the balcony a broad gleaming trail was just visible, like the silver swath of a giant snail track. There was a smell in the air, pungent and subtle.

After a moment's hesitation she went out through the French window and stepped to the edge of the balcony. The earlier fog of the day had gone, and it was a clear, cold night. The metal railing was icy under her hand, wet with a heavy October dew. She rubbed her fingers against the railing and lifted her hand to her face. The heavy, musky smell was pleasant, familiar yet unfamiliar.

Mary looked down, past the edge of the balcony. A low line of bushes marked the edge of the Over The Water's ill-kept garden. Behind a bush she thought for a moment that she could again see the same figure, glistening white through the branches. She moved to one side to get a better look. The figure seemed to merge into the bushes, changing from a pearly, smooth body to a patch of brighter light where the moon struck clear through the line of stunted trees.

She stood for a long minute, watching, motionless, waiting for any sign of movement on the ground beneath. There was nothing. She was still breathing fast and deep, and her pulse was racing. Her odd excitement was more than simple fear and nervous tension.

She turned and went back to the bedroom, closing the window behind her and slipping the bolt. After a moment's hesitation she pulled the drapes across and tied them in the center. As she went across and bolted the door of the bedroom she was beginning to shiver, an uncontrollable spasm of her legs and her lower body. She longed to be back again under the warm covers.

The sheets smelled musky now when she slid between them. There was a new odor of salty sex in the smooth covers, blending with the oily scent that she had brought in from the balcony railing.

Surprisingly, sleep came quickly this time, a rapid swooping descent along a dark plane. But she did not sleep easy. Her rest was punctuated by a wild series of strange dreams. She was in the house on the hill, the house that she had seen so far only as a distant gray mass of stone. But now it was under the sea. She was there with Knowlton, its previous occupant, "poor Mr. Knowlton" as Hamish had described him. He was a faceless figure, leading her through the rooms and passages, searching for Don. When Knowlton disappeared somewhere in the labyrinth of drowned corridors and secret underwater caverns, the gleaming snail track ran on ahead of her, drawing her deeper into the quiet waters.

CHAPTER 5

The legend of the seal people is curiously persistent around the western shores of the Highlands. The seal men, or selkies as they are known locally, are said to shed their skins at will and to assume the likeness of humans. A mortal who can steal a skin during this process of transformation is thereby able to gain magical power over the selkie owner.

The stories have some peculiar features that distinguish them from the general Highland romances. They call to mind other and more famous mythical beings. For example, the seal people (all men, never women) favor nights of the full moon and shun daylight. They are repelled by the crucifix, and avoid mirrors; and they cannot tolerate certain herbs and wild flowers. One is tempted to speculate that many legends of Eastern Europe must share a common origin with the tales of the selkies; or (dare one suggest it?) that the stories originated here in western Scotland and spread east to the Balkans and beyond.

—J. J. JAMIESON, *The Patchwork Quilt of Highland Lore*

Seen from the outside the house did not look encouraging. The dark stone had begun to crumble and flake, like fire-etched charcoal, and the windows were narrow and coated with grime. The twin towers facing west to the sea were exciting from a distance, but Mary's heart had sunk when she came close enough to see the signs of neglect in the weathered stone walls. It was hard to imagine a pleasant or carefree life within that dark structure.

"You know what they say, Mrs. Willis." Walter Campbell seemed to have picked up something from her expression. "You shouldn't judge a book by its cover. Wait until you see the inside, and I think you'll have a pleasant surprise."

Mary nodded. She would have been happy to walk over, but he had proudly produced an ancient car for the trip from the inn. The Riley Monaco (prewar, he had said—but which war?) whined and clattered its way protestingly up the steep road, jolting the two passengers fiercely whenever one of the big wire wheels hit the frequent lumps of granite in the crude road surface.

Mary held on grimly to the door on her left. The glove compartment in front of her held an old tobacco tin and two books; the Bible and a heavy blue-bound volume entitled, *The Quest For The Historical Jesus*. Both were battered from long use. Judging those volumes by *their* covers, Walter Campbell took his ministerial duties very seriously.

"I hope you're right," said Mary as the car pulled up on the paved courtyard east of the house. "I'll try and keep an open mind until we get inside. Anyway, maybe it'll all look a lot more cheerful on a fine day."

Campbell laughed as he switched off the wheezing engine, and they stepped out into the fine drizzle. "Well now, don't hold your breath waiting for that. Not 'till the spring, at any rate. They say in the village that we've seen the last of the summer."

He was still dressed in the same clothes of ancient black. Seen in daylight they looked even older than they had in the inn, with careful patches and mends in both jacket and trousers. If anything could make a man seem grim, those clothes did it. Mary had looked at him carefully as they drove the winding upward road to the house. The left profile was perhaps not enough to go by, but he was both younger and friendlier than he had seemed last night. He wasn't more than forty-five, and in natural light the protruding eyes didn't look so wild—the disconcerting touch of Marty Feldman was still there, but it disturbed her less. Mainly because his manner was much easier, as though he had to keep his worst side public when he came into the Over The Water. He acted

70

relaxed and cheerful now, like a different man. Or maybe, like Dora, he was just a morning person.

Hamish Macveagh hadn't exaggerated at all about that. When Mary crept miserably downstairs at the first light of dawn she had expected and hoped for the kitchen to herself for half an hour. She needed something to chase the cobwebs and the nightmares out of her brain. Tea, or better still coffee, hot and strong and sweet, that was the only salvation—food could come later.

She fumbled her way quietly down the dark staircase, still blinking the sleep from her eyes. At the bottom she paused. The kitchen door was partly open and a light was on inside, over by the stove. The morning was still a pale gleam at the window. Leaning over the stove was the diminutive figure of Dora, fully dressed and with a thick woolen cardigan thrown over her shoulders. She was pouring oatmeal from a fat cloth bag into a heavy iron pot of boiling water. Mary could hear her singing softly to herself, nodding her head over the pot. She looked tiny and very old.

When the oatmeal had been added she began to stir it with a long wooden spoon, still humming and singing in a thin, high-pitched voice. Now Mary could catch some of the words. ". . . *the world was in bloom, there were stars in the skies, except for the few that were there in your eyes . . .*"

Dora paused in her stirring and suddenly went into a little old-fashioned waltz step, still clutching the spoon. As she turned she caught sight of Mary in the doorway, hunched over in her bleary-eyed morning lethargy.

"Good morning, Miss Mary." She smiled and waved the spoon. "You're up betimes. Hamish told me to come on by and bang on the door at half-past six, but there'll be no need for that. Would ye fancy a wee bit o' egg an' bacon?"

Mary walked forward, pulling her robe about her. The kitchen was cold, even with the big stove. "I'd like some tea or coffee, if you could fix that. And I'll eat whatever you're having—there's no need to make anything special for me."

"Tea's easy, if ye don't mind summat that's been stewed a while. It's brewed fifteen or twenty minutes back."

"That will do me fine. I like it strong."

"Strong ye'll get it. An' porritch to eat, then? That's all I can manage, myself, this time of the morning."

"That will be good." Mary felt a sudden twinge of guilt.

71

Dora must have some sort of digestion problem, and here she had the poor old woman waiting on her. "Are you feeling all right?"

"All right?" Dora picked up a pint mug and turned around in surprise. "Aye, I'm fine. Why'd you ask?"

"Well . . . you say you can only eat porridge in the morning?"

"Aye, miss, that's right. Unless I want to go back upstairs and put me teeth in."

She didn't have a tooth in her head! Mary suddenly realized why Dora looked fifteen years older today. What had Don said in one of his letters? "You can tell they all love candy here. The old people don't have a tooth of their own."

She felt like a real fool. "Porridge will be wonderful—might wake me up. You must have been down here for hours."

"Who'd want to hang about in bed in the mornings?" Dora picked up the pink teapot that stood on the corner of the stove, removed the cozy and poured a dark brown steam into the mug. "This is the best part of the day, nice and quiet and clean. In the mid of winter now, I'll mebbe stay in an extra half hour—for the warmth, ye see. But I like to have breakfast on by six."

Mary gave a yawn that stretched the hinges of her jaw, picked up the mug that Dora placed in front of her and took a huge gulp of sweetened tea. It seemed to go directly to her veins, brightening the whole world. She was usually the same type as Dora, bouncy in the morning and collapsing late at night. But with jet lag still on her she didn't know *when* she would feel normal again. She sighed.

"What time is it now? I think I did something wrong with that alarm clock that Hamish lent me. When I woke up it wasn't even going. Hope I didn't break it."

"That auld clock? It never worked right—Hamish is too close to buy another one." Dora glanced over at the window, judging the line of sight of the morning sunlight diffused by the light drizzle outside. "It'll be close on half-past six now, I'd say. Days are drawing in, eh? Be dark to half-past seven in another month or so." She dumped a great ladle of porridge into a deep soup plate and passed it across to Mary. "Now, what would you like with that?"

"The porridge?" Mary stared down blankly at her plate. "Milk and sugar, I suppose—unless you have some honey?"

"No honey here, dearie—'less you count Lochinver Honey. I've seen Hamish use a drop o' *that* in his porritch on cold mornings." Dora sniffed and sprinkled salt from a pewter shaker over her own portion. "I can gi' ye summat mebbe better than the sugar, if ye'll try it. Here."

She did another little waltz step over to the pantry and came back carrying a brassy-gold can with a lift-off top.

"Try a spoonful of this in wi' it. I don't go for anythin' but a pinch or two of salt, meself, but that's the way we was all brought up. There's many as like the treacle for porritch— I've seen Hamish do it hisself, what he thinks I'm payin' him no mind."

Mary stirred in a loaded spoonful of the viscous golden liquid and took a first doubtful mouthful. It was surprisingly good. She began to spoon it down as fast as she could without burning her tongue. "I'm supposed to be all ready for the minister at seven o'clock," she said between gulps. "I'm late."

"For auld frozen face?" Dora sniffed again. "Don't you be worryin' about keeping him waitin' a few minutes. He's a miserable old pape—to my mind he's no more welcome in this house than the Grey Man o' Macdui. Will ye take a drop more porritch there?"

Mary shook her head. "It's very good, it really is, but I've no time for more. But why don't you like Mr. Campbell? I mean, he *is* your minister."

"Aye. Not my choice, he's not. He's an auld bigot, and a papist. An' he's no one of us—he only came in here half a year back, from down south."

"From England?"

"Na. From Glasgow. I don't know what we did to deserve *him*. T' hear him talk, ye'd think we're on our way to hell, the whole lot of us. I told him, I said, Mr. Campbell, I 'spect I've heard more sermons than ye've ever preached or ever will preach, an' I'm tellin' ye, you're foolin' yersel'. There's no more of that dee-ab-o-leezem, or whatever ye call it, here in Laxford than there is wild elephants. 'Tis not a thing but your own silly fancy, I said, and that's all there is to it."

Dora's views of Walter Campbell were quite definite, and there was no way she was about to keep them to herself. Her scornful look when the minister finally appeared in the

73

kitchen, apologizing for his five-minute lateness, would have been hard to miss. There was no offer of tea or porridge, though Mary thought she caught his wistful look over at the stove. She felt guilty about that when they got to the house. Walter Campbell would be showing her round with an empty stomach, and it would take a couple of hours of his time. Looking at him now, she thought again that his public and private personalities were a poor match. He was cheerful and patient, explaining everything to her.

"Here's the low point, you might say, of the whole house," he said, as he pushed open the heavy oak door and led the way into the gloomy hall. "Here we are facing northeast, so there's not much light comes in here first thing in the morning. It's a gloomy start. But wait until we get on upstairs, then see how the house feels to you."

The ground floor had four rooms branching off the main hall. Mary looked around hopelessly. Really, Don had so little gift for description, it was better to ignore what he had said about the house. She couldn't match his letters at all with the place surrounding her. She began her own assignment. This would be the dining room—need a decent-sized table for it from somewhere. And this was the obvious choice for a living room. It was gloomy, but a few lights would make all the difference.

The kitchen was huge and airy, looking westward to the sea, but Mary still regarded it with mixed feelings. There were cupboards galore, and more working surfaces than she had seen in her life. But . . . the hot water came from an old and filthy gas heater above the double copper sink. It made alarming and obscene noises when the minister coaxed it to life. There was no sign of a refrigerator, still less of a dishwasher or a garbage disposal unit. The kitchen implements were vast and heavy, like the equipment of a sixteenth century torture chamber. Maybe she could get used to them in time. But without a refrigerator . . .

"Well, there's a cellar," said Campbell in answer to Mary's question. "It's not a big one, but it's cool enough for your milk and butter. What else would you want to be freezing?"

"Meat and eggs. And I'd like to keep vegetables cool."

"Stick 'em all out by the back door."

"But how do I get ice?"

"For what? You see, Mrs. Willis, you have to remember

this is an old house, and we're not down London way here. The things that you mention, the fridge and so on, you'll find them down in London flats, and down in Glasgie too. But here, it's a wee bit backward. The electricity hasn't been here more than twenty years—an' there was no indoor lavatory in this house 'till three years back."

Campbell smiled. It transformed his face from stern duty to quiet good humor. "Look at it this way. One more gadget means one more thing to break and one more thing to repair. Ye'll find it takes a few days to get somebody up here from Ullapool, and then like as not he'll have to send over to Inverness for the parts he needs. You're safer and easier without too many machines here."

"So what do I do about things like this?" Mary wiggled the handle of the door that led into the backyard. "One good pull and this would come off. I don't think it will even close the door properly. I could have come over here last night and let myself in through here."

"Maybe you could." Walter Campbell bent over and looked at the handle, then turned it once or twice. "There's no problem with it, we've had doors and handles around these parts for a fair time." His tone was full of a dry humor. "We can get spares easy enough from the ironmonger over in Tongue, or maybe in Lochinver. It's the fancier stuff that'll give us the trouble. I'll guarantee that we can find somebody to help you with things like this. We should maybe make a list when we're all done looking around. There's a couple of good handymen here in Laxford, and they won't charge you much. I'll send one over."

There was no bathroom upstairs—modern plumbing hadn't proceeded that far—but Walter Campbell had told the truth. It was like a different house, light and airy, with windows that seemed to draw in more light than their size should have allowed. Mary went from one room to another, enchanted by the leap back to another century. The master bedroom had its own great fireplace, black iron set off by polished brass. Fire irons, tongs and poker and rake, stood in balanced symmetry on either side. Best of all, a tiny door, not more than four feet high, led from the corner of the room up a steep and dizzy spiral staircase to the southern turret.

By the time they were up there both of them were covered with dust. No one had used that stair for years, according to

75

Campbell, not since a visiting professor back in the fifties had set his telescope up on top of it. Mary roved around the odd, unnecessary parapets, looking first east, to the brooding mass of Foinaven, then west to the sea. The early morning drizzle had burned off while they were looking around downstairs. Now the air was clear and chilly, with the sun high enough to strike past the cliff edge and down to the big breakers. A couple of fishing boats were moving on south, half a mile off shore, and gray and white birds were skimming restlessly over the waves between the fishermen and the cliffs.

Walter Campbell leaned on the parapet, breathing in the air. His red face shone in the sun, and he seemed in no hurry to go on with their inspection.

"I wish I'd brought my binoculars up from the car," he said at last. "I didn't know it would be this clear."

"You want to look at the birds?"

"Aye. What else?" His lumpy profile was still, intent on the sea view. "Ye'll see some great ones here on a fine day. Especially when the tide's on the way in. Now, look there will ye." He pointed to a few tiny specks way out beyond the line of waves. Mary couldn't make out any details at all—either his eyes were exceptionally good, or he had a strong imagination.

"Arctic skuas, they are," he said, answering her questioning grunt. "It's a bit early in the year to be seeing them, but there's plenty others to look at if yon's away up north. There's petrels and guillemots down there off the cliff. Aye, an' barnacle geese and puffins and red-throated divers, all in sight of here."

He turned to look at Mary, gray eyes glinting with amusement. "Are you and your husband interested in birds, then, Mrs. Willis?"

"I don't know much about them. Nor does Don."

"I thought so." Campbell was smiling. "You see, Mrs. Willis, your husband and that other man—Roger Wilson, is it?—they came up here and said they were with the Department of Environment, worried about the birds. Well, Wilson knew a thing or two about it, I could tell that. But Mr. Willis, he didn't know a raven from a golden eagle. It was a laugh round here. People saw through that idea in a minute."

Well, so much for Don's idea that they had the natives fooled. How much else did he have wrong—and what else

76

did the locals know, now that JosCo were here and doing the job?

"Did you realize what Don and Roger were doing here, before the news came out?"

"There was a fair rumor. You see, Mr. Petherton, over with the Countryside Commission down in Perth, he's from this area. Born and raised here. He'd told us there might be a power station in the planning."

"Petherton? Not Charles Petherton, is it?"

"Aye, it is. D'ye know him?" Campbell had begun to work his way steadily around the perimeter of the tower, checking each stone in the parapet for the steadiness of its setting. "How did you come to meet him, and you only in the country for a few days?"

"I didn't meet him, not really. But when I was in London on Sunday, Roger Wilson had to meet him in the morning. Something about wild life."

"That'd be Charles Petherton all right. He's real upset about the idea of yon power station—like a madman when you get him on that subject. Me, now, I've seen it coming but I don't fight it. We have to have electricity. Like it or no, Glasgow couldn't live a day without it. But people up here"—he shrugged and dusted off his hands against his dark jacket—"they don't seem to think that way. Don't have any idea of modern needs. Some of them would do anything to stop that power station going in. You wait an' see."

He turned to decend the narrow stair that led back to the second floor. Mary hurried after him. There had been a new note in his voice, one that she didn't like.

"What do you mean, *anything* to stop it? What could people do?"

He halted at the foot of the stairs and turned to face her. They stood, face to face, only a few inches apart. Campbell's mouth was compressed and the muscles of his jaw tight. He stood for a few seconds without speaking.

"Mrs. Willis," he said at last. "You've been here just a day now. I've no wish to worry you, but I said last night that I wanted to talk to you this morning."

His eyes were no longer humorous. There was a new light in them, the look of fiery fanaticism.

"I came here to Laxford six months ago, just six months. Did ye know that?"

"Dora told me. I wondered why you'd left Glasgow to come so far up here."

"Aye. Ye wondered that? You're a clever woman, Mrs. Willis." (Clever? thought Mary; and how long since anyone had said *that* to her?) "I could tell you I came here to look at the birds, or for a bit of peace, and many would believe me. But I'm not one to lie. I like looking at the hills, and the birds are a nice change from Glasgow, but I had other reasons. What have they said down at the Over The Water?"

"About you? Nothing. Really, no one has said anything."

"They will. You'll hear talk. I'm a bit too High Church for most of them—there's talk of popery, and the reader doesn't want to hear about the scriptures, never mind the First Book of Discipline. But there's another reason, one you'll maybe hear about. Last year, down there in the Gorbals, I sat up all night with a sick man. A dying man, he was, and he was ramblin' and rovin' right on 'til dawn. I couldn't understand a lot of what he said, but I understood one thing. He was from these parts, born and raised in Laxford; and he'd run from here, frightened." Campbell's eyes were staring right through Mary, looking back to their own world of recollection. "Aye, frightened he'd been. And he was still afraid, afraid that something from around here could somehow come on down to Glasgow and catch him. He wanted to get out of the country altogether, get to a place as far away from the sea as he could find. But he took sick in Glasgow, with a pulmonary embolism—fear mebbe brought that on him, more than likely—and that's where I saw him, when the doctor realized he was near dying."

He turned abruptly and went on back into the biggest bedroom. "That's all I wanted to say to you. Watch how you go here. There's more to this place, Laxford, than we'll see on the surface."

"But what sort of things? What's it have to do with the power station?"

"I don't know. Not yet. You let me worry it, as my private business here."

"Can't you give me any idea what you're worried about?" After a moment of chills up the spine, sanity reasserted itself. Walter Campbell was one of those people with a mania of his own—no wonder that the staff at the Over The Water had warned her about him. He was a man who seemed normal

78

but hid a point of madness, like a flat-earther or a conspiracy fanatic.

"What sort of thing are you worried *about*?" Mary repeated, keeping her voice as calm and as matter of fact as possible.

"We'll see. I can't tell you yet. We'll have to wait and see." The minister walked to the window and opened it. Long unused, it creaked and screeched as it came up.

"Let's see what else needs doing," he said. His voice was quiet and normal again. "Then I'll let you get a start on the cleanin' up. It has to be a while since Mrs. Macdougal was in here, there's dust around. And this window sash needs replacing, it's frayed through."

The subject had been closed. Mary sensed that Campbell's demons were private ones, worrying to him but hard to talk about to others. He seemed to regret what he had already said to her, now it was off his chest. Maybe he would talk more about it later, after they had finished with the house.

"Got to look at the roof," said Campbell abruptly. "Best if I do that—it's not easy to get up to that attic."

"How do you get there?"

"Through yon trapdoor." He pointed up to a square hatch about two feet across set high in the bedroom wall.

"But you'll need a stepladder to get up there."

"No. There's steps that swing down out of the wall. I'll mebbe be needing a torch to see what's what. I've one with me, out in the car."

He was not looking at her any more. Maybe he was uncomfortable about his earlier confidings. Well, if he needed his own space for a while, there was lots to do in other rooms. Don would be here in a few hours, and she had hardly begun.

"I'll go on down and look at the washhouse. It looked like a mess, and I'd like to get the hot water system working right."

He nodded without speaking. She went back to the gloomy first floor and into the washhouse. Despite its name, it had also clearly served as the general storage room and house dump. There were boxes full of dry wood and peat, ready to be used in the fireplaces. They would have to go—they spread dirt everywhere. And this was no place to store sheets and blankets, even if the boxes were well sealed. Campbell had pointed out another chest of drawers on the upper floor, next to a huge mahogany wardrobe. That's where the blankets ought to be, near the bedrooms. She and Don would only need the one bedroom today. Half an hour of cleaning and dusting would put that into good shape, and the rest of the upstairs would wait for another day.

She heard footsteps at the front of the house and the slamming of the heavy front door. Walter Campbell must have decided that he needed his flashlight for the attic. Chances were that there'd be no skylights or roof windows up there, that wouldn't fit the style of the building. Should she have left him to crawl around all that dust and dirt in his regular working suit? If no one had been there for years he'd get filthy. And those patches suggested that the old clothes were maybe the only ones he had, in church or out of it. She had a clothes brush back at the Over The Water. She must remember to brush him off well when they got back there.

Mary bent over another of the old boxes and lifted the wooden lid. This one held a random assortment of old pottery. She could see everything from chipped glass vases and egg cups to battered chamber pots, decorated with ornate roses, and gladioli that nestled among trailing vines. Hideous. (And probably worth a fortune in New York!)

The temptation was irresistible. Mary began to lift each object out of the box and place it carefully on the dirty stone floor of the washhouse. Ellie's novel would need good background material, they had both agreed on that point. In her next letter to New York she would tell Ellie all about this store of "potted" history—maybe there would be a specially choice item that she could buy from the owner and send to Ellie.

There were more footsteps behind her in the body of the house, ringing hollow on the hardwood floors. According to Campbell, all the carpets had been cleaned and stored in a big cupboard under the stairs. No point in getting them out until she had the floor swept and washed. Would they be too heavy for her to handle alone, once he had gone back to the village? She considered calling him and asking about it now, but that would interrupt his work up in the attic.

The second layer in the box was just as random as the first. Mary frowned down at it in the dim light. There, in the middle, was something that seemed out of place with the rest of the bric-a-brac. What was it?

She leaned forward and lifted out a delicate bowl of paper-thin glass. It was small, only about eight inches across, and it was made with a smoky, cloud-gray texture of swirls inside the material itself. When Mary was a small child, one of her delights had been to take a soap-bubble pipe to her father when he was smoking a cigarette. He would blow a bubble that held a moving cloud of blue gray smoke, drifting through the air until it finally hit the floor and released a puff of gray like a little explosion. That was what the bowl looked like, a smoke bubble cut in half and somehow preserved forever.

There were light footsteps close behind her, back in the kitchen. She took no notice of them. The surface of the bowl was filthy with old dirt, but now she could see that there was a design painted or burned into the thin glass. She peered at it closely, tempted to take it back to where the light was better.

A gentle rub with her handkerchief made a big improvement. Now she could see that it was a picture of a man and a woman. He was naked and hairless, with a smooth ripple of muscle beneath white skin. He was leading the way across a sandy floor. The woman wore a white robe and followed him, eyes closed, toward a low bank of flowers.

Mary drew in her breath. There was a strange sense or blurring and softness in the painting, as though it showed a scene underwater. It suddenly brought back all last night's dreams, of floating on toward some secret pleasure. She turned the bowl slowly around, looking for some sign of its age or its maker.

There was nothing. No maker's mark, no stamps or letters on the smooth underside. She looked again at the picture, trying to see all its details . . .

A large pair of hands passed about her waist and slid up to press her breasts. Off-balance, she found herself pulled backward, back to contact a broad chest. All the chaos of dreams that had filled her during the night flooded back into her mind. She screamed and dropped the bowl from hands that had lost all their feeling. It shattered into a thousand pieces on the hard floor in front of her.

"Shit!" said a voice behind her. "I'm sorry. I didn't mean for *that* to happen."

Close to hysteria, Mary turned.

"Don." She put her arms round him and laid her head against his chest. "My God, Don, you shouldn't have done that. You scared the life out of me."

"I guess I did." He was smiling down at her in delight, then looking ruefully over her head at the broken shards of the bowl. "That was quite a reaction—I just hope it wasn't a valuable vase you had there. Well, honey? Pleased to see me?"

CHAPTER 6

He hadn't seen Mary since she kissed him good-bye in the airport lounge at Kennedy. That had only been two months ago, but now it seemed like years. Don didn't want another day of it, but the drive from Dounreay would be a six- or seven-hour run even if the weather stayed fair and the roads—such as they were—in good condition. The project couldn't afford a wasted day, either. Don had pushed that point hard, and Roger had agreed that it made sense to de-tour the helicopter through Laxford as it took him back to London.

"It will make me late, but we'll do it anyway," he said. He had a strange little smile on his face.

"What's so funny, Roger?"

"Oh, nothing at all." His voice was casual. "If I'd been away from Mary for a couple of months, and she were my wife, I'm sure I'd feel the same way. She's quite dishy."

"That's not why I have to get back!" (At least, it was only part of the reason.) "I've got to get those caves mapped out properly. Didn't you listen at last night's meeting?"

"Sure. You have work to do." Roger's voice still had its amused tone. "You're a lucky man, Don, and I don't know if you realize it. Come on, let's get moving. I have to be back in Westminster sometime today—more blasted meetings with the DOE types."

Don stood for a moment as Roger began to walk casually over to the waiting helicopter. He wasn't quite sure how to take those admiring references to Mary. He didn't feel jeal-ous, of course. Or did he? There was a fine line between Rog-er admiring Mary and doing what he called "fancying" her.

From a few remarks by the work crew, he realized that Roger was a big hit with women. Be honest, though. It had been a long time since he'd seen Mary, and he had pushed pretty hard to get this helicopter ride. No doubt how it must look to Roger and the rest of the gang at Dounreay. Another horny American keen to get back home and jump all over his wife. What was it Lord Jericho had told him, about the British complaint when the Yanks arrived during World War Two? "They're overpaid, they're oversexed, and they're over here."

He hurried after Roger and climbed into the helicopter, where Matson was already at the controls and ready for take-off. As Don leaned back in his seat he realized that he was feeling really good. How long since he'd had this degree of confidence and work interest?

It had started at the first meeting yesterday. Last night had confirmed his original impression. There wasn't an engineer, not one, working for JosCo or for the Central Electricity Generating Board, who had half his feeling for flow problems. He had taken the heaps of computer output that had been available at the first meeting and had spent all yesterday afternoon going over them in detail, marking down critical flow points and anomalies. Some of the runs were inconsistent with each other. He had tagged differences due to models and ones due to input data, and put the whole thing onto a long summary sheet. At the evening meeting, where no one expected him to have much to say, he had offered his analysis.

The chief engineer for the government was a bald-headed, brusque-mannered man named Jenks. Don had already been warned about him. He had a reputation for crudeness and toughness, with a special fondness for carving up contractors. He sat there, eyes half-closed, smoking a big pipe as Don began to present his interpretation of the computer runs done by the different groups. Don was very aware of the heavy-lidded stare as he went into more detail about the government's results. He noticed that the pipe had gone out and not been relit.

"How do you know that?" Jenks interrupted sharply at one point, as Don was about to pass a flow summary around the conference table. He had put down his pipe. Now he was poking thoughtfully at his right ear with a paper knife, digging for wax. It looked dangerous.

Don shrugged. "Experience, I guess. Look at your input rates. They don't even balance. I think you need a new computer simulation for the system I've sketched out there. You'll see I've written my estimate of the temperatures you'll get when you do it again." He paused for a moment. It was time to take a chance, to change the relationship between government and contractor. "I'm happy with my estimates. If I'm off by more than a degree on estimated effluent temperatures for the nominal plant, I'll buy everybody here a drink."

"Hm." Jenks did a little more careful probing into his ear. He seemed satisfied with the result. "That confident, are you? Not many people willing to put their balls out on the table and hand us a hammer."

He picked up his pipe again and looked around the table. "All right, gentlemen. He's calling us, and it's our move, Peter"—his voice was sharp—"how long will it be before you can have new runs back with revised input?"

"A couple of days." Peter was fresh faced and young looking, and he blushed whenever he was called on to speak. "We'll need a priority code to get the machine time for it."

"I'll get that for you. All right, Willis." Jenks nodded at Don. There was no trace of a smile on his face. "We've got work to do here. We might as well call it a day now, and we'll be back in touch as soon as we've done some more homework."

He nodded across the table at Roger and winked. "Bloody know-it-all Americans, eh? Where'd we be without 'em?" He stood up and headed for the door, leaving it to others to clean up the papers. Before he left the room he paused for a moment and nodded at Don, a quick dip of the bald head. "I'm glad you're on the project, Willis."

A few words, gruffly spoken—they were sweeter than all the compliments Don had ever received. He leaned back in his chair, suddenly wondering if he had been right to go so far out on a limb. If for some reason his own estimates were wrong . . .

They wouldn't be. He knew it.

Roger Wilson had watched everything, bright gray eyes flicking from man to man around the conference room table. He knew the players from other work, and he had spotted the critical signal long before Don could have done it. Jenks was a demon for preparation. In any meeting he always had his own crib sheet handy, a summary of results from his own engineers. He had put it to one side after less than ten minutes of Don's presentation. Don was off the bottom of the sheet. He didn't realize it, but there had been no need to go so far with his own projections of flows and temperatures. Roger ought to have a word with him on that for future meetings, tell him what to watch for with Jenks. Unnecessary battles and risks took a lot of nervous energy, and Jericho had a simple business philosophy that he drummed into all the Jos-Co employees. Decide what you have to do to win, and don't go an inch past it. You'll need that extra energy to fight the next one.

Don took one drink from the helicopter bar and refused a second one. When the work was stretching him there was never much temptation. It was when it was slow, or he couldn't get things done because others were slipping their timetables—that was the dangerous time. If this kept going as Lord Jericho seemed to expect, he would be all right.

Roger watched with approval. No doubt about it, Don was riding high; and no doubt where that extra energy would go when Don got back to Laxford.

He thought back to Sunday, when he was roaming around London with Mary. Don was a lucky bugger. When he got back to London tonight he'd have to look up Angela. What the world needed now was a better supply of tall blond-haired women.

He carefully mixed himself a gin with Italian vermouth and added one ice cube.

"You did a good job there, Don. You sounded as though you have the whole thing wrapped up before we've started. Where the hell did you get those flow rates from? I didn't see them on any of our listings."

"You wouldn't have. They came out of my head." Don had spread four pages of blue-and-white computer output over the small table and chair, and was hunched over them, marking key points with a red pencil. "I'm still not happy with them. Not happy at all, once we get into details."

"Well, you sounded it. What's the problem?"

"Tidal patterns. Here, take a look for yourself." He passed one sheet over to Roger, who balanced it on his knee. "That shows the layout of the tidal caves that run in from the sea. The printed X's are the cave boundaries. North is at the *bot-*

tom—you ought to teach your programmers a bit of geography; it's as confusing as hell to read like this. The printed numbers in each cave are the depth values at high tide."

"Where did you get them from?"

"A couple of different places—that's one of our problems. Some of these came from Petherton; they're the official DOE records for the job. The others came from that report that Knowlton made for you before he fell off the cliff. We've got consistency problems there, but they're not too bad. The other numbers, the ones next to the printed stars, those are maximum flow rates for places in the caves. They came from Knowlton and from an old survey, done back in the 1930s."

Roger looked at the listings with the uneasy expression of a swimmer who knows he is well out of his depth. "What units are these in?"

"Feet and feet per second. When are you people going to come into the twentieth century and go metric?"

"Never, if I have my way." Roger smoothed the paper and peered for a moment at the small printed figures. He looked up at Don, eyebrows raised. "You have to look on it as useful knowledge. I didn't learn how to convert from fathoms to furlongs and back for nothing. It's our main line of defense against all you foreigners." He shrugged and handed back the listing. "It all looks fine to me, but don't quote me on that."

"You won't see anything strange in the first two seconds you study it—it takes a while. Take a look at the main caves. See the four that run inland, sort of like a group of four fingers?" Don traced the outline with his red pencil. "Three of the caves are joined here"—he tapped the paper—"about a half mile in from the shore line. They're big caves. They run much farther inland than I realized before I saw Knowlton's report. Laxford village is right here—you can see that the caverns go on underground well past the village. But if they are really this big, there has to be something wrong with one of the variables—either the quoted depths are off, or the flow rates are wrong."

"How do you know that, Don?" Roger had picked up his drink again and was watching the circular pattern of ripples in the glass as the helicopter vibrated its way higher above the Scottish coast. "All those numbers look reasonable to me. Did you show them to Peter Griffiths from CEGB?"

"Tried to. He didn't give a shit—more interested in sitting

there picking his nose. Look, Roger, this is what JosCo hired me for. I'm telling you, you could never get those flow rates with that cubic capacity for the caves and those water depths. If the caves are this big, there ought to be a terrific tidal race in some of them—thirty miles an hour or more. Why isn't it there? The caves don't make sense."

Roger had leaned back in his seat again. "Yes, I noticed that he was picking his nose. Most uncivilized. The rest of us at least wait until we think there's nobody watching." He closed his eyes. "That observation is as far as my brain will take me—you're on your own with those flow rates, I'm afraid. I wouldn't know where to begin. Any idea what you'll do next? I wouldn't like to have old Jenks change his mind about you—he hardly ever says a good word about anybody."

Don looked up briefly from his listings. "First I ought to talk to Petherton. See if he knows anything more about the records he gave me."

"Pethie? Don't hold your breath. He seems to know about wildlife in the Highlands, but apart from that I don't think he'd know his arse from a hole in the ground. Don't expect much from him."

"All right, I won't." Don's voice was vague, attention still on the listings. He whistled softly. "Look at that mother. On a strong incoming tide there ought to be a six-foot tidal bore there. Unless Petherton can come up with some real facts, I'll have to go down in those caves and we'll do our own survey. Maybe I can take a first look today, see how much work we'll have to do there."

"Watch your step if you do. The caves have a bad reputation—people seem to go in and come out drowned. Take diving equipment with you if you go."

"That means I can't do it today."

"Come off it. You won't see those caves today, I'll take bets on it." Roger had closed his eyes and looked pleased with himself. "Two months apart? You'll be off to that house to see Mary, and it'll be the old skirts-up trousers-down game before the front door has finished closing."

Don didn't answer. He was staring ahead out of the helicopter window. Roger finally opened his eyes and turned his head to watch him.

"What's wrong? I'm right, aren't I?"

"I think you are." Don shook his head slowly. "I'm trying not to think about it yet. Mary and I have been separated for a long time—too damned long."

"Want me to come over there and throw a bucket of cold water over you? It works for dogs."

"No. You shut up and go to sleep. I don't know what I'll do when I get to Laxford, but I've got work to finish now."

"Work away." Roger closed his eyes again. "Try and avoid those old impure thoughts."

Good advice, maybe, but harder to follow than Roger knew. His off-hand remark about the way they would pass the rest of the day produced a wild surge of memories of Mary and an instant erection, quite beyond Don's conscious control.

It had been a long time. He stared vacantly out of the window at the purple and dun hillside. He could see Mary, smiling an invitation to him, the secret sign that meant she knew what he was thinking of, and was thinking the same. He bent again over his listings, but the mental picture wouldn't go away. Damn it. For all the good he was doing JosCo at the moment, he might as well follow Roger's example and catch up on lost sleep.

JosCo was different from the places he had worked before. None of his other bosses would have ever dreamed of taking a nap during working hours. All that Lord Jericho seemed to care about was results. He had no time for formality. "You go into some of the big companies, and you'll find they bugger about all day long in meetings. I don't pay a man to sit on his arse for eight hours listening to somebody else and then come away imagining he's done a day's work. The Government lot are worse than anybody. . . ."

Roger followed Jericho's rules. Meetings were short and pointed. He didn't seem to work long hours, but whenever Don was promised products they were there on time. Either Roger worked very fast, or he worked late at night and on his own. The image of the lazy, easy-going man was one that he cultivated—a piece of the same character that denied much formal education.

What a contrast with Don's first job, at Rothstein's down on the West Side. The rules there were clear; get to work before anybody else, be sure that you were still there when they left; come in Saturdays and Sundays, Thanksgiving, and New

Year's. A look of exhaustion was worn like a badge of honor, and the walls were covered with diplomas and degrees and certificates of achievement.

Rothstein's had gone broke soon after he joined them. It seemed to prove there was more than one way to skin the cat—and maybe Lord Jericho's method was the better one.

Whatever else happened, he couldn't afford to blow this one. Don forced his attention back to the listings and began to draw in the outlines that he would expect for constant flow rates. After a few minutes he was back into it completely, moving his mind through the caves as the water would want to move, feeling the tugs and pressures of the bottom and the sides of the caves. This was what he did well, the most satisfying part of the whole job.

He was still busy when they reached Scourie, five miles south of Laxford, where Roger had drawings to pass on to another field team. A short car ride from one of the team members brought Don to the Over The Water before noon, to find from Hamish that Mary had already gone up to the house.

"Would ye be needin' a car ride up there yourself? There's a pack of ham sandwiches back in the kitchen, if ye'd mebbe like to take them. Or maybe a drink here, an' ye stay an' relax and wait for Miss Mary. But then I suppose ye're in a hurry to go on up and see her."

"Yes. I mean, I'll go up there, but I'll walk." Hamish had too many options for him. "I'd like a couple of sandwiches, though, to carry with me. We'll be back for dinner, or supper, or whatever you call tonight's meal."

"Fine. How about your bag, then?"

"I'll leave it here."

He left before Hamish could add any more comments. He was in a hurry to see her, no doubt about it—but did everybody have to point it out? There was more interest here in sex than he had seen in Manhattan. So why were the English always typecast as cold fish? He'd seen Hamish's speculative look as Don was leaving . . .

Campbell's battered car was standing outside the house. The Relic of the Cleric, Roger called it, but actually Don rather admired it. There was no power in the engine, but the lines of the car were superb, and the old preselector gear box had roused all Don's engineering admiration when Campbell had shown it to him.

As he came closer up the hill he saw a pair of legs sticking out of the driver's door. Campbell was stretched out, grubbing around under the passenger seat.

"For the flashlight, Mr. Willis," he said, when Don had identified himself to the hidden body. "It's a very peculiar thing. I'm quite sure there's one here somewhere."

He sat up suddenly. His face and hair were covered with cobwebs, from the car or the house, and his clothes and hands were smeared with dust and grease.

Don bent to look inside the car. "When did you last see it?"

"Oh, a month or so back. Maybe it slipped through to the back here . . ."

He dipped inside again and became a pair of waving legs. "Mrs. Willis is back there in the washhouse," he said between grunts. "I'll be in myself in a minute, as soon as I've found the torch. Let's see, if it's under here . . ."

The idea of sneaking in quietly to surprise Mary had been an impulse, a spur-of-the-moment decision. Looking now at the shattered glass fragments and her paper-white face he regretted it at once. She had no reason to think it was him, he wasn't due back to Laxford until evening. He held her close. There was even a trace of tears in her eyes, and Mary had cried only twice in all the time he had known her.

"I'm sorry, sweetie," he said softly. "I didn't mean to scare you like that. Hey, do you want to go back now to the Over The Water? You look as though you could use a hot drink."

Mary sniffed and shook her head. "I'm all right now. We've got to get this place cleaned up."

With Don here it was hard to recall how she had felt just before those hands drew her backward. Looking at the painting on the bowl made her respond like a lot of the women in Ellie's line of Gothics. There had been a weakness, a mental and physical lassitude that made the long, smooth muscles of her arms and legs seem jelly-soft and nerveless. She had felt that way even though she knew that she was a strong woman. No one ever had to help her with cases, or pry the top off a jar for her.

She couldn't explain any of that to Don, standing there solid and unimaginative. He would think she was feeling ill and prescribe a rest. She put her arms round him and squeezed him as hard as she could.

"I'll clean up the mess in here first, then we can sit in the kitchen for a few minutes."

"I'll help. Getting this place right will take hours."

"Hours?" She shook her head. "You mean months." (The same old Don, not really caring how the place looked if other things were going right.) "Let's at least try and finish the kitchen and the bedroom today. We can live with the other mess for a while."

"I'll agree on the bedroom. Let's forget the rest of it." Don moved his hands down to grip her buttocks and pulled her toward him so that their bellies were in close contact.

"Like that, is it?" She rubbed her hands along the blue-gray sweater that she had bought him last Christmas, feeling through it the muscle of his shoulders. The first feeling of shock when Don grabbed her was changing to a warmth, a stir of affection. A little experimental wiggle of the hips against his groin brought instant results. She could feel what was happening to him, and as always it gave her that odd feeling of power.

"You men are all the same." It was one of their standard games.

"And you women are thankful for it." Don had a half-smile on his face as he picked up the cue. "Hey, don't attach any significance to what happens below the navel. It's not my doing." He leaned forward and gave her their first real kiss for two months.

She responded strongly, then at last pulled away from him.

"Don, we can't. Not now. What about the minister?"

"He'll have to find his own women. Anyway, he's supposed to be celibate."

He was swollen and hard against her lower belly, and there was a look in his eye that she had learned to recognize long before they were married. His left hand had moved slowly up her back and then forward to make a smooth circling motion on her left breast. It felt wonderful.

"Don." She pushed herself away from him. "I'm telling you, we can't. Mr. Campbell is up in the attic, looking at the roof joists."

"No, he isn't. He's out in his car, looking for a flashlight."

"Upstairs, outside, whatever, he'll be back soon." She

looked over her shoulder. "I don't want him to see us doing this. We mustn't do it here."

"So let's get rid of him." He reluctantly released her and turned to look around the dingy washhouse. "I agree, we shouldn't do it here. There's broken glass all over the floor, and I've been circumcised once already."

"Don, be serious." Mary gripped his hands, which were straying back toward her blouse. "You can't just send him away like that, with no explanation or anything."

He nodded thoughtfully. "That's true. I'd better tell him we want to screw, and we're in kind of a hurry. That ought to take care of it. All right?"

"Don!"

He gave her a quick kiss on the mouth and was gone, back through the kitchen. She stayed long enough to take an old broom from the kitchen and sweep up the broken glass. As she dumped it in a trash bin she hoped it wasn't the unhappy end of some masterpiece of glassblowing.

By the time she was done and came out of the house Walter Campbell was back in his car and ready to leave. He flourished a flashlight triumphantly.

"Slipped down there behind the back seat." He switched it on and shook his head in disgust. "Needs batteries by the look of it—though it's hard to tell in this light. Well, I'll be on my way, Mrs. Willis. I'm sorry to hear that you're not feeling too well. Lie down for an hour when you feel off-color, that's my advice."

Mary looked at Don. *You swine. What horrible lies did you tell him?*

He fielded the glare with a bland, neutral smile. *Don't kid me. You're as hot for him to leave as I am.*

Nothing for it but to nod at Walter Campbell in vague and apologetic agreement.

"Don't worry about getting somebody over to fix the house," he went on. "I'll be out and about in the village this afternoon, and I'll be able to arrange for somebody to come over here in the morning. I'll tell them what I think ought to be done, and you can add to it. We've got a couple of fellows in the village who do a good job for a fair wage."

"What about the roof?"

"It seemed to be in good shape." He looked apologetic. "I could tell that without the flashlight. I wanted that to take a

93

look at an old sewing machine up there in the attic. I was thinking, if it works all right there are a couple of old ladies in the village who'd be really glad of it—if you don't want it."

"If it works, it's yours. Come and get it any time." Mary felt guilty, sending him away thoroughly begrimed, but there was no brush to hand.

"Thank you. And when you are in the village with a few minutes to spare, drop in at the kirk and I'll show you the reconditioning work that I'm doing there. We have an old two-manual pipe organ with an eight-foot low C. Not big, but it's a fine instrument, better than many you'll see in bigger towns."

"I'd like to see it. Maybe I'll stop in tomorrow." She saw his doubtful look. "Honestly, I mean it. I'm not just saying it to please you."

"Wonderful." Campbell smiled, and it was a move from cloud to sunshine in his face. "I'll look forward to seeing you. Mr. Willis too, if you have the time and if you feel like it."

He put the car in gear, nodded his head, and drove off, bumping his way down the hill toward Laxford.

"Well, buster?" Mary glared at Don. "That wasn't very nice, telling him I was sick."

"You were sick. You looked terrible a few minutes ago."

"But I'm fine now. You owe me an explanation for what you told him."

"It's just the way the minister said it. If you have the time, and you feel like it, he said. We have the time. Do you feel like it?"

He stood about six feet from her on the old paved yard, still with that half smile on his face. He looked great, tall and straight and handsome. *Damnit all, she did feel like it, no good pretending.* Don was moving closer, taking her by the arm.

"Now then, Don." She put up a mock resistance as he tugged at her, moving them closer to the house. "Do we have to rush off like this, the minute you get here?" She was feeling good, more excited than she had been for years. They were inside the house, moving clumsily, entwined, up the dark stairs.

"Oh, no." She suddenly stopped. Don caught the note of real alarm in her voice.

94

"What's wrong, honey?"

"We can't do it. I don't have my thing with me—it's back in my case, at the Over The Water."

Don was still moving up the stairs, lifting her with him. "We'll just have to improvise. It won't be the first time, will it? Remember back in Iowa, at the picnic? We can get the cases at dinner."

"A lot of good *that* will do us. Talk about closing the door after the horse has gone." She looked at the big bed, then at Don's intent face. (Ellie deserved another letter—she had lied to her. She *did* miss it when Don was away.)

Before they lay down together she made the last token objection. "Don, I didn't have time to make the bed."

"Good. It saves making it twice." He sighed. "Mary Willis, you've no idea how much I've been waiting for this."

CHAPTER 7

Until she married Don, Mary had never given two minutes' thought of sleeping habits. Sure, she had read about Edison, getting by quite well on a couple of hours a night, but that wasn't the real world any more than nine-foot giants or two-foot midgets were the real world. Everyone she knew slept around seven or eight hours.

Don changed that idea. He didn't seem to *have* sleeping habits, not with any sort of a pattern. He'd go for a week scraping along on four hours a night, then suddenly collapse and lie like a log for twelve or thirteen hours, dead to noise, to prodding, everything. He slept more when he'd been drinking, and he was more likely to drop off early; and the next day he'd be surly and silent.

Mary had watched, trying to map the pattern of their lives onto each other. After a while she realized it wouldn't work. She needed regular sleep, had to have it. Without at least seven hours she'd be dragging and grouchy for most of the next day. Back in New York she would fall asleep like clockwork during the eleven o'clock news. Don would move into the living room and watch until the small hours any old movie he could find. Sometimes she'd wake and come through for a drink of milk at two or three in the morning, to find Don chuckling over Errol Flynn or an old Laurel and Hardy short. Other times he'd fall asleep right after dinner, and she'd have to push him off the couch and into bed at eight o'clock.

There was one unvarying feature in his sleep pattern. After sex he would nap for half an hour. He claimed that it was the best and most relaxing sleep he ever got. As soon as he dozed off she would lie there holding him quietly and letting her mind wander away to anywhere it wanted to, a connected but still random thought stream.

The bedroom in the old house was a wonderful place to drift away to nowhere. She watched the shadows move steadily around the walls, marking the quiet advance of the afternoon. Don had been wonderful, urgent and patient and greedy. She had risen to the point where it seemed impossible that she could fail to reach orgasm. Finally it had eluded her, leaving her hanging when Don was already drifting off to quiet sleep. Somehow that wasn't upsetting. Mary had a conviction, beyond logic, that this house would transfigure her sex life. The rooms were soothing, and through the whole building there was always the steady, distant sound of the sea. She listened to its—what were the words? ". . . *its melancholy, long, withdrawing roar . . .*" No doubt about it, tides and moons and sex and sea were all bound together, even if no one could explain how or why. One day they would find out.

She looked at her watch as Don stirred beside her. Three o'clock. Later than she had realized, though her stomach had tried to tell her. She was ravenous. They had made love twice—on an empty stomach. She should have had the sense to bring food from the inn.

Mary rubbed her belly. It felt flat and cool. Damn it, by dinner time she wouldn't be able to think of anything but food, she knew it, and there was all this work to do on the house and it was already getting late . . .

Don had opened his eyes and was watching her silently.

"Hi, gorgeous," he said, when she met his look. "How you feeling? Wasn't it . . . ?"

She leaned over and kissed his bare shoulder. "Marvelous. I'm feeling—what's the word?—starving, it you want to know the truth. I'm absolutely famished, and it's all my fault. I'm sorry, love. I didn't bring any food here for us, and there's nothing in that pantry—not even a can of beans."

"Tin of beans, when you're in England." Don didn't seem worried by the absence of food. "Nothing to drink, either?"

"We could have a cup of tea if you like. That's about all. I could eat a horse. You know what sex does to me."

"I certainly do." Don nodded, looking pleased with himself. "And I planned for it."

"I didn't mean *that*. I meant food."

"So did I. Hamish Macveagh offered to give me a pack of sandwiches to bring over here, and I took him up on it."

"What!" Mary sat up in bed, the sheets sliding down to her hips.

"On the kitchen table."

"My genius husband!" Mary leaned over and gave him a smacking kiss on the lips. He tried to grab her, but she wriggled away and scrambled out of bed.

"You're running out on me?"

"Only for a few minutes." Mary was looking around for her blouse and skirt. She gave Don a quick wiggle of her hips. "You're getting old, old man. I don't want to wear you out too much."

Don lay back and looked at her in satisfaction. She looked her best naked. In clothes there was a bit too much weight of breast and hip. "Stand around like that, and I'll show you how old I am. What the *hell* are you doing?"

"Putting some clothes on." Mary slipped into her panties, then her skirt, trying to keep them away from the dusty floor.

"What for, for God's sake? There's nobody here within miles. You'll be coming straight back to bed—hop down as you are."

"I will *not*." Mary put on bra and blouse, ignoring Don's ogling. "I know you like to show off all you've got, but I was brought up decent."

She had never become used to the casual way that Don wandered about, never bothering to close curtains, never caring who saw him. Miles from anyone, Mary still didn't feel comfortable wandering the house bare. No point debating it. She ran her hands through her hair, pushing it back from her forehead, and headed for the door.

"Hey! What about shoes? Your feet are on display."

"I'll risk that much." She turned in the door and blew a kiss.

"Watch for that broken glass," he called after her.

"Swept up long ago—you know me."

The kitchen was much darker now that the sun had moved farther west. It would be a morning room, a place for hefty breakfasts. She picked up the kettle and filled it at the massive cold water faucet, a pound of solid metal. Would Don like a hot drink? He had certainly earned it—nice to know he

98

hadn't been chasing around with anyone else when he was here on his own. Mary smiled to herself at the memory of his enthusiasm and put the kettle on the stove. It had to be lit with a kitchen match. The North Sea gas that Hamish complained of (It doesna' have the heat of *real* gas, ye see) burned with a pallid blue flame.

Somebody had used a generous hand on the sandwiches. A quarter of an inch of lean ham sat between two half-inch slices of homemade wheat bread, with that fierce mustard (Coleman's, was it?) added to a layer of butter. There were four double rounds, with a big lump of yellow hard cheese thrown in for good measure.

Mary couldn't wait. She was salivating at the sight. She took a huge first bite and was chewing blissfully when the loud knock at the front door made her jump.

Who could it possibly be? They weren't expecting any visitors. She put the rest of the sandwich back on the table and went through to the dark hall. A second knock came as she approached the door, a metallic boom from the heavy iron knocker. She meant to open the door just a crack, but it stuck and finally jumped open wide when she heaved on it.

The man standing there turned to face her, and they looked at each other in surprise.

He wasn't the handyman she had been sort of expecting it must be, after Campbell's promise to send somebody round tomorrow. The stranger was quite tall and broad, maybe running to fat, but that was concealed by a well-cut suit of dark blue serge. He was wearing a wide-brimmed trilby hat pulled low over his eyes, as though to shield them from the sinking afternoon sun. In his mid-fifties, Mary judged, though the smooth babylike complexion (she was beginning to think of it as typically English) belonged to someone much younger. It was not cold, and she was surprised to see that he wore gloves of brown leather.

"Excuse me, ma'am." His voice was soft and cultured. "My name is Petherton. I was looking for Mr. Roger Wilson."

Apparently she was not what he had been expecting, either. He looked her up and down, from her flushed face to her bare feet, then frowned as though trying to remember something.

"Charles Petherton?" The words slipped out of Mary involuntarily.

"Why, yes. Charles Petherton. I represent the Countryside Commission." He slowly removed his hat, to reveal gray hair carefully styled around the forehead and over his ears. "And might I ask how you know my name?"

"I'm sorry, this is very rude of me. Please come in." Mary opened the door wider. "I'm Mary Willis. My husband and Roger Wilson work together, and Roger told me that he had a meeting with you on Sunday, when we were both down in London."

"I am delighted to meet you." Petherton looked over her again, this time sweeping his gaze up from feet to head. Mary felt herself blushing. "Actually, Mrs. Willis, it was your husband that I was really hoping to see. Is he here?"

"Yes. He's upstairs at the moment."

"Is there any chance that he might be available for a few minutes?" He was looking again at her feet. She wondered what he might be thinking. Well, there was no way to disguise a naked foot.

"Just wait a minute, will you. I'll call him." She went over to the stairs. "Don?" There was satisfaction in her voice. "Don, we have a visitor. Mr. Petherton is here to see you." *That ought to make him jump into his clothes.* Mary was going to ask Don to bring her shoes down with him when she realized that would make things look worse. Better if Charles Petherton assumed she went barefoot all the time (. . . just another eccentric American . . .).

"I'll be right down," called Don. There were hurried and desperate scuffles from above.

"Please, ask him to take his time," said Petherton. His speech was almost free of Scots accent, but a little too carefully produced, the sort of sound that often comes from a person with an early speech impediment under constant and tight control. "I came here unannounced, it would be wrong for me to disturb your afternoon."

"No problem," said Don unconvincingly. He was coming down the stairs, smoothing his rumpled hair.

"Don, dear, this is Mr. Charles Petherton from the Countryside Commission." (*See. Now do you understand why I won't roam around the house bare-assed naked, the way you tell me to?*)

100

"We've talked before, but only over the telephone." Don held out his hand. "I'm very pleased to meet you in person. Those data plots that you sent us have been really valuable." He turned to Mary and looked at her feet. "You know, dear, you shouldn't go around without shoes like that. If you're not careful you'll get a splinter." (*Go on then, explain what we were really doing—I dare you.*)

"That's why I'm here, about the data." Petherton (thank God) didn't seem to be catching the looks passing between Don and Mary. "I was over in Scourie an hour or two ago, and the crew there mentioned that you had questions about some of the data values."

"I do. I'd like to talk about it. Why don't we sit through here." Even as he led the way to the living room, Don felt a twinge of perplexity. Why should Petherton drop everything he was doing and rush over to the house, just because of a second-hand report that Don wasn't quite satisfied with his data?

"We haven't had time to stock up on food yet," he went on. "So about all we can offer you is a cup of tea."

"The kettle's already on," added Mary, seeing Petherton's hesitation.

"Then I will take a cup, if you please." He was staring at her again, through thick-lidded blue eyes. His look was disconcerting. It was not bold or heavy with sexual interest, direct or hidden, yet all the same there was an element of evaluation and judgment that she found disturbing. It was a look that spoke of . . . something. But what?

Mary watched as he seated himself on the brown sofa. There would be dust on the back of that blue serge when he stood up. (Better vacuum as soon as she could get her hands on a cleaner—so much to do in the house.)

Petherton adjusted the crease in his trousers with a precise, fastidious movement, and placed his briefcase neatly by his feet. She was conscious of his gaze still on her as she walked through to the kitchen. What *was* he thinking? Did he know they'd been having sex—how could he know? She suddenly worried about her smell. There had been no place to wash upstairs, even if she had felt the inclination, and no time since she came down here.

When she came back with the teapot and cups, Don had taken a sheaf of new papers from Petherton and was placing check marks on one of them with a borrowed pencil. He didn't look up as she put down the tray.

"All of these, for a start," he said. "They just look too low to me. You'd have to have some kind of controls down there—locks or floodgates—to keep the flow so low through this part of the tunnels."

Petherton stared gloomily at the marks Don had made. He looked worried. The tea that Mary gave him was accepted with an abstracted nod.

"It can't be. I know those caves—I've been right through them several times."

"All the way through them? They're big."

"Certainly. I was there just last spring. You must have made some wrong calculation. Maybe your computer made a mistake."

He looked up just as Mary, catching Don's eye, impulsively stuck her tongue out at him. There was a long, embarrassed silence, while Petherton took a sip of his tea. He coughed.

"I wonder if I might have milk with this," he said at last.

Mary shook her head. "I'm sorry. We don't have any yet—I still have to arrange for delivery. Would you perhaps like some sugar?"

He thought for a moment. "Thank you, but no . . ." Just as well. Mary had sniffed at the crusted contents of the bowl, and tasted it, but it was anyone's guess as to how long it had been sitting in the pantry—or what had nibbled at it while it was there. Maybe Petherton had the same worry. He had reached out as though he intended to take some, then paused and withdrew his hand without picking up the spoon.

Don had been quietly rechecking his notations on Petherton's work sheets. "I don't think I'm wrong here." He shook his head. "And I don't think there's been a computer error. Knowlton's figures and mine agree pretty well, even though he didn't look at the total flow. My bet is that the cave sizes are wrong in the records. That's where we ought to be checking."

"Cave sizes?" Petherton said blankly. He raised his eyebrows at Don. They were gray and bushy, thick like his hair. Mary, standing to his right and a little above him, happened to be looking at his forehead as the eyebrows lifted.

She frowned. *Lordie, I think he's wearing a toupee. That*

102

would be really weird—but his scalp didn't move at all when his forehead went up, it looked as though the skin was sliding under the hair. She peered more closely as the smooth skin moved down. *Surely real Englishmen don't wear wigs—or do they?*

Mary had an urge to reach out and tug at the graying locks in front of her—just one quick pull. Don had caught her peculiar expression. He looked at her questioningly, but she gave him a wink and went across to sit and drink her own tea. He was too wrapped up in the tides to be distracted for more than a few moments. He leaned back over the listing and went on, "I think it's the sizes. Somebody who worked on the caves made a mistake. I've done it myself—it's hard to judge distances underground. The best thing we could do is go down there and take a look."

Petherton was silent. He sipped his tea quietly, a model of British decorum and dignity. *But he doesn't like the taste of it,* thought Mary. There must be a special way of making it that she hadn't learned yet. Petherton looked as though he was sniffing a dead rat, and he had that other expression, too, the one that Don had warned her about in his letters. It said, come now, those measurements must be right—after all, they were made by *British* surveyors.

He finally seemed to reach some decision. "You know, those caves are dangerous."

"So I've heard. I'm experienced in this sort of work. I still think I ought to take a look."

"Not alone." Petherton had put down his cup and his hesitancy was gone. "You need someone who knows the caves to accompany you. I must be back down south tomorrow morning, but I would be happy to go with you today."

"What about your suit?" said Don after a moment's pause. "You'll ruin it down there."

Petherton laughed. It sounded too loud. "I have others, you know, and I don't expect we'll be there for more than an hour or two." He stood up. "Actually, I keep an old suit of clothes in Laxford, ones that I use when I go bird-watching."

Don nodded and flashed a look at Mary. *Do you mind?*

"Go ahead. I'd prefer you to be there with Mr. Petherton rather than have you go in on your own." She smiled at him. *There you go, just like a man. Use me for what you want, then run off and leave me.* "Don't forget we're having dinner at six o'clock at the Over The Water. I'll walk down and meet you there."

Don turned to Petherton. "But what about equipment?"

"Flashlights and marker rods are all we need. We'll pick them up easily enough in Laxford." He looked at his watch. "As a matter of fact this is an excellent time to go into the caves. It's almost low tide—forty minutes from now."

"Let's go." Don stood up. "I'm ready now. We've had no lunch, but I'll grab something to eat while you're changing your clothes and getting the flashlights."

He started out of the room. Petherton paused for a moment in front of Mary and took her hand in both of his. His grip was warm and soft, with smooth pads of muscle along the thick palms and fleshy fingers.

"It was a real pleasure to meet you, Mrs. Willis. I hope we will see each other again in the near future."

"And you can teach me how to make tea properly, eh?"

He squeezed her hand. Mary was conscious again that he was assessing her, studying her. He smiled down and nodded. "Perhaps even that. When we are all less busy."

Mary stood up and followed him to the door, where Don was waiting impatiently. "Six o'clock, Don—and don't be late, or you'll find I've eaten yours too."

When she went back inside the house, it suddenly seemed lonely and too quiet. Without Don, it was just a dingy old place in bad need of a good spring clean. She went through the kitchen and found her abandoned sandwich. While she was eating she noticed her feet, black and dusty from the floors. No wonder Petherton had given her some odd looks. She would have to do something about it.

The bathtub was a monstrosity, over six feet long and ridiculously wide. It stood separate from the other furnishings of the bathroom, solid on four clawed feet. Hot water had to be coaxed from another vast gas heater, suspended menacingly above the end of the bath. Mary found a scrap of hardened soap by the sink, took off her clothes again, and stretched out in the half-filled tub. It was a unique luxury, a bath that was longer than she was. She lay there in splendor until hunger, cooling water, and conscience combined to drive her out. She had no towel. Back upstairs, naked and dripping wet (a treat for Don if he could have seen her!) to the chest of drawers, then collect a towel and her shoes and back down to wash

104

her feet again. No doubt about it, there was a lot of work to be done on this house before it was fit to live in—beginning with the bathroom and the bedroom.

She put on the same clothes (beginning to feel distinctly grubby) and ate the rest of the sandwiches. The cheese went as a dessert—Don could get all the food he needed when he was in Laxford. Finally she felt ready to face the house again.

After a quick look at the kitchen (no mop and no detergent) she decided that the bedroom won as top priority. They had to have a clean bed for the night. The washhouse held an ample supply of clean sheets and blankets, and when she was putting them away upstairs she found a drawer with a dozen candles and a supply of matches. A bad sign. How reliable was the electricity up here? That was something to discuss at the Over The Water when they got there.

. The bedroom was growing darker as the sun moved lower in the sky. The area near the bed was gloomy and shadowed. Mary turned on the light—a stronger bulb would be nice—and made up the bed. She dumped the old bedding on top of the chest of drawers, then went to the wardrobe that stood next to it. They would need a place to hang up clothes when they got back. That would be later tonight. The house might be dusty and neglected, but it was better than another night at the Over The Water with nosy Hamish peeping through the keyhole. She giggled to herself. The image of the little inn proprietor sneaking up inquisitively to see what they were doing was too plausible to reject.

. The old wardrobe held its own share of junk. There was a shabby old raincoat, two pairs of mildewed shoes, and a great stack of yellowing newspapers. Mary went back downstairs for the metal trash can.

The coat and shoes went into it at once. She started to pick up the papers in one load but found there were too many to handle all at once. The first batch went into the trash, then she bent over to pick up the others.

A name in a headline sprang off the page at her. NIXON: THE FINAL ECLIPSE. It was an English newspaper, *The Guardian*, for August 9, 1974.

Mary picked up the heap and carried it over to the bed, dust and all. The light made it a lot easier to see what she had found. Someone had saved pages from special events.

105

Most of them were British politics or sports, with names and faces that meant nothing to her, but occasionally there would be American news. Archibald Cox's resignation had been considered worth keeping.

The ones that had first caught her eye were still the most intriguing.

NIXON CASTS DIE ON RESIGNATION—*The Daily Telegraph*.
EXIT NIXON—*The Daily Express*.
MR. NIXON RESIGNS AS PRESIDENT OF U.S.—*The Times*.

The photos worked even better to stimulate floods of memories; Nixon jubilant, Nixon dejected. Beneath that pair, in the *Telegraph*, the final assessment: *Never glad confident morning again.* The pictures were like a direct pipeline from the present to college days in Iowa. Mary carried the whole stack back to the chest of drawers and put them on top of it for later reading.

While she was dividing them into two heaps she found the folder.

It was in the middle of the stack, overlapped above and below by newspapers. Inside the brown manila cover were fifty or sixty sheets, most of them of lined yellow paper. Mary's first temptation was to carry it over to the trash, but the name on the cover stopped her. Patrick Knowlton again, that shadowy figure that not even Hamish Macveagh seemed to want to talk about.

She went back and sat on the bed. Each of the sheets was in the same neat handwriting, in blue and red inks.

The first sheet. A meaningless mass of arrows and crisscrossing lines, joining patterns of letters. The same characters were repeated many times, *R*s and *D*s and *X*s and *H*s and *Y*s. The next three pages were more of the same, with lots of crossing out and over-scribbling. They were just as confusing as the first one.

She flipped through a couple more pages, just about ready to consign the whole thing to the trash. About ten sheets in, something flickered past her eyes as she rifled through. She went back and turned, one page at a time, until she came to it again.

It was a scrap of white paper, about seven inches square, with a brown stain—tea? whisky?—along the left-hand edge. There were no words, but a single drawing, crude and amateurish in technique but painstakingly executed. Mary shivered. That squat body was familiar. And the hairless skull, and the ears flat to the head. Last night's dream at the Over The Water had been full of the same shape, the white presence at the balcony window.

She looked around her nervously. The house was very quiet, nothing here to be worried about. Moving quickly, Mary flipped through the rest of the sheets. It was past four o'clock and already getting dark outside. She would arrive there early, but she wanted to get to the Over The Water and to Don. When he was here the house was a different place.

A few other pages caught her eye as she skimmed through them. One bore the single word *allergies!* in triumphant red ink in the middle of the page. Another held a pair of drawings. The first was a set of complicated closed curves in blue ink, and the second was a copy of that, with another set of dotted red lines and bars added to it. The first drawing was like a deformed human hand with webs of skin between some of the fingers. It made no sense at all, any more than those first four pages of gibberish.

The last pages were different again. A penciled note, "Eureka—but how many of them are there?", followed by the final sheet, a news clipping from an Inverness paper:

YOUNG EXPLORERS DROWNED

The bodies of Joseph Walker (19) and Mark Hamblen (17) missing since April 14, were found yesterday on the shore north of Ridsdale. The youths had announced their intention to explore the tidal caves of the northwest shore. They had carried with them a variety of exploration and caving equipment. None of this was found with the bodies, which showed evidence of immersion in seawater for at least several days.

Tidal caves. That made Mary suddenly become doubly edgy. That was where Don was now, looking through them with Petherton. But maybe he was already out again—they had mentioned a short trip. With luck he would be down at the Over The Water by this time.

107

She shuffled all the pages roughly back into sequence and stuffed them into the folder. After a moment's thought she went over and put it into the bottom of the wardrobe again, then ran downstairs without giving herself time to think how quiet the house seemed. The light in the hall didn't work—another chore for tomorrow's handyman. After a moment's hesitation Mary decided that she would leave the light on in the kitchen for when they came back. It was nearly dark, and she wanted all the light she could get on the way to the front door.

As usual, it stuck. She took a deep breath, jerked it open, and stepped outside. It was almost dark now, with colors muting to a single tone and the sea beyond the cliff a blur of gray. There was a faint red glow to the west, where the sun lingered just below the horizon. Mary walked a few paces closer to the edge of the cliff and looked toward the setting sun.

The evening was mild. The shoreline had retreated far from the cliffs, exposing a wide strand of shingle and pebbles. The air was full of smells, of weed and stones and shells and driftwood. The road that led to the village wandered along the cliff edge, sometimes just a few yards away from the steep rock face.

Keeping well away from the rocky edge, Mary began to follow the dark gravel path down to Laxford. She felt shivery, wound up, unwilling to look across toward the cliff. Inside every big woman there seemed to be a small and nervous one who was trying to stay hidden.

"There are dozens of ways in here when the tide is out. But you come back here in a few hours and you'd ask yourself if there were any caves in these cliffs at all."

Petherton was leading the way, moving easily along a tunnel that slowly sloped downward under the land. The surface was slick and uneven, covered with clots of decaying seaweed and sharp shells.

"Heading downhill." Don was panting along behind. "Tide must run at a rare rate through here in a while."

"It does. You wouldn't want to be anywhere near this cave once the tide has turned." Petherton was amazingly sure-footed for a man of his height and weight. He was carrying the fifty-pound set of markers and measuring rods and having

108

no trouble at all with the slippery floor. Where the tunnel began to curve south, he paused and waited for Don to catch up.

"Keep on going," gasped Don. "I'll have to learn how to move faster, or we'll never be through in time."

He was slipping and puddling along over the uneven surface. It was a chaos of broken boulders and deep cracks full of black water. Don had lost his footing a couple of times, and his shoes were squelching with salt water. At each breath, a stitch of aching muscle stabbed along his right side, and the air in the caves seemed to burn its way down to the bottom of his lungs.

"You need more experience, that's all," said Petherton. His clothes were unspotted and he was breathing slowly and easily. He worked through the most difficult places with casual ease. "It's like everything else, technique, When you've walked on this sort of surface for a while, it's not difficult. Try and use the sidewalls to balance you. We're almost to the first branch point."

He swung his flashlight to show the path ahead, curving to a bigger chamber. "This one will be full at high tide, all the way to the top. If you were in here in a couple of hours you'd drown like a rat." He sounded cheerful and relaxed. "Do you want to check the tunnel height here? That paper you're carrying should have it plotted there."

Don pulled the work sheet out of his pocket and shone his torch on it. "I don't think we should take the time. I'm not worried by this one. Let's move on and go farther in."

"Very well. Let me know if you feel I'm going too fast for you." Petherton smiled. "You're quite right, we should keep moving, or we'll have to turn back too soon and won't see the whole cave system."

"Let's go." Don's pulse was hammering away like a pump inside his ears and the stitch in his side as bad as ever. *Shouldn't have bolted my food like that. My own damned fault.* He had wolfed down four cheese and onion rolls while he was waiting for Petherton to change clothes, then (the big mistake) washed them down with a couple of pints of brown ale. There was no time for digestion before Petherton was back at the Over The Water with the measuring rods and they were on the way to the openings at the foot of the cliff.

Why the devil wasn't Petherton panting and groaning? He

had to be twenty years older than Don, and he was carrying all that damned equipment. That bulk under his coat was deceptive. He was like a good weightlifter. What looked like rolls of fat was sheer muscle, hiding places for power and energy.

As though to drive home that line of thought, Petherton lifted the pack of markers in one hand and transferred it to his other shoulder. He shone the flashlight ahead of them again.

"We're coming into the second big cave now. The roof here is a lot higher than the other one." He turned the torch upward. "See up there, the ceiling is barely wet. Over on the left you can see the spring tide marks. I'd say the depth in the channel will be less than three feet now—we're right on low tide."

Don peered for a moment upward at the roof of the cave, then at the black walls, encrusted with barnacles and periwinkles, glistening like jet.

"Can we do a measurement here?" His voice was hoarse, echoing back along the irregular chamber's roof.

"Very easily. You stay there and catch your breath."

They were standing on a natural shelf of rock that ran parallel to the main channel of the cave. Petherton laid down the bundle of rods along the shelf and pulled three of them out of the pack. Each was about eight feet long. He attached two of them halfway up the third one, then used them as remote handlers to set it upright in the tidal channel. About two and a half feet of rod was covered when the lower end scraped on the bottom.

He looked across at Don. "Will that satisfy you?"

Don nodded. He was staring around the cave, swinging his flashlight from one end to the other and matching the shape and size with his recollection of the computer printout. There was an unpleasant smell in his nostrils, a blend of decaying animal life, drying seaweed, and musk. "Two and a half feet at low tide? That certainly seems about right. But there's still something peculiar here."

"What? The charts show it exactly like this at low tide."

"I know—but look at the way the cave widens and then *narrows* again up near the high water mark." Don shone his torch on the curving wall. "See, it comes in tight up there. That means at high tide we ought to be getting really fast

110

flows through here—not the ones that the records show." Don began to pace off along the length of the cave, still peering at the walls.

"Watch your footing there," Petherton warned. "It's very slippery."

Don was still edging along the natural rock shelf beside the channel, with Petherton following. Don could tell how close behind he was by the light of his flashlight, which threw Don's shadow like a gigantic black insect on the wall ahead. He turned when Petherton was a few feet away from him. The other man abruptly swung his torch down to shine it on the dark, slow-moving water.

"Tide's near the turn," he said. "Watch your step here, footing's bad all the way along. I don't know what you mean by a slow flow through here. You'd think it was fast enough if you were in here in an hour or so. It would be over your head then."

"How would you get back from here if the tide was in?"

"Swim." It was hard to tell if Petherton was joking. "Or you'd go through one of the other connecting caves. Come on, we have to move fast. As soon as the tide turns, things in here seem to change very quickly. Look at it now."

He turned his flashlight down again. The sluggish water moved like black oil. As Don watched he saw that the current was beginning to reverse itself, to flow back into the cave. He allowed Petherton to move on past him and again lead the way, passing into a third cave that was bigger yet.

"Satisfied with the size of this one?" Petherton was splashing through a couple of inches of still water.

"It's about the right size." Don was beginning to breathe more easily, and the stitch wasn't troubling him as much. "I'd say it's as the charts show, even without bothering to measure it." He shook his head. "Something's still bugging me. I can usually tell the size of channels from the flows alone. Here I'm having trouble tying them in to the depths and the boundary shapes."

"I see what you're saying." Petherton's tone was noncommittal. "If your theory disagrees with the measured data, certainly one of them needs to be modified."

Don sensed an undertone behind the reasonable words. *How can you come here*, said that voice, *and try and tell me what should happen in caves that you have never visited be-*

111

fore? You don't know anything about this country. Doesn't that deserve a prize for arrogance?

"Just one more minute," said Don. He mustn't let Petherton's impatience interfere with the main job. He turned for another look along the walls and ceiling.

"What are you looking for?" Petherton moved up beside him again. He carried the marker rods like a handful of feathers.

"Directions." Don felt as though he had a lump of lead in his stomach, but even if it meant more hurry later he wanted to make sure of what he was seeing. "Where's this cave's main axis pointing? Can you give me a compass bearing?"

Petherton shone his flashlight on his wrist compass. "Northeast, or close to it. You know, we don't have much longer. We have to be on our way out of here in less than twenty minutes. I am not being alarmist, but it would be foolhardy to stay here longer."

He was right. Don could hear the chuckling and gurgling of the incoming flow, the first sign that the new tide was on the flood. He swore under his breath.

"I feel we've hardly started here—we have to be a lot more thorough. I'll have to come here again when I have more equipment and better clothes."

Petherton was silent for a few moments. "Let's go quickly now," he said at last. "There are just two more sizable caves and a couple of crossbranches, then we can head out again. What happened to you?"

He was staring at Don's left hand, which was red in the flashlight's glare.

"Fucking barnacles back there. I scraped against them—they're sharp as razors." Don put his hand to his mouth. "It's just a surface graze. I'll be all right—I heal well."

They were moving on into the long tunnel of the third cave. This one was much more complex, with side turns and crossing tunnels curving through the black rock. Petherton shone his torch along one of them as he came up to it.

"This is another place where the flows become complicated. There are four caves all running together here, each one with separate connection to the sea. They all flood at different times."

Don shone his own flashlight along the curving tunnel and walked a couple of paces along it. He noticed a curious

112

formation up near the roof and stepped closer to it. The rock seemed to have been chipped and gouged away in a fashion that didn't seem possible with the natural steady force of moving water.

"Was there ever any sort of mining done down here?" he said.

"Mining?" Petherton had walked on, flicking his own torch beam around the walls and ceiling of the main cave. He was about fifteen paces ahead. His laugh echoed around the cavern. "Why would anyone want to mine down here? This isn't the place for prospecting."

"There's a place here that looks as though stonecutting has been done," said Don. He had to raise his voice above the increasing busy noises of the rising waters. There was a chilly flow past his feet, tugging gently at his ankles.

He stepped a couple more paces in for a last closer look at the branch that ran away to the left. There were chisel marks in places where the narrow tunnel seemed to have been widened to a more uniform dimension. He shone his flashlight on it again. It was hard to be sure. Could the force of a tide do that, sweeping pebbles and rocks with it and scouring the solid wall for hundreds of years?

Don turned back reluctantly and splashed his way into the main cave again. He looked up ahead.

There was no sign of Petherton, no glow of a torch anywhere in the cave.

"Petherton! Where are you?" Don's voice came echoing back to him, a shrill re-sounding off the bare rock walls. He shone the flashlight ahead and began to run, his feet sliding and skating over the rock and splashing up dark water to wet him from head to foot.

"Petherton! *Peth-er-ton!*" Echoes of his own voice answered him.

He was emerging into another big cave. Don forced himself to stand quite still and played the beam of his flashlight in front of him. So far as he could tell from the moving light this one was long and straight, until the reflection failed forty yards farther on. There was still no sign of Petherton, no sound except the threatening chuckle of running water. The odor of decay was stronger here, a sickly smell of rotting weed. He began to move slowly forward.

There was no answer to his cries. The cave ahead twisted

113

and branched, so that now the beam of the torch carried only twenty yards in front of him. Don realized that he had lost any sense of the direction he was heading—and Petherton had the compass. Along each side passage he could hear and see the rising, moving water, picking up speed as the tide advanced.

Which way? It was no good trying to backtrack, the caves there would fill to the roof in a few minutes. He would have to keep moving forward. He swung the torch upward. The ceiling was wet. This part of the cave system would also be submerged at high tide.

"Petherton!" Only the rush of waters answered.

No wonder that people drowned here. It was so easy to get lost, to be robbed of all sense of east or west, of general direction. For all he knew he had already doubled back on his tracks, heading for the hopeless area where they had entered the cave system. The water had reached mid-calf, tugging harder at him with persistent cold fingers.

He was emerging into another big cave. Don forced himself to stand quite still and look around it. This one also seemed long and straight, as far as the flashlight beam would carry. There was still no sign of Petherton.

What was the layout of the caves? Don put his hands up to his head. Think, man, think of the output listings. Which one was this? It had to be the center one, the longest and straightest, with its long axis running north east to south west. He looked down again at his feet. The water was pushing the back of his legs, moving past him along the cave. Logically, he should turn about and head against the tide, follow a direction opposite to the flow of the water. Was that right?

Don closed his eyes, forcing his attention inward. Remember the calculations that he had showed off so proudly in Dounreay—could that have been just yesterday? He had marked the flows for all the caves, pointing out the unusual cases. Wasn't this cave, the third one north, a situation where the flow ran *opposite* to the way you might expect? When the tide was rising, the flow in the third cave was *outward*, toward the sea. Pressure gradients from some of the other caves dominated the flow, made this one run backward.

Don turned slowly. He pointed his torch at the restless water. Now it was up to his knees, sucking at him with a cold mouth. Common sense ordered him to turn round, to walk

114

against the flow, to force his way counter to the incoming tide. It took all his will to force himself to pace forward, following the current along the cave.

Soon the water was up to his thighs. He paused. Mary would be waiting for him by now at the Over The Water. Soon she would wonder where he was, wonder why he was late . . .

He made himself start walking again, hugging close to the wall of the cave, where the turbulent flow was the weakest. If he was heading deeper into the tidal labyrinth there would be no chance for a second try. Behind him the caves would be filling to the roof. The water was still rising. It grasped his crotch with an icy hand, lapped up to his waist. He kept moving.

After twenty more yards in the rising flood he heard a new sound added to the swift-running water. It was ahead of him, an uneven crashing and booming—like the surge of breakers on a pebbled beach.

He staggered on, close to exhaustion, and emerged at last into the dusk with a setting sun still casting a faint light across the water. There was a beach to the left. He forced himself across toward it, dragging himself free from the clutch of the tide. Soon he was slipping and staggering his way onto the wet pebbles. He sank onto his knees, shivering in the fresh sea breeze.

"Willis!" The cry came from the left. Don lifted his head and looked around. Petherton was standing by the opening of another cave, a dark round in the gray face of the cliff. He walked across toward Don.

"What the devil happened to you? My God, I thought you were still in there. You were walking behind me, then next thing I knew you'd gone. I've been back in three times trying to find you. How did you get out?"

Don let his head fall forward. "With a lot of luck. I don't know how we got separated. I stopped for a minute to look at a tunnel, then I couldn't see where you had gone."

"You see now why you should never go there alone?" Petherton was lifting him to his feet.

"I see why." Don coughed, leaning to steady himself against the other man.

"Come on. You're in bad shape." Petherton himself was looking battered. His clothes were marked and stained by

115

weed and water, and the arm of his jacket had been cut and shredded by contact with the barnacled walls.

"Come on," he repeated. He bent and picked up the pack of marker rods where they had been dropped carelessly on the shore. "We'll be all right now. We have to get up the cliff—the steps are over there—and back to the village."

He shone his torch for a second on Don, studying his staring eyes, wet hair, and pale cheeks. "You need a drink, old man, before you need anything else. And I wouldn't say no to one myself after this. Get your breath for a second, then let's be away from here."

CHAPTER 8

The edge of the road that led down to Laxford was bordered on the sea side by rock cairns, rough heaps of stones about four feet high and three feet across. They were made of the same broken granite that Mary had seen all around the village. It was used for dry walls, for walkways, for patching up the sides of the houses—for anything that could be done with stone rather than scarce wood.

There was still enough light to see the cairns and keep well to the land side of them. As she walked down the hill, Mary's nervousness left her. She quickly began to feel disgusted with herself. A batch of old notes, a rough drawing that reminded her of something she had dreamed about, and away she had gone in a panic, out of the house without finishing the cleaning or even switching off the lights.

She paused and turned to look back up the hill. It must be nearly five o'clock but Don wasn't due at the Over The Water until six. Did she have time to go back now and do anything useful at the house?

The deepening gloom decided her. If she waited another hour before she went down to Laxford, the cairns by the road would be completely invisible and she would be groping her way along the cliff edge. There was no sign of the moon—either they would have to get good flashlights or she and Don would have to learn the rise and set times. She hadn't taken any notice of the moon for years. In Manhattan you never saw it.

Mary started down the hill again, following the dim outline of the rock piles against the edge of the cliff. She had gone another hundred yards when she stopped again.

117

The smell. It was there again, elusive but unmistakable, rising from the sea. She hesitated for a few seconds, then angled her path toward the cliff so that she continued toward the village but came slowly closer to the edge. This was a place where the road came to within a few yards of the steep drop to the sea. The rock pile here was taller and wider than usual, warning the passerby that there was danger close to the road. Mary walked up to it, conscious of the scrunching of her flat-heeled leather shoes on the rough gravel.

The smell seemed to be stronger, the penetrating odor of musky lavender. It was coming from the shore beneath her. When Mary was close enough she could see that the tide was still far out. She inched closer to the edge, putting her hand on the cairn and leaning out to see the shore closer to the cliff.

"Careful now, Mrs. Willis."

The voice spoke almost into her ear. She straightened up with a jerk, her shoes skidding on the bare rock.

"Who's that?" Her voice wouldn't come out right. She felt as though there were no breath in her lungs.

"It's me, Walter Campbell."

The slight form of the minister appeared suddenly from behind the cairn. He must have been crouched behind it, down at the very edge of the cliff.

"I hope I didn't startle you, Mrs. Willis. I heard you coming down the hill and I would have called to you, but I was interested in trying to see what's been going on down there."

It was too dark to see his gesture, but she realized he must be pointing over the cliff.

"What do you mean, going on?" Mary had her voice under better control now.

"I'm not sure." His words were soft, almost whispered. "I come up here most nights, looking at the sea and the sky and marveling at God's works. Usually it's the quietest place you'd ever find, just the birds and the waves. Tonight, though, I was thinking that something was happening down there. Here, would you take a look? I don't see too well when the light's bad—Mrs. McNair tells me I need new spectacles, and I dare say she's right. Can you see anything there?"

He had come alongside Mary and leaned far out over the cliff.

"Careful!" She grabbed the back of his dark jacket. "Mr. Campbell, you'll be over the edge if you go another inch."

He drew back a few inches and shook his head.

"I'm all right. Here, take a look."

He urged her forward. Mary took a reluctant step and leaned out as far as she dared. She frowned down into the darkness. He was right, there was *something* down there, a faint moving light patch near the base of the cliff. She forced herself forward another few inches, conscious of Walter Campbell close behind her, breathing noisily through his mouth.

"You see, my dear," he whispered. "Isn't that—"

He broke off suddenly as there was a loud clatter of falling rocks to their left and a shout of alarm. It came from half-way up the face of the cliff. The light patch beneath seemed to flicker and vanish. Mary jerked back from the edge and collided with Campbell who was crouched inches behind her. For a terrifying moment they swayed on the edge before they could move back to a safe footing.

"What was that?" said Mary.

"I don't know." He went again to the very brink and leaned far over. "It must be somebody on the steps—there's a sort of rough set of ledges down that way, where you can get from the cliff to the beach. I can't imagine who'd be there at this time of day, with the tide on the rise now." He raised his voice. "Hey! Is there somebody down there?"

The answering call made Mary cry out. It was Don's voice.

"We're stuck here. We'll need help to get the rest of the way up. Could you get a rope?"

"Get one from the inn." That was Petherton, hoarse and uncertain. "Hamish has fifty foot of good rope. We're safe enough here but we daren't climb farther without some support. Who's up there?"

"Walter Campbell. I'm with Mrs. Willis." He turned to Mary. "You stay here and make sure they don't try to climb until I get back. I know this road well. Give us ten minutes."

Mary was suddenly alone at the edge of the cliff, peering out and trying to see the two men below her. They were invisible—what had happened to the flashlights they should be carrying?

"Don, be careful." Her cry echoed down the cliff face.

The nervous words sounded ridiculous. But he could be

119

killed, with one wrong step he could be smashed on the rocks beneath them. Suddenly the safe and routine job of an engineering survey looked different. It was filled with hidden dangers, swirling around them like the black waters below. For the first time since she left the city, Mary longed for the comfortable boredom of her life in Manhattan.

"My fault completely," said Petherton. Propped against the corner of the bar in the Over The Water, dressed in his neat blue suit and with a pint of mild held in one well-manicured hand, he was a picture of calm and urbanity. "I lost my head for a moment there as we were climbing up. There's a lesson in that, don't try and make a rock-climber out of an old fogy like me."

Don shook his head vigorously while Mary sat opposite and bit her lip with anxiety. He was white-faced and over-tired—work, sex, and the exertions in the caves had been too much one after the other—and his left hand was one ugly big blotch of bright pink where the skin had been scraped off the back of it.

You deserve a drink or two, Don, said Mary to herself. *But stop now, you've had four whiskies and Hamish is pouring doubles. Please stop before you lose track of how many you've had. I can't make a scene here in front of everybody, not after the scare you had in the caves and on the cliff. No more, please, please, PLEASE.*

She could not catch his eye. He was bright, too animated and active. There was still a fine tremor in his hand as he held the glass. Twenty people were crowded round them, listening in fascination.

"Not your fault at all," he said to Petherton. "I shouldn't have let myself get left behind. Then we'd have been back up the cliff while there was daylight. I thought we were goners when you slipped and dropped those flashlights. If I hadn't been well placed, hands and feet, we'd both have been over the edge."

His glass was empty again. A tiny nod to Hamish Macveagh had it refilled. Mary wished that Walter Campbell had stayed in the Over The Water, but he had paled and excused himself as soon as Don described how near he had come to drowning in the tidal caves. Campbell might have done what Mary could not, and told Don he was on the way

120

to drunkenness. But would anybody else ever notice it? Don didn't show the usual signs, no slurred speech or staggering walk. He would go on, more and more affable and easygoing, until he passed out. Thank God he was eating well. That would slow things down. While Don's eyes were on Petherton, Mary slid her own biscuits and cheese over to the other plate, where Don could reach it easily.

The talk around them was getting louder, other villagers joining in. The dangers of the caves, the strength of the currents, the bodies that had come floating out of there over the years, the time that three men had been killed falling from the path up the cliff . . .

Another double whisky for Don. And another. Now another. That was—what? Seven? Eight? Mary felt as though she would be physically ill.

"Don!"

The loud and cheerful talk around the bar halted. Faces turned to her questioningly.

"What's wrong, honey?" Don's eyes were still much too bright, but his voice sounded perfectly normal.

"Don, I—I don't feel well." (It sounded silly, but it was all she could think of). "I don't want to rush you, but could we go home now?"

"Home? You mean back to the house?" Don looked round the bar and when his eyes came back to Mary they were suddenly dulled. She felt a quick anger. He didn't want to leave, and he was trying to think of some way to justify it.

"Yes. Soon. I don't feel good at all." The bar had fallen silent.

Don looked at his almost empty glass, then up to the faces that were clustered around them. "Well, I guess if that's the case we'd . . . Time for one more, do we have that?" He wouldn't meet her eye. "I'm sure I haven't paid my share here. I ought to buy another round for all of us. One more round—"

"Tomorrow. We won't forget—we'll make it up double." Mary stood up.

The pallor on Don's face had been replaced by a flush of resentment. The men standing round them had begun to back away, sensing the silent argument between them.

"All right." Don drained his glass and stood up suddenly.

121

"Come on, let's get out of here." Without waiting to see that Mary was ready he headed for the door.

"Don, we'll need a flashlight." She turned to Hamish Macveagh. "Could we borrow one? Just for tonight?"

"Aye. Hold on a minute, Mary." He slipped through into the back room. By the time she had the flashlight and could leave the bar Don was already striding up the hill. She hurried after him, shining the beam on the road ahead of her. Petherton's words as she left the bar seemed to follow her up the hill. "Don't rush up there in the dark. Laxford has seen too many accidents already on that piece of road."

What did he mean, too many accidents? That was a worrying comment, one that she would explore when the opportunity arose. If this piece of road was really dangerous, perhaps that was one reason that the house had been standing empty until Don signed the lease.

He had slowed down a little, letting her catch up with him, but he had still not looked around. Mary could replay the next couple of hours from memory. The indignation—of course he hadn't been drinking too much, that was sheer nonsense. The sullen look around, when there was no more drink to be found anywhere in the apartment. Finally, the rapid drowsiness and the fall to a deep, stupefied sleep.

Her words at the inn were proving to be no sham. She felt ready to vomit, with the misery and nausea rising from her belly. Here it was, their first night together in Scotland, something she had fantasized about for months. *The fucking drink.* If only she could banish every bottle of it to the bottom of the ocean.

Mary's fingers were clenched hard on the flashlight. She didn't notice the coast road as she hurried after Don, nor the odor that was wafting up to her, stronger than ever, from the shore beneath. The tide was rising still, filling all the caves far beneath their feet with the clear green waters of the North Atlantic.

One window of the kitchen was angled to the east. Mary had been up soon after sunrise, watching the hills emerge from the morning mists. Now they rolled away in the distance, green and brown and purple, washed with the soft-edged sunlight of a fine Highland morning. She went outside to empty out coffee grounds and breathed in the smell of the

122

bracken and the heather. When she came back in, she went to the window to push aside the white lace curtains and open it a crack. The steam from cooking breakfast had misted the inner surface with condensation.

"Leave it closed, please." Don was still sitting, head down, at the kitchen table.

She looked at him uncertainly. He was hunched over a heavy mug of black coffee, the stubble on his face marking his pallor and skin-sagged look. He had said only a handful of words since he came down just a few minutes ago. Mary's early trip to the Over The Water, to struggle back here with clothing, food, milk and coffee, had gone unremarked. He had taken the mug of coffee without a word. Mary, ready to forgive and forget, was beginning to lose her own resolve to make peace.

"Why leave it closed? It's a marvelous day out there—you should get a breath of air." Her voice was carefully neutral.

"Yeah." Don yawned. "In a minute. Haven't got my eyes open yet. Boy, do I feel shitty. Look at that."

He held up his left hand, where a huge scab had formed. "Fucking barnacles. I hope it doesn't fester."

Mary came over to the table and took his wrist. "I don't like the look of that. You ought to get it to a doctor." She felt a twinge of guilt. Don had been drunk all right—but look what he had been through yesterday. "Will you promise to have somebody take a look at it?"

"Who? I don't know if there's a doctor within twenty miles of here. I'll be all right."

That was one thing in Don's favor, you didn't hear him complain over minor ailments. She had seen him in New York coughing his lungs up and still insisting that he was well enough to go to work. Maybe that was why he would always get a good reference, even from the places that had fired him . . .

Mary looked guiltily over to the shelves on the other side of the kitchen. When they arrived back at the house last night, she had had to help Don up the stairs and into bed. He had gone out like a light. It had not yet been nine o'clock, and Mary had gone dejectedly back downstairs and sat at the old kitchen table. She'd had it with him. When other people talked about Don's drinking, she was always defensive, explaining that it wasn't a physical addiction, just a response to certain situations and pressures. But the simple truth was that he could never refuse a drink once he'd *had* a drink and the people around him were drinking. It was a social disease.

She had taken her notebook, the one that Roger had filched for her from JosCo stock, and written her heart out until she found herself beginning to nod off over the pages. She told Ellie everything that happened to her, about the day with Roger Wilson in London, the trip up to Laxford, the house, the old papers that she had found with their strange notes, the reunion with Don, the frightening moments on the cliff edge, and the events later at the Over The Water. When she was finished it had felt like a catharsis, a cleansing of all her worries and complaints, and she had been ready to begin this morning with Don on a fresh basis. Only he didn't seem willing to cooperate.

The letter to Ellie was sitting over there on the shelf. Should she send it, or should she recognize it for what it was—her own safety valve—and tear it up in favor of a bright and chatty one?

She sighed and patted Don's forearm. "JosCo must have a doctor handy. Make him take a look at that. Please?"

Don shrugged his consent. A grudging truce? She went back to the stove.

The thick-sliced ham there was sputtering nicely in the massive iron frying pan. Dora had cut it herself from the line of great hams that hung in the pantry at the Over The Water. She had nodded and cackled happily at Mary's request for the makings of "a real Scots breakfast."

"By rights you'd get nothing but porritch an' cold water," she said. "But I'll do ye better than that. Come on, let's see what the auld skinflint has up in the pantry."

Half a dozen eggs—newly laid, according to Dora—were ready to go into the pan, and alongside it the porridge was bubbling sluggishly, little bursts of steam like exhalations from a bowl of molten lava. Mary had managed to refuse the smoked fish ("The best finnan haddie in the North," according to Dora), but the idea of scones from the freshly made dough made her mouth water. She had eaten them the previous evening at the inn and knew she had to learn the recipe. Half a dozen of the scones were in the oven beneath the range. She cracked open the door to see if they were

124

browning, and the smell was heavenly. If this didn't restore Don to life and civilized behavior, nothing could.

"What time do you have to go to work, Don?" The kettle was boiling again, and she poured the water into the pot. She was drinking Earl Grey—Don swore it wasn't tea at all, it was bordello sweepings and perfume.

Don was sniffing the air. He caught her eye and wrinkled his nose—the first sign of friendship since he came down from the bedroom.

"You'll poison yourself with that. I'm amazed they drink it up here." He sipped coffee for a moment and sighed. "I'll have to be off to meet Roger by half-past nine. More site checking. Well, at least it's not raining this time."

"You must be having trouble with it, finding level places round here. It's all terribly rough."

"I'll say." Don started to shake his head, then thought better of it.

But not as rough as the Scotch, thought Mary. She bit off the comment before it could get out and turned to cover the teapot with a knit tea cozy. It reminded her of something else.

"Don, I can't find a tea strainer in the kitchen here. Did you see any sign of one when you first looked round?"

He looked around him vaguely as though a strainer might suddenly materialize on a wall or ceiling. "Don't remember. I was too worried about foundations and structural walls and damp. I've never seen anybody bother with a strainer up here. They slurp it right down to the tea leaves and swear when they get a mouthful of 'em."

Mary poured carefully from the pot, frowning when she saw a tea leaf come from the spout. "Good business up here for the fortune tellers. Everything's all ready here. One egg or two?"

"Start me with none—I haven't got the motor running yet, to quote Roger. Give me a few minutes. I'll just have one of those bread things and some more coffee. And jelly, is that?"

"Marmalade."

"That's fine." Don watched as Mary opened the oven door and peered inside. "They done?"

"A bit over." She began to lift the scones out as fast as she could, leaning back from the heat. The back of her hand touched the side of the oven for an instant. "Ouch. No pot

125

holders either. We'll have to buy a few or I'll be all burns in a week—this thing gets hot."

Mary put the plate of scones on the table and looked at them with satisfaction. They looked as good as Dora's—maybe a tiny little bit overdone, but it was the first try with an unfamiliar oven. She picked up her cup and took several swallows without lowering it.

"Think I could read my own fortune from this?" Mary peered down into the cup for a moment and then put it down while she helped herself to porridge, ham, and eggs. If Don didn't feel up to his food, there wasn't much chance it would go to waste. Dora had warned her about the effects of Laxford air on the female appetite and waistline.

After a couple of tentative bites Don had started in enthusiastically on the scones. "You ought to talk to Lord Jericho," he mumbled with his mouth full. "Did you know he believes in that bullshit?"

"What bullshit?"

Don shrugged and leaned across the table to steal a piece of Mary's ham. "You know, palm reading, fortune telling, tarot cards—all the mumbo jumbo stuff. I think I could do as well as they do without the tea leaves. It's all common sense and guess work." He leaned over and speared another slice.

"Here." She swung the frying pan off the stove and placed it between them on the table. "If you're going to steal mine, you might as well do it the easy way. I wish somebody would read my fortune there. Ellie still thinks I ought to write a book while we're in Scotland. I'd like somebody to look in the crystal ball and tell me if it'll be any good."

Don looked up for a second, dark hair hanging uncombed over his forehead. He had dropped marmalade and butter down his undershirt and stuffed his mouth too full to speak. "Hmph." He swallowed hard. "She wants you to do a Capitol book? If it is any good, it'll be the first. Those things are *supposed* to be lousy—junk food for the brain. The damned things never get into the real book stores, they stick 'em in the food stores with the rest of the groceries."

"Well, I'd like to see *you* write one that somebody would buy." Mary stood up angrily to pour herself more tea. The old argument. According to Don "any idiot" could write and sell a novel of the kind that Ellie's company published. Since

126

he would never dream of trying to do it, she had no way at all to convince Don how hard it was.

"She hasn't bought yours yet. When are you going to start writing it?"

"I'm collecting material." Mary cringed when those words came out—she and Don had known people in New York who had been "collecting material" for forty years and never written a line. Don didn't seem to pick up on that one. He nodded and looked at his watch.

"Got to get a move on. Jericho's flying in later this morning. Here." He handed his mug across the table. "If there's time before I go I'd like one more mouthful after I've showered and shaved."

He hurried through into the bathroom leaving his dirty dishes on the table. Mary looked at them. Should she feel pleased or annoyed? He'd eaten lots of ham and eggs and scones after saying he wasn't interested. True, but there hadn't been one word of appreciation for the fact that she'd conjured up a complete (and delicious) meal in a house where yesterday there wasn't a scrap of food. Don must think it had materialized from the air while he lay there snoring.

"Hey." His call came through from the bathroom. "Do you know how to make this thing work? I'm trying to get hot water, and it just stands there farting at me. What's the trick?"

"Just a second." Mary loaded a double armful of dishes into the sink and adjusted her apron (hideous, but all she'd been able to find in this house. How about looking in that place under the stairs?). She went through to the bathroom. "Mr. Campbell showed me. You have to coax it at first."

He was standing there dressed in just his undershirt, frowning at the heater. Mary came round to the side and showed him how to turn the nine-setting, adjustable dial on the base. The gas roared inside the big cylinder, and a stream of hot water poured out into the bath, steaming where it met the cold porcelain.

"See? You can set the temperature here, or you can run it as hot as it'll go and use the cold tap down there to get the right mix." She stepped out of the way.

"Wish we had a shower here—maybe we can add one later." Don splashed into the bath and began to fiddle with the faucet, hopping from one foot to the other, storklike, as the water ran first too hot and then too cold. Finally he sat down cautiously and looked at Mary.

"So what are you going to do while I'm working? Collect more of your 'materials'?"

There was an unpleasant edge to his voice. She could see how bloodshot his eyes were, and how the bags under them were more prominent than ever. Still hung over? Sure he was—but even making allowances for yesterday's experience there were limits to what Mary could take.

"It should be obvious to you what I'll be doing if you've got eyes in your head. I don't need dumb cracks like that." She waved her arms at the room around them. "This whole place is like a pigsty, dust on everything. I'll be weeks and weeks just trying to get the damned place to look decent and clean. So don't give me any of that hard-working-man-with-sit-at-home-wife horseshit, all right?"

Don looked surprised at the anger in her voice. He picked up the soap. "I'll see Roger about a cleaning woman. He says he knows a good one locally—young woman who needs work. I'll get in touch with her if I can. OK?"

Not an apology, but as close to one as Don would ever come.

"Thanks." Mary looked thoughtfully around her at the old bathroom fixtures. "You know, Don, if it were clean I really *would* like this house. It's run down and battered, but it feels as though it belongs here, like part of the ground. I want us to put something of us into it, make us feel more . . . I don't know, more comfortable. I've started to clean rubbish out of that little room upstairs next to our bedroom. It ought to make us a terrific study when either of us wants to work there."

Don sat panting. The water was a good deal hotter than he expected, but it felt good, flushing out his pores and relaxing the band of dull ache that ran round his skull. He closed his eyes and lay back slowly at full length.

"Do you think we could rent a typewriter from JosCo?" said Mary. "If we don't, I'll have to do my first drafts in longhand. I used to do that, but now I think a typed version looks a lot more professional. Do you think Ellie would mind which way I do it?"

Don opened his eyes for a moment. "For Christ's sake, woman, how do I know? I'm not a writer. I had a hard enough time scribbling those letters to you. Write to Ellie and ask her."

Mary thought of the letter sitting out on the kitchen shelf. "You might at least try and act interested in what I'm doing." *There. Now she was being defensive.* "You've got your job but what about me? I dropped all my friends, my job in New York, the whole bit." Even as she said it, Mary knew how it sounded. The whining wife, the sort of person she couldn't stand. No wonder Don had that pained look on his face.

"We'd better talk about it when I get back." He picked up the soap again and began to soap himself carefully all over, not looking at her.

He was right. Talking now would make it worse. Mary turned to leave and paused when she was at the bathroom door. "By the way, I found a lot of old papers when I was cleaning up the bedroom yesterday. They were by somebody called Knowlton. Didn't you say something about him yesterday afternoon?"

Don sat up, soap still clutched in his hand. "Knowlton papers? Did you look at them at all? I mean, were they technical?"

"Not so far as I could see. They had a few pictures, clippings from papers, notes about things that happen around here. Do you want to see them?"

He ought to look at them. But not now, not when he was feeling so relaxed and he had to go over to meet Roger in a few minutes. Don shrugged and lay back again in the bath.

"Sometime, maybe. I doubt if it's anything important. We've got all his reports in London, and Roger tells me Knowlton had a reputation for being off his head about a lot of things. He spent a lot of time on the cliffs drawing and scribbling." *And drinking.* Better not mention too much about Knowlton to Mary, or she'd start to worry that he'd fall off the cliff like his predecessor here. "Chuck 'em out if they get in the way."

"You don't want to see them?"

"I've got to shave and get out of here—I'm late already."

He closed his eyes again. Mary went back to the kitchen and plumped down into the straight-backed wooden chair. She wrapped her robe about her forlornly. Don was in a real morning-after mood. That's how it had been in New York, too many times to count.

She poured another mug of tea and helped herself to left-over porridge and bacon. The sad thing was that she tried to be supportive and understanding all the time when he drank, but she couldn't get that across to him. He clammed up. It was obvious that he liked his drink, always had, even back during the time when they had first dated. In those days it had been an element of maturity, of solidity. Dad had been a hard drinker, no doubt about it, but he had always been a solid, lovable human being as well. The sweet, astringent scent of alcohol on her father's good-night kiss had sent her off to sleep feeling warm and secure. When Dad had died suddenly, back in college days, Don had for a time seemed like an extension of her father. A ten-year age difference became an advantage instead of something to worry about. And at first their weekend drinking had been a load of fun . . .

Mary looked down at the dark brown leaves in the bottom of her cup. Who could have told her fortune then, to prophesy marriage, then lost jobs, and the bad periods, and the time when the smell of alcohol on Don's breath would make her insides clench? *Strong drink.* That first word was well chosen. It described what it could do, how it could make or break the bridge between them.

She ought to get to work on the house. Don was still banging about in the bathroom, the water running again and the gas heater rumbling.

"Mary." The cry was plaintive, a little-boy-lost lament. "Where's my clean underwear?"

"In our bedroom. On top of the chest of drawers." She smiled as Don flashed out of the bathroom and up the stairs, completely naked and parboiled-looking. He'd have to learn how to handle the hot and cold water. And she'd have to stop nagging him. *Let him do his job.* Right now, that was the only thing that really counted. If he could succeed at this one, her book and Knowlton's papers and the dirty house were all trivial. How could she help him? It wasn't easy. Don said she complained too much, but he was the other way round. He wouldn't have a heart-to-heart talk about what was happening at work until too late. *After* it was too late, when he had lost a job, then they could talk while she nursed him back to enough self-confidence to begin to look for another one. She still didn't understand what it was about the jobs that made him start drinking—was it work pressure, or tough technical problems? Don always seemed to thrive on those. So what was it?

Maybe she was more to blame than he was. She found it hard to talk about his drinking until anger or real worry triggered her, and by then it might be too late. She heard the clatter of his footsteps on the stairs.

"Don? What time will you be back?"

"Early this afternoon, say about two o'clock. Oh, and I might have Roger and Lord Jericho with me. We need a quiet place to talk."

"Don! You can't bring Lord Jericho here. Not with the way that it looks now. We'll have to get the floors cleaned and a new—"

The slamming of the front door interrupted her. She went through to the living room and peered out of the narrow window, watching Don hurry off along the gravel road to Laxford. Then, dismayed, she turned back and looked around her. Another four or five hours, and Don would reappear here with a genuine English lord. She ran through to the kitchen, threw her robe across the chair and began to load dishes at top speed into the sink. Washing up could wait until later. She had to get the living room looking good, and if she had time she'd do the kitchen. And she'd have to make time to change into a decent dress and put on some makeup. Lord Jericho and Roger Wilson might take a Lordship lightly, but Mary didn't want to disgrace herself at her first meeting.

A real, live Lord. That's what she needed for her novel. She had the mental image already established. Tall, fair haired, distinguished, with the natural grace that came only from centuries and centuries of good breeding . . . Mary smiled to herself as she rummaged for cleaning equipment. She knew where that image came from—reading too many of Ellie's Gothics slushpile. So let's see how the real thing stacks up to the traditional picture. But hurry, hurry—you've only got a few hours, then it's into the nice clothes and sit here all prettied up waiting to meet Prince Charming-Jericho.

CHAPTER 9

"Mrs. Willis?"

The man standing in the doorway smiled at Mary as she swung the heavy door open. She looked at him, disconcerted. This wasn't Lord Jericho, whoever else it might be. The newcomer was too young, probably only a year or two older than she was. The early afternoon sun lit up the highlights of his light-brown hair. It was almost blond, with just a trace of curls.

"Yes, I'm Mary Willis," she said after a few moments.

He looked at her thoughtfully. He seemed to have caught the surprise in her voice.

"You were expecting somebody else? Mr. Campbell told me he'd talked to you about this. My name's MacPherson, James MacPherson. Everybody round here calls me Jamie."

He smiled at her confidently. His presence had smacked her as soon as she opened the door to answer the strong, self-confident knock. He had a healthy, ruddy complexion as though he spent most of his time outdoors, and that fitted with the broad, strongly built frame. His eyes were long-lashed and blue, looking straight at her and demanding full and total attention.

"Of course, you've come about the work on the house." Mary hesitated. She had been expecting somebody else, but to say that other person was an English lord would sound ridiculous. "I've been busy, and I forgot what the minister told me. Come in." She held open the door. Four years of Manhattan living made her instinctively add the safeguard: "I'm expecting my husband and a couple of his friends any time now."

He smiled again. Mary realized that she was staring at him too hard as he nodded and swung a bag of tools over his shoulder. He looked up at the second floor before he came in. "Roof's gone skew a wee bit since last I was up here. I think ye'll need a few new tiles, too, when we get up there. Best get that out of the way before we worry too much about the insides, eh?"

"I made up a whole list of things that have to be done, but you'll probably find a lot more when you look." Mary noted the way that his eyes did a quick scan of her body as he walked past her into the hall. His manner was informal and casual, very aware of his own presence. He was dressed in comfortable work clothes, with a worn leather jacket filled out by a thick chest and wide shoulders. His wide corduroy trousers tapered from a thin waist and narrow hips to long legs and his unscuffed leather boots. The clothing sat on him as naturally as if it had been cut by an expensive tailor.

"I didn't realize you'd done work in this house before," said Mary. "That ought to help us a lot." She was suddenly pleased that she had taken care over her own appearance. The dress she was wearing showed off her full figure, and she had applied lipstick and rouge discreetly, just enough to show off her mouth and cheekbones to advantage. The touch of perfume behind the ears had been an afterthought but she was pleased by the result. It had all been designed for Lord Jericho's benefit but that was all right. Looking nice could be spread around as many people as came to the house and saw her.

His bright blue eyes were still fixed on her, calling for her attention. "Aye, I've been here before. It's a real old house, this one, an' there's often been a bit of work for me here. Mind you, I'm not so often in this area."

"You don't live in Laxford?"

"Off and on. I like t' wander around a bit, see the country. Last time I was here must have been, oh, a couple of years back. I'll be glad of some work now, though." He nodded at his bag of tools. "My sort of work's been a bit short lately. Nobody can afford to pay a general handyman when times are hard. I can use a few days fix-up work, if that's what ye have here."

"I think I do." Mary stepped into the house and closed the

133

door only part of the way. She caught his eye. "I like to let the fresh air in here."

"Aye." He was smiling again, some private joke.

"Well, should we have a look at the house? I don't want to get dirty now, because visitors are on the way. Could you look over the attic and roof by yourself, Mr. . . . er . . . I'm sorry, what did you say your name was?"

"James MacPherson. But I'd rather ye call me Jamie."

"James MacPherson." Mary paused. "Strange, that's the same as the man who owns this house. Are you related?"

"No ma'am, not as far as I know. It's not an uncommon name in these parts, ye'll find." He walked past her, looking around the hall. Mary stepped back nervously. There was something disconcerting about Jamie MacPherson. He was only an inch or so taller than she was, but she felt dwarfed by him, as though he occupied all the space in the room. She took in a deep breath.

Got to get this situation sorted out. He was somehow giving her the eye without any of the usual signs of it. She'd seen more handsome men before without ever losing her composure. It was part of the New York game, the boy-girl jousting that she had only recently learned to play. Like with Roger Wilson. She had parried all his subtle moves and enjoyed it greatly, even lured him on a little bit and made it clear that it wasn't unwelcome. But this fellow . . .

Mary watched him stick his thumbs in his pockets, tool bag hung over his shoulder, and saunter around the sparsely furnished room. He hadn't said a word out of place to her. But communication involves a lot more than conversation.

"Thinking of doing any painting anywhere?" he asked. He turned back to Mary and smiled. "Don't worry, I'm not trying to make work for myself that doesn't need doin'. But this hall's awful gloomy. D'ye think mebbe a coat would cheer it up? Little bit of warm yellow, say. Make a big difference in here."

He ran a muscular hand along the wall, then dusted it against his trouser leg. He turned again to Mary, who had been standing by the door. "What do you think, Mrs. Willis?"

That broad grin again, and those bright eyes. He had nice, even teeth, with a smile rather like Roger's. Another exception to Don's rule, that the English and the Scots had all ruined their teeth by eating too much candy. Mary smiled back at him, trying to create her own space in the room.

"I think we ought to worry about other things that need taking care of first. Let's do the necessities. We're only renting here, and we'll only be here for a year."

"Fair enough. I could have got you a really good bargain on paint, though. I know the fellow at the ironmongery in Ullapool and he's got paint coming out of his ears—especially yellow. Only here for a year, eh? From America, right?"

"Yes. My husband . . . my husband has a position with a survey group that's going to be doing work near Laxford."

He nodded as though only half-hearing her words. "I'd like to see America some day." His voice was suddenly wistful. "I like the music—specially the women singers. There's nobody here that comes up to them. Old Shirley'll belt it out, but it's not the same."

"And I prefer English music." Mary smiled and walked across to the door of the kitchen.

"Oh, aye? What do ye like?"

"Any of the groups. Old ones like the Beatles, on up to Roxy Music and the Boomtown Rats."

"That lot! They're a bunch of poofs. Why, they need their tonsils out. But you take somebody like Linda what's-her-name, from California."

"Ronstadt?"

"Aye. She sings well and she's good-lookin' with it." He chuckled softly, as though it was just to himself. "Aye, she looks like a real armful. Well, mebbe we ought to take a look at what needs fixin' here, or your husband'll be back before we get started. Why don't you lead the way and I'll take notes."

He pulled a notebook from his jacket pocket and stood waiting. Mary noticed that he showed no signs of impatience. He seemed like a cat, willing to wait all day long without moving or fidgeting. She led the way to the second floor.

"All the window sashes here ought to be replaced. See, I can hardly get the windows up and down." She jerked one open a few inches, then struggled to close it.

"Here. Let me do it." Jamie MacPherson came close and leaned across to the wooden frame. He closed the window with a single effortless movement. "Nice perfume you've got on there."

She had been conscious of it herself for the past few seconds. Say what you like about the smell of what Ellie had bought her, but you couldn't deny that *Climax* was good value on a drop-by-drop basis. It seemed as though the longer she wore it, the more penetrating the odor became.

"It's something that was made here, locally."

"That right?" He was jotting a note in his book. "Didn't know we went in for that sort of thing round here. The only liquid most of the lads care about is Lochinver Honey." He closed the book. "Seen any of the Scots pubs yet?"

"I only just arrived here. I don't know how typical the Over The Water is, but I liked the atmosphere there." Mary led the way through to the next room. "Can you do anything about the molding here? It looks as though something's been chewing on it."

"Mebbe they have. I'll bring a couple of traps, just in case." He was watching Mary's look with a twinkle in his eye. "Don't worry, there's no harm in a wee mouse. They have plenty of those at the Over The Water, too."

"I didn't see any. And I'm not scared of mice. I was brought up on a farm. But I don't have to like the idea. Bring the traps as soon as you can."

"Right." He was crouched down by the wall, measuring the length of a section of skirting board. "I'll be by tomorrow with a couple of 'em. I thought ye had the farm look when I first saw ye." There was a calm, sideways look at her legs. "Ye'd pass for a lass from these parts, no trouble at all, did ye know that? Colorin', build, looks. But I don't know of a local lass so good-lookin'!"

"Thank you, Mr. MacPherson."

"Jamie."

"Thanks, Jamie." Mary was absurdly pleased by the simple compliment. She felt that he was undoubtedly a connoisseur of experience when it came to Scots womenfolk. "Hamish Macveagh said I'm one of his relatives. My maiden name was Vayson—he claims that's the same as Macveagh."

"Right enough. I'd say there's good Scots blood in ye." He straightened up. "Mary Macveagh? Aye, it sounds right for you. An' ye like it here, do ye?"

"I love it." The words had just spilled out. "I love this

136

house, and I love the scenery round it. But it makes me feel lonely."

Damn. That sounded like a crude come on. Jamie MacPherson was standing quite still, his expression unreadable.

"I mean," she hurried on, "I've just come over from New York. I've lots of friends there, and there's people around all the time. Here . . . well, it's all sky and sea and hills, isn't it?"

MacPherson had turned to go to the window. He pulled back the curtain and stared out at the cliff. "Aye, that's the problem with city folk. But are they really friends, the people you're missin'? Me, I'll take the sea anytime."

He had a point. All the people she and Don knew, and how many of them did she miss? And how many missed her, or even gave a thought to the fact that she had gone from the New York scene? Only Ellie. She ought to get that letter off to her as soon as she could.

"I don't know the sea yet." She laughed self-consciously. "I have to get used to it. I'm originally from Iowa—not much sea there."

"Where's that? Inland?"

"A long way inland. I never saw the ocean until we moved to New York."

"Ah, then ye don't know yet what ye've been missin', all those years." Jamie MacPherson's voice was soft and deep, like the purr of a cat. "Ye'll learn it when ye've been here a while. Some night, when the moon's lookin' down all quiet and there's just the ghost of a breeze, driftin' on from the west an' easin' the sea onto the shore like a babe in its mother's arms . . . Aye, then ye'll find ye can talk to the sea." His eyes were bright and almost hypnotic. "An' then if ye wait a while it will answer you. An' then ye'll not want that inland life again."

There were a few moments of total stillness and uneasy silence. He was still holding the curtain open as though inviting Mary to come and gaze out of it. She suddenly saw the ocean as he described it, the cool, moist sand between her toes, the brackish taste, the wind whipping at her long loose hair and easing her forward to meet the endless sea waves reaching up the beach.

Mary fought against the feeling of pleasant lassitude that had been sweeping over her. She coughed to clear her throat

137

and said haltingly, "You must love this land and this shore very much, the way you speak of it."

"Aye. It's life and death to me." He let the curtain fall closed. "Someday ye'll learn it for yourself—if ye stay here in the North."

Mary took a deep breath and rubbed her hands together nervously. "I hope that I will—someday. Well, let's take a look at that bathroom now. There's lots to be done there, starting with the faucets."

She led the way downstairs, deliberately not looking back to see if he was following her. "In here."

"Right. I know this place well enough." He slipped past her through the doorway. She felt a sudden moment of dizziness, as though she had lost all feeling in her hands and feet and was standing on artificial limbs. As she swayed there was a powerful hand on her arm and his voice spoke softly into her ear.

"Mrs. Willis? Are you feeling all right?"

She regained her balance and her breath, and leaned against the rough wall. "Yes. Yes, thank you, I'll be all right. I think I haven't recovered from the trip over here yet. Jet lag does funny things to people." She smiled to cover her feelings. "That, or Hamish's whisky. I think Lochinver Honey's stronger than I bargained for."

"You'll get used to that. Do ye need to have a bit of a sit down, maybe?"

She went on into the kitchen, deliberately putting more distance between them. "I think what I want is tea. A few days in England and I'm already an addict. Would you like a cup?"

"I would, Mrs. Willis—on one condition." He had followed her into the kitchen. The mists were clearing from her head, but she still didn't feel quite right. It had to be that damned perfume again—she'd had that same feeling back in New York and here the smell seemed stronger than ever. But it *couldn't* be the perfume. There was no way that a few drops of scented liquid could make her so dizzy. She was beginning to feel worried, almost scared. What diseases began with occasional dizziness? Her hand was trembling slightly as she picked up the kettle.

"What's your condition for a cup of tea, then?" She tried

to concentrate on Jamie MacPherson, lounging in the doorway.

"Ye have to remember where you are. 'A few days in England,' ye said. But here it's not England, it's *Scotland*." His voice was friendly and good-natured. She thought she could hear an edge of worry in it, wondering if she was feeling all right. "Tell me ye'll call it Scotland, an' I'll be happy to drink tea with ye."

"Thanks." She forced a smile. "I'll remember. Why don't you take a quick look round on your own while I'm making the tea? There's probably things that need doing and I didn't even notice them."

"Now this chair, I think it will do just fine for the desk, once that wobbly leg's fixed." Mary wiggled it back and forward. "It looks like a real antique, you should be real careful with it."

"I will. I'll handle it like the vet with a baby lamb." MacPherson looked again at his notebook. "That's the end of my list for today. There's a couple of other things that should be looked at, but I'll need t' get ye estimates for materials before I think it's worth your time to look at them. Ye've given me more than a week's work right here."

"You can start on it at once, can you?" Mary felt tons better. The tea had washed away all the queasy, dizzy feelings, and Jamie MacPherson had made her feel very much at ease when it came to estimating his prices for the work. He talked it out with her, every step that needed to be done to put something into good shape, and he talked over the price list for materials, pointing out where he could get discounts for her and what the profit factor was on wood and paint and nails and paper. His earthy, common-sense manner was relaxing, and his conversation was interesting. She had underestimated him in their first few minutes together. If women fell into his arms, it wasn't because of simple animal charm. He had a lot more going for him. Under pressure from her—he'd talked about structural wall removal too casually for her comfort at one point—he admitted that he had a college degree in architecture and designed buildings as a hobby and a side interest, whenever things were quiet. But he much preferred the casual life that work with his hands permitted him.

"Laid back, that's what you are," she told him.

He looked puzzled. "Come again?"

"It's a life style. Much prized out in California." She shrugged. "You do what you want, when you want it, and you don't let anybody pressure you into anything. Isn't that what you want?"

His sunburned face became serious. "You might think that. But Mrs. Willis, I—"

"Call me Mary. If I'm going to call you Jamie that's only fair. Women's lib—you have that here, don't you?"

He smiled a secret smile. "Aye. Ye might say so. But, Mary, I'm not really the way you describe it at all. I've got responsibilities—big ones."

She felt a sudden sense of disappointment. "A wife and children?"

"Oh no, nothing like that." He laughed aloud. "Perish the thought, eh? No, sometime when ye've nothin' to do for an hour or two I'll tell ye, but just take my word for it. I've got duties, same as anyone else, and I live up to 'em. And I can't start work here right this minute, the way you asked me to."

More disappointment. Jamie MacPherson was a great source of knowledge about the area. Mary had hoped to snare him in to share lunch with her over the next few days and use him as a source of research material for her book. Ellie had taught her that much, the need for real background to give a novel any sort of feeling of depth. Well, she could sketch out more plot and let the back-up details wait.

"When can you start?"

He sucked in a breath and looked up at the ceiling. "A week today? I'm committed for the next three or four days to the minister, for work on the church roof. Then I'd like a couple of days off."

"You'll still be in this area?"

"Aye, but I'll no be working. A man needs a day off now and again, eh?"

"Certainly." She thought of a question, decided it was none of her business, then asked it anyway. "What do you do on your time off?"

"Oh, this and that. Hike about. Read. See a lassie every now and then. Not much to interest anybody from the big city." His tone was dry. "Ye don't read much over there, do ye? It's all parties and watching the telly."

"You watch too much TV yourself, by the sound of it, if

that's your view of life in America. I never saw a program more than once a week in New York except for the news in the morning."

"So how do you spend your time?"

Mary realized that he had switched the question on her, but she answered it anyway. "I'm a writer." (*There. It was a half truth, and maybe in a few months it would be an honest statement.*)

"Are ye now. I'd like to read something you've written."

Mary saw her chance. "I'll do better than that. You can help me write it. I'm doing a novel about the Highlands, and I'll need all the background I can get. How would you like to help me with it?"

"I'm no writer. How could I help?"

"Sit there and talk to me—or just answer my questions when you're working on the house. It won't be difficult for you."

He pursed his lips. "If you think it would help you, I don't see why not. Mind you, I like to do most of my work in the evenings—the day's too nice to waste indoors. Could we talk then?"

"If you don't mind, it's fine with me. You can maybe tell me where all this furniture came from when you're repairing it. Oh, that reminds me. I didn't show you the washhouse." Mary led the way toward it.

"I took a look there when you were making the tea. There's no work to be done."

"Not on the walls and ceiling, maybe. Take a look at this though."

She led the way to the darkest corner of the washhouse, where there was a shelf of ornamental bric-a-brac. It was mostly rubbish—an empty pipe rack, two battered picture frames, a set of chipped and ugly pieces of porcelain. Behind them, covered by a dirty piece of cloth, stood a candelabrum. It was made to hold five candles, but two of the holders were so bent out of shape that no candles could be fitted into them.

Mary picked it from the shelf and blew the new dust off it. As she turned with it in her hand she saw Jamie MacPherson's expression change from a puzzled look to a frown. He stepped back a pace and shook his head.

"Here's what I wanted to show you. Is something wrong, Jamie?"

"Not really." He was smiling again. "Depends what you want me to do."

"Fix this up for me." She tapped the bent parts with her finger. "I'd like this straightened out. All it will take is a bit of banging. You could do that, couldn't you?"

"Yes and no. I can get it done for ye, easy enough. But I can't do it myself. It'll give me a rash, a bad one, if I work on it."

"From this? It's only silver plate."

"Aye, I know that. I'm tellin' ye, it would give me a really horrible rash if I started to handle it. Wrap it up for me an' I'll take it on down to Ullapool with me and arrange to have it done at a metalsmith who comes by there every month."

Mary put the candelabrum back on the shelf. "There's no hurry, we can do it that way. But I've never heard of such a thing. An allergy to *silver?*"

"Aye. What's so odd? There's people allergic to everythin' from face powder to pickled onions. I'm lucky—in my job it's not too often I run across silver. Suppose it had been iron? Do ye want to wrap it now, an' I'll take it with me?"

"But what will it cost? Suppose it's too expensive?"

"Then I'll bring it right on back to ye. How much are you willing to pay?"

Mary put her finger up to her chin. "For a good job? How does ten pounds sound?"

"Ridiculously high. I'll get ye a fine repair job for no more than three."

"And you'll help me on the book, right? If you'd like to talk over lunch I'll be glad to pay for it, maybe some day down at the Over The Water?"

Mary got a sharp look from Jamie's bright blue eyes. "Now then, a married lady like you has to worry about her reputation in a little place like this, don't ye think? An' I've always been told there's no such as a thing as a free lunch. I'm not sure what I could give ye about this place that would earn my food."

"But you'll do it?" Mary stepped closer to him and met the look he gave her. She needed to establish herself as his equal, as someone who was not asking a favor so much as trying to offer a fair price for a service.

142

He was smiling broadly and looking her full in the face. "Oh, aye, I dare say I'll do it. But it won't be for the price of the food ye'll be giving to me, now will it?" He laughed. "I'm after seein' myself in a book. Would ye have a place in the plot for Jamie MacPherson?"

"I'll make one." Mary laughed delightedly. "See if you recognize yourself when I've done with you. Don't you realize what power a writer has over her characters? I can make you wise or stupid, or married or single, or good or bad. You ought to be worrying about how you'll come out."

"No matter on that." The smile on his face was serene. "Ye'll do me proud, I'm sure of it." He stood quite still, his head cocked to one side. "Now then, I ought to be away. Your visitors are here."

"Not yet. I'd have heard them—they'll be coming by car, I expect."

"Aye." He seemed to be listening intently. "By car it is. Come on now, ye'll be in time to meet them at the door."

"But you can't possibly hear anything out there—" began Mary. She was interrupted by the sound of a car door slamming, carrying clearly into the house. "You must be psychic."

"Just good ears." They went together into the kitchen.

"Mary! Mary!" Don's voice was loud through the half-open front door. "Are you in the kitchen? I've brought guests."

Jamie MacPherson shook his head humorously. " 'Tis His Master's Voice. An' do ye have a servant's costume to go on out an' greet them?" He gave her a wink.

"Now then, mister," said Mary solemnly. "I'll have you know that American women are very liberated. I'm in here alone with a man, and you'll not hear Don say one word."

While she was still speaking Don poked his head inside the kitchen door. "There you are. Could you make some tea? And bring out some of those scones we had at breakfast." He was gone, while MacPherson looked at Mary and raised his eyebrows.

"Well, I was wrong on the liberation and right on the rest," she began, when Don's head reappeared around the door.

"Who's this, then?" He was frowning. "Are you Mr. MacPherson? The minister told me you'd be dropping by some time." He looked at the empty plates and the teacups. "You two seem to have been having a good time."

143

"Just been looking around the house." Jamie MacPherson stepped forward and held out his hand. "Pleased to meet you, Mr. Willis. I'm sorry I got here when you weren't here, but your wife has been kind enough to point out all the things here that need attention." His manner was brisk and businesslike. "I'll have a complete estimate for you, itemized, the day after tomorrow."

"That's very good." Don hesitated. "I appreciate the speed you showed getting out here—we want to make the place livable as soon as we can." He lingered in the doorway for another moment as though unsure whether he should stay or go back to the other room. "Come on in as soon as you can, Mary," he said at last.

A perverse satisfaction filled her. Don was never jealous (more's the pity!), but he'd sensed the rapport that had been growing between her and Jamie MacPherson. On the strength of the past few hours she was getting along better with Jamie than with Don. Maybe Don was feeling a bit guilty about his behavior at breakfast?

"I think you ought to go now," she said, looking first at Jamie and then at the door to the other room.

"Aye." He didn't seem annoyed. "Best if I go the back way, eh, through the kitchen here?"

Mary nodded. *So MacPherson had felt Don's reaction, too.* Well, he had nothing to blame himself for in his behavior— Don could stew for a while and serve him right. It would be nice if he thought somebody else was giving her the kind of attention Jamie was willing to offer. (But remember what Ellie said—the most dangerous men of all are the ones who make you feel that *you* have power over *them*.)

"You'll be back with the estimate in a day or two?" she said.

"That's right. As soon as I've worked it up for ye. Now, I'll be away through the Tradesmen's Entrance here. Be seein' ye."

He hefted the tool bag easily on to his shoulder and opened the kitchen door.

"Don't forget we're going to talk about Laxford," she called after him as he turned toward the south side of the house.

"I'll not forget. An' maybe we can look at a couple of lo-

144

cal estates, too." His voice was faint. "One or two of 'em have castles that are worth seein'."

Mary closed the door and made a quick dash to the mirror by the southern window. She touched up her makeup, tidied her hair unnecessarily, and quickly loaded the tray with teapot, cups, saucers, milk, sugar, and plates. The scones would need a few minutes to warm, and she'd come back for them and the butter. Walking very cautiously she navigated her way with the loaded tray from the kitchen to the living room, thankful that Don as usual had left doors open behind him.

The men were talking when she came in. She went across to the low table by the window and set the tray down on it. The jingle of the silverware stopped the talking over by the fireplace. Don remained seated, but the other two men stood up and stepped toward her. The nearer of the two had to be Lord Jericho—Roger looked as relaxed as ever, giving her a nod and a pleased smile and waving the other man forward.

"My wife, Mary," said Don. His voice sounded a little bit stiff and unsure. Mary realized that the man standing in front of her left Don feeling unsettled. She held out her hand and looked at him closely. Well, there went the tall, fair and elegant mental image. Lord Jericho was stocky, bald-headed, and blunt-featured. He looked to be in his middle fifties, and more British than English—Mary's ideas always made *English* people rather reserved and often effeminate; *British* men were big, hearty, direct, and able to handle the Empire On Which The Sun Never Sets.

"This is Lord Jericho," Don added after an awkward pause.

Jericho took her hand and shook it with a single, vigorous up-and-down movement. "Pleased to meet you. I'm sorry we've been running Don all over while you're trying to settle in here. You seem to be doing very well."

"Thank you, your . . . Lord . . ." *How did one address a lord?* "Thank you, Lord Jericho. Things are still a mess, but we're working on it."

"Not Lord Jericho." He shook his head. "That's me title, but me name's Joshua. You should call me Joshua, right? Then I won't feel bad calling you Mary."

"Thank you." Mary couldn't bring herself to use his first

name. "Don't any of your friends call you *lord*? I'd have thought they'd maybe call you Lord Jerry."

She was astounded at the reaction. Don said "Mary!" in embarrassed tones, Lord Jericho looked astonished, and Roger put his head back and gave a great guffaw of laughter.

"I hope not, lass," said Jericho. "I wouldn't encourage it if they did."

Mary put her hand up to her mouth. "What did I say?" She looked from one to the other of the three men.

"Lord Jerry," said Roger, and laughed again. "Marvelous, eh? Mary, do you know what 'Jerry' is slang for in this country?"

Jerry . . . Jerry. Something in World War Two movies? That felt right.

"Doesn't it mean a German?"

"It does." Lord Jericho was grinning. "An' that's not all. You haven't been exposed to enough rude seaside postcards yet. To lots of people in this country, a Jerry is a po."

"A po?" said Mary blankly. Things were getting more confusing.

"A po is a chamberpot," said Roger gravely. He was having trouble keeping his face straight. "So Lord Jerry would be . . ."

"Oh, Lord." Mary felt herself flushing. "I'm sorry—I had no idea."

"That's all right, lass." Jericho chuckled. "It's one way to break the ice." He turned to Don approvingly. "Well, now we all know each other, right? I must say your missus looks lovely when she's blushing. Let's all have some tea."

Mary poured tea and did a quick run back to the kitchen for the scones. Lord Jericho seemed like a nice old man, not at all the slave driver who came across from Don's descriptions. When she came back they were again into their interrupted project discussion. Mary passed scones, butter, and marmalade around quietly and did not speak. When she came to Lord Jericho he handed back his empty cup.

"Nice cup of tea, lass. Any more in the pot?"

"Lots." That was a relief. "I was going to give you coffee because I'm still not sure how to make tea the way you do here."

"You're well on the way, Mary," said Roger. He handed over his cup also. Don was looking distinctly relieved. He had

146

seemed on edge when she first came in, but as she listened to their conversation she began to get a feeling for the different roles that the three played. Lord Jericho was brusque, no-nonsense, and definitely the overall boss. Roger argued with him on questions of procedure, skirting the line between familiarity and deference, rephrasing Jericho's comments to be sure they all understood the same thing. They seemed to be a good team. Don kept his remarks to technical issues, and he handled Lord Jericho well, with a sharp and knowledgeable air that steered well clear of a yes-man role. If he didn't agree on a technical point he said so, quickly and clearly. And the other two men listened. This was the first time she had heard Don really working. It was an impressive new look at him. He knew what he was doing, and the reactions of the others made it obvious that he was a valued voice in the discussions.

Mary tiptoed away to reload the tray with more scones. *Pray God, this job would be the turning point. We need a win so badly now . . .*

The conversation drifted in to her through the open door. "Interesting that you should say that, Willis. That bit of land was picked out in the first look that we took at this site. You remember, Roger, when Knowlton came on up to London, and we had to tell him no because of the DOE people? But if Don here thinks we have to have it . . ."

Knowlton again. Mary instinctively turned her head to look up toward the bedroom where she had left Knowlton's papers, and tripped slightly with the tray that she was carrying. She staggered through into the living room, a couple of scones falling off the china dish onto the tray and the tall marmalade jar teetering precariously. She had a moment's terror that she was going to dump the whole thing into Lord Jericho's lap, then she managed to balance herself again.

"Are you all right?" Roger had moved with catlike speed to her side and was supporting her by the arm. He released her self-consciously as soon as it was clear that she had regained her footing.

"I tripped on the step there."

"You have to get used to these old houses," said Lord Jericho. He seemed to be in a very good humor. (Thank Heaven!) "The blasted floors aren't flat. You'd think they

147

were put up by a bunch of shop stewards." He looked up. "Not a right angle in this place, I'd say."

Mary put down the tray and caught Don's eye. When the conversation moved from technical to social comment, he was much less at ease. He looked worried now, waiting for her to bungle further and embarrass them both. She tried to handle herself with special grace as she collected the teacups and piled them on the emptied tray. The best thing she could do for Don was keep out of his way—he was holding his own well with the other two men.

"Do you mind if I smoke this?" Lord Jericho was holding a thin black cigar out toward her. His tone surprised her more than his question. He looked and sounded like a small boy asking parental permission, rather than the Big Boss—and he was asking *her*, not Don.

"Of course not. Do you need matches?"

"No. I've my lighter here, thanks."

He nodded, and Mary lifted the loaded tray to carry it to the kitchen. It occurred to her that she had just seen an interesting commentary on English life, or at least on Lord Jericho's perception of it. Had it been born in his own working class background? He would order Don around in work, but this place was *her* property, and what went on here was decided by the woman, not the man. *An Englishman's home is his castle.* Or should it be *Englishwoman?*

Friendly farewells, and the Bentley purred off into the late afternoon twilight. Don stuck his hands into the pockets of his cardigan and watched the big car drive away, a breath of exhaust pluming up behind it.

Mary waved good-bye and turned to go back inside. "I've never heard such a quiet car. Pity we couldn't have it instead of the Austin." She looked at the green car parked outside the house. "Coming in?"

"In a minute." Don walked to the side of the house and looked around him while Mary went indoors to sort through the cases he had brought with him from the Over The Water. They had a big sorting and storing job ahead of them.

After she had gone Don leaned against the stone wall of the house and thought back to the meeting. It had gone well, if Jericho's vigorous nods and Roger's sly sideways looks of I-told-you-so were anything to go by. Only Don remained unsatisfied, edgy. *Caffeine attack, maybe?* He had to watch how much tea or coffee he drank, especially later in the day. He'd had four or five cups there with Lord Jericho and Roger, and plenty of coffee earlier. He felt a tensed-up, nagging worry. *God, wouldn't a quick Scotch go down well now—or better still a martini.* That would pull him down from the caffeine high in a minute and let him enjoy the rest of the evening. But there wasn't a drop of drink in the house—he ought to have brought some with him from the inn but he didn't want to hold up the others while he loaded beer and whisky into the car. Anyway, it would look bad.

He watched a seagull hanging in the air close to the cliff and heard its ugly, croaking call. The air was rapidly losing heat, and the wind had moved from landward to seaward. The sunlight was gone, and the clouds on the western horizon were red and orange. *Red sky at night, sailor's delight.* Not off this coast. The currents and reefs and ripping tides made the sea dangerous at any time.

That was what was nagging at him. Those damned tidal flows. Petherton didn't believe him; Roger was politely sceptical; Lord Jericho was noncommittal. The jury would stay out until Jenks and his group over at Dounreay had their own calculations finished. Meanwhile, he'd be hanging here, sure he was right, sure something strange was involved, and unable to prove himself.

He turned and went back to the front door, hesitated, then entered. Should he talk to Mary, tell her what was worrying him? No. She'd bounce it back to him for an answer. He was older—quite a bit older, as she'd told him several times. So he had to make the major decisions, balance the checkbook, do the worrying. It had been that way from the beginning, big Don, first lover and then husband and new Daddy. He couldn't match what Mary expected from him—confidence, and success, and all-knowing strength. Instead when things got bad he slipped off the pedestal and could only offer silence and tenseness.

"Mary?" The house seemed very quiet.

He went through to the kitchen to find the back door standing open. Mary came back in as he walked toward it.

"What were you doing outside there?"

"Potato peelings. I stayed out for a while to have a look at

149

the sunset. What do you want?" She had the ugly apron on over her dress.

"Nothing." Don stuck his hands back into his cardigan pockets. Now that the other men had gone he ought to grab her and tell her how gorgeous she was looking. Only the memory of her sitting in this outfit with MacPherson held him back. He couldn't remember the last time he and Mary had sat together and just *chatted* the way that she seemed to be doing with the Scotsman. And he was a damned handsome fellow. *And* he was young, no older than Mary. Age difference again—and one of the hopes he'd had when they came here to Laxford was that he'd have Mary just to himself for a change, away from the involvement with her friends in New York. He slumped down at the table.

"Fish and chips suit you all right for dinner?"

"Eh?" He looked up absently. *One quick Scotch would work wonders.* He could almost taste it sliding down, burning away the jittery tension. Roger and Lord Jericho would be in the village until at least seven o'clock. . . . He frowned at the bowl of peeled potatoes that Mary was holding.

"You don't know how to cook fish and chips, do you?"

"I can learn easily enough—it's only deep-fried fish and french fries. The fish was caught this morning." She was watching him closely, noticing the way that he kept his hands in his pockets. Was he upset about something? If he was, could he be persuaded to talk about it? "Well? I don't have to cook it if you don't want it."

Don stood up. "Look, why don't you wait a while before you start the cooking. I told Roger that I'd try and dig out some papers on the Dounreay meetings and drop them off for him at the inn. It shouldn't take me more than half an hour—an hour at the outside."

The easy lie twisted his guts. Not just telling it—the way that Mary stood there, simple and trusting, nodding her approval. It for some reason filled him with irritation. Better if she gave him a hard time, yelled and screamed at him for ruining her dinner plans. He watched her standing there, her long hair pleasantly mussed. She had taken off the high heels and changed to slippers, but the care she had taken to be ready for his arrival still showed in the careful makeup and well-pressed blue dress. He felt a helpless love fill him as he looked at her. She was still an innocent as far as he was con-

150

cerned, young Mary Vayson, cooperative co-ed, sitting there
listening to him show off back in Iowa with her big-eyed interest and enthusiasm. New York had taken her natural shape
and laid over it the confines of a sophisticated woman but
here in Scotland the old Mary was blossoming again. He
ought to stay here and have dinner and a quiet evening together.

The knot in his stomach tightened again. Hour after hour,
sitting here waiting while Jenks and his idiot programmers
tried to reproduce his estimates on the flows and temperatures. There was a spasm inside him like a sharp cramp, and
he gritted his teeth to fight back the tension. If he were
wrong, and he'd made a fool of himself back in Dounreay
. . . Could he be wrong? Not unless he was wrong all the
way—unless all his ideas and experience had failed him here.
He was spiraling inward, the tension feeding on itself inside
him. He had to get out of here for a while. There was no
choice.

He stood up. Mary had been watching him in silence, a
shadow across her face. "Do you have to go, Don? You've
been working such long hours, and the meeting here seemed
to go so well."

"It went well. I told you old Jericho is a devil for work.
We got a lot done, and I'm holding my own." *That at least
was true—unless he had goofed on the flow patterns in
Dounreay*. He felt his fists clench inside the pockets. "Look, I
won't be long—just take me an hour or less. All right? I'll
take the Austin."

"But drive carefully. I don't like the look of that road at
night." She wanted to add the plea: *Don, please don't drink
while you're there*. She couldn't bring herself to say the
words. Nagging him would make it worse, deepen whatever it
was that he had sunk himself into. She watched as he
stumbled upstairs, came down with his brown jacket on over
the cardigan and hurried out, eyes averted. How real was the
appointment with Roger? When Don got into this mood she
felt like hitting him—not to hurt, just a tap to relieve her
feelings and tell him to behave sensibly.

Now it was too late. Mary eyed the ancient telephone on
the kitchen wall. It ran only to the Over The Water, a relic
from some previous occupant of the house who was too sick
or too lazy to go down to the village for supplies. The gro-

cery and general goods store was an attachment to the inn, run as part of the Off Licence liquor service. Should she see if the old phone worked now? Call the inn in a few minutes and ask Hamish Macveagh if Don was there, what Don was doing?

Mary forced the temptation away. The word would spread through the village in a few hours: the American woman doesn't trust her husband. Hamish might have his virtues but aversion to gossiping wasn't one of them.

She went across to the table where the raw fish, batter, and sliced potatoes were waiting. As she poured herself a cup of reheated breakfast coffee a new worry hit her. If Don did drink, he'd be driving the coast road in the darkness. Wouldn't it be better for *him* if she called, and if necessary walked down to the inn to make the drive home herself—or at least persuade him to walk back and leave the car overnight? Fretful, Mary picked up her notebook and tried to write outline notes for her book. Meaningless words. She finally gave up trying and sat miserably in the uncomfortable chair, wondering what Don was up to at the inn. Was this the pattern for her whole year in Scotland—worried days and lonely nights? That hadn't been the plan back in New York. She needed some fun and laughter. There must be a way to find it, even here in the empty Highlands. Mary sipped her coffee and made up her mind. Somehow, wherever it was, she *would* find it.

CHAPTER 10

> Till a' the seas gang dry, my dear,
>   And the rocks melt wi' the sun:
> I will luve thee still, my dear,
>   While the sands o' life shall run.
> And fare thee weel, my only luve!
>   And fare thee weel a while!
> And I will come again, my luve,
>   Though it were ten thousand mile.

Mary turned the page and looked again at her watch. Eight o'clock. Nearly three hours since Don had left. It was all very well for Burns to be away in the tavern writing those happy poems about the joys of boozing—who was home looking after the empty house? As for his "wee, sleekit, cowrin, tim'rous beastie," she couldn't wait for the mouse traps to arrive. She had imagined scufflings and scratchings around the skirting boards and paneling all evening. Mary laid down the book and looked around her.

The house was somehow changed at night. She had noticed it yesterday and later blamed her strange dreams at the Over The Water on Monday night, followed by Knowlton's disturbing collection of notes and drawings. But the feeling was still here tonight. When the light of morning drove out the shadows, the place was airy and friendly. Now, alone in the house, she felt that the meager light of the low-wattage bulbs (someone was a miser for the electric bill) could not keep out the sense of gloom and decay. She was tempted to go from room to room, switching on every light and setting matches to the candles that she had found in the upstairs drawer. The night had closed in like cobwebs, shrouding her in a private and claustrophobic uneasiness. And it was getting colder, as the chill of the October evening seeped in through the old stone walls. She had asked Jamie MacPherson about ways to heat the house for the winter but he'd laughed at her.

"I'll try and make sure the windows and the doors all fit well, that much I can do. But that will be near the end of it for useful work. As for central heating, there's more than likely no such thing through all Sutherland County."

"So how *do* you keep warm up here?"

"Aye, that's a fair question. Warm hearts, that's all we have to rely on."

A funny enough answer at the time, but now she was feeling chilly—and she *never* felt cold back home. Was it just a question of getting used to it?

Mary stood up, intending to go and bring a sweater from the chest upstairs. Her eyes went again—the hundredth time—to the black phone on the kitchen wall. She had resisted the constant urge to call the village, to try and track Don down there. She had invented reasons why he was late—all of them weak. Perhaps he had gone out for a drive to test the car that JosCo had provided for their stay in Scotland (but wouldn't he have come back here to take her with him?); perhaps the meeting with Roger and Lord Jericho had taken much longer than they expected (but if that was the case why hadn't he called her and mentioned it?—it would only have taken him a couple of seconds). Mary looked at the soggy fish and browning sliced potatoes. To hell with this. She walked across to the telephone. Let Hamish think and say what he liked, she had to know what had happened to Don.

When her hand was within inches of the receiver the phone jangled with its peculiar buzzing ring-ring, pause, ring-ring. She jumped and hurriedly took it off the hook.

"Hello."

"Hello?" The voice sounded as though it was coming from thousands of miles away, indistinct and crackling. "Mary? This is Don."

"Where are you?" (A ridiculous question—the line went only to the Over The Water!) In a fraction of a second all her worry evaporated and was replaced by a seething annoyance. "Why didn't you call me? Our dinner is completely spoiled, I suppose you realize that?"

"I'm sorry, honey." Don's voice was more cheerful than apologetic. "I should have called you. I was going to call you and tell you to go ahead and have dinner because I'd be delayed for a while here."

"Why didn't you? I was here." Mary was listening closely, trying to hear the sounds of drink in his voice. "I've been sitting here waiting."

"I know. You've heard how it is with Lord Jericho, he works long hours." Don paused. There was an indistinct sound of laughter in the background, and she could hear him talking to someone else away from the mouthpiece. "Mary? Honey, I'm sorry. We're all finished now, and I thought you might like a break from being in the house all the time. You must be going out of your mind, working there all day."

"Or waiting for you to come back." Mary's tone was chilly. "I happen to like it here."

"I told you I was sorry. Anyway, there's a sort of party going on here at the inn. They have one here most Wednesdays. The others suggested that you might like to come along and join us."

"Did they now? And who is 'us'?" (Weren't Roger and Lord Jericho supposed to be going on to another meeting this evening?) "Do you mean you and some of your drinking partners?"

"Look, I'm *sorry*." Don still sounded cheerful. "I know I behaved like a real asshole, staying here and not calling you. And it's not *my* drinking partners—it's MacPherson and his friends."

"Who?" Mary stared at the receiver as though it was garbling the message. "You don't mean Jamie MacPherson?"

"How many other MacPhersons do you know around here?"

"But he wasn't at your meeting."

"No, he wasn't." There was another sound of a voice in the background, and again Don spoke to someone away from the phone. "You see, after the meeting I stuck my head in the bar here for a minute—"

"For how long?"

"Will you just let me get in a few words? I looked in and MacPherson was sitting here, and he said he'd like to talk to

155

me for a minute about the estimates he was making up for the house—he's not sure how much we want to do if we're only here for a year. It was *his* idea for me to stay here, not mine. What should I have done? Told him I didn't want to talk about it?"

"Is he still there now?"

"Of course he is—he's the one who suggested that I try and get you to come over and join us. He's here with his girl friend. We've all been talking, and he bought me a drink, and I feel as though I ought to buy them one. She's very nice— very amusing—and they've both been very friendly to me."

"That's more than you were. You were rude to him this afternoon."

"I know I was. I explained to him, I was feeling a bit uptight, worried about bringing Lord Jericho home, I guess. Anyway, that's all in the past. We've been having a good time—"

"I'm sure you have." Mary couldn't keep the anger out of her voice. He had been sitting there boozing while she sat alone and worried. "So what are you suggesting? If you think I'm going to trail down that awful road at this time of night you should think again."

"Of course I'm not suggesting that. I'll come over and get you. I'll leave this minute. What?" There was an interruption and another inaudible exchange at the other end before Don's voice came back on the line. "Mary, we've a slight complication. Liz says I promised to play darts as soon as the board was free."

"And who the hell is Liz?"

"She's Jamie's girl friend's friend. She's been making fun of Americans, saying we're a decadent lot. I told her one American could beat three Scotsmen any day of the week, and she challenged me at darts, best out of—"

"Don, if you think I'm going to sit here and wait while you get pissed and make passes at some Scots tart you've picked up in that bar, you ought to go and see a good shrink. You can tell—"

"Will you hold on and *listen*. Calm down. Jamie says he'll come and get you at the house, this minute, on his motor bike. He'll be there for you inside five minutes. And while he's on the way I'll order you a meat pie and chips—Hamish says this is the best batch of pies he's had for months. Dora

156

baked them this afternoon. Honey, please say you'll come. You'll have a good time here."

"Well . . ." Mary frowned at the wall. If she didn't go she might—a slim chance—be able to persuade Don to come home to her now. If she went she'd be able to have at least some control over how much he drank. And she wanted to go—wanted it very much. The laughter she could hear in the background was what she needed, the thing she was missing here in the house. "All right. I guess I'll come."

"Terrific. Jamie'll be along in just a few minutes." There was a swell of music in the background. "Mary?"

"I'm still here."

"There's no need to dress up much for this. It's a young crowd here tonight, and they all seem to be pretty casual. Just keep it comfortable."

"All right. See you later."

Mary hung up the phone and went through to the bathroom. Don seemed to have survived into his late thirties without learning a single thing about feminine psychology. *It's a young crowd here tonight . . . don't dress up much.* He was out of his mind. That's when she needed to look her best.

Mary ran upstairs to the wardrobe and picked out her nicest blouse, a silver blue cotton with short sleeves. And she'd wear high-heeled black pumps—if the Scots men all had to look up at her, that was their bad luck. As she changed she puzzled over the conversation with Don. He seemed to have buried the hatchet with Jamie—this afternoon he'd seemed ready to bury it in him. And there was a *crowd* at the Over The Water? The whole village didn't have more than a hundred people in it. Where could you get a crowd from?

She put her dress in the laundry bag and dropped it in the wardrobe on top of the package of Knowlton's papers. When she had time she'd have another look at them, even if Don and Roger both said he was a lunatic. She'd read a fair number of strange documents that had been submitted to Ellie's paperback house—flying saucer booklets, documented proof that cattle deaths and mutilations in the west were the work of subterranean races, demented ramblings about Lemurians and Atlanteans and gods in spaceships. She had wanted to throw them away at once. Ellie wouldn't let her—even the handwritten ones with their warped drawings and semiliterate

157

ranting. The neatly typed ones with their beautiful diagrams and extensive technical appendices, like the hand-scrawled ones, were all given a full reading.

"Look," Ellie had said. She was insisting that Mary work her way through a text that promised a method to teach animals to read and to spell written English. "You're forgetting something. Look how many nuts there are out there. We're in the *minority*. Good crackpot pieces sell as well as anything—just take a read through the list and see how many kook books get on the best-seller lists."

"But he says his dog and cat helped him to prepare the text."

"So what? I don't care if he thanks Kermit the Frog for editorial assistance. Here." She handed back the stack of pages. "Read it. See what else he says. Some of the crap I've seen come in here could have been written by a retarded hamster."

But Knowlton's papers were neither easy to understand nor neatly packaged. Only one fact gave them some credibility in Mary's eyes: the man who wrote them had been Don's predecessor at JosCo. Would Jericho and Roger Wilson employ somebody who was really off the wall, unless he had some special talent?

Mary heard the sound of a motorcycle roaring its way up the hill. Jamie was driving fast—faster than she'd let him go if she was riding on the pillion! She closed the wardrobe door, ran downstairs and did a quick repair job on her makeup. She jerked open the balky front door (one of Jamie's first repair priorities) just as the bike skidded to a halt on the gravel in front of the house.

"Ready for the death ride?" Jamie grinned at her cheerfully, hatless and without goggles. He had changed to a red lumberjack shirt and gray woolen pants. "Come on, hop up behind."

"Not unless you promise me that you'll go slowly." Mary realized that she was looking at the same red motor bike that she had seen when she first arrived at the Over The Water. "You were going too fast coming up here. Will you take it slowly?"

"It's a promise. I hurried on the way up because I wanted to get back and see Liz hammer your husband at darts. But there'll be lots of time for that later. Come on, sit tight and grab hold."

Mary was beginning to enjoy herself. Jamie MacPherson's enthusiasm and cheerfulness was infectious. She straddled the seat behind him and put her arms around his chest, gripping the cloth of his thick shirt.

"No need to crush me flat. I'll take things easy."

"I'm sorry." Mary moved back, realizing that her breasts had been pressing into his back.

"The pleasure was all mine." He let in the clutch and took them steadily down the hill, keeping well to the shore side of the road and not moving at more than about thirty miles an hour.

"So you think Liz will beat Don, do you?" Mary had to speak into his ear to be heard above the rush of air. "I don't think she will—he's good at games."

"Mebbe he is—but ye've not seen Liz. She's won more pub dart games than ye've had hot dinners."

The chilly wind whistled past them, and Mary crouched for shelter in the shadow of his broad back. Even moving at this speed it was a scary but an enjoyable ride. The road seemed to sweep back from the headlights and rush away into darkness, blurring past too quickly to see more than occasional rocks and posts.

"Here we are then." Jamie slowed down. "Short but sweet, eh? I'll take ye for a real ride someday. We'll go off and take a peek at some of those auld ruins all you Yanks seem to be so fond of. Come on."

As soon as he switched off the engine she heard the music. It was a rhythmic bass resonance driving into the night air from the Over The Water. She looked at the inn in disbelief. What was going on here?

"Jamie, I didn't know there was anything like this in the village. Who's inside there?"

"Lots of people. All the young 'uns from all over the county."

"You mean they drive over to Laxford?" There were cars in the road below the inn, scores of them.

"They've been coming these past ten years or more. It's a bit of a mystery how it all started but now ye'd have trouble stopping it."

"What does Hamish think of it?"

159

He laughed, pushing his bike up on to its stand and leading the way inside. "What d'ye think? He sells more beer and lemonade tonight than he does all the rest of the week put together. If ye want to find somebody who doesna' like it, go and seek out Walter Campbell. He can't make his usual speech about the demon drink—there's too much noise inside to hear him."

The main bar of the inn was a crush of young bodies. As they elbowed their way through Mary saw that the average age was from eighteen to twenty-five.

"Keep right behind me," said Jamie. He seemed to slip through the press of people like an eel. "Don't ye get lost now—we'd never see ye again in this lot, eh?"

"Where are you heading?"

"Away from the music. Over to the back there."

"That's Don's choosing, I'll bet. Right?" She grabbed the back of his shirt and let him tow her along. "Anything besides classical and Dixieland jazz and he won't listen to it."

MacPherson turned for a second and eyed her appraisingly. "You know your old man real well, don't ye?" There was a possible slight emphasis on 'old,' and his eyes had the conspiratorial glint of youth. *There's him and us*, it seemed to say. *But we really know what life's all about, don't we, missie?*

She could feel the cheerful insistent thump and drive of the music lifting her up, banishing the last trace of depression that she had felt while she was waiting at the house.

"I think this is great." She smiled at Jamie. "Thanks for picking me up and bringing me here."

"It's as I told ye, the pleasure's all mine. Good noises, eh?"

A pair of hundred-watt speakers had been set up at the end of the long bar. They were blasting out sixties rock and sixties-inspired New Wave revivals. The old walls of the inn scarcely seemed able to contain the volume of sound. Mary could hear the Pretenders' version of an old Ray Davies song, "Stop Your Sobbing," echoing round the rafters, while the striding bass came to her as a vibration of the whole room. The music fought its way through the young voices chattering happily over tankards of dark beer and glasses of Babycham. The old inn was brighter-lit than usual, with added wall fittings of red and yellow lights. In spite of all the noise the room felt less homey and comfortable than before. There was no fire in the hearth, no muted shadows, no regulars enlarging upon the world as they saw it. Hamish was still behind the bar, but he was much too busy serving customers to join in the conversations or to distribute the blessings of Lochinver Honey.

"C'mon. Nearly there." Jamie took her arm to guide her through the crush of tables. They were heading for the far corner, where Mary could see Don holding forth expansively, arms waving and face animated. She realized that Jamie MacPherson had a curious way of holding her, powerful but still gentle. It made her feel good, relaxed and self-confident. *See what a little attention does to your self-esteem!*

The aromatic smell of pipe tobacco wafted past her nose in a bluish haze. Suddenly they were at the table. " . . . and so one Saturday, I said to myself, let's give it a try. So I bought a token—just one token, mind you—and I stayed on the trains most of the day." Don was leaning intently over his nearly empty mug, eyes a little bleary and voice a touch too loud. "I did 'em. Manhattan, Brooklyn, Queens, and the Bronx. Did 'em all." He finally caught sight of Mary. "Whoa now, who do we have here? That was fast. I'm just explainin' to the 'wee lassies' here all about New York City."

Fibs, thought Mary, trying to disguise her amusement. Don had never ridden far in a subway—he detested them. He took cabs and buses whenever he could, rather than descending into the bowels of the city streets.

"Oooh. It sounds an awful scary place," said the attractive auburn-haired girl right across from him, craning her neck around to look at Mary and Jamie MacPherson.

"Oh, absolutely, it is," agreed Mary, nodding her head with exaggerated seriousness. "You know, I was afraid to go out of my apartment at all."

The girl turned big blue eyes to Jamie.

"Everybody lives in flats," he explained. "What wi' the price of houses an' all. Now, Mary, I want ye to meet Liz Carlin, a sweetheart of mine."

"Jamie, go on now." Liz wrinkled her snub nose at him. "In front of Jeanie there, what a nerve ye're havin'."

"But ye are, my love." Jamie put his arm lightly round her. "If ever Jeanie gives me the boot, I swear it, ye're a shoe-in for next in line."

Don leaned back and laughed uproariously. "You just want

her because she's a bloody darts queen. You should have seen the way she did for me."

"Ah, now." Liz smiled modestly. "Ye were a wee bit tipsy, Mr. Willis. You know what that does to a man's aim."

"Not true!" Don turned to the woman sitting at his side. "You're my witness, Jeanie. Have I had more than a couple of pints?"

The woman's smile was slow in coming. She looked down at her own half-pint glass, which scarcely seemed to have been touched. "No, Mr. Willis—"

"Don, you mean. For Christ's sake, aren't we all friends now?"

"Aye. Well, Don, I haven't *seen* ye drink more than a pint or two, that I can say."

She was a tall woman, broad hipped and full breasted. The makeup she was wearing was in fashion in London—heavy around her eyes, with bright red smears on the cheeks to highlight her cheekbones. Mary felt that it didn't quite go with the thick, red-gold hair, but she could see that it was a big hit with Don.

"Here, Mary, you have to meet Jeanie." He patted her arm. "If she didn't belong to Jamie here, I don't know what I'd be doing now."

Mary nodded in greeting. The other girl looked to be about twenty-two years old. Don's tone had been joking, but Mary couldn't help feeling there was an undercurrent of truth there. He was quite taken with her, or he would never be so relaxed. But the drink helped there—and it was hard to believe the two pints that he claimed.

"Now, then, no poachin' there," said Jamie. He sat down next to Liz. "As for the pints, who's doin' the countin'? That's how I see it."

Don clapped his hands emphatically. "Quite right. I'm going to buy us all a round. Mary, what's for you?"

"Same as you—a small one." She tried to catch his eye, but he was avoiding her gaze.

"And how about you, Jeanie?"

"Nothing." Her eyes seemed a little glazed. Mary took another look at her. She'd seen the expression often enough in New York. But here? If she were on drugs where on earth could she be getting them?

Jeanie's refusal seemed to make Don think again. He

162

looked across at Mary, and there was some kind of new tension in his face. It was as though he had suddenly been able to move outside the group and evaluate his action from some other point of view.

"I'll get the drinks," he said at last. "I'm going to skip this round for myself, Mary. What would you like?"

She smiled her relief. "Just a lemonade, Don. Want me to help you to carry?"

"No. I'll get them."

While Don was away Jamie came around the table and took his seat. As he sat down he kissed Jeanie lightly on the forehead, then put an arm jokingly around both women.

"There we are. A rose between two thorns. Did Don say he'd be getting you food while he was up?"

"No. Will it be ready?"

"Mebbe—Hamish only had to serve it up. Hold on a minute."

He slipped away through the door that led out of the bar, back to the rear of the inn. By the time he came back carrying a loaded plate Don was threading his way through the crowd with a load of glasses.

"Now, who gets what?" Don came across to Mary. "Here's yours. Did you introduce yourself to Jeanie Inglis yet? She's Jamie's fiancée—they'll be getting married soon." His voice was eager, with almost an apologetic tone to it. *Sorry, dear,* he seemed to be saying. *I got the wrong first impression of him.*

Jamie MacPherson was leaning over the table with Mary's plate of food. He straightened up as Don spoke and looked at Jeanie.

"Now, dear, you've been tellin' tales again." There was an edge to his voice, and he smiled coldly at Don. "We're not quite there yet—think of us as very good friends. Jeanie sometimes mixes up wishes and facts. We've talked marriage but nothing's decided yet."

He hadn't lowered his voice at all. Jeanie bit her lip and looked down at the table top. After a moment she said, "Jamie, I'd like a whisky."

"And why not?" MacPherson rubbed his hands together cheerfully. "I'll be right back with it."

As he turned to go to the bar, Don slid back into his old

seat. Mary patted his thigh under the table. "Have you eaten, Don?"

"A little bit." He picked up a french fry from her plate and ate it. "Is it all right? I'm sorry I didn't come home. It was just—"

"Don't worry about it. I'm not angry—not any more. We can talk about it later."

"So do you want to stay longer?" Don's voice was cheerful again. "It's a really good way to see what the locals are like. They come in from all over the county."

"So they're not much like the people in Laxford, are they?" Mary patted his thigh again. "That's all right. I'm not complaining. Course we can stay."

Liz had somehow picked up her last words from the general noise around them. "That's wonderful. I told Don I'd like to see you try your hand at darts. He's really good for somebody who's not been brought up with it."

"I've never played." Mary looked doubtfully across at the board, where a team of four youths was arguing over the best combination to finish a game. "It looks hard."

"It's easy. So long as you don't let one slip and stick it in Jamie—that's what happened a couple of weeks back. Ye'd have thought he was mortal wounded."

Don laughed. "It's you women. Always trying to stick us men with something."

He didn't seem to realize that his words might upset Jeanie, but Mary saw a quick look pass between the other two women.

"Come on now, Jeanie," said Liz. "You and Jamie'll be all right, won't you?"

"Ye'd better ask me that later." Jeanie had her eyes focused on her half pint of ale. She took a single small sip, then placed it back on the table. Her manner was a sharp contract to Liz's sparkle and bright chatter.

"He's really all heart, Jamie is." Liz leaned across the table and squeezed Jeanie's hand. "He always has been, as long as I've known him—and that's a long time."

"You were raised round here?" asked Don. Liz seemed street-wise, hardly like a Scots Highland girl at all.

"Since I was ten. I knew Jamie back before I had anything *here* at all." She put her hand to her chest. "Lordie, I had a *monstrous* crush on him then—lasted for years, it did. Just

164

my luck, though, we were too young for him to do anything about it." She laughed. "But he was nice to me."

Liz lowered her voice and leaned toward Don. "We still have a bit of fun now and again, Jamie and me—he's a good sport. Mind you, lately he's been seein' Miss Pout across the table there, steady. Don't pay her no mind just now. She'd like to pin him down permanent, and Jamie's a hard one to peg. But he's a fine man."

"So they're not engaged at all?" Don's voice was thoughtful.

"Well, that's a word that means different things to different people, right?" Liz raised her voice to include Mary in the conversation. "You two are married, though—that's the nicest condition. You'll make a stir here in Laxford. We've had a few tourists drop through here, but having a couple of Americans here for a long time should make the old biddies' tongues flap."

"Why should that be?" asked Mary. She hadn't noticed Liz's abrupt change in subject.

"Oh, ye have to live here a while an' then ye'll see it. Any change at all flusters the old people." Liz took another drink. She was using a pint tankard and emptying it as fast as anyone. "That's one reason I'd like to get out of this place."

"But you've lived here most of your life," said Don.

"Most of it so far—but not most of the rest of it. Come next year I'm headin' out. You watch my smoke. Glasgow, Edinburgh, London—here I come. Folks around here say that ye'll never get the Highlands out of you, but here's one body that's going to try."

"Does Jamie feel the same way?" Mary could see him standing at the bar, watching Hamish fill his order for a double whisky. Was this one point of disagreement between Jamie and Jeanie—a wish to leave Laxford?

"Oh, he's a real local," said Liz. She had emptied her glass and raised it high above her head to catch Jamie's eye. After a few seconds he nodded, and she turned back to the table. "A real local. His parents had a wee place a mile or two south of here. Just a cottage, wi' a path down to the sea and a few acres to farm for themselves. There's not much to be pulled out of the land round here, I'll tell ye that. But I've had some marvelous great times up in that barn they had." She looked across to Jeanie to see if she was listening, but the

165

other woman seemed to be lost in private thoughts. "Some high old times. That was before his parents died—must be nearly ten years back. Drowned. The currents off the coast here are murder. Jamie changed some after that."

"So he's a *farmer*?" Mary couldn't fit the handyman she had seen to a farmer's image.

"Lordie, no. He hates farming, Jamie does. He sold everything there except the boat—he's at home on the water." Liz shook her head. "Bein' tied to a farm would kill Jamie. He's a man who was born to roam an' range an' have fun. I've not seen a happier fellow this side of Lochinver. He earns his money all over the county, and he spends it as it comes, here or down in Inverness. He's taken me with him a couple of times." She paused as though she had said too much, then turned to look at the bar. "Where the devil is that man? He must be buying out the whole inn. Maybe I'd best stop talking about him. He's not happy when there's gossip behind his back—and for a man who wanders as he does, there's a fair amount of that."

"He doesn't live here at all?" said Mary.

"Oh, he has a place here. He rents the old place, the one he sold. Some English people bought it for a summer home, but they're only here for a couple of months of the year. Jamie keeps it in good shape and lives there for next to nothin'. But we shouldn't keep on talkin' all about him when he's not here."

"Fair enough," said Mary pleasantly. She had missed Don's gesture to Jamie at the bar. "So what about you? What do you do around here?"

"Plan to get away." Liz laughed. She was full of energy, moving to the beat of the music that carried through the crowd. "And dance. Oh, and I'm polishing up my shorthand and typing. As soon as I get past sixty words a minute I reckon there's a job for me somewhere down south. My future's rosy, don't doubt that—rosy as Jeanie's cheeks, right, love? I don't have the same urge to settle down to holy wedlock—funny how people are different in that. I want to have some fun before I put down roots. Well, Lord save us, here's the man at last."

Jamie was hovering over her, holding a tray. "Clear a way there. Here's an unidentified flying object comin' in for a soft landin'."

Liz moved glasses quickly round the table to make space for the tray. Jamie handed a pint of bitter to Liz and a double whisky to Jeanie. To Mary's dismay he passed another double whisky across to Don.

"You didn't order that, did you?" She kept her voice low.

Don shrugged. "I guess Jamie thought he owed me a drink or two. I can't send it back now, can I?"

She looked at him unhappily, one hand stretched out to the glass of whisky. "You'll make it last, then? I don't think I could drive that car up—"

"Listen to that," Liz interrupted. "I've been waitin' for it all evening. Come on, if you don't want to dance to this ye have to be a dead man. Jamie!"

The record had changed and the beat of a Stones classic, *The Last Time*, was making Liz twitch and rock in her seat. Jamie shook his head and sat down at the table.

"Not just now, Liz. Let me have a sip of beer first. There's your man." He nodded across the table at Don. "He's ready, eh?"

"Come on, Don." Liz was on her feet, reaching across to tug at his arm. "You don't mind, do you, Mary?"

Mary hid her moment of irritation. It would do Don good to get some exercise—and while he was there he couldn't do any drinking. "Not at all. Go on, Don, let's see you dance."

"I've no *idea* how to dance to this." Even as he protested, Don was allowing himself to be pulled to his feet. "I've never done it."

"Dead easy." Liz reached up and unbuttoned the top of his shirt. "You'll need breathing space when I'm done with ye. Come on, ma bonny laddie—let's show the locals how real dancin' is done."

There was no stopping her. Jamie and Mary looked at each other as Don was hauled away through the crowd, to the cleared dancing area at the far end.

"Does he dance?" asked Jamie.

Mary laughed. "*Now* he does, by the look of it—but he never has before, not while I've known him."

As she was speaking she saw Jeanie raise her glass and drink her whisky in two gulps, grimacing as the liquor went down. She looked very moody, ignoring the conversation. Jamie had caught Mary's look. He shook his head. *Leave her alone. She doesn't want talk right now.*

167

They watched Don and Liz for a couple of minutes, getting off to a couple of false starts and then moving with reasonable coordination on the dance floor. Jamie was watching with a critical eye.

"He's doin' all right, eh? He knows how to move."

"I told you, he's good at sports."

He inclined his head toward the dancers. "How about us, then? Would ye dance this one with me, if Liz has stolen your husband."

"I'm sorry. I don't dance, either."

Mary felt the old sinking feeling. She began to explain to Jamie, that she had been too tall and thin in high school and had never learned to dance. He cut her off before she could get out a complete sentence.

"*Now* ye do, eh? Come on. If it's sauce for the goose it s sauce for the gander." He took her arm and stood up.

"I can't—and what about Jeanie?"

"You go ahead." Jeanie looked up and forced a smile. "I'm happy to sit here for a few minutes. But I'd like another drink, Jamie, if you can get me one."

"Here." Mary pushed Don's untouched whisky across to her. "Take this one. We can get another one for Don later if he wants it." There. That act seemed to commit her to dancing. Wasn't it well worth it, though, if she could keep Don away from more drink? She ignored the thrill of excitement that came with her action. She was going to be forced to do something that she had desperately avoided for years.

Mary could feel a mixture of emotions as they made their way through to the dance floor. Fear of embarrassing herself and Jamie. Pleasure at the idea that Jamie had asked her. Sorrow on Jeanie's behalf—it was clear that she was having a terrible time.

"Your fiancée, eh?" She said in a quiet voice as they came to the edge of the tables and moved toward the dancers. "What have you been telling her?"

"Don't laugh. I'm thinking it over, really I am. And don't judge Jeanie by the way ye see her now. She's sweet an' she's kind. She just takes a lot for granted. I like her a lot."

"Like her a lot?" Mary watched Jamie and began to follow his movement as best she could. The style of dancing made it easy to achieve a passable effort, and she could see from the

168

people around them that there were a fair number of beginners. "Do you love her?"

"Sure I love her." Jamie was dancing much closer than most of the men. "I'm like any man, I love all beautiful women."

"Maybe. But they don't promise to marry them." Mary concentrated on matching her movements to those of the people around them. Some of the tricky spins and breaks called for a lightness of build she would never have—not if she dieted to starvation. That confirmed something she had learned long ago, all the best dancers were short and lightly built. "Does Jeanie like to dance?"

"No. She's daft about it—says she's too big and fat for dancing."

"She's no bigger than I am."

"I know. You've not had much experience, but you've got better balance than Jeanie. She's a wee bit top-heavy."

"She has a marvelous figure, if you ask me." (So Jamie didn't like people to talk about him behind his back? Why didn't he learn the golden rule?)

"She does—but so do you. You're like two peas out of a pod when it comes to figure. Mind ye, there's a difference in the face. She looks like a Southerner, an' ye look as though ye were born and bred in Laxford." He had moved in close and was dancing with her at half-speed, his right arm around her waist. She glanced over toward Don, but he had moved away across the dance floor.

"Hamish thinks I'm from local stock. He's been claiming me since I first arrived here."

"Old Hamish?" Jamie laughed. "Aye, then ye'll be in real trouble. Better not let him get too close to ye, Mary Macveagh, or there's no tellin' where it will lead."

And that goes for you too, buster. Mary didn't say it aloud. It was too nice to be the object of an undivided attention. No doubt about it, when Jamie looked at somebody they got the whole two hundred volts. As the music stopped she gently removed his arm from her waist and moved toward the edge of the dance area. She came up behind Don as he was leading Liz back to the table.

" . . . yes, yes, it's fascinating stuff, bird migration," he was saying. "And we've been studying the terrain, too."

"Birds?" Liz looked back at Don and saw Mary behind

them. "Who gives a bugger about *birds*? Unless you mean the human kind." She flashed Mary a grin of conspiracy.

"No, the feathered sort." Don was weaving a little. "We saw all sorts up here. Seagulls and terns and—er—guillemots. And lots of others."

Mary reached up and stroked the back of his head. "Give it up, Mr. Darwin. Can't you tell she's seen through you? You couldn't tell a turkey from a tomtit unless it was served with onion stuffing."

Don swung round. "Mary? Oh, didn't know you were there. I was just explaining to Liz—"

"I heard you." Mary tried to ignore Jamie's gentle rub along her bare upper arm. "No wonder everybody in Laxford knew you were here to build a power station. The minister said you wouldn't have fooled a ten-year-old who'd grown up on this coast."

"Campbell said that to you?" Don didn't seem much worried by the news. "That makes him a sneaky old bastard. He sat there by the bar and pretended he believed every word we said."

"Maybe he thought ye were talkin' about *human* birds," said Liz, winking at Mary. "Unless ye're tellin' us ye're not interested in them, either?"

Don put his arm round her and gave her a quick hug. "You're as bad as Mary. It's all you think about, sex and—and—"

"Sex?" Liz was snuggling up to his side. "Course it is, you know that. It's all we think about, right, Mary?"

"Day and night, night and day," said Mary gravely. Jamie was still quietly touching her arm and back. Was Don beginning to feel the same way she was feeling? It looked like it, from the way he was reacting to Liz. Well, that was fine, too. She wriggled her shoulders where Jamie was stroking them. "It's all we ever think about—our whole pathetic lives. We're all sisters under the skin, Don, you know that." She winked back at Liz.

"Dreamin' of tall, dark men who'll love us forever." Liz turned to link arms with Don and Jamie, so that Mary was in the middle of the three of them. "Carry us to ecstasy at the single snap of our painted fingernails. Aye, it's a hard and lonely thing to be a lovely young woman. So delicate an' fragile we are, like the flowers in the forest."

"Aye," said Jamie. He had put his arm around her waist and was grinning down at her. "Ye're a flower all right, Lizzie Carlin. But I doubt it's maidenhair—an' more likely it's marry-gold. Better watch her, Don, she's a real wicked one."

Mary could feel the erotic awareness rising around her, each of them sensing the mood. Was it caused by drink? How could it be, when she was cold sober and Don was certainly nowhere near drunk? It was a shared resonance, a warm feeling of desires that could be enjoyed at a completely nonverbal level.

"So who gets you for the next dance, Jamie?" said Liz. She was stroking the back of his neck. "See now, if ye go an' scare Don away like that, I ought to be havin' you instead, eh? That's fair trade. So ye should give us—"

She paused and took her hand sharply away from his neck. A group of people had moved out of the way in the aisle in front of them. Through the gap Mary saw Jeanie moving slowly and unsteadily toward them. The makeup on her prominent cheekbones stood out like a crimson flare against her pale face. She came straight up to Jamie as the others moved away from him.

"Jamie. I want to go home. Take me home."

Mary saw that the whisky glass on the corner table had been emptied. Two doubles in a couple of minutes. If Jeanie wasn't much of a drinker . . .

Jamie was standing quite still, his expression unreadable. "It's early yet, love."

"I want to go." Jeanie was swaying slightly on her feet.

"But what about—" began Jamie, but Liz had stepped close to him and said something in a quiet voice.

"All right." Jamie nodded and took Jeanie by the arm. "Come on, lassie. We'll be on our way." He turned back to Liz. "Are ye sure?"

She nodded. "Talk to Jeanie. You'll see."

"Aye. I believe ye, Liz." Jamie turned for a second to Mary. "We'll have to postpone that other dance, eh? But some day when Don's off on his bird watchin'"—he winked—"don't forget that the two of us will be off castle-hoppin'. All right?"

Without waiting for an answer he turned back to Jeanie and began to lead her away toward the entrance. Liz sighed. "Aye, there goes the fun. I knew Jeanie was feelin' off, but I didn't know it was so bad. So bang goes the dancing." She looked shrewdly at Don and Mary, who had moved closer and were holding hands. "I know how you're feelin'. Lucky you. I don't know if I've got the energy to start over with one of these lads." She waved an arm at the crowd around them.

"Will Jeanie be all right?" asked Mary.

"Oh, aye—after she's had a bit of a throw-up. Poor lass, she's never been able to drink more than two drops without gettin' bilious. I'd feel sorry for Jamie, too, but I think it's part his fault. Well, he'll see her home safe enough." Liz was still watching Don and Mary. "Look, if ye feel like that, go on an' do somethin' about it. I'm not one to play gooseberry on ye."

Don looked at Mary and raised an eyebrow. She nodded, and instead of sitting down again at the table they stepped back toward the exit.

"Night, Liz," said Mary. She had to raise her voice. "Good hunting."

Liz was looking at the men around her. She lifted her hand to wave Don and Mary away. "Off ye get to bed, an' leave me to see what happens." She laughed. "If it's good, Mary, don't forget to give me part of the credit. I was the one started the pot boilin' there."

As they left, Mary saw a sudden image. Jamie making love to Jeanie Inglis, running his hands through her thick, gold-red hair and over her soft body. She squeezed Don's arm hard. "Come on. Let's get back to the house. I forgot to tell you something yesterday afternoon."

"About the boiling pot?"

"Wait and see, sweetie. You'll find out."

CHAPTER 11

The heavy ticking of the grandfather clock in the other room was loud through the house, so loud that Jeanie Inglis wondered how anyone could sleep through it. She lay there, counting its steady march toward daylight. One o'clock had struck, and then the quarter and the half, and still she could not sleep. Even though she was exhausted, even though she was empty, drained by tears and vomiting and more tears. Jeanie lay scrunched up in the big, comfortable bed, her worn Pooh bear the single companion of her misery. It was tear-soaked, a straggly bundle on the side of the bed, too damp now to be huggable.

He had *promised*. Sworn with all his heart, months ago, before she had ever asked for anything from him. And now . . . now that he *had* to, he was backing off, saying they shouldn't rush into something, shouldn't marry just because of this.

Had Jamie been joking? He still had that little half smile on his face when they left the others, still spoke as though it was nothing serious.

"Now then, Jeanie Inglis, don't be a little twit. Ye're gettin' too worried an' there's nothing to worry about. It can be fixed, ye know that. I'll arrange it for us."

"Fixed? Jamie, I don't want it fixed. I want us to get married, the way you said we would." The liquor had been burning inside her, making her head spin and her stomach shiver. She leaned her head helplessly on his shoulder, while he patted her cheek.

"Take it easy, Jeanie. Ye're gettin' overset and there's no need for it."

173

No need. So casual, when there was a bit of him growing inside her belly. She had been the one who worried about precautions, he had never wanted to bother—and she was the one worrying now.

"Just tell me ye love me, Jamie." He hated her to cry but she couldn't stop the tears from flowing. "I need ye now, can't you see that? Don't you know what they'll say to me, Mam and Dad and Gran? Jamie, we have to get married."

They were walking back to the house, away from all the lights. She couldn't see his face, couldn't tell what he was thinking. "Jamie, ye were tellin' me true, weren't ye? About us?"

He took his hand and ran it gently across her cheek, where tears had cut their salt rivulets through her makeup. He licked the tears away, as he always did if he found she was crying.

"Of course I was, love. I always tell ye true. But I never said we'd be marryin'—not for a while yet. Jeanie, ye must have imagined it—I've *always* wanted to wait an' see."

Anger made her feel sick and dizzy. "Ye've waited and seen all right, Jamie, that ye have. An' it's no my imagination that says ye made love to me, and it's no imagination there's a babe on the way." She turned her head away from him. "There's proof of that."

"Who knows about it?"

"Who the bloody hell cares who knows about it? Isn't the fact of it enough? What are we goin' to do?"

He had stopped in front of the house. It was silent inside, her mother and father long asleep. Gran would be awake, but she was so deaf now that there was no danger of being overheard. Jamie shook his head.

"Ye have to trust me, Jeanie. I'm tellin' ye, we've made a mistake and it can be corrected."

"Corrected? Ye think ye can change things back, as though there were a—an *eraser* for this? Jamie, what will we do?"

"Give me a day or two. Just a day to think. We've both got liquor in us now and can't think straight. Go on in, now, an' I'll come by for ye tomorrow night. I promise."

"Aye. Like your other promise."

"I *promise*, on my soul. I'll be here tomorrow."

"Jamie, I need you now. Come in for a minute."

"Not now, Jeanie, I have to think. An' ye have to trust me."

"Trust you?" The bitter words welled up in her. "Trust you, when I see ye there with your arms round Liz and around that American woman? Jamie, I know ye too well. I know I'm not the first an' I know how ye think. But now there's somethin' else ye have to add to the thinkin'. Ye can't walk off an' think this will be goin' away on its own, so a year from now there'll be just memories. A babe's a babe, an' don't you ever forget it."

"I know, lass, I know." His voice was soft. "I'm tellin' ye, come tomorrow night there'll be an answer for ye. Now, will ye trust me or will ye no?" There was a colder edge to his voice on the final sentence.

"I don't know." She was crying again. "I don't know what to believe now. Oh, Jamie. Say we can be wed. I can't stand it to face them an' say there's a babe on the way an' no father for it."

"Jeanie, I told ye—" He had paused, struggling for control. When he spoke again his voice was tender. "I know it's hard for ye. We'll sort all this out between us—tomorrow."

He touched her and softly kissed her. She clung to him hopelessly. She could never think straight or hear or see anything else when she was with him. But then he had gently pulled away from her and was gone, off along the night-shrouded road that led back into Laxford.

After a few moments she called his name and ran down the road after him. He was gone, swallowed up by the October ground mist. He had taken a short cut across the moor, making his way by instinct over the blind heather and rocks. Jamie MacPherson knew Laxford, knew it in a way that Jeanie never would. They had wandered the county together, and he seemed to know every rock and every fell.

Jeanie went into the house and off to bed, loving and wanting him despite herself. Jamie was like the land and the sea, beautiful and still unknowable. No wonder that so many found him easy to love.

She had sat up, wrapped in a heavy gray shawl, until nature asserted itself and she brought back up the whisky she had drunk. Retching made her stomach ache, and she felt icy cold and shivery. Before she went back to her bed she turned on the small night lamp on the tallboy in the corner. She needed some light to cheer her. The lamp threw long shadows from the knickknacks that covered the battered dressing table—the Hummel statuettes, tiny dolls, and slim bottles of perfume. They had been collected and treasured over the years. What was the point of them now? They couldn't offer comfort.

Instead of climbing into bed Jeanie went across to the long mirror that stood in the corner. She stripped off her warm nightgown and turned side-on to examine her naked reflection. Her face was still marred by streaked makeup and tear-swollen eyes but that was not her concern.

Was she beginning to show yet? It was just two months now. Wasn't there a shade more bulk to her breasts, an extra fullness around the nipples? She rubbed her hand over her stomach. It always bulged a little, now there seemed to be an outward curve under her stroking hand. Inglis women always showed early, that she knew. In another month her condition would be obvious. Jeanie went back to the bed and sat down on it. In spite of the cold she did not put her nightgown back on. The sickness and drunkenness had all gone, and if she could not sleep she could at least think.

Jamie loved her, she was sure of it, even if he was having trouble accepting that. Weren't all men that way, easygoing until it came to settling down, then getting scared of responsibility and the ties to one woman? Hadn't that been what Mam always told her, that a man had to feel he had enough rope to move around, even after he was married? Jamie didn't realize that he would still have some freedom—she wasn't one to tell him he'd have to stay home every night of the week. She'd let him breathe.

After a few minutes Jeanie stood up and went to the chest in the corner. She put on jeans and a flannel shirt, then a warm sweater and shoes and socks. She went to the water jug and wiped her face clear of all makeup, dried herself and walked quietly to the door.

Jamie would have to be *made* to understand. She could explain to him.

At this hour the road was deserted. Jeanie hesitated. Should she take her bicycle or go on foot? The road out to Jamie's place was rough, and the night was dark. Best to walk it, even if it took a few minutes longer.

As her eyes became used to the dark the stars overhead

grew brighter. The ground fog stopped at waist height, and the sky seemed to swarm with stars, twinkling in the bright, clear Highland sky. Jeanie knew the path very well. She could look up as she walked and wonder how people who came to Laxford as visitors could stand it, going back to air so dense and dirty that stars were hidden from your sight. A tiny breath of wind from the sea made her face feel pleasantly cool and soothed her tired, aching eyes.

What was she going to say to him? Best to have that straight in advance and not be tongue-tied, the way she was when first they met. He'd walked into the shop next to the inn last year and looked at her as though he had never seen her before. Well, maybe he hadn't, not in that way. When he stopped and talked to her she felt like fainting away. She'd never seen anything to match the light in Jamie's eyes. And then—explain that if you can—he'd gone to the back of the shop and asked *Dad* if he could take Jeanie out sometime, for a walk or a ride on his bike.

Her life had seemed to hang in the balance, waiting for Dad to answer . . . Why hadn't Jamie asked *her*, she'd have said yes in a minute, and now if Dad started to hem and haw and dither about it . . .

She hadn't understood her Jamie, not then. If there was anything that could make Dad trust somebody from the start it was that asking for permission. How could he say no—or how could he feel bad about somebody who thought his opinion was so important? From that point Jamie could do no wrong, he was welcomed like one of the family. Even Mam said the same thing, he was a wonderful young man.

Jeanie looked down at the road ahead. *Jamie could do no wrong*—but he had. It would kill Dad if he found out and Jamie wouldn't get married. It would kill Dad to even realize what Jamie had been doing with her these past few months, in his house and hayloft and out on the cliffs at night. Dad still thought of Jeanie, his little girl Jeanie, as young and innocent. If Dad just knew . . .

She reached the crest of the hill and could see the outline of the stone cottage against the skyline. The sea lay beyond it, very calm and smooth tonight. Now that she was so close there was an urge to dawdle, to think again what she could say to him. That they'd live in his cottage, him and her and the baby? That she'd make him as happy as she could? He must know all that, he'd known it for a while. And it hadn't been enough for him. She had to offer more than that. What?

She walked quietly to the rough west wall of the cottage, through the long weeds that grew there and around to the door. It was a simple two-room building, a combined kitchen-and-living area and a single bedroom. There was no light inside the place, but she didn't need it. Jeanie eased past an old rose briar, careful not to tangle her sweater on the thorns, and approached the old knotted oak of the door.

It was slightly ajar. Surprised, she stood there for a moment with her hand on the door knob. Could Jamie still be out? But where would he be, at this hour? Jeanie was feeling the first prick of jealousy when she heard the low voices inside the bedroom. Instead of announcing her presence she stooped at the door to listen.

"—other measures now." The voice was just a whisper in the darkness. It was impossible to tell if it came from a man or from a woman. "Are you sure of it?"

"Positive." That was Jamie. "She's usually as regular as clockwork."

"And she hasn't come totally under control?" There was a breathy sigh. "Then it will be a female. Again. That's bad news. You'll have to try something new. My time's coming along fast now—more loss of hair every day. It won't be more than another few months before I have to go and join the Elders. We have to start one before I'm into Second Change—once that happens there's nothing I can do to help you."

"Aye." Jamie's whisper was somber. "But who? Who'll we try?"

"The Carlin girl is barren?"

"I'm sure of it. An' she's not close to a Macveagh, so there'd be other troubles."

Jeanie was held motionless by a mixture of emotions. If that was a woman in there with Jamie she wanted to surprise them. If it was a man, she wanted to hear more—even though at the moment it wasn't making much sense. She pushed the door a fraction farther open.

"There's one other possibility." The second voice was thoughtful. "I don't think we dare rush into it, but we have to think about it. What about the new one?"

"I thought of her too. What about the husband?"

178

"Leave that to me. Are you sure that she's a Macveagh? I'll have to go and tell this to the Elders."

"Not sure." Jamie was very respectful as he spoke. "Everyone says she is, but how can we tell? Even if she is not, do we have anything to lose by it?—assuming that ye can handle her husband, I can handle her."

"I don't know." There was a long pause, a heavy breathing. "This has to be discussed by the Elders. I'm on my way there now. How soon can you join me with them?"

"Tonight? Well, I wasn't planning to be going out again—"

"How soon? This is important."

"Ten minutes." Jamie sounded resigned. "Give me ten minutes."

"I'll meet you there. Remember, my time for Second Change is coming fast. I have to make many arrangements and every day is vital."

There was a long silence. Jeanie listened, hardly breathing, but she could hear nothing more spoken in the bedroom. After a few moments she thought she could make out a steady rhythmic noise, smooth objects being rubbed together. All her suspicions came rolling back. If it was a woman in there, she knew Jamie's powers, and the strength of his persuasion.

She hadn't been a virgin when they went out together. There'd been Dieter who was hiking through the Highlands and who later sent her the Hummel statuettes. He'd been the first. Then Will Strickland, the fisher's lad who drowned two years ago off Cape Wrath in a freak squall. Looking back on them, they had been just grunts and groans and amateur gymnastics. She had enjoyed it well enough, accepting that giving was a woman's role and not knowing there could be more to it than that.

Jamie had changed everything. A week after they had first gone out together he had taken her one evening to the slopes of Foinaven, riding his bike far off the trails and popular ways. What had he done to her there? When she tried to think of it, in detail, she couldn't get a clear memory. All she knew was that he had made sex into something that was better than any of her fantasies. Even now she couldn't describe what they did together. When he had her it was like magic, she just swam away into a different world of pure sensation. Everything he did to her seemed to fit, the close holding, the gentle and persistent nibbling at her arms and shoulders and

179

neck and breasts, and the inevitability of his steady penetration and her own flooding climax. And all around it and over it and mixed in with it, the disturbing male smell of him, drawing her like a parched field drawing in the drops of rain, crushing all her fears and reservations and worry about the consequences.

Was she as special to him as he was to her? Or could he leave her and then take some other woman to his cottage and lift her to the same heights? Inside the bedroom the rhythmic, liquid noise had not stopped.

Jeanie pushed the door open wider. There was a rattle in the bedroom and the clatter of something falling to the hard floor.

"Jamie?" Even if he was with somebody else, it was his own fault for cheating.

There was no answer. She felt her way inside, stumbling over a pair of shoes that had been left in the middle of the kitchen floor.

"Jamie? Are you in there? Is somebody in there with you?"

There was still no answer as she felt her way past the couch and over to the bedroom. The door to it was open. Her eyes, fully accustomed to darkness now, could make out vague outlines of the bed and dresser. Was that Jamie by the bed? The form had risen up, no more than a pale outline.

"Jamie, why don't you answer?"

Something *shusshed* on the floor ahead of her, a greasy, sibilant sound of liquid contact. An unreasoning terror ran thin fingers up the base of her spine. She reached out and picked up the oil lamp and the matches that always stood by it. Her fingers were trembling as she tried to run the match head along the side of the box. A coughing grunt came out of the darkness, as though someone being strangled was trying to say her name.

"Jamie. Are you all right?" She was filled with new emotion, a concern for him. And it *was* Jamie, now she was quite sure of it. Her nostrils were full of that smell, the smell that only Jamie had. Usually it was there only when they were having sex. . . . Suspicion flared again as she drew the match into flame. It took a second to light the oil wick, then she could lift the lamp and hold it out into the bedroom.

"Is that some woman—" she began, in the moment before

she was accustomed to the brighter light. Then she gasped and sagged back against the frame of the door.

"Oh, my God."

The awful thing was that it was still Jamie. His skin seemed to be covered with pearls, bright beads of light that caught and reflected the lamplight. He was moving toward her, slow across the floor, his mouth working to form words.

"*Jeanie. Jeanie, do not move.*" It was a rasping hiss, struggling to release itself from his throat. She backed away, wanting to vomit, feeling again the emptiness of her aching stomach. There was nothing there but bile.

"*Don't move, Jeanie. Turn . . . off . . . light.*" The voice was like the hiss of rough surf on the shore, advancing into her consciousness, reinforcing the paralysis of fear. She knew the sound, knew that it was familiar and comforting to her—but the revulsion was still in her, dominating the smell of sexual pleasure that filled her nostrils.

Fight it! The thought was rising from deep in her brain. *Fight it, or it's the end.*

Jamie was still shambling forward. He was squat and powerful, his face so engorged with blood that his eyes were like hollow pits. Swollen veins marked the chest and arms, and his hair had slicked back to a glistening, flat layer. He reached out one thick arm to touch her cheek. The beads covering his skin were like sticky pearls, oozing onto her where his club fingers touched her face.

"*Turn . . . off . . . light.*" He was gaining more control of his voice, assuming a more human tone. "Jeanie, don't move. It's all right, darling. Don't move. I love . . ."

The viscous liquid slid down her cheek. It had a powerful and pungent smell, a mixture of musky oils and rotting detritus from the sea bed. Jeanie felt it filling her nostrils, the effluvia of warm sex and cold sea-death.

". . . love you," said the gargling voice.

Jeanie screamed, shuddered, and screamed again.

Her wail of horror and disgust broke the trance. She stepped back one pace and hurled the oil lamp at Jamie MacPherson, turning as she did so toward the cottage door.

There was a brief flare of burning kerosene and a scream from MacPherson as the lamp threw hot oil over his shoulder. As the room was plunged into darkness Jeanie turned and ran blindly for the door. Jamie was screaming behind her, still in that high, gargling voice. She crashed into a chair, then into the kitchen table. The whole room seemed to whirl about her in a maelstrom of confusion, but convulsions of terror drove her legs forward, scrambling her way along the wall until she found the opening of the outer door.

The cool night air hit her as she emerged, and she ran on with the speed of desperation. The chill outside was like a slap of cold water, moving her away from the unreality of what had happened in the cottage.

Was she dreaming?

The breeze and the crash of sea breakers answered with indecipherable whispers. The rising moon seemed to stare down with bright, chill indifference.

Run. Don't look back, just run.

She had to get away, far away. Far enough to be safe from the thing in the cottage. The fluid from its hand had trickled down her face and now it oozed into the corner of her open mouth. With a spasm of mingled disgust and inexplicable pleasure at the peculiar taste, she wiped it off with the arm of her sweater as she ran. When the heather that tore at her legs nearly tripped her at the foot of the hill, she turned for a moment to catch her breath and to see if she was being pursued.

The hill behind her looked empty. There was no pale form shambling along on her trail.

Jeanie breathed deep and looked around her. She had run south, away from the village and parallel to the sea. Somehow she had to get back and find help. The significance of what she had seen in the cottage was creeping into her mind, telling her what she must face. *The thing growing in her belly now had come from him. It was part of him, carrying Jamie's form within her.*

No, no, mustn't think that way now. Must get to the village, get to where it was safe, to where he couldn't follow her and find her. She began to run through the heather and the yellow autumn grass, circling her way around the cottage. The gorse clutched at her and tugged her legs, cutting through her socks and hurting her ankles. She welcomed the pain, welcomed the relief it brought from thought . . .

Don't run, Jeanie. There was a voice inside her head, whispering its message. *I love you, Jeanie. I'll make everything right for us. Don't run away from me.*

She was running up a steep path strewn with stones. They

rattled away down the side of the hill, noisy in the still night air. She had to ignore that voice, deny the feelings deep inside that called out their demand to turn and walk back to the cottage. Something internal—something in her own nature—was telling her to abandon the flight. *Don't fight this any more. Don't run. It's your purpose, what you were made for.*

Stop.

Her legs bore her onward, carrying her around the path that led down to the cottage. It must be nearly three o'clock, after a night that had been filled with misery and sickness and terror. She plodded on, her pace slowing.

At the crest of the next hill, the taste of ooze that lingered in her mouth seemed to explode, driving pain and weakness into every part of her body. She put her hands down to her thighs. The muscles there felt numb and stiff.

The sky seemed to be changing, with stars and moon collecting into a single spotlight that tracked her staggering progress down the other side of the hill. She couldn't go farther without a rest. The darkness congealed about her so that she felt as though she were running through an inky murk that held her back and clogged her movements. Claws reached out and raked her legs as she ran, cramping them with agony. Bat wings were fluttering and brushing close to her thighs. Something was chittering at her from the darkness, and she could taste fresh blood in her mouth, like a wave wafting in from the sea.

Gravity seemed to roll her down the hill, leaving her standing exhausted at the foot of it. It was the end. She would fall down here and fight no more. The barn ahead seemed to swim into view.

Somewhere to hide. Somewhere to rest.

She shot a fearful glance behind her. Still he did not follow.

Jeanie struck out across the cleared field, her breath a furnace of pain in her chest. The agony in her legs made her weep. She kept her eyes set on the barn, her only goal, and forced herself to keep walking.

Its familiar form reared before her. Two stories high, of stone and mortar, with a wood and shingle roof, it squatted like an old, gigantic toad, about a half mile away from Jamie's cottage. The roof was in poor repair, sagging and twisted like a half-melted candle. She stood at last in the open doorway. Spills of straw lay all about, with clumps and bundles stuffed into the broken windows. Jeanie felt a twisting coldness in her gut as she thought of the first time she had been into this barn.

Jamie holding her, taking her. Tangled in the hay, her nose full of the sweet smell and her body full of delirious pleasure, racked by spasms of fulfillment . . .

She had been *used*. He had done exactly what he liked with her, and she hadn't been able to resist—even to think of resisting. She had to get back to the village as soon as she could, but only rage and fear had pulled her this far. Before she could go another step there would have to be some rest.

Jeanie took a final, careful look around her. She could see nothing in the fields behind, no pale form gliding after her in the moonlight. And she was so tired, she really had no choice. She went in.

The moonlight streamed in through the upper level windows and filtered its way down through the cracked floor. She could see the solid shadows of hay bales and farm equipment along the far wall. As she moved forward something scurried ahead of her into the corners. She froze. *Rats or mice.* That's all it could be, rustling away from her in fear. Jeanie shivered and scanned the interior. There ought to be a ladder leading to the upper loft, where most of the hay was stored. That would be the place to hide. She could push the ladder away so that no one else could climb up and if she had to she could even jump clear out of one of the windows. It would be an eight-foot drop to the rear of the building, no more.

She felt disoriented as she looked around her. Her mind had the strange remote feeling that came with total exhaustion, as though she were decoupled from her own body. Her chest still rose and fell with her rapid breaths, but she could no longer feel pain there. Her nostrils had dilated to take in the stale barn air. The rich smells of old manure and hay and straw made no direct impact on her thoughts.

Where was the ladder? The inside was crammed with materials. Piles of sacks, empty or filled with fertilizer and feed. Bales of hay and straw. A big harrow attachment for a tractor, its long tines upright and set away from the wall like a huge set of grinning teeth. Rakes and scythes. Jeanie moved past the implements of Scots farming, piled into the barn with no particular organization. She could see them as hiding places for skulking figures, waiting to pounce as she came past. She tried to shake off that thought, edging her way through. She paused when she came to the scythes.

Did she need a weapon? A large scythe would be useless, but she could handle a sickle with no difficulty. It was unwieldy in a small space, but better than nothing. She found one hanging on a peg on the wall, tested the blade against her thumb. Sharp enough. Jeanie shuddered at the idea she might have to use it.

She stepped carefully around the harrow and found herself at the foot of the ladder. Gripping the sickle securely in her left hand, she started up. The stair was made of sturdy oak and held her weight easily as she went up, step by cautious step. As she neared the top she felt it wobble beneath her. As she had thought, it was not attached at the upper end. She could arrange it so that no one could reach her from below. The angle was so steep that she had to climb sideways to the upper floor. On the left, bales of hay made an effective barrier. She put the sickle down in front of her and edged to the right, making sure she was balanced before trying to transfer any weight. During daylight it would have been easy. But in the gloom here she had to feel her way along, testing every step.

Finally she had herself in a comfortable position, her back against one bale and two more underneath her. Through the window she could see the lights of the village—not far away, but she dared not go there now. When had she last looked out from here? After she and Jamie had made love in the hay—two months ago, had it been? Maybe that was the time that she had failed to protect herself. She thought of him, as she had seen him in the cottage, and of the baby she carried.

What was he? Dear God, he didn't even look human. How could he have made her pregnant when he was like that?

There was a sound outside the barn. Jeanie froze, not even turning her head. She hadn't moved the ladder away and now it was too late. She would be announcing her presence instead of concealing it by moving now.

There was another squeaking sound down below, a sliding sound on the wood.

Inch by inch, Jeanie moved her arm along toward the sickle. Her hand was trembling when it met the cool wood of the handle. The feel of the weapon calmed her a little, helped her to sit motionless.

Someone was at the base of the ladder. She had to move away, out to a point where she could jump from the window if they came up here. But how could she do that without betraying that she was here? The ladder beside her creaked as a heavy weight was applied to its base. Someone was coming up. If she moved now, her sound might be drowned by his.

She stood up stealthily and began to tiptoe across the wooden floor. The old boards cracked and groaned beneath her feet. She was too heavy to pass across the surface without the structure announcing her presence. She halted.

"Jea-nie."

The soft voice from below still had that muffled, gargling quality. The memory of the cottage drove her over the edge of terror. Her skin crawled and she had to move, to get away from the top of the ladder.

Her earlier caution had deserted her. She started out for the window and was only halfway there when the rotten boards crumbled beneath her feet. Her right leg went straight through, smashing her pelvis down to the edge of the hole and breaking away more wood. She dropped the sickle and scrabbled desperately at the edge. Wood splinters broke under her nails, and her cheek banged hard against the floor as she slipped down. With a cry of fear, she swung for a moment and then fell through to the lower floor.

She landed almost flat and face down. The impact splashed white lights across her vision and drove her to the edge of unconsciousness. Only the driving, blinding pain that lanced up her abdomen forced her back to awareness. She gasped, wondering how she had landed. Instinctively, her body tried to roll away from the pain.

She could not move. Her legs and arms still had feeling, but she could not move her body at all. As she tried to do it, another jab of white-hot pain painted the back of her eyes like a lightning flash. Again she was at the limit of consciousness, waiting for her senses to connect with her brain.

Each ragged breath was agony. She reached down with her right hand to her midriff. Instead of the floor she felt cold, rusted metal. A warm liquid was seeping from her belly and running down her hand. Suddenly, as though from a great

186

distance away, the thought came to her. She knew what had happened when the floor had given way beneath her.

She had landed on the harrow.

Three of the long, murderous tines had driven into her belly, with the rest of her body lying on either side of them. Every time she moved the foot-long tines were driven deeper.

O God, O Father, help me. Even now, with the darkness growing in her brain, her strongest urge was to try and get free and run away. *Don't let me stay here. I can't bear to face it again.*

She reached down again with both hands, grasping the tines. They were slick with blood, and she could not get a purchase on them. After a few moments she moved her hands to the side to grip other parts of the harrow and tried to lever herself upward. The crushing pain in her abdomen had ebbed slowly to a throbbing ache.

The tines were each about twelve inches long, but they had not pierced her all the way. Part of her weight was taken by the harrow's shaft. If she could raise herself about six inches she would be clear of the points and could move back over the body of the harrow. Grunting with pain, Jeanie began to lever upward. She had always been strong in the arms, now it might save her life.

A flashlight beam bobbed around the inside of the barn, playing its way from side to side. Jeanie went motionless. Maybe he would not see her, would think she had fallen to the floor and run off outside.

The light went out again, and she heard soft footsteps descending the ladder. She hung there, lifting again at the tines that impaled her. Each time she moved she felt the rusty spikes churn inside her, moving as she moved. But she was winning. Inch by fraction of an inch, she was raising herself higher on the harrow. In a few more seconds she would be able to pull herself completely free.

A heavy foot came down on her back, forcing her lower than ever. She cried out as the central tine plunged deeper into her viscera. It was impossible to hold herself up with that force pressing down on her. She groaned.

"Well, Jeanie. There's been a nasty accident, I see. Ye might even want to call it a harrowin' experience, if ye've a mind for that kind of joke."

The voice behind her was quiet and reflective, as though

there was an abstract problem to be solved here. But there was no pity in it. Jeanie prayed that she should lose consciousness, to free her from her agony and fear.

"But in a way I can see this might solve a whole lot of problems," went on Jamie's voice. "Aye, I'm sad for ye, Jeanie, but mebbe it's all for the best."

She was sobbing softly, unable to lift her head or turn it to look at him. "What . . . *are* . . . you? You're not human, are you?"

The flashlight snapped back on and played its way over her. He was leaning forward to see how she had landed on the harrow.

"Human?" Jamie's voice was reproachful. "Now, Jeanie, don't say that. I'm as human as you are. Isn't that my baby you're carryin', and wasn't I the best lover ye'd ever met? I'm human all right, an' we had our fun, eh? Ye've been one of the best, Jeanie—nobody likes it more than you do."

The boot on her back lifted and was replaced by a powerful hand, holding her in the same position. He leaned over farther, and she could see his face. It was the same handsome Jamie that she had always known, bending over to see her tears.

"I dare say this isn't quite the sort of skewering ye like, though." He licked away the tears and the sweaty blood that oozed from the cut in her cheek. "Ye should never have followed me home, Jeanie. Ye know that now. If only ye'd done as I asked, given me a day to arrange things . . ." He shrugged. "Ye've only yerself to blame, lassie."

Her vision was fogged, black patches swimming across the field of view. She tried to turn her head to look at him. "Jamie . . . ye'll have to help me here. Help me off. I'll do whatever ye want me to, anythin' . . ." The pain in her belly was growing, filling the world. Jamie's voice sounded fainter.

"Aye, but it's too late now, sweetheart. I told ye, I could have taken care of all of it, no problem. If ye'd given me a few days there'd have been no babe to worry about, an' ye'd have lost your interest in Jamie MacPherson. I'd be just a nice memory for ye, somebody ye once had a nice affair with an' then cooled off on—same as the way that Liz thinks of me now. But no, ye had too much jealousy an' too much possessiveness. My way, none of this would ever have come about. Ye've got to take the blame for all this, Jeanie, every scrap of it."

"The baby," she gasped. "The baby . . . what will it . . ."

"Quite right. The baby, that was the start of the trouble. If ye'd started what I want inside of ye, I'd be savin' ye even now. I'm no murderer, now or ever."

"What . . . what in God's name did ye want of me?" There was not much else left in the world except the pain, forcing her apart.

"Why, I wanted a son for ye—an' ye're all set to bear a girl child."

"How do ye know? Maybe . . ."

"I know. Even there, if ye'd had patience, we might have tried again when this one was out of the way. But it can't be. We're at the partin' of the ways now."

"They'll . . ." She grunted but could not speak more.

"They'll what? They'll *know*, ye mean? Now Jeanie, ye're not thinkin' clear. What we're lookin' at here is an accident, a tragic accident. I'll be desolate for a while, that I can promise ye. An' it was an accident, wasn't it? Playin' in the hay, after ye'd had a drop too much at the inn—there's witnesses to that—an' ye have the bad luck to fall on a bit of rotten board. There'll not be a dry eye in the parish for me when this gets out."

Jeanie could feel her arms and legs weakening and a chill rising from the bottom of her belly. She looked up with a final effort. The sickle was gleaming in the flashlight's beam, just in front of her. She could reach it easily.

"Jamie." She strained upwards and turned her head, at the same time as she groped in front of her for the sickle. "Jamie, ye know I really loved ye."

"Aye, Jeanie, I do know that." His voice was tender. "An' I'm not lyin' when I tell ye I loved ye too. We love women, me and mine. We couldn't live without them, and that's an honest word. *No, Jeanie*"—he had seen her hand close around the sickle—"I'm afraid that just won't do. It won't do at all. An' I've got other business to attend to—I should have been meetin' there long ago."

He stood behind her and began to press his full weight on her back. Her arms buckled, and the tines thrust their way deep into her body, the middle one scraping against the bones of her spine. She gave a scream of pure agony.

189

"No good, Jeanie. There's none here to hear ye. Best if ye just go quiet an' peaceful. Good-bye, lassie. Ye'll go quicker an' easier if ye relax now."

The pressure on her back became heavier and heavier. It pushed Jeanie Inglis steadily all the way down to a final peace and oblivion.

CHAPTER 12

Fear God, and keep his commandments; for this is the whole duty of man.

For God shall bring every work into judgment, with every secret thing, whether it be good, or whether it be evil.

Walter Campbell closed the Bible and laid it on the ledge inside the lectern. He looked at his hands, palms down, as they gripped the smooth wood. The tremor was almost too fine to see—certainly too controlled to be noticed from the pews in front. *Forty-five years. Forty-five years old, to the very day—and what a birthday.*

He remained motionless, head bowed, waiting for the doors at the end of the nave to be closed. A few latecomers were still straggling in, shaking the water from their overcoats and rain hoods. After a fortnight of Indian summer, the lease of autumn had expired in Laxford. Yesterday had been the sharp eviction, and today winter took over as tenant. The temperature had dropped fifteen degrees in twenty-four hours. Storm cones had been hoisted on every weather station from the Shetlands to Anglesey, and now the winds were sweeping in from the northwest. They carried a mixture of rain and drizzle and salt spray, driving in from the gray sea.

Fit weather for a birthday. Fit weather for a funeral. Campbell looked up. The doors were being closed, and the inside of the church was darkening, unlit in the dull afternoon. The bell, muffled by the walls of the kirk, still sent its mournful call out across the fell.

For-ty–five–years. For-ty–five–years.

191

That was it, a birthday greeting, telling him that he was on the way to joining Jeanie Inglis and already more than half-way there. How could consolation for the family come from someone who was himself so afraid of death? Behind him, Campbell could hear the grunts of Johnnie McBride, pumping up the organ ready for the service. Mrs. Paisley would be already poring over her music up in the organ loft. Soon the music would swell out . . . "A Mighty Fortress is Our God," his own favorite. Luther's old inspiration had carried him through other difficult times; the hymn would carry him through this one. A brief ceremony here, then down the hillside to the newly dug grave.

For a thousand ages in Thy sight are but as yesterday when it is past, and as a watch in the night. Thou carriest them away as with a flood; they are as asleep; in the morning they are like grass which groweth up . . .

He looked more closely at the congregation. Sunday-best worn on Saturday, black suits and dresses of decent gray, with dripping overcoats still huddled round them. The faces were blank, unrevealing. It would shock them, the innocent as well as the guilty, but he must go through with his resolve. They must face something of Laxford life that they had closed their eyes to.

Campbell half-turned and nodded his head. Mrs. Paisley caught the cue and played the opening lines as the tones of the bell died away outside. The people in front of him (his flock—but who then guides the shepherd?) rose noisily to their feet, heavy shoes on the stone floor.

The words after the hymn came to his lips without need to look at the open prayer book.

"Man that is born of a woman hath but a short time to live, and is full of misery . . ."

Forty paces away, at the far end of the church, the coffin had been placed. It was a gleam of smooth elm against the heavy black doors. Jeanie had lain at home in the cottage until this morning, then had been carried over here in William Inglis's old carriage. (Even for the dead, there was no sense in wasting money.) The county police and the medical examiner had finished their work by Thursday afternoon, up from the county seat in Golspie and back away again the same day. He had spoken with the examiner, heard the questions, and seen the looks of doubt. "Strange wounds. She looks as though she squirmed about on those blades, trying to lift herself up, then fell back." A baffled shrug and a shake of the head. "Wriggling about like a butterfly pinned to a board. What a way to go!"

But a lot better than Campbell's own fears, the ideas that came in the night and could not be banished by prayer or labor. Thirty years ago the rented rowboat had tipped over half a mile off shore in Scarborough Bay. He had gone down five times (forget those who say you surface only thrice) choking on the cold salt water. At first he had kept his eyes closed, but as the life was wrung from him by his need for air, the reflex to blink had slipped away. He had seen green, dreamlike images of the sea floor, shells and waving weed and faint moving slender shapes. After consciousness had already left him, a teacher managed to catch hold of his shirt and raise his head above water until they could be rescued by another boat of summer visitors.

Campbell looked down again at his hands. The tremor there was stronger now, controlled only if he gripped hard at the edge of the lectern. The church swam with watery green and waving sea plants. *Who would fear a harrow, when this might be the way he went?* The best antidote was the powerful ritual of the burial ceremony itself. He drew in a deep breath.

"In the midst of life we are in death . . ."

In the congregation, Mary stared up at the minister's white face. He looked like the Angel of Death, hovering above them. The inside of the church was freezing cold—so what must it feel like for the old people here? They said nothing, but they had to feel the body heat being sucked out of them. At least they came prepared with thick, drab clothes. Mary had watched them enter, one by one . . . *in customary suits of solemn black*. And one by one they had paused by the coffin, set off from the aisle by a polished ebony railing near the main church door. *Emprisoned in black purgatorial rails*. No wonder that memory turned up such sad images. Less than a week ago Jeanie had been blooming with health and beauty. Liz had seen the body and told Mary that even in death Jeanie looked like a sleeping child, ready to wake up and enjoy life again tomorrow.

Mary stood, sat, and kneeled, taking her cues from the people in front of her. She could see Liz, two pews away,

193

with her brown hair drawn back from her face and tied in a bun under her dove-gray hat. She had not lifted her head at all during the ceremony. She seemed to be taking this very hard, more moved than Jeanie's parents or her brothers, the twin boys who had driven back on Thursday from their profitable jobs as masons in booming, oil-rich Aberdeen. The Inglis family had sat last night in the Over The Water, stone faced, quietly drinking and ignoring the other patrons.

Mary took another quick look up and around. There must be a hundred people in the church, everyone in the village and some from neighboring towns. Nothing like a sudden death—especially of someone young and fit—to draw people to the church. (*Never send to know for whom the bell tolls; it tolls for thee.*) Walter Campbell usually preached to a handful. Now his face was twisted with some strong emotion that Mary could not read. He was having trouble controlling his voice as he led them through the first part of the burial service.

She felt that his eye had sought her out, fixing on her and on Don at her side. Could he tell that Don was only listening with half an ear? She knew it well enough.

Don had moved into a mood of relief and strong satisfaction early in the morning, when Hamish Macveagh had called through from the inn over the antique telephone line. "Mr. Donald? There's word come in here from the Laird Jericho. I hope ye can take his meaning, for I'm bound to admit to ye that I cannot. He says, 'Jenks confirms, now it's our move again.' Mister Donald? Is that you?"

Don's rebel yell must have almost blown Hamish's ear off. Ever since, he had been muttering to himself, watching the weather and the surging seas. That's all he had talked about on the way down from the house. He had gone on whispering to Mary as the gusts shook the open church doors. "I wonder how often they get a blow like this? Maybe I ought to call Roger and have him put me in touch with the people working for Mobil. They've been doing deep-water drilling exploration off the northwest coast—they must have looked into the patterns here. If it's like this too often here, we'll have to think again about our construction plans."

He was still fidgeting next to her now. She felt like nudging him to pay attention to the ceremony. Everyone around them was completely motionless—and how odd that no one showed

194

visible signs of grief. It was like being surrounded by robots with fixed features. Didn't they *care* about Jeanie's death?

She had asked Roger that question a couple of days ago, and he had answered it, at least to his satisfaction. He had been leaning against the kitchen table, cheerfully eating a piece of cheese and a slice of her homemade bread.

"You're seeing a difference in life styles. Death's like a close neighbor up here. He might drop in whenever the weather's bad and the boats are out. You learn to live with a neighbor, even if you don't like him. Over in the States you've sent him off to live down in Florida, or in the old peoples' nursing homes."

Maybe he was right, but some people round here still shrank from Death's touch. Just look at Walter Campbell up there—something had a hand around his heart. Mary suddenly realized that the people around her were beginning to button up their coats and rise from the hard wooden seats. Surely the service couldn't be over already? She looked at Don.

"What's going on?"

He jerked his head toward the aisle. "Been daydreaming? We all go outside now, the rest of the ceremony will be at the grave side."

He stood up, started to put on his floppy fur hat, then realized that he must go bareheaded until the burial was over. The rain was still beating down on the lead roof of the church.

Mary caught his thought. "Let's hope that Campbell can keep it short out there. It's worse for the old people than it is for us."

The cemetery was fifty yards down the hill from the kirk, set at the closest place where the soggy turf covered the depth of soil for a deep grave. Walter Campbell had come through the nave of the church and was leading the way down the slippery path, head bare to the sleet and the wind. After him came the Inglis family, then the coffin carried by six men from the village. Next came Jamie MacPherson, his usual casual dress replaced by a dark gray suit and polished black shoes.

Don and Mary were a dozen people back. She was having trouble with her hat. It wanted to take off and fly away in the strong gusts of wind. The only thing that saved it was the no-

tice she had when an extra strong blast was on the way. The
heather on the hillside would ripple, like a wave on a gray,
tilted pool, and then moments later the wind would rip at her
coat and hat and make her eyes water.

The going underfoot became more treacherous as they
went down the hill. Sometimes Mary was plunged to her
ankles in cold brown water as the soggy surface yielded to
her weight, then she would be sliding on hard rock cover.
Twenty yards from the newly dug grave, one of the men supporting the left side of the coffin slipped and was forced to
release his hold as he fell. The other two in front of him
could not adapt to the increased load. They were slipping
aside to avoid the tilting casket when Jamie MacPherson took
two quick steps forward and placed his shoulder under the
coffin. The men on the other side stopped in their tracks.
There were a few perilous seconds where Jamie was holding
up three hundred pounds alone, the muscles under his coat
bulging with the sudden strain. He grunted but stood firm until the other pallbearers could get back to their positions.

When he could finally move back to take his place in the
procession, Mary caught his eye and smiled at him. Jamie
nodded casually. He didn't even seem to be breathing hard.
For the final twenty yards the funeral procession went even
more slowly.

Where the grave had been dug the bedrock was no more
than five feet down from the surface. Peaty brown earth had
been piled away well to the side, leaving the mourners free to
surround the pit completely. Walter Campbell looked at the
circle of friends and relatives before he began the final part
of the ceremony.

The shell of apparent indifference was finally breaking.
Jeanie's mother had begun to cry, her face blotched and
reddened by her tears and the cutting wind. Four or five of
the women relatives had followed that example and were
weeping openly. But William Inglis still stood without expression, as pale and frozen as though he were himself the
corpse. The medical examiner had confided to him what
would be told to no one else in Laxford: Jeanie had been
pregnant when she died. Inglis had begged for secrecy, even
from his wife. No one must know it. (But someone else *did*
know it. Had the unborn bastard been fathered by Jamie
MacPherson? If not, then who?).

196

When he looked at the coffin, ready now to be lowered into the grave, William Inglis felt his heart shrink and twist with sorrow. Even a week ago he would have said it to her: Better ye die than bring a bastard into this house. But now . . .

"We therefore commit her body to this ground . . ."

The coffin was descending into a slick, oozing cavity that now held six inches of standing water. Walter Campbell had shuddered again when he saw that. To be lowered into that—almost as bad as if Jeanie were alive in the casket, to think of the resting place in stifling, gluey clay.

"Earth to earth, ashes to ashes, dust to dust; in sure and certain hope of the Resurrection to eternal life."

The hands that held the Prayer Book were trembling and shivering, part of the tremors that shook his whole body. The difficult part was almost here. He had to carry through with it, or risk his own soul. William Campbell stepped back from the side of the grave, lifted his head and spoke directly to the gathered mourners.

"We meet in grief today, for the loss of a lovely young woman. Less than a week ago the whole of Jeanie's life seemed to lie ahead of her. But no one among us can ever know the measure of our days. Jeanie is gathered now to the company of Our Lord, Jesus Christ."

Campbell cleared his throat, hardening his resolve for what must follow in a few minutes. "Even as we grieve for Jeanie, we must remember that she now enjoys a happiness beyond our measure or understanding. Just as in the midst of life we are in death, so Jeanie Inglis, in that state that men call death, holds eternal life."

A ripple of uneasiness was spreading through the group by the grave. A eulogy should have been given in the shelter of the kirk, not out here on the cold hillside.

Campbell met their stares unflinchingly, facing them down.

"Jeanie's death was an accident, a terrible accident. Aye. But in a world where God knows all and sees all, can there ever be such a thing as a true accident? Does not God order events on earth as a sign to us, as a signal and warning?"

The words seemed to be ripped from his mouth and carried away on the icy wind. Mary was close enough to see the veins in his neck, congested and purple, and the staring, protruding eyes. The fanatic gleam filled them again. Mary lowered her own eyes and looked down at the coffin. *Never ask to know for whom the bell tolls.* Its brazen voice had begun again at the top of the hill, calling their sorrow across the desolate fells. While Campbell was silent, Mary looked far up, to the hill above the church. Someone was standing there, a bulky and motionless figure in the relentless, beating rain. Who could it be? The whole village was here. She peered upward through narrowed eyes. The man on the hill did not move. Mary turned her mind back to Campbell's words.

"The resurrection to eternal life was promised to us, if we will wear the shield of faith, by Jesus Christ himself. *Resurrection,* our own rising to a second and a better life." He stared down at the coffin as though he expected the lid to creak open and Jeanie, clad in grave cerements, to sit up in the clammy depths. "Since that is true, why do we fear death and why do we grieve at death? It will come to all of us at last, and then in a moment, in the twinkling of an eye as St. Paul puts it, we will be raised to life everlasting. Why do we fear? Because if we have sinned in this life, we will be held accountable for those sins. If we have acted from lust, or vanity, or pride, or if we have turned our backs on virtue, we will pay for it. For sinners, there will be punishment."

Campbell stared around him at the chilled and pinched faces. No one moved. "For any among you who have sought the dark ways, who have turned back to the Old Religions and set them against the words of Christ Our Lord, remember that those sins will be measured and weighed. Again let us heed St. Paul's words, when he tells us 'for we wrestle not against flesh and blood, but against principalities, against powers, against the rulers of darkness of the world, against spiritual wickedness in high places.'

"*Sins must be punished.* 'Whom the Lord loveth he chasteneth'—not as mindless vengeance, but to bring us to our senses and make us fight shy of evil.

"I have seen the signs, here in Laxford. Signs of the old evil, signs that we are not true Christians here. Some of us imagine that we are still pre-Christians, no more than Picts and Celts. Some here still wander the dark ways of blasphemy and mouth the gibberish of the Antichrist. *You* will be punished. It may happen today, or in torment in the hereafter. You *cannot* escape."

Campbell had raised his hands high above his head, fists

clenched. The eyes in their pale, bony sockets were blazing as he glared at the hushed circle of wind-flayed faces. And as they watched, it seemed that a light went out behind those eyes. Walter Campbell slowly lowered his head and stood there, bent and silent, while the rain trickled unheeded down his forehead.

"That is all." His voice was tired, scarcely loud enough to hear above the wind. "If any among ye now wish to come to the kirk and tell me of these things, I urge you to do it—speedily. If ye value the immortal soul within your breast. And do not be afraid to come. There is nothing new about sin. Remember, 'all have sinned, and come short of the glory of God.' Forgiveness is infinite. Now . . ." He was shivering, the thin body bowed forward in the cutting wind. "And now . . . peace be with ye."

He turned and began to walk slowly up the hill, past the neglected, moss-grown headstones and crosses, on toward the dour outline of the church. At the graveside there was an uncertain silence, broken by the quiet sobs of Maureen Inglis.

Don took Mary's arm. "Come on. Let's get the hell out of here. I don't know about you, but after that I need a quick drink." He started to walk diagonally across the hill, back toward Laxford.

"Hold it a minute." Mary saw that Jamie had not moved from the grave side. He was standing, head down, staring into the coffin at the bottom of the pit. She went across to him.

"Jamie, I want to say again that I'm sorry. Come on, now. There's nothing to be gained now by staying here."

He slowly looked up at here. There was no expression in his blue eyes. "Aye. Sure enough ye're right on that." He began to walk away from the grave, not looking back to it. "They'll all tell me that, I know it."

He turned to Don as they came up to him. "An' I owe ye a real apology, Mr. Willis. These past few days I've not been able to mind my work at all. It's way behind, every bit of it. Would it be all right if I came over to the house in a week, maybe, an' start in of an evenin'? It's not so good for you and Mrs. Willis, but it'd be quicker that way."

Don patted Jamie's shoulder sympathetically. "Whenever you want to start, that's fine with us. And it's not Mr. and

199

Mrs. Willis—it's Don and Mary, right? Come on with us now. We're going to the Over The Water for a drink. You look as if you're frozen."

"Aye. There's parts of me that are. But no drink for me today. I'll walk on over there with ye, then I'll have to be away on business."

His eyes flicked up toward the hill above the church. Mary followed his look, but the figure she had seen there earlier had disappeared. The rain was easing off, leaving the hills to the east shrouded in fog and clouds. She began to untie her raincoat belt, then felt at her pockets.

"Hold on. I've lost my purse."

"You didn't bring it with you. Don't you remember, up at the house you decided you wouldn't need it."

"That was my big handbag. But I had a little purse with me, one with my keys and some small change in it. I don't know where I could have lost it."

"Then don't bother with it. It will turn up." Don had stopped by a headstone, waiting for Mary to catch up with him. "All these things seem to read the same. In fond memory of Aggie, or Annie, or Bertha. Where do the men in the village get buried?"

Jamie inclined his head to the west. "Ten fathom down. Half the men folk in Laxford are lost at sea—the kirk's full of memorial plaques, but there's no body for the minister to bury." He turned his head back to Jeanie's grave, where two villagers were preparing to replace the sodden earth. "Maybe it's better that way."

"Come on," said Mary quickly. "You two go on to the inn. I'll go and take a look in the church. My purse may have fallen out of my pocket when I was kneeling down. I'll be with you in a few minutes."

"We'll meet you in the bar."

Mary angled her steps back up the steepest part of the hill. The main doors of the church were still closed when she arrived there, but the small inset door on the left was unlocked, with the key still in the padlock. She slipped inside. It was darker than ever within. She walked quietly along the central aisle, past the ornate baptismal font and along the nave, peering along each row of pews. Her footsteps rang through the silence of the church, echoing off the vaulted stone ceiling.

There it was. The little brown purse was lying almost under one of the rows of seats. Mary bent to pick it up with an unreasonable feeling of satisfaction. It would save the hassle of sending a key to Ullapool for another copy and being completely keyless while it was away. Now it was only fair that all her loose change in that purse should go into the collection box as she left the church. Maybe William Campbell could use it to buy himself an overcoat or a decent suit. Back home she'd given things better than he wore to the garbage men.

"Who is there?"

The voice from behind the chancel screen was high and tense. Mary jerked upright and banged her elbow hard against the wooden back of the pew.

"It's me—Mary Willis."

Walter Campbell appeared from behind the screen. He had taken off his dripping coat and was rubbing at his wet hair with an old yellow towel.

"Hello. Can I help you now?"

"I came back to look for my purse." Mary held it up to him. "I found it. I can leave now."

"Right." Campbell leaned against the carved wooden pillar that stood at the end of the sanctuary. He looked exhausted, drained of all his fire and energy. "I was thinking for a minute that it might be one of the people from the village. But that's maybe too much to hope for."

"You mean . . ." Mary hesitated. "To talk about what you said just now, at Jeanie's burial?"

"Aye." Campbell sighed. "I told you before, there's somethin' going on here in Laxford, but devil a man or woman here will admit it. Don't ye see it when ye look around at them? There's something secret. It scares me."

"I'm too new here to notice, I guess. They don't seem very cheerful, but I thought that was the hard life they lead." Mary began to edge toward the door. "I'll watch now and see if I can notice anything peculiar. Do you mean they behave strangely here in church?"

"Here? No, this is sacred ground. That's what 'kirk' means—a thing belonging to the Lord. The things I suspect might be any place but here. There's dabblin' in things out on the cliffs—ye'll never get a villager out there when the

201

moon's full, try it and ye'll see what I mean." Campbell shook his head. "It's beyond me. I've wanted to get back to your house and talk about this with ye, but the last few days I've had to concern myself with poor Jeanie. An' there were things there I didn't like the looks of—the lass shouldn't have been out in the middle of the night . . ."

He jerked his head up. "I'm ramblin' here. I'll let you be on your way. Did ye think any more about the sewing machine—the one in the attic?"

"It's yours if you'd like to come on by the house and collect it." Mary noticed a wrapped parcel standing on top of the baptismal font. "Is that yours, or did somebody leave it behind?"

"This?" Campbell laughed softly. "It's mine. There's still a lot of good in this village, never mind what I say about it. This here's a birthday present from Mrs. Macdougal—a fruit cake, from the size of it, same as she gave me back at Harvest Festival. They seem to think I need lookin' after. Mebbe they're right." He picked up the brown paper parcel. "I would like that sewing machine—poor Mrs. Morrin's a widow, she could use it very well. Sometime next week, maybe?"

"Anytime." Mary hesitated at the door. She wanted to put her loose change into the box, but now it would look phony with the minister looking on. Better to do it another day when no one was watching.

She stepped out through the little inset door set into the huge main doors. "Just drop in when you want to for the machine. I'll ask Don to bring it down from the attic and put it in the kitchen. That way you can take it even if I'm not there—that kitchen door still doesn't lock properly."

As she walked away she knew that Campbell was still standing just inside the church, his birthday present in his hands. When the religious fire left him he was a gray, aging man, worn down by years of deprivation and disappointment, As Mary headed down the hill to the inn she realized that she was looking about her at the crofters' cottages with a new eye. Walter Campbell couldn't be right about the village—but the suggestion of it was enough to start you thinking. She began to hurry, keen to reach the warmth and cheerfulness of the inn and the people.

Mary's progress from the church to the inn was watched closely from the hillside. Her future role had been decided a few minutes earlier. Now it was necessary to consider the best timing for events, and the placement of the other actors.

CHAPTER 13

Well, Ellie, that takes care of most of it, but you'll have to come here yourself to catch the atmosphere. I went out for a walk yesterday, up to Ardmore Point, and in four hours I saw exactly one person. Roger told me when we were on the way up to Laxford that Sutherland County's the emptiest part of Britain (fifteen thousand people scattered over an area the size of Delaware), but that's just words until you get up here. The hills over to the east of us are so craggy you'd think the word was invented for them, and when you get up on top of one, the sides dive down vertically into the lochs. You'll *have* to get over here to see for yourself. Can't you somehow wangle a trip to London to buy books or sell them or something? If Blocker bumped you last month so he could carouse at the Frankfurt Book Fair, he should have that on his conscience (does he have one?) and let you come over later.

We have lots of room for you at the house, and we've even got it so there's enough hot water now. I'm falling in love with it. Don's job is going well still, and he's not drinking too much (I'm trying to type with my fingers crossed). The people at JosCo and the DOE treat him as though he's God when it comes to flow problems—good for ego rehabilitation.

I'm not going to wait for your comments on the first three chapters, on second thought. The material for the next two is in my head, and I'll just keep going and write them. You can expect to have them in another week after this lot. Do you know how much it costs to send stuff to you airmail? Take it into account when you fix the terms for *The Mistress Of Laxford* or whatever we finally decide to call it.

More soon, hot off the pen.

Love, Mary.

P.S. When I say I'm not waiting for your comments before I write the next two chapters I don't mean I'm not keen to see what you think of what you've got—I'm dying to get your reaction.

The ribbon of the typewriter had been catching on one of the little metal pieces at the side. Mary removed the letter to Ellie before she began to fiddle with it—there were enough black smear marks on the manuscript without putting some on the letter. If this was the best machine they had over at JosCo they were in trouble. It was an old electric Smith-Corona, with a clean type face but a nasty habit of skipping two spaces whenever you hit the space bar. (But JosCo had probably loaned Don the worst one they had—they'd keep the good ones for company reports. And if Ellie's main criticism of the first three chapters was the word spacing, she'd be buying them drinks all round at the Over The Water.)

Mary read the end of the chapter for about the twentieth time. How many fiction works were real people and places, disguised enough to keep you out of court cases?

She was too engrossed in it to look up as Don came into the "study," the little room upstairs that was really beginning to deserve the name. She had recognized his footsteps as soon as the front door opened.

"You're home early. It can't be later than about three."

"Yeah. You busy?"

"Medium." Mary suddenly caught the tension in his voice. She swivelled round on the cushioned chair. "Hey there. Is it good news or bad news? Tell me all."

He came up behind her and put his hands on her shoulders. "I'm not sure which—it depends some on you. You know that I've been working over those pump sizes, the ones that the preliminary design has for the heat exchangers?"

"You have? Now how would I know that?" Mary waved her hand to the table that sat over against the study wall. "I mean, apart from the fact that you've talked about nothing else for the past week. And the fact that every square inch of the kitchen and bedroom and the living room is covered with your notes and numbers. Maybe it's because you've been sitting with *Kent's Mechanical Engineering Manual* open to 'Heat Exchangers' at every meal we've eaten together since Monday. That could have given me a little bit of a hint."

"Bitch." Don leaned forward and kissed the back of her neck. "Have I been that bad?"

"At least that bad." Mary stood up and put her arms round him. "But don't worry about it—I've been doing my own thing with the writing. Mary Stewart, move over. It's been going well for you, hasn't it? I thought you went off for a final briefing on all that this morning."

"I did."

"And it went well?"

"Too damned well. Somebody at the Department of Environment seems to have decided that I'm Mister Fluid Flow for 1980."

"That's great—they really are impressed with what you've been doing?"

"Looks that way—but it's not as great as you think. They've asked me to serve as contractor representative to a nuclear plant design workshop that starts at the end of the week."

Mary frowned up at him. "But that's *wonderful*. Why the heartache?"

"The damned thing's in Oak Ridge, Tennessee. It lasts for five days. I'd be gone for at least a week."

"I see." Mary tried hard to hide her own drop in spirits. "Wouldn't it be good for you at JosCo if you go?"

"Well, sure. But I don't want to leave you here on your own. We've only just got back together."

"Nonsense. I'll keep a while longer—and I'm as capable of managing here on my own as I was in Manhattan. Lots less likely to get mugged." Mary made her tone determinedly cheerful. "I'm really proud of you. It's an honor that they asked you—you definitely *have* to go. Whose idea was it—that man at Dounreay who thinks you're a hot shot?"

"Jenks, you mean? No, Roger says it wasn't him. Jenks agreed at once that I was a good man to send, but I know from his people that he'd be just as happy to have me around and keep an eye on what they're doing on the design. The request came up from Petherton at London Headquarters of DOE. He's pretty senior—that makes it even harder to argue with the idea. Even Joshua says it's unusual for the government to ask a contractor to go instead of one of them, and he says we'd be fools to miss the chance. He thinks I must have made a good impression on Petherton when he was here."

"Well, if the Laird Jericho says you'd be a fool to miss the chance, then it must be right—that's what Hamish keeps telling me. I think Lord Jericho must have hypnotized him or something when he was staying at the Over The Water. Anyway, that makes it definite, you'll have to go. When will you be leaving?"

"Soon." Now that he had got over breaking the news to her, Mary could see that Don's own pleasure and excitement was beginning to bubble up. It was clear that he had desperately wanted to go.

"I'll have to fly down to London a couple of days from now, then over to New York."

"My genius husband." She gave him another squeeze. "You impress Jericho, then you impress Jenks, then Petherton—but none of them's as impressed with you as I am. And don't you worry about me. I'll be fine."

"That's what I *was* worried about." Don went across the table and picked up the calendar. "I didn't like the idea of leaving you here on your own."

"Don't worry about that—I know the place now. I'll be hopping into bed and having fun with all the Laxford laddies, just like Dorcas Macveagh here." Mary patted the fat package of typed pages that was sitting next to the typewriter. "Hey, here's a thought. You say you'll be flying out through New York?"

"Just a connection on the way to Oak Ridge. I think I'll have about three hours at the airport. But I'll be in New York overnight on the way back. Why?"

"Could you maybe play mailman and save me some time and money? If you could give these to Ellie, or even just stick them into the mailbox when you're at Kennedy—"

"Dead easy. Hand 'em over. I'd quite like to see old Ellie again."

"Not too much of her, all right?" Mary folded her manuscript and letter into a brown envelope and passed it to him. "Tell her I'm writing hot and heavy. While you're away I should go even faster. She can expect another fifty pages, and I ought to have them in the mail a week from now. You're home early, so what about a fancy English tea? I've got pickled herring and a cream cheese."

Now that the first reaction of dismay at Don's absence was fading, Mary could feel a sense almost of freedom. She'd been writing hard, but it had been guilty writing, sneaking away in the evenings since Jeanie's funeral, when neither Mary nor Don had felt like going to the pub. Not too guilty, because Don had been very busy as well. But the house still needed attention, and she thought she ought to be spending more time worrying about the repairs. Jamie MacPherson didn't seem to need supervision or directions. He had been arriving at six or half-past, worked his way quietly until nine or ten, cleaned up any sign of his labors, and left. The windows now opened and closed miraculously smoothly, the washhouse had been reorganized and all the cracks in the walls plastered over, and the hot water heaters produced more water and less symptoms of extreme flatulence. Jamie had even managed to sweep the chimney without putting a layer of soot over everything. He was obliging, intelligent, and inexpensive—but shouldn't Mary be keeping a closer eye on it and show more interest in the result of his labors?

Perhaps she was imagining a problem. Jamie didn't seem to feel any need for praise and pats on the back.

"You'd make your fortune if you ever went back to the States," Don had told him as he left one evening. "You can't find people to do what you've been doing at any price."

"Is that right?" Jamie had stood there and listened politely. He was covered with a thin film of white powder, the result of a sanding operation on the wall of the kitchen, but Mary could see no sign of a mess in there. "Who knows? Someday I'll mebbe pull up my roots from Sutherland County and go off an' see the rest of the world. I've always fancied the idea of America."

"So what keeps you here?"

"Oh, ye know how it is. This an' that." Jamie hadn't reacted to the possible implication of Don's question—that with Jeanie dead, he might now want to leave—but Mary thought that he had caught it well enough. "I've got my responsibilities around here. Maybe in a couple of years I'll spread my wings an' take a look down south."

"The way Liz plans to?"

"More like the way Mr. Petherton did it. He's from here, ye know, used to live not a mile south. That's why he's back regular from London and the Commission."

His tone was polite, but Mary felt that Jamie was humoring them. He didn't intend to leave this area, for America or

London or for anywhere else—the roots here were too strong.

Mary wondered about Jamie as she followed Don down from the study to the kitchen. He was still holding the calendar, looking at dates and feeling his way down with one hand against the wall.

"Should I have Jamie keep coming in while you're gone? If I do, you ought to leave me a list of the things you've talked about with him. What's the order of priority for the outside repairs?"

"Let's take a look. I don't see why he ought to stop just because I won't be here. You'll need company here in the evenings, or you'll begin to feel lonely." Don went to the list that he had pinned on Mary's cork board. She had scrounged it from JosCo and hung it on the kitchen wall over near the door (the lock worked now but they seldom bothered with it—with so few people about, the danger of theft seemed negligible). He studied it for a few moments and shook his head.

"He's done all the ones that we thought were the urgent ones. Except the insulation, and that's going to be a long job. I think everything that's left will depend on when he can get the materials, and we can't decide that for him. I'm willing to let him set his own priorities. Do you trust him for that?"

"Sure. Jamie's a gem."

"Then we ought to let him organize things for himself. That's another one of Lord Jericho's rules: don't organize somebody who doesn't need organizing."

"He seems to be a great one for maxims—you ought to write all of them down and publish a book of them. You know, *The Wit And Wisdom Of Joshua, Laird Jericho*. It ought to sell a million."

Mary was over at the sink filling the kettle at the tap. Could Jamie maybe do something to get rid of that moaning gurgle in the pipes? Don said it sounded like somebody trying to throttle the family ghost.

"I've seen worse books. It's not as crazy an idea as you might think."

"I know it. You don't need to tell me that, I used to do the blurbs for some of them. 'Thermodynamic Dieting—the effortless way to the new, slimmer you.' God, those blurbs. Broke me bleedin' 'eart—that's what Jericho's helicopter pilot says about Little Susie from Highgate. With any luck, some wretch in Manhattan ought to be doing one for me in a year."

"So you've got to get on and finish it. I'll give this to Ellie."

"Good. Hey, that reminds me. What about those papers of Knowlton that I gave you? I thought they might have some good background in them. You said you'd take a look and tell me if they made sense to you—what have you done with them?"

Don had gone back to the calendar and was marking off a rough schedule on it. He grimaced and looked vaguely around the kitchen.

"Oh, shit. I forgot all about 'em. What the hell did I do with 'em? I guess they're still stuffed in the bottom of my briefcase upstairs. Look, let me have them for one more day. I promise you I'll look them over before I leave. All right?"

"Fine." Mary was cutting thick slices from a loaf and looking at the outside of it critically. "Just a minute too long in the oven, I'd say. Look, you don't *have* to bother with Knowlton's stuff if you don't want to. I thought it might have something in it that was useful for the job. But I'd like to take another look because they're sort of odd." Mary thought again of the strange symbols on the first pages. "Maybe I ought to let the minister have a look at them as well. He's interested in anything around here that seems sort of peculiar."

"He ought to. He's peculiar enough himself. Here." Don passed Mary the calendar. "That's my best guess as to when I'll be going and coming back. I'm vague on the return because I don't know what the government people may have set up for me to see and do in Oak Ridge. I'll leave this here with you and pass word via JosCo if things start to get screwed up."

Mary put down the butter knife. "You've made a real mess of this. You should have done it in pencil. If you'll be flying to London, do you think I could hitch a ride?"

"If Matson's still the pilot it should be easy. How will you get back here?"

"Train. I still want to try one. And there's things we need in London that I don't see us getting round here—a tea strainer, a spare iron. You need a new electric razor, and I need some more gunk for the diaphragm. I don't know what the locals use for birth control, but whatever it is you can't buy it at the store in Laxford. How's our finances?"

"Let's take a look at the checkbook. We should be doing all right." Don went through to the living room leaving Mary to put a shovel of coke into the oven and curse again at the amount of grime that it seemed to generate.

That was something else that had to be done. The coal shed behind the house was huge, enough to hold a couple of tons of fuel. But where did you order it from? Hamish would know—or maybe ask Jamie next time he came out here.

"Four hundred to spare." Don had the checkbook in his hand. "I'm assuming we can get JosCo to swing for a double room for me in London. Want to try and take in a show while we're there? I'll have Friday evening free."

"Anything except *The Mousetrap*." Mary rattled the poker among the coals, and a shower of hot ash fell through to the pan beneath. "Pour the water into that pot, and let's plan the trip. I've been wanting to get at the London shops ever since you told me you'd won the contract. Don't put that checkbook away."

The road from the village ran flat and due west for the first half mile. When it reached the cliff it angled sharply back northeast and began to rise steadily, so that by the time it passed the front of the house the cliffs on the left stretched nearly fifty feet to the sea below.

The rock cairns along the edge were a warning, but a dangerous one to an unwary traveler. By the time they were visible from a fast-moving car it would be too late, and at night it would be doubly easy to go over the edge when the autumn ground mists scattered and blurred the beams from the headlights.

Mary slowed to a crawl as she made the sharp right-hand turn at the cliff. In the four days since Don had left, she had become used to driving the Austin alone, but the gears still gave her problems. There seemed to be something wrong with the synchromesh, grating unpleasantly as she went between first and second gear. Did it need repairing? Probably not— Don didn't seem to have had any trouble with it. She'd have to learn the car's little peculiarities now that he wasn't here to drive her around.

The sight of Walter Campbell's old Riley already standing

in front of the house made her swear to herself. He must have arrived right on time. (Punctuality in others was a virtue—unless you were late yourself.) Mary had wasted a few minutes with Liz Carlin, chatting to her about the spoils of the London trip. Next time they'd do Regent Street together. But that delay had eaten up the margin that would allow a quick bath and a bite to eat before the minister arrived. Would he be interested in sharing a meal?—he didn't seem to eat well. Mary smiled to herself as she shifted to neutral and set the handbrake. The bath would have to wait—but the thought of Walter Campbell's reaction if she suggested sharing *that* as well as the meal was one to dwell on. She heaved the canvas bags of groceries out of the back of the Austin and went over to the other car. There was no sign of Campbell near the Riley—no pair of legs this time, sticking out of the door. Where was he?

Mary went to the front door and opened it with her big key. She managed to push it open one-handed but it was a real effort. That was one thing that Jamie still hadn't managed to fix, even though he had oiled the hinges and fiddled with the hanging. It would probably have to come off and be rehung completely.

"Mr. Campbell?" Mary's voice echoed off the wood paneling and dark wood floor. "Are you in here?"

"I'm upstairs. Up here in the bedroom." The voice sounded a little guilty. A moment later the minister poked his head out under the banister. With his scrawny neck and the stiff clerical collar a size too large, he looked like an anxious turtle peering down at her. Mary smiled up at him.

"Hi there. How did you get in here? I thought I'd left it all locked."

"I was a few minutes early, Jamie let me in." Campbell came down the stairs. His frayed jacket had its shiny elbows and most of the front covered with big patches of gray dust. "I knocked and there was no reply, so I went round the back. He was there and he let me in. I hope that was all right?"

"Sure it is—we've nothing worth stealing here, I don't know why we even bother to lock up." Mary put the bags on the kitchen table and started to sort through the contents. "Jamie has a key. We gave him one so he could start work if he got here before we got home. But I didn't know he was going to be here tonight. Do you know what he's doing?"

"Replacing rotted boards on the side of the coal shed, at least he was when I found him. Er . . . I hope ye don't mind me wasting a few minutes of his time, but as ye weren't here I took the liberty of asking him to give me a hand to move the sewing machine out of the attic. It's heavy, and he's a lot stronger and younger than me—and I didn't want to trouble you with it. We put it in the big bedroom."

Mary unloaded three pints of milk and put them down on the cool stone floor. "Don't apologize to me for that—I'm just as happy to stay out of that attic altogether. It's filthy. Last time I was up there I got all sorts of allergies, fluff and dust and Lord knows what. Here, let me get you a brush for your coat."

"No, no, that's quite unnecessary." Campbell waved his hand to dismiss the idea. "I'll get just as dusty when I carry it out of here to the car."

"Do you think it works all right? It must have been up there for years."

"I'll know for sure in a day or two—it looks all right. Now then, if ye'll just hold that door open for me in front, I'll carry it down and be off on my way. I don't want to trouble you, or take up more of your evening."

"It's not trouble. I meant to have you come over and get it before we went off to London." Mary hesitated. When Campbell was in his vague and relaxed mood, it was hard to recall the fiery preacher who warned against hellfire and torment. Was now a good time for it?

"I was thinking about Jeanie, and what you said at her funeral." Mary paused to see his reaction.

Campbell cocked his head on one side and looked at her noncommittally. "Oh, aye?"

"I was thinking," went on Mary, "did anyone ever come to you from the village—the way that you asked them to? You know, for the things that you said had been happening here, around Laxford?"

"Not a one." Campbell's tone was grim. He turned and led the way up the stairs. "Why do you ask me that, Mrs. Willis?"

Mary followed him to the bedroom and crouched down next to him by the old sewing machine. It was an ancient Singer, operated by a foot treadle. The body was so coated with grime that the model number and name was invisible, and the wheel on the side had been bent out of true. Campbell took the wheel and began to turn it slowly. His hands were curiously delicate as he worked, and he talked as he touched the old gears.

"Come on now, there we go. Ye're a little stiff there, an' it's no surprise. It's been a long time. Let me get at ye with a drop of oil and the little spanners, an' we'll have ye as good as new in no time." He blew fluff away from the inside of the case and rubbed absently at the underside of the treadle.

"Never a word, Mrs. Willis." His voice took on a different tone, softer and sadder. His eyes never lifted from the old machine. "No one said a word. I pray for patience, but it comes hard to me. I'm too used to city speed, quick actions. Round here ye have to wait for things to creep up on you, slow and quiet. It's a different world, an' it's up to me to learn it. But I'll say it again, why do ye ask me about that— what I said at Jeanie's funeral?"

Now that he was asking, the whole thing seemed ridiculous. Mary couldn't bring herself to talk about it without more reassurance.

"Mr. Campbell, you were quite serious, weren't you? That there's something bad in Laxford—I don't mean just *ordinary* bad, like greed and sex, but really bad."

"I'm sure of it." The minister was bowed forward on his knees in front of the machine, as though it were some strange idol of a mechanical age. He looked up for a moment at Mary, and there was a glint in his eyes like the reflection from a deep pool of water, far-off and cold. "Ye didn't hear what I hear, back there in Glasgow, or see the fear in a dyin' man's face. There's something here, near Laxford—maybe in the village itself. I want to know what it is, an' I want to help cleanse this place. But I'm no nearer to knowing than when I came, six months back."

"Can't you *make* people tell you, when they come to see you in the church?"

"Mrs. Willis, we parted ways here in the North from the Catholic Church a long time back. Over four hundred years ago. That's mostly been a blessing, and I'll never say different, but there's one thing of theirs that I wish we still had, just now and again. I wish we had confession. With that, maybe I'd have been hearing things about this village—things that people are ashamed to talk about in the open. Maybe I'd have an idea now what I was seeing in Bruce Maclane's eyes, the night he was dying back there in the Gorbals. I don't know what he was scared of, but I know this. He was too far gone to be makin' up a story."

Mary stood up without speaking and went over to the wardrobe. She picked up the folder of papers in the bottom of it and came back to squat on her heels next to Walter Campbell.

"Here. I'm probably wasting your time as well as mine, but I can't get my mind off this, ever since you spoke to me in the church after the funeral. I'd like you to take a look at these papers and see what you think of them."

"Certainly." Campbell's polite reply was automatic, but Mary caught a quickly erased look of scepticism there. (Come now, Mrs. Willis. You've been here in Laxford for how long? All of two weeks. And now you think you've got something that explains what I've been puzzling over since the day I arrived here, and before that. Really, Mrs. Willis?) The minister took out an old and bent pair of wire-framed reading glasses and hooked them carefully over his prominent ears.

"Papers, eh? And did ye write these yourself, then?"

"No." Mary felt obliged to hit out at the way she was being humored. "They were written by a man called Knowlton. He used to work for the same company that my husband does—JosCo—and he wrote these when I think he was living here in this house."

"Recently?" Campbell's voice showed a trace more interest.

"A couple of years ago. I found them when we were clearing out the old stuff in the house."

Campbell straightened up with the folder and took it closer to the overhead light. He rubbed his grimy hands on his trousers, nodded, and opened the file at random. The page was covered with Knowlton's careful script, neat notation in red ink. The minister began to read it silently, following the lines with a grubby and horny finger and mouthing the words beneath his breath. After a couple of minutes he shook his head.

"I know ye mean well, Mrs. Willis, an' I appreciate that ye showed this to me. But it's nothing, not to my eye. Look, it's all some sort of engineering talk. See, 'they must have been in the place for hundreds of years to make that system of

215

sluices and flood gates. Maybe I can date it from the materials and design that they've got down there? Check the old texts and see when steel was first used up in the north.' " He shrugged. "Ye see, there's more like this. It's the sort of thing I can see Mr. Willis wanting to look at, but not me. Ye should have shown this to him."

"I did. I asked him to read it first. He only gave it back to me a couple of days ago."

"So what did *he* have to say about it?"

"He said it's nothing important to him." Mary did not take the folder that Campbell was holding out to her. Had Don really read it? He said he had, just before he left—but that might have been his way of sliding out if he hadn't done what he said he'd do. "Is it all about sluices and gates? Or is it just that page you happened to pick?"

"I don't know." Campbell opened to another random page of the folder. "This Mr. Knowlton, he's an engineer too, is he?"

"He was. He got killed when he fell off the cliffs on the way from here to Laxford. He drowned."

The folder in Campbell's hands trembled. "That was Knowlton? Aye, I heard of that death when I came here, but I didn't recall the name."

He looked down again at the pages of careful script. "See here, it's still all some sort of science, same as before. Knowlton's off on something else. *'Why do they have to transfer proteins after fertilization? Anti-bodies, maybe, or maybe a difference in hormonal makeup? Note: call Jack and see if he can find any analogues for insect species—and ask him about species split with mutations on Y's alone.'* Mrs. Willis, I don't know what this is, but I know what it *isn't*. There's nothing here that makes me think of Satan and his works."

"And you don't remember Knowlton?"

"You're forgetting, Mrs. Willis, I've only been here myself for half a year. All this was before my time, and even the rumors have been odd. I swear it, they're a funny people round here—close and guarded."

"You mean like Hamish Macveagh?"

He smiled. "There's the exception that proves the rule. Anyway, thanks for passin' this by me. I think now I ought to be off on my way—it's getting dark out there, an' the lights

216

on the car aren't what they should be." He cleared his throat. "Don't think I'm over-inquisitive, but what gave ye the idea that there might be somethin' in here"—he waved the folder—"that might interest me? I'll fix up the Riley, if I have to, but I'm no engineer."

"Well . . ."

Now that Mary had heard Campbell read from it, the folder seemed less and less significant.

"I didn't realize that it was engineering. You see, there's a picture in it, near the front of it, and it made me wonder if Knowlton had been drawing a—well, I don't know what else to call it. Drawing a sort of demon?"

"In this folder?" Campbell looked surprised. "Whereabouts?"

"Here, I'll show you." Mary skipped back and forth around the first ten pages until she had found the drawing. With Campbell standing next to her it seemed a lot less scary and suggestive than it had on first sight. "That's it—what do you think of it?"

Campbell dropped his glasses back off his forehead and studied the drawing closely. "Aye, that's interesting, I'll not deny it. So Mr. Knowlton was a student of the old legends round these parts, was he?"

"Not as far as I know. What makes you say that?" Mary found the drawing was pulling her eyes to it, carrying her back to the first night in the Over The Water, back to the strange submerged dreams.

Campbell's manner remained casual. "Oh. I've seen figures like this drawn in quite a few places around this area. Once in an old history, written a couple of hundred years ago and all about the Minch and its legends. And ye'll even see one like this carved on a stone, over on Handa Island. Maybe that was even where Knowlton copied it from. Ye see, this part of Britain has a lot longer history than ye might think. There's legends and superstitions going back for the longest time—way before Christianity came here. But I don't belittle those pre-Christian times. That's one of the things that I worry about around Laxford—some of those pagan notions are still running round the countryside now, as much today as they were a thousand years back."

He turned his head suddenly to face the stairs. "Now, what was that?"

217

"What?"

"I thought I heard a noise down there, a bang on the door."

"Maybe it's Jamie—he sometimes stays later than this." Mary went to the head of the stairs. "Jamie? Are you down there?"

There was no reply. The house below seemed to be perfectly quiet, even when Mary went halfway down the staircase and stood for a moment listening. She came back up to Campbell.

"He must have gone already. How's the work that he's been doing for you on the organ reconditioning coming along?"

Walter Campbell did not answer. When Mary left him he had been turning over the pages of the folder, idly looking at the notes and occasional drawings. Now he was staring at one page with a total cold concentration. His mouth had tightened until the lips were white and bloodless.

"What's wrong?" Mary couldn't have missed that change of expression. "Mr. Campbell, are you all right? What are you looking at there?"

"Why didn't you show me this at first?" said Campbell at last. His voice was breathy and intense, with an edge of fierce excitement.

"Show you what?" Mary leaned over so that she could see what he was looking at in the folder.

Without speaking, he held out a single sheet to her. His hand was trembling and his protruding eyes were blinking rapidly.

It was one from near the front of the folder, one that Mary had looked at briefly and at once dismissed as unintelligible and probably unimportant. A network of lines connected a pattern of repeating letters, Xs, Ds, Hs, Ys and Rs. They were repeated in an irregular and yet systematic way, and alongside every node of the network a string of numbers had been written. Sometimes it would be a single digit, but more usually there would be four or five symbols and numbers, all written with great care. At the bottom of the page were the only words she could find—*"unto the third generation!"*—written and then several times underlined.

Mary regarded the page for a few seconds. She was clearly supposed to see something in it—but who could say what? She

218

shook her head. "Maybe I'm dumb, but I don't understand any of this. For all I know this is more stuff about engineering—that's all that those numbers make me think of."

Campbell laughed, a dry and humorless cough. "Ah, Mrs. Willis, ye should thank God that you're still an innocent. Ye've never heard then of gematria, or of the Kabala?"

"Never." (Not quite true—Kabala sounded vaguely familiar, but she couldn't say why.) "What are they?"

"Look here now." Campbell took back the page. "Ye see all those numbers, written in all over the pattern of lines. That's gematria, but to understand this page completely ye'd have to know how to read it. Gematria's an old mystery, thousands of years old, an' it's a method for matching up words and numbers. Each of these groups"—he tapped the page with a finger whose nail had been bitten down almost to the quick—"everyone will have a word equivalent. The lines are like a tree, like a drawing of the Tree of Life. Every branch carries its own meaning."

"But what does it mean?" Mary looked again, but it was still a meaningless set of squares, polygons, symbols, and numbers. "How do you read it?"

"Aye, that's the real question. The Kabala's full of old patterns like this, if I remember it right. Ye know how these would be used? In the old ceremonies for conjuring, containing, and banishing demons."

"Demons." Mary felt a sense of relief so strong that she felt like laughing out loud. "So you mean that Knowlton had been writing out methods for raising demons? He must have been out of his mind—there's no such thing."

"Mebee not—I wish I had your certainty." Campbell's face was grim. "Our church would mainly agree with you, but there's others around the world that would tell ye different. But ye see, that's not the point. The main question is never that simple one, do the incantations work and raise demons, or do they not? The real question concerns the minds and the hearts of men and women. *Are they trying to raise demons here?* If they try and succeed, then we should have no fear. Demons cannot stand against the power of Jesus Christ. But the souls of *people*, the ones who are trying to bring Satan into this world—that's my worry, an' it's all my worry."

He began to turn over more pages, shaking his head as other diagrams were revealed. His nervousness and tension

219

had gone now. The look that filled his eyes was one of pure belief and conviction.

Mary didn't know how to react. Surely this all had to be nonsense, the idea that someone might be trying to conjure Satan here in peaceful Laxford? But why had she been so afraid, here alone in the house the first day? And if she really believed all this was impossible and ridiculous, then why had she wanted so much to show this to the minister?

There had to be some level within her that thought as Campbell thought, believed as the minister believed. She handed the sheet of paper back to him.

"So what *does* this mean? I still don't know how to begin to interpret those numbers and symbols."

Campbell shook his head, but he did not look up or take the page from her. "You're asking a difficult question, an' one that I can't answer. But look there, now, that's a pentagram and a hexagram, clear as day. I wish I could interpret these myself, but it takes years of experience. Ye see, there's accepted abbreviations, where a single number will stand for a whole group of words, and then there's other cases where ye have to get back to the original Hebrew before ye know which version of a letter or a word is the right one. The man who interprets this is somebody who's made a life's work of it, an' knows Hebrew backward and forward."

"A rabbi?"

"No." Campbell closed the folder and held it close to his chest. "Most rabbis will get less out of this than I would. I tell ye, we need an expert, a real specialist."

A specialist. Mary found that strangely reassuring. For someone who wasn't very religious it was a comfort, the idea that you could call on an expert on satanism and demons, and ask him to identify something just as though it were a problem of treating a disease or deciding the species of an unfamiliar plant. Specialists and experts connected all this to the real world. But surely Knowlton . . .

"Mr. Campbell, I don't see how Knowlton could have been much of an expert, himself. I mean, he was an engineer, and he'd only been here for a short time, less than a year, when he died. How could he have been able to invent all this?"

"I don't think he could have done it—but I don't think he did, either. Ye see, he might well have been able to *copy* this from somewhere, an' watch some ceremonies without people

220

knowin' what he was doing. We've got a different question here. If we can't say what Knowlton was doin', or where he got his knowledge, what ought we to do with what we have—with his notes here?"

Campbell rubbed the back of his hand against his forehead, leaving a gray streak here. Mary slipped the paper she was holding back into the folder.

"Mr. Campbell, couldn't you get help from people higher in the Church—from a bishop, or somebody?"

He looked hard at her. The tension in his face relaxed a trifle. "Ah, Mrs. Willis, ye'd better not be lettin' the people round here hear ye talk like that. Not if ye want to stay popular. Didn't ye know we've no bishops—that we're not Episcopalians here? Anyhow, there's not a bishop in Britain that has the knowledge to help us. I picked up what I know before I came into the Church, when I stayed in the Middle East after doin' my national service, twenty years back. But I'm too rusty on all this. I'm wonderin' who we should call on. There's Macrory, over in Edinburgh, but I think he's out of the country. He was, last time I had word of him. I'll call there in the morning. An' if he's not there, I think Duncan down in Cambridge would be the best choice." He tapped the folder thoughtfully. "This isn't his period—he's more a specialist on the sixteenth century mystics. But he knows so much in the whole field . . ."

Campbell nodded to himself. "That's our best tack. Macrory or Duncan. Ye see, Mrs. Willis, there's no way we could sort this out, just the two of us. We have to get these papers in the hands of somebody who can really tell us just what they mean and what we have to do next. This is deep waters we're in."

Unconsciously he glanced over to the window. It was completely dark now outside. The house was creaking a little as the walls carried the cold of the autumn night to the inside. Campbell went to the head of the stairs, listened for a moment, then came back.

"This might be a bad business. I'd like your permission to carry these papers with me, over to Edinburgh or down to Cambridge. This isn't a thing that I'm easy talkin' about over the telephone, and Laxford is full of ears."

Mary hesitated. Now that the request had come she was

strangely reluctant to let the papers out of her possession. "How long would you want them for?"

"A few days. I can leave the day after tomorrow, an' back by the weekend or Monday at the latest. Don't worry, I'll take good care of them."

"All right. But let me find something better than this old folder for them—it's falling apart at the seam."

"No." Campbell shook his head violently. "I want to take this exactly as it is. We're not qualified, either one of us, to say what's significant and what's not. Even something like the color of the folder and the paper could be important. Aye, an' one other thing, while I'm gone don't be tellin' anyone where I've gone, or what I'm doin'. Who knows about this?"

"Just you and Don."

"Fine. Keep it like that 'til I'm back here. Come on now, there's a lot to be done."

Now that the decision was made, Campbell was impatient. He started down the stairs, clutching the folder. Mary followed him, suddenly aware that she hadn't been exactly truthful. Ellie knew all about the papers, she had mentioned it to her in her letters. But that was way off in New York, nobody here would ever speak to Ellie.

"Don't go without the sewing machine," she warned, as Campbell seemed set to dash straight off to the door. He stopped, halfway across the hall.

"Oh, aye, I was forgettin' all about that. If ye'll hold the front door for me I'll carry yon out to the car. There's no sense leaving it here when there's a use for it."

Mary felt another twinge of unease as she stood, holding the door open. What was it that her college teacher in first year humanities had warned them? *"When a man has spent his life thinking a certain way, beware when he meets a new situation. Most of the time he'll evaluate it only in terms of the things he already knows and believes."* Wasn't that what Campbell was doing, seeing the Knowlton papers in terms of what he expected, satanism and "gematria"? Suppose there could be another interpretation?

She watched as Campbell staggered out carrying the heavy Singer sewing machine. It was clear that he was completely preoccupied with the folder of papers. He heaved the machine into the trunk of the car, tucked the folder under his arm and climbed into the driver's seat. The brief nod that he

222

gave Mary suggested that he was hardly seeing her in the moonlit dusk.

"Ye'll hear from me in a few days, as soon as I've had the chance to talk this through. I'll not tell the housekeeper where I'm goin', but I'll let her know as soon as I'm comin' back."

Mary nodded. "Drive carefully. Let me know if I can do anything to help."

"Aye. If I'm to be away on Sunday I'll need help with those services. It's got to be one of the kirk elders, or have Jackie drive on up here from—"

Mary lost the rest of the sentence as the Riley's engine clattered to life. The ground mist had deepened so that now it covered everything around the house. She watched the old car disappear, cutting its way through the fog like a ship through quiet water.

"Bye." Her voice was swallowed up by the pressing fog. She turned and hurried back into the quiet house, suddenly aware again of how hungry she was feeling. Somehow when Campbell was there it hadn't been possible to think about food. Mary was thoughtful as she began to put away the groceries that were still out on the kitchen table. Was there something diabolical in Laxford? If there was, Walter Campbell's unshakable confidence in the cleansing powers of his church was a definite comfort.

Before she went to bed, Mary went around the house and carefully checked that all the doors and windows were securely fastened.

Tomorrow night. No later.

The voice was soft, a whisper against the splash and gurgle of lapping waters. The figure standing there alone bowed its head, a silent assent.

And when this is done, the papers must come here. Nowhere else. You are sure they are there now? It was a second voice, rising like the first from the quiet water. *You should have stayed longer to be sure.*

"There was danger that I would be discovered." The figure spoke quietly and a little defensively.

Then there must be a second plan. For their recovery if they are not at the house. Promptly.

"I know. I may need help."

223

There was a long silence in the echoing darkness, no sound but a muttering and bubbling that continued beneath the smoothly rippling surface.

You will have it, said the first voice at last. *The guardian will help you. But remember that he is approaching Second Change. He cannot go far from here without harm.*

"I know. I will remember it. The papers will be here two days from now."

Swear.

"I swear."

Drink.

CHAPTER 14

The sky was like a solid blanket of dirty wool drawn over a sodden bed. Wind whistled over the roof, rattling and flapping the shingles in a mordant rhythm. Beyond the house, less than a quarter of a mile from where she was sitting, the sea was like a nervous animal, all shakes and spasms, pawing at the beach with white talons. Among the heather and the hard, stone-filled ground the remorseless drizzle had begun to pool and rivulet, down from the high ground. Dorcas watched dolefully as moisture trickled steadily down the window pane, creating the watery bars to her self-imposed prison. A gust of wind wailed its banshee warning, spreading a moist film to dissolve the Scots coast before her like a—like a—

Like a what? Mary swiveled her chair and gazed blankly out of the window. Damn it, all she had to do was write about what she could see out there. The weather was horrible enough to match the harshest description. She turned off the typewriter, hugged her cardigan about her, and went across to the bedroom window. Maybe she should forget the machine and go back to the Bic pen and the fat notebook of lined green paper. At least she felt as though things were moving faster that way, at a couple of paragraphs to a page. She had to get beyond the stupid scenery and into the meat of it. There was a bit she was itching to write, the scene where Dorcas met the smugglers' chief, and he realized that she wasn't a young boy at all . . .

She went over to the head of the stairs.

"Jamie?"

225

"Yes, Mrs. Willis?" After a couple of seconds he appeared at the door of the kitchen, still holding a hefty wrench. Mary noticed again how careful he was to avoid calling her 'Mary' when Don was away. Well, that was all for the best.

"Busy?"

He grinned, but Mary fancied she could see the sadness behind his eyes. "Aye, busy enough. But no progress. Still groanin' an' moanin' through the pipes like Gran Gull's gizzard." He stood motionless, waiting to see what she wanted.

"Jamie, I'm stuck again."

"Are ye now?"

It wasn't a question—merely a neutral response.

"I am." Mary leaned on the stair rail. "Did I tell you that Dorcas Macveagh couldn't get off the boat, and she had to go with it to the Hebrides?"

"Surely. Along with Scully an' the others, right?"

"Right. Well, I was wondering about the boat they'd be on. Do you think that it would have cabins, or would it be all open like the fishing boats that come into Loch Laxford? And how would the men talk when they were at sea?"

It was the elaborate game that they'd been playing since Jeanie had been killed. Jamie MacPherson had come to the house, just as he had promised, and worked on the maintenance. But he had been like a zombie, pale and stoic. No jokes, and only a polite and guarded response if Mary or Don tried to draw him into conversation.

Don's departure for Oak Ridge had provided a new lever to pry Jamie out of his shell. If Don wasn't on hand to give advice on male behavior, then clearly Jamie would have to be a substitute, as the only male who was around when she was trying to write. (Forget the fact that Don's only contribution to plot line seemed to be "Have him screw her"—Jamie didn't know that.)

"Well now, there's a fair question." Jamie had been painting earlier, and his overalls and cap were spattered with droplets of sunshine yellow. "Ye'd probably have a small cabin on it, even for the fishing boat. And as for talk at sea . . ." He paused and gave it serious thought. "There's not much place for chat. It's the sea itself, an' easy first, an' after that ye'll hear talk of drink an' women. On a fine day it's more women than drink, an' the other way round when the weather gets bad."

226

That was his longest speech for weeks. Maybe he was coming out of the black, guarded shroud that had seemed to enfold him when he'd looked down into Jeanie's open grave. Mary racked her brains—anything would do that kept him talking.

"Is that the yellow paint that you told us about—the same color as you've got on your overalls?"

He glanced down at his arm. "Aye. I've been touching up my place with it—it's good quality, an' the price is rock bottom."

Mary advanced halfway down the stairs. "Maybe we'll change our mind about having the hallway painted with it. It's a lovely color. Could you put a brushful on a bit of board and bring it next time you're here? I'd like to see how it goes with the floor and the paneling."

"I'll be glad to." He stepped out of her way as she went through into the kitchen. "Tomorrow all right?"

"Sure, there's no rush." Mary looked back at him as she went over to the stove. No doubt about it, he was more relaxed than she had seen him for quite a while. It was worth a few minutes to keep him that way—the writing was going slowly, less than thirty pages in the last week, so what did an extra hour or two matter? (She could hear Ellie's answer to that. "Thirty pages in a week? Damn it, woman, you've written me *letters* longer than that.") No denying it—two days after the funeral she had sent a description of that dismal affair that ran ten single-spaced pages. Maybe it would encourage Ellie to come and visit, to see the locals and their strange and quirky ways. And there was plenty of local color to be collected, all over the country.

She could imagine Ellie's comment on *that,* too. "You can't write a novel running all over the place. Get your ass stuck on a chair in front of the typewriter and let your fingers do the walking. Shit, a sixty thousand word novel is *nothing.* Why, did you know . . ."—and then would come the stories of Sir Walter Scott, scribbling out four long novels a year while holding down two full-time jobs and editing nineteen volumes of Swift's works; or of John D. MacDonald, sitting down in the Florida sunshine and beating out ten thousand words a day of smooth, final-draft prose. While Mary—to borrow Ellie's phrase—was short on literary Ex-Lax.

Mary pushed those thoughts to the back of her mind.

Jamie had been working hard. He'd said he didn't want to mope around at home, and he didn't want to spend his time sitting in the pubs, either. Chatting with him while they ate lunch and trying to draw him out of his shell a bit gave her some kind of motherly feeling. It set up a different type of relationship, one she'd not had before with any man. His chattiness today felt like a personal victory, one that was worth a few pages of writing.

She turned from the stove intending to fill the kettle over at the sink. It was the first time she had glanced over to where Jamie was working. Her spirits dropped like lead. So much for the idea that Jamie was coming out of his gloom. Next to his toolbox stood a bottle of whisky, half-full and with the cap taken off it.

Mary turned back to the door. "You might just as well be going to a pub, Jamie," she said softly.

He had followed her glance and shook his head without speaking. She sensed a new hint of vulnerability behind his bright eyes, a look that brought the feeling of compassion to a lump in her throat.

"Won't you try some coffee instead?" She picked up two mugs from the table. "If you want to keep out the chill, this ought to do it as well as the whisky. Here."

He came to the table and silently accepted the mug. Mary spooned instant coffee and sugar into it, knowing that Jamie wouldn't take cream. He walked over to the open whisky bottle and added a hefty shot to the cup, looking back at her defiantly. "Any reason I shouldn't have both?" His voice had a flat, mechanical tone to it.

Mary poured boiling water into both cups before she answered. "You do what you want to. Get drunk if you feel you have to, I can't stop that. But don't you think you owe it—"

It took a big effort to cut off her next remark. She musn't try and lecture—it was his life.

"To Jeanie?" He stood there, his eyes blinking. "Ye think I owe it to Jeanie to be sober? Is that it? Don't worry, I'll not get drunk. I can hold liquor, that's not *my* problem. Why don't *you* look out—"

This time he seemed to bite back the cutting question, something about Don. Tit for tat. Mary was speechless as she watched him walk over to the table and sit down there, looking away from her. Had she been ready to say that Jamie owed it to Jeanie to behave well? Surely she meant he owed it to *himself*, not to his dead girl friend. Mary felt helpless, like a child who has been accused of doing something wrong, when she knew she hadn't but couldn't explain it. It wasn't fair.

"Jamie, I'm sorry. Listen, we've not really talked since . . . you know, since the accident. I know how you have to be feeling, I honestly do. I . . . I've lost loved ones, seen them die."

He looked up at her, and she recoiled before the intensity of his gaze. "Ye have, eh? Ye've seen them die the way that she died, with foot-long spikes shoved through her guts? Tell me that, if ye can." His voice broke. "God, I couldn't do a thing for her. Couldn't stop the pain, couldn't stop the blood. It ran down the tines, flooded out of her . . ."

Mary felt as though she was ready to vomit. The image swam before her eyes, the bloodied harrow and Jeanie's ruptured womb and torn viscera. Don had talked for a moment with the medical examiner and came back shaken and sickened. And poor Jamie had seen it, had been the one who pulled his dying girl off the harrow. No wonder he couldn't face the memory.

She looked down at her own hand as it held the coffee cup. It was shaking. Maybe what she needed herself was some of that whisky. She walked over to the open bottle and poured an inch into her own mug. As she drank, the warmth spread through her, calming the tension in the pit of her stomach. She took a deep breath.

"I'm sorry, Jamie." She swallowed another gulp of whisky-laced coffee. "I didn't mean to make you think of it again. Forgive me, if you can."

To her horror he put the cup blindly in front of him on the table, dropped his face to his open hands, and began to quiver and tremble uncontrollably.

Without pausing to consider what she was doing, she went across to him and put an arm lightly around his shoulders.

"There now, Jamie. It's all right. You'll be okay." Even as she was speaking she felt a new sensation run through her. Instead of soft despair and helpless grief, she felt flowing from him a tingling excitement, a current of emotion that passed to her like electricity.

229

It was a steady warmth moving along her veins. She wanted him.

Her emotions had leapt far ahead of her thoughts. She checked herself and pulled back her arm. Her instinct was to take him in her arms, to pull his head to her breast. She could feel how easy it would be to be sucked into the maelstrom, to take the irrevocable step with Jamie. The emotion that pulled her back was an odd one: she wanted him to feel that someone understood the problem, with a real sympathy for his loss.

He stood up abruptly and went to pick up his bottle of whisky. "It's not right, not bloody right." He began to drink straight from the bottle, but now she knew that it wasn't going to make any difference—he wasn't going to collapse, to be a weak alcoholic. His despair was a cry of rage, not of weakness. "People think they know what I lost, but they don't—none of them do. Nobody says it, but I know it. Jeanie was pregnant—she was carrying my baby in her."

He held out the bottle to her. As she took it a new image, of Jeanie and Jamie making love together, blossomed in Mary's mind. She felt as though she could stand above and watch it, as though her consciousness had been split into two parts. Her skin felt warm, stifled under the wool cardigan.

"It's tragic, I know that. You see, we have to accept . . . we can't change what things are." She was stumbling along in her words, making them up as she went, knowing that the platitudes she mouthed made no difference to the reality that was growing in the old kitchen.

Jamie was staring straight into her eyes. "I feel like going out on that hill. Digging into the grave and takin' Jeanie out, an' tellin' her she's not dead, that she *can't* be dead. She's so soft and warm, like summer itself."

A thin film of perspiration had started out on Jamie's face and neck. Mary looked at it with that same split-consciousness that she felt when she thought of Jeanie and Jamie together. Part of her pulled away, moved to a distance and told her that she belonged to Don. He was the only man she had ever cared for. The other part had no abstract thoughts. It was all senses, seeing each tiny drop of sweat on Jamie's forehead, feeling the vibration of his touch when he reached out to put one hand on her shoulder. There was a scent in the air, a growing perfume that surrounded her and was like an

230

echo of *Climax*, cloudy green droplets from the tiny hunting-horn flask.

The walls of the kitchen seemed to have receded, far away from them. Mary felt a giddy thrill run through her, a lazy knowledge that he was sinking into a deep pool of sensation.

Jamie moved his hand slowly down her arm. "Ye do understand me, don't ye? I see the kindness in your eyes."

His voice was thick, as though something had stuck in his throat. Mary nodded, unable to break contact with those blinding blue eyes that moved closer to her and never blinked.

She fought for words. "I—yes, I understand, Jamie. I do."

He sighed. He leaned forward, sat down at the table, and moved his head against her belly. She put her hand to the shock of wiry, light-brown hair, feeling him press gently against her.

"I can't imagine living without her." His deep voice set up a vibration inside her. His words were muffled, still with that rough thickening in his throat.

Mary fought back against it. The two parts of awareness were warring inside, one telling her to break away at once, the other to stay and comfort him. Her mouth was dry, and she could hear the pulse hammering in her ears. The rise and fall of her breast was something that she could look at from a distance, as she might watch the breathing of a stranger.

"I—I must go. Jamie, let me go. Don't touch me. I love Don, he's all I want."

As she was speaking her hands continued to stroke Jamie's smooth cheek. The perspiration seemed to diffuse through her skin and into her hand and arm, spreading a wave of warmth up her body. He hadn't moved against her since the moment his head had fallen forward.

"Jamie. I'm sorry . . . I must go."

It was like being blind. The kitchen was there around her, but it made no impact on her senses. Her eyes were not focusing properly, so Jamie and the table in front of her were no more than vague blurs. She began to pull herself gently away.

Mary. Don't leave me now. I'm so sad.

His words seemed to drift into her mind, vibrating through her whole body. She felt his hands move to rest on her hips.

"I *must* go now. Let me go."

Her mind was still split in two, with abstract intelligence hovering above them. But now a peaceful languor was drifting into her thoughts. It was like the last moments before sleep came, when the conscious mind surrendered pleasurably to the world of dreams.

Don't go, Mary. I need comfort. You know that you're the only person in the world who can give it to me. Stay now.

It was true. She alone could ease his sorrows. Mary felt the conviction growing within her and worried about her own inadequacy.

"Will I be enough, Jamie? I can only do so much for you. Suppose I fail you?"

You can do anything you want to, Mary. You know that. You can help me, and you are the only person who can. Help me, Mary.

Tears were overflowing from her eyes and running down her cheeks. She cradled his head against her. It felt so good to be holding him, knowing that she could bring him peace.

She felt a sudden uneasiness, like the memory of past sorrows.

"I mustn't do this. What about Don?"

He lifted his head from her chest and moved forward until his face was against hers, a pale blur through the tears.

You're not for him, Mary. You are for me. He was only a foreshadow of what will be, just as Jeanie was no more than a dream of you. I am your Don, all that we need is each other.

A rough tongue licked the salt tears from her cheeks and touched her eyes with a gentle flickering motion. The contact left a tingling on her skin. She stood there in an aching darkness as he kissed her on the lips with a soft, firm embrace. The last trace of tension was slipping away from her temples.

Relax now, Mary. Admit it to yourself. You want me as much as I want you. Stop playing games and accept that. For once in your life, do what your feelings tell you to do.

Mary felt herself breaking, like an ice floe melting in a warm southern current. She was being sucked into him through her open mouth. Each breath that she took came minutes after the one before.

Come with be, Mary. Comfort me now . . . now . . . now . . .

It was as though a trap door had opened in her head, plummeting her into the dark cellars of her body. Her legs were moving her out of the kitchen, up the dark staircase, following a pale form that seemed to float upward. She had no control over those limbs that carried her onward, into the big bedroom. The hands that removed the warm cardigan were not hers—they belonged to the new being that had been created from herself and Jamie, a four-handed, two-bodied, single-minded animal. The rough cotton blouse seemed to fight against impatient fingers that were no longer gentle. When it came off, she reveled in the feeling of strong arms against her bared skin, slick with a warm and perfumed oil.

The smell of the paint and sanded wood was gone from the bedroom. There was only Jamie's smell, his touch, a warm breathing and fiery bloom against her neck and shoulder. His lips were like cool fire roaming over her skin.

Four hands slipped off her bra, skirt, and panties, stroked her full breasts, unbuckled the belt of his jeans. His mouth moved lower, sending impossible pulses of feeling through her erect nipples.

Now, Mary. You are ready now. You know the words that move you most. Take them from me, pull them from my mind. I will see you as you want to be seen.

Words rose in Mary's mind, vibrated between them, and returned to her more intense and exciting. The touch of blankets against her back was a new caress. Unclothed, she was not cold at all in the sharp air of early November. The words came back to her.

and her veined breasts like hills—the swallow islands still on the corn's green water: and I know her dark hairs gathered round an open rose . . . her pebbles lying under the dappled sea . . .

Mary was covered with a weight of pleasure, pressing her closer on the bed. An old instinct spun her back a million years.

. . . and I will ride her thighs' white horses.

The bed sheets were twisted chaotically around them, frozen waves of white. She looked at them with half-open eyes, her head still snuggled in to his thick shoulder. Though the passion had subsided, her mind was still sluggish and relaxed. She felt as though she was submerged in Jamie and lovemaking.

Her eyes wandered idly across the sculpted muscles of his body, across to the alarm clock over on the dresser. Nine o'clock. For four hours she had been away in another world. As night fell a strong wind had arisen, sweeping in off the sea and rattling loose metal now on the roof of the shed. She had not noticed it at all, not noticed that the sun was gone and the house was dark. Who had switched on the small lamp by the bed? It must have been Jamie, while she lay dozing.

He lay quiet now. He had seemed insatiable, devouring her at the same time as he created her own hunger. He seemed to have a perfect knowledge of her every want and need, of hidden springs of feeling that she had never known existed. He had touched her, with his hands and with his tongue, until everything had become hazy and off-focus. Not until her feelings had crested, driving her to a higher level of feeling, would he enter her. Then his erect penis had begun to lift her, up and up, driving her over the top of a wall that had always been too high to climb.

Her hand moved slowly down his body, touching his smooth belly and heavy genitals. Five bouts of lovemaking had still left him swollen and engorged, long and thick against his abdomen.

He stirred at her touch.

Again?

She shivered. Her stomach muscles tightened at the thought of his embrace. He turned, moving his mouth down to her right nipple.

You are mine, Mary. Do you need me again?

She felt the glow inside her. Even through the film that had dropped over her mind, she knew that they were meant to be together. Even without the sex they would belong to each other. She shook her head.

"Tired. I'm tired. Jamie, hold me close."

Do you know what has happened, Mary?

His strong hand was gently stroking the roundness of her belly. She couldn't think properly while he did that.

"I came. It was the first time ever, Jamie."

Her nostrils were still filled with his strong, sexual smell. She had a sudden flashback to the first orgasm. It had been like a wave on the beach, full of a deceptive strength that

234

could lift her and tumble her beyond any power to resist it. She could feel the surge inside her, with the violence and the mystery of the sea. Her second orgasm had seemed like a blending with nature, an easy moving of her body in a kind of liquid dance that ebbed and flowed as Jamie drove deep inside her.

"Jamie. I came. Hold me close."

Mary, listen to me now. I have to ask you something.

She lay, silent and waiting.

Walter Campbell came here yesterday and you showed him some papers, right?

"Yes."

What were they?

"Notes." His soft hand kept her relaxed and waiting, reveling in the touch.

Patrick Knowlton's notes?

"Yes." A question floated into her mind. Why was Jamie asking about this? The thought dissolved and disappeared when he moved to nibble and tongue her breasts and shoulder.

Mary, why did you show them to Campbell?

"They were about something in Laxford. Something strange."

Mary, I want those papers. Where did you put them?

"I gave them to Campbell."

Jamie's body stiffened against her, and his hands ceased their steady work on her thighs. Mary felt a sudden uneasiness, like the prickle of pins and needles inside her head. What had been happening to her? What had he done to her?

Campbell has them now? The soft question forced itself to the center of her attention, pushed at her growing discomfort.

"Yes. I—I think—"

What will he do with them?

"Take them to his friend to ask what they mean." The reply was pulled from her, beyond the control.

When?

"I don't know. Soon. Maybe tomorrow. Jamie, stop it. Let me—"

His face came down close to hers. She saw his bright, unblinking blue eyes, destroying her identity and securing her in their depths.

Mary, I must go now.

235

"No!" The protest was wrung out of her. "Don't go."

I must go. Mary, I will come for you tomorrow. Rest now.

She lay back as his lips moved softly along her cheek and neck. The drowsy numbness was returning to her mind, carrying her away in a drifting pattern of half-thoughts and memories.

"Don't go, Jamie." The words were a faint murmur.

She felt the shock as he moved away from her. Her eyes filled with tears as their bodies broke contact, and he rolled away to stand up by the side of the bed. She watched as he pulled on his shirt and jeans, hiding the powerful muscles and the smooth white skin.

"Don't forget, Mary." His voice was gentle. "I will come back here tomorrow night. Stay in the house tomorrow. Don't talk to anyone from the village about Campbell and the papers."

He leaned forward to kiss her, and the touch was like another shock through her body.

Don't talk to anyone.

He pulled on his shoes and his jacket. Then he was gone, moving silently and swiftly down the old stairs. Mary did not hear the door open and close. She was lost in the sorrow of separation from him. Tomorrow seemed an eternity away from tonight.

She lay there dozing for nearly three hours, until well past midnight. When she finally rose, it was to go down to the bathroom and climb slowly into the big tub. The fine, silvery residue on her body seemed like her only memory of Jamie, something that she would wash off but be sad when it was gone. It dissolved away in the hot water leaving a heavy perfume on the damp air.

She slipped on a flannel nightgown and went back to the bedroom. The heaped sheets were still damp, and touched in places with the sheen of greenish-silver splotches of mucus.

Mary did not think them strange. Detached and dreamy, she quietly stripped the sheets and put clean ones in their place. When she finally lay down to sleep, Jamie filled her thoughts. Even now, the bright eyes held her to him and banished any questions. Sleep came easily, full of soft dreams and contented memory.

CHAPTER 15

Crucifix—gold, *silver*, iron, wood, brass
Mirror—*silver*, brass, coated glass, steel
Bullet—lead, bronze, *silver*
How simple can it get? Allergic reaction would explain aversion to all three. Check histo-compatibility
next trip to London. *Note for when write this*: anti-
histamines as cure for vampirism?
          —From the *Knowlton Papers*, page 29

"Hello? Operator? Look, could you try it again. There's
bound to be somebody there at this hour. I'll hold."

Don looked at his watch again while he waited impatiently
for the connection. Six here, so eleven o'clock in Laxford.
The pub would be closed, but Hamish must still be up and
about—it took an hour to get all the place cleaned up and
ready for morning. He heard the slow, broken buzz as the
phone rang at the other end. Ten rings. The operator came
back on the line.

"Still no reply. Would you like me to try later and call you
back?"

Don looked at his watch again. "No thanks, I'm going out
to dinner. I'll have another try tomorrow morning."

He paced up and down the hotel corridor as he waited for
the elevator. Four tries in four days, and he hadn't been able
to talk to Mary. Hamish swore that he'd passed on the
messages to be at the Over The Water just before opening
time in the evening, but she was never there. If Hamish
hadn't sworn also that he'd seen Mary, and she was doing

fine, Don would have dropped everything and jumped on the first plane out of New York.

The streets were fairly quiet. It was breathing time in Manhattan, the hour when the rush of commuting workers was almost over and the night life had not yet begun. Don decided that he would walk the ten blocks, and stretch his legs. He had spent eight days in airplanes, rented cars, and day-long meetings, and he was beginning to feel stuffy and out of condition.

He walked straight down Madison, opposite to the flow of traffic. After a couple of months away, New York didn't seem too bad—you could get a meal in less than two hours, which was more than anyone could say for Northern Scotland.

Ellie was already there, waiting for him on the sidewalk and looking uncertainly in all directions. She didn't spot him until he was only a block away. They walked toward each other and paused a couple of paces apart.

"Well . . ." Don reached out his hand and stepped forward. "You're looking good."

She took it in both of hers and studied him for a moment, her head tilted. "And so are you." She laughed. "Well, so much for the social amenities. What now?"

"Luchow's. I've been dreaming of a lingonberry pancake or whatever it's called for months. Let's walk a block over and get a cab."

Ellie seemed even shorter than he remembered her—a full head and more lower than he was. He looked down and saw that she was not wearing her usual high heels. She caught the look and shrugged.

"I didn't know how much walking we'd be doing. It seemed safer to wear my flatties."

Her manner was just a little too formal. It was the first time in two years that they had been together without Mary. Don thought back to his frustrating phone calls of the past few days. Surely Mary would want to know what Ellie thought of what she'd sent over?

"Did you get the manuscript all right?" he said abruptly. "I dropped it off at the Pan Am desk at Kennedy."

"Sure."

"Is it any good?"

238

She turned her head and gave him a quick look from carefully made-up dark eyes. "Don't waste any time, do you?"

"Might as well get the bad news over all at once. How is it?"

"Not bad at all. Good story, and some good bits of background. I'll have to do a few things to it with my fine Italian hand, but that's what I expected. What I want to know is, where the hell's some more of it?"

Don had paused on the corner and was busy flagging down a cab. "Hell, I gave you all I was given. What do you mean, where's more of it?"

"Mary said she'd be rolling right along with it, that she'd send me another fifty pages—that was in the letter that you brought with the package. She's been writing to me every few days, talking out what she wants to do next. But since you came over here I've not heard a peep out of her—no letter, no manuscript. I even tried to call her a couple of times, and couldn't get her. The old man at the the other end insists that she's in the village and doing fine, but I'm damned if I can get her to call me."

Don's uneasiness returned with doubled force. He gave up his attempts to capture a free cab.

"You too? Damn it, I've been trying to get her over there for four days. What do you think's wrong there? Last time we spoke she sounded fine. You haven't spoken to her at all?"

"Not directly." Ellie saw a cab with its light on and automatically waved an arm to bring it to the curb. "I did leave a message, though. I told her we'd be seeing each other and having dinner when you came back through New York."

They looked at each other carefully as Don opened the door and she climbed in. The atmosphere between them changed again, a subtle move that made them more formal and more intimate at the same time.

Don shook his head. "I know what you're thinking. I don't think that's it. Mary knows that's all over years ago."

"She knows it. Do you think she *believes* it?"

Ellie was perched warily on the edge of the cab seat, with two feet of bare space separating her from Don. She could tell that he was beginning to feel annoyed.

"Hell, she ought to. She was the one who asked me to

bring her story and give it to you. What does she want us to do, take a damned chaperone along with us?"

His manner was just a shade too indignant. Ellie wondered if it was really her fault. Maybe she had sounded a bit too enthusiastic when he had called from the airport and suggested dinner. But what was she supposed to do? Pretend she wasn't pleased at the idea of seeing him again? She pulled her shaggy coat closer around her and stared straight ahead out of the cab's front window. They drove the rest of the way downtown in silence.

Dinner helped a lot—or maybe a cocktail and red wine helped even more. By the time they had finished the entree they were no longer avoiding each other's eyes across the small table. Ellie shook her head and pulled out her cigarettes when Don suggested dessert.

"Coffee and a couple of these. Are you calling them fags yet?"

Don was studying the menu. He looked up without raising his head, wrinkling his brow. "I forgot about that—you've spend time over in England yourself."

"Just in London."

"That's the civilized part—you get up to the north of Scotland and it seems like a different country. Hell, it *is* a different country." He grinned at her. "Did I tell you what an old man in Aberdeen said to me when I said something about being in England?"

"No, but I have some idea. Tell me anyway."

"I'm not sure I ought to—it's pretty disgusting."

"That does it, now you *have* to tell me."

"Well, first I have to set the scene." Don looked around the tables near them. "Don't make it obvious, but take a look at the little man with the bald head two tables over. See him? Now, imagine that he's wearing a kilt halfway down to his ankles, and he's missing most of his teeth . . ."

By the time he had finished, Ellie's eyes were tightly closed in her efforts to suppress her laughter. She leaned across the table and patted Don's arm.

"No more of those. You'll get us thrown out of here."

"So what?" Don was leaning back in his chair, long legs stretched out under the table. "We'll go some place else. Come on, the night's young. You should plan the rest of the

240

evening and really show me what New York can offer a visitor."

Ellie sat for a few moments looking down at the tablecloth. When she finally met his gaze, her expression was an odd mixture of resignation and anticipation.

"Sure. Just let me finish my coffee, and you get the rest of that dessert over with. Then I'll show you the highlights."

"I'm sorry, Walter. It was all arranged, and then we had this emergency on the services here. Two people down with the flu." The telephone line was crackly and full of static, but the apologetic tone carried through. "I'm sorry to tell you so late."

Walter Campbell looked down at the black receiver in his hand and grimaced his disappointment. Hamish Macveagh was standing over by the bar, pretending to be polishing glasses but obviously listening to Campbell's end of the conversation.

He leaned closer to the mouthpiece. "Never mind, Jackie. Don't worry about it at all—it was my fault for askin' ye to come here on short notice. I'll manage."

"Ye can find somebody else?"

"Ah, sure I can." (But where?) "Don't give it another thought. Thanks for tryin' an' give my best to Maureen."

Macveagh was watching as he hung up the receiver. "Problems, Reverend?"

"Ah, it's nothin'. I was thinkin' I had Jack Hastie comin' in for the services tomorrow, an' now he's got problems of his own."

"So ye'll not be goin' on holiday?"

"Sure I will—but maybe not tomorrow. It can wait a day if it has to. Could I be makin' one more call here? I'll pay for it, ye know that."

"Aye, of course ye can."

Campbell waited for a few seconds, while Hamish went on polishing the glasses. "If ye don't mind, Hamish, this one's a wee bit private."

"Oh, aye?" Hamish's sharp nose seemed to sniff the air. "Well, I'll be off, then. Let me know when you're done, eh?" He gave a look around as he reached the door, as though hoping to be invited to stay, then went out. Campbell waited for a few seconds before he placed the call through the Inverness exchange and was connected with the number in Cambridge. As it was ringing he stepped quickly to the door and confirmed that Hamish had gone out of earshot.

" 'Lo?" The voice on the other end sounded as though the speaker was just waking up.

"Mr. Duncan?"

"Yes?"

"This is Walter Campbell, up in Laxford. I'm sorry, but I won't be able to come on down to Cambridge until Monday. I have to stay here tomorrow."

"Well, bugger it." Duncan didn't sound particularly worried by the news. "I'm looking forward to seeing your stuff. But you'll be down here Monday, will you?"

"Monday or Tuesday, I'll have to see how busy I am tomorrow."

"Well, I'll be here." Toby Duncan laughed cheerfully. "Pity about tomorrow, I'd have had all day free. Look here, Tuesday's a lot better than Monday. I've got two lectures to give on medical primitivism. All rot, you understand, but that's what I'm here for."

"I'll come on Tuesday."

"Great. I'll arrange a guest room for you here at Johns. Know how to get to the college, do you? Never mind that," he went on before Campbell could answer, "Give me a tinkle when you get to the station, and I'll zip on down there and pick you up. Tuesday, then?"

"I'll be there."

"Bye, then."

Campbell was left holding a dead phone. He shook his head as he hung it back on the wall. If Toby Duncan hadn't enjoyed an international reputation, Campbell would have been more than ready to cancel the trip to Cambridge. After three conversations, Duncan still sounded as though he was permanently intoxicated.

He left a fifty-penny piece on the bar counter and left without waiting for Hamish to come back. The evening outside was another miserable one, steady gray rain and random gusts of wind. He bent his head and splashed rapidly through the puddles on the cobbled street, too preoccupied to take much notice of the damp ring that grew around the bottom of his trousers.

"Here, steady now." An arm reached out to grab his shoulder and avoid a head-on collision. He skidded on the pavement and almost fell. The firm grip on his shoulder kept him upright.

"Oh, it's you, Mr. Campbell," said a very English voice. He found he was staring up into Roger Wilson's cheerful face. "You ought to watch your step there—I could have poked your eye out with the umbrella if I'd been a bit slower."

They moved closer to the wall of the inn, where the overhanging eaves shielded them from the rain. Roger Wilson looked closely at Campbell's white face.

"Here, are you all right? You're shivering."

"It's nothing." Campbell looked around him. From the moment that he had decided to go down to Cambridge he had felt a growing uneasiness, a steady movement of cold through all his veins. His bag was packed, his ticket bought, and in the morning he would have been on his way. Jack's absence would change all that, he'd have to stay here days longer. He thought back to the packet of papers in their safe hiding place. The more he had looked at them, the more he felt their significance. Dear God, to be held here when all was ready to leave, with the housekeeper alerted to his absence in Cambridge (but not to tell anyone else) and his secret knowledge bubbling within him like a heated cauldron. He lifted his head and looked up at Roger's concerned face. "I'll be all right. I may have a bit of a chill, that's all."

"It's this damned changeable weather." Roger looked at the minister's dark threadbare clothes and thin rain slicker. "You need oilskins to keep it out. I'll be away from it for a few days, thank heaven. Here, you're still shivering." He hesitated. "I know you don't drink, but come into the Over The Water and have a cup of hot tea. I'm not being nosy, but honestly you don't look too good."

"Bit of a chill." Campbell allowed himself to be led back into the inn, to the safety and the warmth. They moved together to the fireside. It was still too early for the regulars to be coming in for their beer, and they had the room to themselves.

Campbell held his cold hands out to the flames. The finger ends were almost white in the ruddy light. "D'ye say ye'll be leavin' Laxford, then?"

"Oh, only for a few days." Roger loosened his overcoat.

243

"I'm going down south for the weekend, to watch the Bumps."

"Oh, aye?" Campbell looked at him with polite incomprehension. "The bumps?"

"On the Cam." Roger caught the other man's expression. "It's like the boat race, but you have to catch up with a boat that starts off in front of you. This is just a practice, but I told them I'd help coach."

Campbell was nodding, his head leaned forward. "Well, I hope ye'll enjoy that. Ye'll be down in London, then?"

"Not London. On the Cam—I'll be in Cambridge, back at my old college."

Roger was surprised by the minister's reaction. He lifted his head and looked at Roger open-mouthed. There was a sudden light of triumph in his eyes, and he seemed to be muttering "O ye of little faith" under his breath. "Mr. Wilson, when are you leaving?"

"Early in the morning. I'll get a helicopter ride down to London, then on up to Cambridge by train early tomorrow afternoon. Do you know Cambridge at all?"

Campbell ignored the question. The color had crept back into his cheeks, and the shivering had stopped. "Mr. Wilson, do ye know Toby Duncan? He's down there in Cambridge."

"Duncan?" Roger shrugged. "Doesn't ring a bell. Do you know which college?"

"St. Johns."

"No, I'm still drawing a blank. I went to Peterhouse, so I wouldn't know him unless he was there the same time as I was. He's a friend of yours?"

"Not exactly." Walter Campbell hesitated and looked at the red heart of the fire. Was it worth the risk? To get the papers safely away from Laxford, he would have to entrust them to the hands of a comparative stranger. But remember, it was a stranger to Laxford, too, not someone who would be part of the village and its ways. The big danger to the papers was surely here, where they could be stolen—and this was a God-sent opportunity. He took in a long breath.

"Mr. Wilson, I promised to get some papers down to Cambridge, down to Professor Duncan. He told me on the phone that he'd like to look at them as soon as I can get them there." (Almost the truth, and surely this justified a half-lie.)

244

"I'm wondering, do ye suppose there's any chance—any way that ye might . . ."

"Take them on down with me? Good Lord, man, that's nothing to ask me. I'll be glad to." Roger had rung the bell over on the bar, but no one had come. Now it didn't seem so important. Campbell's color was good, and there was no sign of the tremors that had been shaking him a few minutes earlier. "I'll take 'em, that's easy to do. But what's in 'em? Not valuable, are they, so they ought to be insured or something?"

"No need to think of insuring them—but they are very valuable." Campbell looked around him, tempted to tell Roger much more. The other man's calm made him seem like a strong ally. "Mr. Wilson, I don't want to give you details, not now, but I'll assure ye that those papers are important." He dropped his voice to a whisper. "Ye remember the death of a Mr. Knowlton, a man who worked for your company a couple of years back? Well, I'll not be surprised if these papers turn out to be connected with his death. Now, will ye take good care of them? An' I promise ye, inside a few days ye'll have the full explanation from me."

He halted as Hamish Macveagh appeared in the doorway from the back of the inn. "Ye're back, Reverend. I thought you were gone for the evening. An' will we be seein' Mr. Hastie tomorrow, then?"

Campbell gave him a reproving look. So there was clear evidence of eavesdropping! "Maybe ye will, an' maybe ye won't. Come by the kirk tomorrow, an' see for yersel'." He turned to Roger. "Here, Mr. Wilson, I'll be off on my way again. Ye'll come on by for the package, then, or d'ye want me to drop it by for ye?"

"I'll get it." Roger nodded to Hamish. "I'd like a pint of best bitter. We were going to ask for tea, but if the minister is leaving I'll change that." He turned to Campbell. "Best for me if I come and get it. In a couple of hours time, or if I get tied up on the phone with Lord Jericho I'll make it first thing in the morning. How early can I come round?"

"Anytime after five will be all right. If that's early enough for ye?"

Roger shuddered. "I *think* that ought to do it. You won't stay and have a quick drink?—it's only beer."

"Thank you, but no." Campbell bit back the words of reproof that came so easily. (Roger Wilson would be going on God's work, be thankful for that—*thou shalt not muzzle the ox when he treadeth out the corn.*) "Good night, then, or maybe I'll be seein' ye a bit later on."

"Maybe."

"Let me go on to the other room and use the phone again. I'll tell Professor Duncan to expect ye, and I'll be on down there myself in a few days." He paused a moment longer at the door. "Mr. Wilson . . . I'd much appreciate it if ye'd hold this to yerself for a while. It's important to me, an' I think it's important to this village."

"I won't say a word." Roger turned back to the fire as Hamish hurried in, holding a full tankard with foam streaming down the sides of it. Campbell hovered in the doorway for a moment as though wanting to add another remark, then finally went on through to the other bar.

When he emerged from the inn the air no longer seemed at all cold. He walked with his head high, savoring the night air on his face, and instead of going home went straight on to the kirk. First he checked beneath the lectern (the package was still safely there), then he went to kneel in the sanctuary. He felt a strong confidence that the worst was over. No matter if there was devil's work in the village, God's mercy would provide, as it always provided. There was no force of evil that could resist the power of the Cross. As minister of the parish, God's workman here, he could defeat any evil, banish it from the earth.

He stayed on his knees on the hard floor for over an hour, so that when he finally stood up, his legs were cramped and stiff. Instead of going out by the small inset door at the front of the church, he headed through the sanctuary to the side door. It was a shorter route to the house, but there was no light here away from the village. The rain had come on hard again. He shone his electric flashlight through the heavy drops, letting its cone of light flicker across the wet, stony hillside. The spatter of spreading droplets made flashes of reflected light across the ground, patterns that seemed to connect themselves by bright, instantaneous lines.

He thought again of the diagrams that Knowlton had drawn. Duncan would know how to read them, how to interpret the Devil-speak that lay behind them. By the time he reached Cambridge, perhaps the whole cryptic pattern would be laid open. And then? Then he would face another difficult

246

decision. The cleansing of Laxford, with all its real or imagined demons, would be his problem to solve—Toby Duncan could not do that for him.

He crested the top of the hill and walked on thoughtfully to the front garden of the stone house. Bigger than the crofters' cottages, it was still far from a luxury home—but it was more than enough for his needs; a man who wished to serve God should not ask for material possessions. He ducked in under the shallow porch and fumbled with wet hands for his keys. The patter of drops dimmed to a faint thrum as he opened the front door and slipped inside. He sighed as he took off his slicker and hung it on the hall coat rack. His case was still standing there, but now he wouldn't be able to make the trip tomorrow. He pushed his wet hair back from his forehead. His knees still ached from kneeling in the church, and the damp was bringing twinges of arthritis in his shoulders and back.

The wooden sign in the hall caught his eye and he straightened up. *Gird thy loins in the armor of God!* He would do it. All he needed now was the sword of knowledge, and soon he would have that from Toby Duncan.

Lord. How long had he been dreaming in the church? Suppose that Roger Wilson had already been to the house, and gone away again? He should have come home here at once—there was time for the church after Wilson left.

A slight noise coming from the living room reassured him a little. There were damp footprints leading in there—Roger Wilson had at least had the sense to come in out of the rain to wait, and not stood about out there in the cold.

He went across to the door and opened it. "Sorry, Mr. Wilson. I wan't thinking what I was doing, and I've been over in the kirk and . . ."

He halted. There was no light in the room, but he could still hear movements, and feel the breeze from an open window. Furniture scuffed against the stone floor as it was slightly moved.

Campbell felt for his flashlight. It was back on the coat rack.

"Who's there?"

No answer. The room was filled with a strong smell, a musky, animal scent. The room was silent now but for his rapid breathing. He backed away from the door.

"Mr. Wilson? Is that—? Who is in there?"

He knew it was not Roger Wilson. His eyes were growing used to the darkness, and he could make out two dim forms, one hulking over the desk in the corner and the other at the chest of drawers. There was a white spill of papers over on the floor.

No doubt about it. Whoever this was—*whatever* this was—they were seeking Knowlton's papers.

"Take him." The words were slurred, thickened in the throat to where they were scarcely intelligible. Campbell stood for a moment, paralyzed with fear, then turned and ran blindly for the door. There was a noise behind him, a slither of feet across the wooden floor.

He crashed into the coat rack and fumbled for a second at the shelf, trying to grab the flashlight with fingers that would not respond. The sliding feet were only a step away from him. With a groan of fear and despair he flung the door wide and ran headlong out into the darkness.

Where could he run to? He turned first up the hill, then down it, his feet sliding on the slick surface of mud and turf. As his eyes went back and forth he saw the shadow of the steeple, a darker black against the rain-filled sky.

The kirk. He would be safe there, protected against whatever pursued him.

He thought of the sanctuary, a haven of God's creation. The rain pasted his hair down as he skidded back up the hill. The wind drove through his thin clothes, suddenly much stronger. It felt as though the elements themselves were conspiring to slow his progress. In a few moments his clothes were soaked and tight against his body.

Behind him, the door to the house crashed wide open, hitting hard against the stone wall.

He tried to run faster, crouching close to the ground. For the first time as he reached the crest of the hill he felt the cold seeping through him. It added to the feeling of his wet clothes, constricting his movements and binding his limbs to a labored trot.

His chest was hurting, stabbing him with every breath. The random thought came to his mind—suppose that he were to have a heart attack, now, on the cold hillside? There would be no medical care, no rush to the hospital. Only the creatures behind him, and whatever attention he could expect

248

from them. He could imagine clawed hands on his shoulders, the Devil's clutch reaching inside his chest and tearing out his heart each time he took another breath.

The church was closer. It reared above him. He lifted his gaze from the ground to angle toward the side door, then turned to look behind him.

That was a mistake. He fell full length along the sodden ground as his leather-soled shoe hit a slick patch of stone. He landed heavily, biting his tongue. That pain masked the feelings in his left ankle until he tried to get back to his feet. He crouched on all fours, gasping at the shooting agony that ran suddenly through him from the twisted ankle. There was the unmistakable taste of blood in his mouth from his bitten tongue.

He turned his head. The hillside behind him seemed to be silent and deserted, but he could not be sure through the darkness and heavy rain.

Keep moving He began to scramble forward, hobbling to favor the injured ankle. After a few steps it became a little easier, the pain shrinking until it was no worse than that in his aching chest.

The church was before him, looming over him. He felt a new hope and strength. As he reached the side door he looked again behind him and thought he could see two pale blurs near the top of the hill. Then he was fumbling with the door handle, turning and pulling. It would not move. He had locked it, as always, when he left the church.

The key. Where was the key?

He fumbled and tore at his pockets, imagining again that his pursuers were close behind. The key ring that he pulled from his left jacket pocket carried half a dozen keys of all sizes. He couldn't see them, only feel at each and try to tell which one he wanted.

He selected one and tried it on the padlock. It would not fit.

The sound of feet, flapping and squeaking across the sodden ground, was closing behind him. He dared not look round. Keys jingled on the ring in his shaking hand. This would be his last chance . . .

He held a key in numbed fingers, thrusting it into the padlock and turning desperately. It moved easily, opening the padlock with a loud click of metal. Pulling the key from the lock, he yanked open the door and slipped through. There was the usual screech from the unoiled hinges, loud enough to hear from anywhere on the hillside.

Walter Campbell pulled the door closed and slipped the double bolt into position.

Sanctuary!

The door was heavy oak, poorly fitting but sturdy. He leaned against it for a moment, then limped forward to rest on the wooden bench that lay along the wall. He knew the inside of the church so well that the faint light from the lamp high in the nave was unnecessary.

There was a noise at the side door, a shaking of the door handle and a rattle of the frame. He watched in fascination as the bolts moved back and forward in their settings, resisting the pull from outside. They held firm.

He took a step forward, searching his mind for the words of exorcism. They were never used in the Presbyterian faith, but he had studied them, long ago, when he had first considered a life with the ministry. What was it . . .

The bottom of the door had a gap more than half an inch wide near the jamb. For months he had intended to ask Jamie MacPherson to come in and add a strip to it, to keep out the persistent drafts. Now he watched in horror as pale fingers curled in through the gap, taking a firm hold on the side of the door. They tightened and pulled, and the gap grew wider, to permit a second hand to join the first.

There was a squeal of twisting metal. Some great force was pulling the door outward, steadily drawing the bolts from their seats in the dark oak. He could see the screws being pulled from the wood.

Adrenalin pumped through him, overriding his aches and pains. He moved quickly forward and grasped the door handle, pulling inward as hard as he could. For a moment the door closed tighter again, then the terrible power of those white hands asserted itself. The door was open an inch, then two inches. The bolts screeched and moved. He pulled harder at the handle.

Another hand moved through the gap between the door and the jamb and groped toward him. He shuddered as it moved to touch his cheek, questing like a blind worm. The touch was cold, a smooth oiliness against his skin. The fingers were thick and hairless, and there was a deformity to their

250

clubbed ends. The pungent aroma that he had noticed in the house filled his nostrils.

He gasped in horror and recoiled from the touch.

The door swung open with a last squeak of strained metal. He groaned and turned to move back through the sanctuary, toward the protection of the center of the kirk.

As he reached it and sank to his knees, the door behind him crashed shut with a sound that reverberated through the interior of the church. They were inside! He had prayed that they could not enter this holy place, that the sanctity would be enough to keep out any evil forces.

Crouching by the lectern, feeling the smooth cloth drape under his hand, he grew calmer. He had prayed that the cup might pass from him, but that was not the Lord's will. If these devils were banished, it would be by his actions, by the faith of a man who was the guardian of this church. He must take the initiative.

Shivering with a new resolve, he fumbled for the simple crucifix that he kept by the pulpit. He had to operate by feel alone. For the seond time that night, he wished that the Presbyterian church permitted some of the trappings of the Catholics. Candles and an altar would give him added strength, would help to defeat any creatures spawned from the darkness.

Footsteps, soft and steady, padded through the sanctuary and approached the pulpit. He raised the crucifix in his right hand, the silver surface gleaming faintly in the dim light. The heavy metallic bulk beneath his hand felt comforting, like the sword of knowledge that he had wished for earlier. He held it forward.

"In the same of Jesus Christ Our Lord." His voice sounded cracked and uncertain through the empty, echoing church. "I command you to leave this House of God."

He could see them now, two naked male forms. As he spoke and thrust the crucifix toward them, the one closer to him grunted and retreated a pace. The pungent, musky odor of them filled Campbell's nostrils as he stepped forward. His voice took on new strength and confidence.

"In the name of the Father, the Son, and the Holy Ghost, I bid you be gone from here."

He took another step toward them. The nearer creature recoiled again, but the one behind stood its ground.

"The papers." Its voice was a thick croak, hard to understand. *"Where are Knowlton's papers?"*

It took another pace toward him, ignoring the cross between them. Campbell felt a surge of triumph. He had been right. Knowlton had uncovered the truth about the devils that had been raised in Laxford, and for that he had paid with his life. Well, if the cup would not pass from his hand, he too would be prepared to pay with his own life to let the truth be known about the village. His personal safety was nothing, what mattered was the defeat of evil.

He took another step forward and brandished the crucifix in the creature's face. It recoiled, avoiding its touch. *They were affected by the power of the Cross.*

He thrust it forward further.

"In nomine Patris, exorciso te . . ." The unfamiliar Latin words came garbled over his swollen tongue. *"Pello te.* Leave this holy place."

The creature in front of him growled and smashed the cross from his grasp. It spun away into the shadows, slid toward the lines of pews. While Campbell stood gaping, the nearer creature lunged toward him, gripping his old jacket with its powerful fingers.

He jerked backward, overbalancing and feeling the thin cloth of his coat tear as he fell. Instead of trying to stand up, he rolled under the line of pews, feeling unsuccessfully for the crucifix.

This was wrong. All wrong. The crucifix had slowed them, but it had not stopped them. And they seemed to be immune to exorcism, immune to the power that ruled within this church. It must be that his own faith was not strong enough, that doubt still lingered within him. He was the vessel that held God's power, and if he had faith, that power was irresistible.

He began to pull himself along the line of pews, back through the nave toward the big doors at the front of the church. They were following him, but clumsily, unfamiliar with the church interior.

The baptistery was at the far end of the nave, set off from the rest of the church by a low railing. Inside it, the baptismal font was old and ornate, a relic of a time when infant baptism was done by total immersion of the child. The carved bowl of gray stone was deep, with an embossed lid of heavy wood.

He moved to it, praying that it was still unlocked. Sometimes Mrs. Paisley came in after the ceremony, and checked all the locks for him. He hadn't seen her today or yesterday, and he had opened the baptistery then . . .

He lifted the lid with a tremendous feeling of relief. His pursuers were more than halfway along the nave, moving cautiously but remorselessly toward him. He plunged his hand deep into the basin of the font. The water was cool and comforting to his hands. He bent his head and said a brief prayer for strength and guidance, then straightened his shoulders and stood waiting for them. When the nearer of the creatures was close enough to be reaching out for him, he scooped a double handful of holy water and flung it straight into its face.

It raised its hands to its eyes, coughing and growling, and retreated a step.

God's will be done! It was working.

"In the name of the Father and of the Son and of the Holy Spirit, I command you to leave this place, to be gone to that foul hell—"

The creature shook its head, lunged forward and caught him in its powerful grip. He felt himself lifted off his feet and moved to within inches of its staring eyes.

"Where are the papers?" The fetid smell from the thick-lipped mouth made Campbell gag, wriggling in the strong, oozy grip.

"Satan, exorciso te!" he cried out in a cracking voice.

His bones were breaking, his upper arms screaming in pain from the creature's strength.

"Speak. The papers. Where did you put them?" He felt himself being lifted, turned in the air. With some dark corner of his mind, he prepared himself to resist any torture that they would inflict on him. Even if they broke his bones, he could not speak. Then he felt that resolve die within him, as he was plunged headfirst into the baptismal font. The old, impossible terror enveloped him as the cold water closed around him and filled his eyes and ears.

He writhed and kicked, fighting against the hands that held him under. Water was in his mouth, filling his lungs. His mind began to reel and spin, waves of darkness dimming the horror and the fear.

He was still holding a thread of consciousness when he was lifted above the surface, out to the same world of pain. He coughed and gasped the water from his windpipe, while they turned him in the air and held him retching until he was breathing again. Water streamed down his face and dripped from his soaked hair.

He was looking into those same bright eyes, hard as sapphires.

"Speak. Where did you put the papers?"

He shook his head feebly. "I don't know what you mean." He was lifted again, turned in the air so that his head was inches from the water in the font. "No, in God's name, don't. I don't know what you want. I can't help you."

"Think. Think hard." He scarcely heard the slurred words as his head was plunged back under. This time he managed to hold his breath as water rushed into his ears and eyes. Sounds beneath the surface were muted, as though in a tomb. He prayed, trying to force his mind to rid itself of the dark, consuming cloud of terror. Pain grew in his chest, and he could hear his own pulse inside his head, beating louder and louder.

Even as the waves of darkness came rolling in again, he held his breath. The agony in his lungs was better than the unendurable cold clutch of water. The idea that grew deep in his mind had to be fought away. If he told them, they would end his torture, release him as the price for his secrecy. . . . *Tell them. Tell them.* The pulse in his head was speaking the words, louder and louder, as his consciousness began to fade. *Tell them! Tell them!*

He did not feel them lifting him out again. All he knew was the welcome fire of a new breath, and spots of light and dark swimming in front of his eyes. The bone-crushing grip had turned him upright again, was shaking him to new consciousness.

"The papers?"

He shook his head weakly, aware of the traitorous thought that still ran in his mind. The building spun about him as he was turned again in the air, moved forward to the terrible dark surface.

"No!" The words burst out of his mouth, beyond his control. "No more. I'll tell you. Let me go and I'll tell you."

The hands held him poised an inch above the surface. He tasted blood again in his mouth. *Father, forgive me. It is more than I can bear. God, give me new strength to fight.*

"Where are the papers?"

"Under the lectern." The words burst out from his mouth as a gabble of sound. "At the end of the church. Under the lectern."

He felt as though he were fainting. The inverted image of one of the creatures was padding off along the nave, down toward the pulpit. Its movement was smooth and steady, somehow irresistible. He tried to pray as it disappeared from sight, then finally came back into view gripping the bundle of papers. The misshapen head nodded to the one who was holding him.

"You have them now. Let me go." Campbell's voice was no more than a whisper. Suddenly he realized that it was not over, that the cup would not pass. His head was moving down again, into the infinite dark water. This time he had not taken a deep breath. The grip that held him was unbreakable, as though he were trapped within solid rock. There would be no escape.

His screams bubbled past his ears. Walter Campbell learned the road to Calvary.

All day long Mary had felt an unnatural lassitude. The house needed work, and she was running low on milk and butter, but she could not summon the energy to get fully dressed and go down to the village. She had spent the day in a dream, pulling on a thick skirt and warm sweater when she felt cold, eating randomly when she felt hungry.

She had taken no notice of the time. Hamish had called to give her another message from Don, asking her to be at the Over The Water for his call, but somehow it had not felt important. She stood in front of the bathroom mirror, idly noting the Venus collar of red contusions around her neck. Jamie's love bites. The thought made her feel warm inside.

She went to bed soon after dark, to fall into a waiting half-sleep that lasted for several hours. It was close to midnight when she heard a soft footstep on the stairs. A few moments later he slipped into bed beside her. Even before he touched her his exciting smell was enveloping her, rousing her.

She sighed as he nuzzled again at her neck.

"You're so late." Her voice was a sleepy murmur. "I was afraid that you might not come."

I had business to attend to.

"I was afraid that you might not come. I worried that you might have something more important."

She let her hands wander down his smooth body. Already he was tremendously aroused, throbbing powerfully to her touch.

Never fear that. I will always come to you. There is nothing in the world more important than this.

He seemed to be laughing inside her mind. She felt her skin becoming slick with his oils.

"Will you stay with me tonight?"

I will stay. But we must sleep after this. The night has been a full one already for me. Come, my Mary. Open to me.

He had moved on top of her and was steadily penetrating her eager body. Already the tide was rising, beginning to lift her and shake her. After a few exquisite minutes Mary relaxed completely and allowed herself to be carried away on it. Wherever Jamie wished to take her, she had to go.

CHAPTER 16

How do we get a handle on the first Selkie branch point? If separation of the lines was near Laxford, and not somewhere else in the country, then first records seem to appear about A.D. 800. Check dates of carvings on Handa Island? Maybe thousand-plus years old. Note: old drawings look same as the recent ones, so basic form has been steady for many generations—suggests true species. Q. How can it be new species, if breeds self-true with human female? Re-define species? Two male forms for single female?
—From the *Knowlton Papers*, page 37

Don finished sorting the reports into three piles, then picked up the middle heap. "This is it. It should have everything that affects what we're trying to do."

"That's all?" Lord Jericho looked quizzically at the other two piles. "There's some big bits of stuff in them. What's the rest of it?"

"Regulations—U.S. Government regulations. I picked them up at Oak Ridge so somebody over here could compare notes." Don shrugged. "It's not my line at all, you know that, but I thought we ought to know how permits and impact statements look, here and in the States. There seems to be a tendency for the countries to follow each other's leads."

"Mebbe you're right. Aye, I s'pose that's sound thinking." Jericho rubbed thoughtfully at the monk's border of gray hair around his bald head. "But the way I see it, in another few years none of us will be allowed to build a damn thing—we'll be up to our arses in paperwork. Anyway, I'll have Bill Matthews look them over and see if we ought to be bothered. What else did you see that we ought to be worrying about?"

Don thought for a moment and then shook his head. "I can't think of anything else, not at the moment. I'll be doing a trip report, of course, and I've got pretty good notes."

"Right. Keep it short. Nobody reads those bloody trip reports anyway—and if anything important happens, people always come out with it the minute they step off the plane." He peered at Don's bloodshot eyes. "You look pretty knackered. There's a bunk back there, and we won't be picking Roger Wilson up for another couple of hours. Why not take a nap now?—you'll want to be awake when Roger tells us what Petherton and the buggers at the Ministry are asking for on special building codes. Rest while you can—sleep anytime and anywhere you can."

Don shrugged. He gathered up his papers, stuffed them quickly back into his case, and went to the rear of the helicopter cabin. The bunk was narrow, and there was a good deal of vibration. But it felt good just to close his eyes for a while. He was certainly ready for a rest now. Jericho had sucked him dry of information—fifteen minutes briefing him felt like a day's work. There was no chance to make a point twice, and no need to.

It had been two days since Don had managed any real sleep. Dozing off on the plane over from New York, interrupted every half hour by people moving in and out of the seat row, he had arrived in London feeling more tired than when he started the flight. But now he felt past the point where he could sleep. He seemed to have moved into the uncomfortable hyper-state, too tired to relax and nod off.

He closed his eyes for a moment, wondering what time it was now. Then he opened them again because Lord Jericho was standing by the bunk and shaking him gently awake.

But it was Roger Wilson, not Jericho.

Don squeezed his eyes shut for a moment, opened them again, and sat up. The inside of his mouth tasted coated and foul.

"Feel all right?"

Don shrugged and sat up reluctantly. His jaw was aching, and there was a dull pain across his forehead. "Not too bad."

258

He was surprised to find that they were still airborne. "How the devil did you get on board?"

"The usual. Walked on, when you landed at Cambridge." Roger grinned. "That was a couple of hours ago. Joshua said we ought to let you sleep for a while. He says you look shagged out. If he's right, here's sympathy and congratulations. We woke you up because we ought to talk some more, before we get to Laxford. Here," Roger passed him a cold glass. "I know how you feel. Try this. Rose's lime juice, water, and ice. It's not quite as good as fresh orange juice for a pick-me-up, but it's the best that we've got on board."

Don swilled the tart drink around his mouth for a second before he swallowed it. He stood up.

"I'm ready." He moved unsteadily past the partition and sat down at the little folding table, where Lord Jericho was quietly marking off stock prices in a copy of the *Guardian*. He looked up as Don sat down and slipped the newspaper into a rack on the cabin wall.

"Feel a bit more lively now? Right. I don't think you need to go over what you told me—you and Roger can beat that to death after you get to Laxford. But I'd like your reaction on what the Ministry's doing here. Honestly, I sometimes think they don't want this station at all, the way they've been fiddle-farting around with the specs on it. Roger, why don't you fill Don in on Petherton's latest?"

Roger nodded, still standing and leaning back on the cabin wall, head bent forward. As he spoke, Don tried to force his attention to follow every word. It wasn't easy. Either Roger was having his own troubles organizing his thoughts, or Don's brain was like a piece of fluffy cotton. He gritted his teeth together and struggled to concentrate.

"How's it sounding to you, Don?" said Jericho. He had let Roger speak for nearly ten minutes before interrupting—close to a record.

"I have to agree with Roger." Don looked thoughtfully out of the side window, where the Grampians were swelling beneath them as a steadily rising succession of bare peaks and valleys. "They're giving us unnecessary static. We were supposed to have had full answers to all those questions months ago—now they're starting again. It looks as though they want to slow us down with a lot of fake report requirements. It could cost us."

259

"I agree with both of you." Jericho sounded grim. "I'd better see what I might be able to do a bit higher up. If somebody's trying to bugger about with the schedule, I can tell you one thing—it's not something that the Minister approves of. I had dinner with old Fergie last week, and me and him agree on this all the way. We want this one to be a showcase for how to do it right."

Don looked at him questioningly. "If he's for us, who'd try and throw a curve at us?"

"Petherton." Jericho sniffed. "Him and his bloody band of bird watchers, that's who. It's no good telling him that all the right facts are already in the file; he still thinks we've not done our homework right on flows and temperatures. Daft bugger. Let me have a go at this one."

He banged his hand down hard on the table. "Right, change of subject. You've been away longer than we expected, Don—it was the Ministry's idea that you ought to drop in on Brookhaven as well, not ours. But now Roger has Jenks and his lot breathing down his neck for the second phase of the design, and Morry's group in Manchester are asking me for some kind of implementation timetable for the whole thing. I can hold 'em off for a few days, while you get your feet back on the ground here—but you're going to have a busy week or two. Any problems with that?"

"I'm looking forward to it."

It sounded phoney. Don listened to his own words, and suddenly realized that there was nothing fake about them at all. He was getting a big kick out of the bustle and the feeling of action. *Anything* was better than a project that went too slow.

Jericho had watched him and listened to him carefully through Roger's briefing. Now he nodded at Don approvingly and turned back to Roger.

"One other thing while we have a few minutes. What's all this about the bloody vicar up in Laxford? I couldn't make head nor tail of it. I had Matson check on the phone call you made, and he says there's no trouble that he can find out about. What's been happening?"

Roger shrugged and sat down at the table. "Wish I knew. I met Campbell on Saturday night, in Laxford, and he asked me if I'd take a packet of papers with me down to Cambridge—*important* papers, he said. I went round there on

260

Sunday morning to pick them up and he'd gone. No sign of him—taken his case, too, according to his housekeeper. So I thought when I left Laxford that he'd changed his mind and taken the papers down to Cambridge himself."

"He must have. That's what Matson found when he checked the village—Campbell had gone. Here, I'll get Matson to come back here for a couple of minutes, and you can ask him about it for yourself."

Don looked dubiously at Jericho's back as he went forward to the front of the helicopter. "Does he have a license to fly this thing?"

"He *says* he does—and he owns it, you know." Roger watched as Jericho slipped into the copilot's seat and Matson moved back to join them at the table. "Got it on autopilot up there, have you?"

"Naw. Not for a helicopter. I've got old Kamikaze flying it for me." Matson flopped down at the table and pulled a packet of State Express out of his jacket pocket. "What's up then?"

"Probably nothing." Roger was still looking puzzled. "You say that Campbell left Laxford, right, and hasn't been back? Well, I looked up Duncan yesterday in St. Johns College, and he's not seen or heard of Campbell since Saturday. Did you happen to find out who took the church services in Laxford on Sunday? Was it Campbell?"

"Naw. He'd gone, buggered off down south elsewhere. The Elders had to fill in for him in church. They was madder than hell about it." Matson lit his cigarette and pulled a long drag deep into his lungs. "So he was supposed to go up to Cambridge, was he?"

"He was expected there. Does anybody in Laxford seem to know where he went?"

"No ideas I could find out about. Sly old bugger, eh? Probably off for a dirty weekend, right? Here—" Matson looked forward as the helicopter suddenly yawed and lurched off the vertical. "I'd better get back up front and see if the boss has us headed for Norway yet." He stubbed out his cigarette on the metal table top and stuck the long unsmoked stub back into the packet. "You wait and see, we'll find out all about old Campbell in a while—just watch the *News Of The World*— 'Vicar denies grave charge,' it'll all be there."

He stood up. "We'll be in Laxford in ten minutes. One

261

other thing about Campbell. His car has gone as well. That's why the housekeeper is convinced that he left to go down south—he needed his car to get to the train station. But I called the station, and his car's not there now. Maybe he decided to drive it all the way?"

"I don't get all this, Roger." Don watched as Matson moved back to the pilot's seat. He apparently began arguing at once with Lord Jericho over the control settings. "What's the big deal about where Campbell went to? You've never shown much interest in the movements of the Scottish clergy before."

"I'm not interested in *Campbell*—he can be in Brighton with a dozen Chelsea Pensioners for all I care. It's the *papers* I'm interested in, the ones that I was supposed to take to Cambridge."

"Why were they so special? Did you see them?"

"I never did—but I had a quick look round for them on Sunday morning at Campbell's house. You see, he told me that they had something to do with Knowlton's death, a couple of years ago—you know, the JosCo fellow who got drowned. And Toby Duncan—Campbell's friend in Cambridge—he told me that Campbell was convinced that there was some sort of devil worship going on around Laxford." Roger laughed self-consciously. "All right, I know—it sounds like a daft fairy story. But Campbell was dead serious when he talked to me—serious and *scared*. And right after that he disappeared. I'd give a lot to have a look at those papers. Better yet, I'd like Toby Duncan to see them."

Don sat for a moment, drumming his fingers on the table top. There was a sudden surprised look on his face.

"How much would you be willing to give, Roger?"

"Come again?"

"You say you'd like to let Duncan see those papers. Did Campbell tell you where he got them from?"

"Not a word. He really didn't want to say one word to me more than he had to. Look, what are you getting at. Do you think you know what was in those papers?"

Don shook his head. "I wish I could tell you I did. Damn it, I had them for a couple of weeks, carried them about with me—I'm sure they were the same ones. But I never really looked at them. I took a quick look at the first couple of pages, and they seemed to be a lot of rubbish. Mary kept asking me to read them, but I was so busy with work I just put it off. I gave them back to her the day before my trip started." He paused for a moment. "She said she wanted to loan them to Campbell."

"I'll be damned." Roger pushed back his chair. "You mean you actually had your hands on them?"

"I did. And now they're gone?"

"Completely. I called and asked the housekeeper to check everywhere that she could think of. There's no sign of them, not in the house, and not in the church either—she took a look there. Either he took them with him . . ."

"Or somebody took them, and him too? It sounds way-out."

"Maybe." Roger stared gloomily out of the window, watching their approach over the eastern end of Loch Laxford. "Look, do you think there's any chance that Campbell gave the papers back to Mary again? I never thought she might be in this at all."

"Why would he?" Don shook his head. "You say that he had to get them to *Cambridge*. Mary couldn't do that for him. Anyway, if you think it's all that important, there's still a way that you can get the contents of those papers to Duncan—not the originals, I can't help there. But the information in them—that we can get."

"How, for God's sake? We don't know where they are—unless you've got a bright idea?"

"I've no idea—not for the papers themselves. But before I left Laxford for the States I knew I hadn't had time to look at the damned things. And I told Mary that I'd read them all. I thought that some time she might catch me on that."

"So?"

"So I took them down to the JosCo trailer in Scourie, the one that we use as a mobile office—"

"You mean you—"

"—and I had a copy made. I thought I'd look at them one day when I got back. I stuck them in a file there."

Roger was looking at him with an expression of disbelief. "You *copied* the bloody papers, just so Mary wouldn't catch you out?"

"Sure I did." Don grinned sheepishly. "Hell, you know how these things go. You have to do things like that to keep a marriage in one piece." (The uneasy thought came right

263

behind the words. *Was* the marriage in one piece? Mary had never been there when he called the Over The Water, and she didn't place any calls to him even though he had left numbers . . . had Ellie written to Mary, or maybe called her after Don left New York?)

"—the hell are they?" Roger was saying. "Why didn't you say that at the beginning, instead of waiting all this time?"

"Well, you know how it is. No one wants to be caught telling lies, and it didn't seem important. But if you think it is . . ."

"It might be. Where are they?"

"Still in that trailer in Scourie, as far as I know. It's a really terrible copy, by the way. The machine wasn't working right, so there's smears and lines all over every page. I *think* it's just about readable, but I didn't try for myself. Some pages may be hard going."

"It's a damn sight better than what we have without it. Now we've got nowt, as Joshua puts it. I'd better get over to Scourie."

"All right." Don sighed. "I'll come with you and make sure you look in the right place."

"No need for that. You're tired. I'll do it—you grab the afternoon in bed."

"I'm not all that tired. But I'd like to spend some time with Mary before we start work again."

"Spend it with Mary, spend it in bed. I'll check in Scourie. Where's the copy?"

"Filed under 'Knowlton.'"

"I should have known it—a literal-minded engineer. Do you think you could meet me for an hour later, at the Over The Water? If this still looks important I might hitch a ride back to London with Joshua, late tonight, and hop up to Cambridge tomorrow to see Duncan."

"Roger, it can't be *that* important, surely."

"Campbell thinks it is. He believes there was some real funny business about Knowlton's death—and he sounded pretty scared when he said that to me. How much more important can a thing get? The only thing we really need to screw up our project completely is some kind of murder investigation going on while we're trying to work out the plant design." Roger looked at his watch. "Two o'clock now. How about meeeting at nine? That should give you a break."

Don hesitated for a moment. "You really think I can help on this?"

"I'd like to have your thoughts on it—don't forget you saw the original, even if you never read it. Anyway, you know what the locals say, twa heads are better than yin. We can drop you off at your house and then head over to Scourie."

"All right." Don felt suddenly uncomfortable when he thought about his next meeting with Mary. "Are you going to brief Lord Jericho on this?"

"Sure am. When he hears the pieces he'll be as worried as I am—and you know Joshua, he has a built-in shit detector. If there's a flaw somewhere he'll be on it before you can wink. Nine o'clock, in the bar?"

"All right."

"Say hello to Mary from me."

"I'll do that." Don felt again that unreasonable sense of gloom. Was it just a guilty conscience working inside? He picked up his cases from the luggage rack along the wall. The helicopter was preparing to land on the cliffs next to the house. Where was Mary? She hadn't even come outside to look.

As the 'copter touched down, Don climbed out, bent low, and moved quickly clear of the rotors. Almost before he was out of the way it took off again. He put down his cases and watched it swing south to head for Scourie. In a few seconds it was a roar in the distance. Then it was gone completely.

Don straightened up. For the first time that day, he really saw the weather. The sky was an unclouded and glorious blue, and the hills to the east were clear in the clean air. He turned toward the sea, and the calm surface threw back the color of the sky. He was suddenly back in Laxford. He picked up his cases and walked slowly toward the house.

Mary was upstairs. She had moved one of the comfortable chairs so that it stood in front of the main window of the big bedroom and was sitting there now, brushing her long, blond hair and staring out through the open window at the shining blue sea beyond.

Don watched her for a moment before he spoke—softly, knowing that she was unaware of his presence.

"Hi there. Didn't you hear me open the front door?"

She started at his voice, turned her head, and came quickly

265

to her feet. She was wearing a light, sleeveless blue dress—a perfect match for the sea and sky. Don thought it seemed too summery for the season, but Mary looked wonderful in it. Her usual creamy paleness of complexion was set off by a new healthy glow in her cheeks. Her eyes were brighter than usual, and even the carriage of her body seemed better, more poised and upright.

She stared at him in surprise.

"Don?" Her voice was puzzled. "I guess I was dreaming, watching the scenery out there." She put down her hair brush on the window ledge and walked forward to Don's open arms. "Did you have a good trip?"

He nodded and pulled her to him. She met his kiss for a second or two (*act naturally*) then drew back as Don moved his hands gently down to her breast and thigh.

"No. Don, don't do that."

"What? Hey, what the hell's going on here? I've been trying to reach you for a solid week, then when I get home I'm not allowed to touch you. Why didn't you answer my goddam phone calls?"

"Phone calls?" Mary sounded vague. "I didn't even know you were trying to reach me. I've been out of the house most of the time, looking around the headland."

"Mary, are you feeling all right?"

He had sensed her reserve even before she pulled away from him. It wasn't quite the usual kiss that followed a separation. His eyes followed Mary's glance over toward the bed. On the little bedside table he could see an airmail letter. Had she been looking at that? He noticed the address written in the orange-red felt tip pen that Ellie had always used for copy-editing. It took an effort to pull his eyes away and back to Mary.

She gave him a half-smile. "I'm not sick. But it's that time of the month again just now." She took Don's arm and drew him with her toward the open window. *Treat him normally,* said the voice inside her.

"Already?" Don seemed puzzled, then he shrugged. "Well, I guess you're the expert if anyone is. I'll take a rain check. Here, how about a cup of tea or coffee for us? I slept some on the trip up here, but my head still feels as though it's stuffed with feathers."

"I'll make something for you." Mary started at once for

266

the bedroom door, then turned and came back to pick up the letter on the bedside table. She tucked it into her dress pocket.

"That a letter from Ellie?" Don winced at the uncertain tone in his voice. "What's she have to say? Did you know we had dinner together in New York?" (Might as well get the worst over now instead of dragging it out).

"Yes. You said that you were going to." Mary's voice seemed to Don to be unnaturally calm and dispassionate.

"Do you want coffee or tea?"

"Coffee." Don took a deep breath. "Mary, I bought you a present when I was in New York. Let me get it for you while you put the kettle on."

"All right." *Treat him completely normally*. Mary came back and gave him a quick kiss on the mouth. "Bring it down and surprise me."

Surprise me. He suspected that Mary may have been surprised already. He tore at the straps on his suitcase, his feelings an odd mixture of worry and guilt. His fingers were trembling as he took out the little black case. Surely Ellie wouldn't have been insane enough to write something stupid in a letter to Mary?

He thought back to that last conversation in New York and felt suddenly sick. He had meant what he said, every word of it. That hadn't been deception. But it had been unthinking, a spur-of-the-moment statement. Now it might come back to haunt him here.

Don remained crouched by his open suitcase, his mind back again in New York. The contrast between Mary and Ellie couldn't be greater, physically and emotionally. He loved Mary. He had nothing more than powerful physical attraction for Ellie. But it worked both ways, and that was part of the problem. After making love to Mary there was always a feeling of failure. It was hard to rationalize that away, especially when Ellie responded to his lovemaking with such open, exuberant pleasure. Don had always been turned on most by small, lightly built women, and the body chemistry between him and Ellie created an almost impossibly urgent reaction.

They had found that out years ago, and got over it. So how had they slipped back into it again? It was easy enough to invent excuses—no cabs, the weather turned bad, his hotel was crummy, her apartment was close by and comfortable. Excuses were easy.

She had suggested the nightcap; he had suggested that they drink it at her place, that the bars were a rip-off. All right. But who had made the first contact, and how had they got to be naked, lying on the couch? That didn't happen by magic. And if he could half-explain their lovemaking by urgency and physical need, how could he account for the second time, and the long hours of physical gloating and shared pleasure that had filled the night together?

"Don!" The soft call broke into his train of thought. "Coffee's ready down here."

Well, the hell with it. Don took a deep breath. Mary didn't sound angry with him—if anything she sounded too damned cool and reasonable. Maybe that could be worse than rage.

Don stood up, still clutching the small black case. And as he came slowly down the stairs, his mind began to function rationally again. His time sense and his brains must be all screwed up from fatigue and the long trip from New York to Laxford. He ought to have realized it at once—even if Ellie had sat down the moment he left and mailed a letter to Mary within the hour, there was no way it could have got here yet. Hell, it wasn't forty-eight hours since he had left her. That must be an old letter from Ellie, mailed to Mary before he arrived in New York. As for the telephone, how could Ellie have succeeded when all his own efforts to get through to Mary had been total failures?

Very relieved, Don walked into the kitchen and sat down on one of the wooden chairs that flanked the old table. Mary had made a whole pot of coffee and heated milk, and was quietly sitting at the table now waiting for him to join her. He handed the black case across to her.

"Here, honey. Something to make up a bit for my being away too long."

As she slowly opened it he was struck by another thought. He had spent far more than usual on the gift. A true present, or the workings of a guilty conscience?

The earrings were turquoise in a white gold setting. As Mary opened the box, Don realized that he had, quite by accident, chosen something that exactly matched the dress that she was wearing. Had Mary realized that? She was smiling to herself as she carefully freed an earring from its fastening in the box.

Then she frowned and sat motionless.

"Are they all right?" Don knew that they sometimes differed in their taste for jewelry. "Is there something wrong with them?"

"Is this a silver setting?"

"No, it's white gold. Do you like them?"

Mary was suddenly smiling again. "I love them. They're absolutely beautiful." She stood up to lean across the table and gave him a quick kiss. *Behave as usual*. "Thanks, Don. That's the nicest present you've ever brought me. I can't wait to wear them."

Don relaxed and picked up the coffee pot. As Mary put on the earrings he realized again how good she was looking. It would have been nice to just laze away the rest of the day and go to bed early together. Damn Walter Campbell, wherever he was.

He put down the coffee pot.

"Honey, I'll have to go out again for a couple of hours tonight. Roger Wilson and I have arranged to meet at the Over The Water, at nine o'clock." He looked at her anxiously. Her face was unreadable. "Look, why don't you come along, too? It won't take long to get our talking over with."

Mary was carefully pouring more coffee for herself. "Oh, I don't think I will. I've got used to the evenings here. What time do you think you'll be getting home?"

"Eleven?" He watched for any sign of irritation, but Mary's face remained totally impassive. "Is that too late?"

"That's all right. I'll be here." Mary looked up. *Act naturally*. "So how is Roger?"

"A bit harassed. He's in a funny mood over something he was supposed to do for Walter Campbell. Do you remember those papers that you gave to Campbell? The notes that Knowlton made?"

"Of course."

"Well, Campbell didn't give them back to you, did he?"

"No." Mary at last seemed to be fully awake. "He kept them."

"Well, Roger had promised to do something with them for Campbell, but now they're gone and Campbell seemes to have gone with them."

269

A neutral, guarded look. "I heard that he hasn't been in the village for the past few days."

"But he didn't arrive in Cambridge, either—that's where he was supposed to be going. Roger's been quite steamed up over it. It should be all right, though. I made a copy of them, and Roger can take that to London with him if he wants to." Don frowned. "Did Campbell ever talk much about what he thought was in those papers? I mean, what he thought they meant?"

Mary shrugged and yawned. "He had some idea about devils or demons in Laxford. It sounded silly to me. You know that Campbell's a fanatic, you told me that yourself. I don't believe him. I've never known a place that made me feel so at home and at peace with everything."

She was fully relaxed again, super-casual in her manner. Any idea that she was jealous or suspicious of him and Ellie looked ridiculous. Don nodded.

"It's quiet up here, I can't argue with that—it makes me feel sleepy just to breathe the air. You've no idea how noisy New York seemed after two months in Scotland. I'm going to have a nap now, before I have to go out. Want to come with me?"

Mary leaned back and stretched. "Not right now. You go and get some sleep. I'll clear up here and maybe I'll come on up later."

As Don stood up he noticed again the bulge of Ellie's letter in her dress pocket.

"How has your writing been going the past couple of weeks? Ellie says that she's waiting for more from you."

"The writing." Mary was thoughtful. "Oh, yes, she mentioned that in her letter, too. I've not been doing much of it recently." She yawned again. "You know, it all seems rather silly now. Maybe I'll have another look at it tonight or tomorrow. It's not urgent."

Don watched as she picked up the coffee cups and carried them toward the sink. She moved smoothly and gracefully, less stiffly than he remembered. There was no doubt about it. Mary was blooming here in Laxford.

Don felt another twinge of guilt and uncertainty as he turned to go back upstairs.

CHAPTER 17

"Beer or whisky?" Roger turned from the bar and waited.

"You know, I think I'll just settle for a ginger ale." Don licked his lips. "I'm feeling a bit jet-lagged—you know that sort of metallic taste that you get in your mouth?"

Roger looked at him shrewdly. "Why don't you go and bag us a table. There's a free one over in the corner there. I'll bring the drinks in a minute."

Don nodded and turned away. It was a tiny victory, but he had proved that he could do it. The resolve had been forming as he came over from the house. He was tired, he was overworked, and he was worried about Ellie and Mary. If he could refuse a drink this time, he could manage without whenever he chose to. It hadn't been easy, but he had done it. He opened the packet of papers that Roger had handed him and looked again at the first couple of pages. It still seemed completely gibberish, meaningless diagrams and random symbols.

"Well," said Roger, as he came up to the table. "What do you see?"

Don shook his head gloomily. "It's garbage. Take it down to Duncan if you want to, but don't expect much."

Roger slid onto the bench across from him. "Ginger ale and a long face. You don't seem to be exactly bubbling with joy to be home."

"I'm a bit tired now."

Roger nodded. "I see. Lucky Mary, eh?"

Don shook his head again without speaking. Roger took a long swig of bitter from the tankard and leaned against the red back of the bench.

"Bad as that, eh? I won't ask for details. I don't know if this will do anything to cheer you up, but Joshua couldn't find enough good things to say about you after we dropped you off this afternoon. He thinks that you and this job were made for each other."

"Yeah?" Don sipped the ginger ale. He resisted the thought of how much better it would taste with a good shot of bourbon in it.

"Yeah." Roger did a passable imitation of Don's flat, Midwest accent. "He thinks you've come a long way since you arrived over here. Two months ago—pardon this un-English candor—he thought that it would be touch and go with you. To be honest, I thought the same myself. But you seem to be enjoying the job, and you seem to have that"—he nodded at Don's glass—"licked." He saw Don's look. "All right, not licked yet—shall we say, under control?"

"I just hope so. Was it all that obvious when I was first here?"

"Everything's obvious when people have told you about it in advance. The people you'd worked for all said its a problem—hinted around it delicately, but the message was clear enough. But you seem to be in good shape now. And I've seen more real boozers than I like to think about, enough to turn your liver green. How long now since you had a skinful?"

"Three weeks and three days. I ought to cross my fingers when I say that."

"I'll do it for you." Roger took a look at his watch and then a quick look around the bar. Nobody seemed to be within earshot of them. "Don, I know it's not drink—so what the hell is it? You don't have to talk if you don't want to, and it's none of my business. But if you want to tell me, it won't go any further. What's wrong? You've got a face as long as a yard of black pudding."

Don shrugged. "You can probably guess."

"Mary?"

"Right in one."

"Ah." Roger picked up his glass. "I thought that it might be. I've noticed that she was acting odd the past week. There was nothing I could put my finger on, but she seemed a shade standoffish and distant."

"What?" Don paused with his ginger ale an inch from his

272

lips. "Here, you're misunderstanding me. It's not what *she's* been doing that I'm talking about. It's me."

"She's mad at you?"

"I don't know. Look, Roger, what would you think of a man who goes off for a business trip for a week and a half and fucks his wife's best friend when he's on the way home?"

"I'd say she must have had her tongue hanging out for it. It takes two to tango, you know that." Roger was looking a lot more serious. "But if the wife we're talking about happened to be Mary, I'd say you've got sawdust where your brains ought to be. Don, she's one of the best wives in the world."

"Thanks. That makes me feel a whole lot better."

"Steady on—you didn't tell me you were asking for my approval. What are you going to do about it now?"

"I don't know." Don looked sick. "Roger, that's not the worst part. I asked Ellie—just before I left her—if she'd come over and see us here in Laxford."

"You did *what?*" Roger shook his head in disbelief. "I can't hear right, there's no way you would have said what I thought you said. Don, did you ever read what old Samuel Pepys wrote in his diary for a thing like you've done? 'It is as though a man should shit in his hat, and then clap it onto his head.' What in God's name did you think you were doing?"

Don sighed. "I just wish I knew. I've said some stupid things in my time, but that has to be the topper—and I wasn't drunk, if that's what you're thinking. Now I'm hoping that she won't come, but I've got this terrible fear that she will. She has to talk to Mary about this damned book she's writing."

"Does she now?" Roger cocked his head to one side. "Don, pardon my Latin, but how good was the fucking with Ellie?"

"Great. Really great, if you want to know the truth."

"For both of you?"

"I think so. What's that got to do with it?"

"Are you sure that she wants to come over here to see Mary—or try something again with you?"

Don did not answer. He shook his head again and sat there gloomily sipping the ginger ale as though it were a cup of hemlock. They both sat in silence for a couple of minutes, while Roger looked again at his watch, finished his beer, and leafed slowly through the pages of his folder.

"You're right about one thing," he said at last. "This is a really terrible copy. If we make many of them this bad, we deserve to get our records messed up. I can only just read most of this."

"You still want to take it to Cambridge?"

"Tonight—we're late already. Matson should have been here a few minutes ago. Did you ask Mary about all this?"

"Yeah. Campbell didn't give them back to her. Look, did you say that Mary has been acting strange *for a week?*" Don's brow was furrowed in thought. "If that's ture, she can't possibly be acting that way because she's suspicious of me and Ellie. We didn't even have dinner together until two nights ago—and that was as far as I ever thought it would go. Mary *can't* have known."

"So she has something else on her mind. You ought to keep more of an eye on her now you're back. Maybe she's feeling lonelier here than she's willing to admit to you. Nobody goes up to the old house, only a couple of delivery men and Jamie working on the house repairs."

"How's he bearing up? Still having a hard time over Jeanie?"

"So they say. He's never in here any more at night. But he's young. He'll start to snap out of it soon, and find somebody else. He's—"

Roger broke off as Matson hurried through the door, looked around, and waved his peaked cap at them as soon as he saw them.

"Come on, Mr. Wilson. We're late—we have to get going."

"I know damn well that *we're* late." Roger stood up. "Where the hell have you been? I've been expecting you for the past half hour."

"Not my fault. We spotted a car as we were flying back from Lairg. Lord Jericho was sitting up front with me, and he recognized the model. That's a damn sight more than I would have done. It was Campbell's old Riley Monaco— Lord Jericho used to have one like it himself, back in the forties."

Roger was standing quite still. "Where was it? Nobody else round here seemed to have seen it—I asked them."

"They wouldn't have, not from the ground. It was hard to spot unless you were up above it. It had been run into a gully

274

between two rocks up on the side of the Arkle, that big hill south of Foinaven."

"Did you take a look at it?" Roger flashed a quick glance around them, but again no one was near enough to be listening. "I mean, was there any sign of Campbell with the car?"

"Naw, no sign he'd even been there. We looked at it all right—Lord Jericho made me land right next to it. That's why I'm so late. You should have heard him crooning over the bloody thing."

Matson stuck out his chest and tucked in his chin. He dropped his voice half an ocatve. " 'By gum, Matson, I've not seen one like this in donkey's years. Look at them overhead valves and that al-yu-mini-um engine—and they built it back in the thirties.' " He put his hands down to the table. " 'See how you can lift the engine cover off here, and get right at the valve tappets? Aye, we'd run one like this all day—no fan belt, but she'd never boil over. I'm telling you, they don't build 'em like this any more. Not wi' the bloody shop stewards and thirty-hour weeks.' " Matson shrugged. "I could hardly tear him away. *That's* why I'm late."

"Very good." Roger looked as though he wanted to laugh but didn't think it appropriate with Hamish Macveagh standing at the other end of the room. "Let's go. I'm sure Lord Jericho would like to see more of that impersonation."

He tucked the folder under his arm and turned to Don. "Stick in there, and keep an eye on Mary. I don't think she's happy now. And don't worry too much about the other thing—it'll all blow over."

"And blow me with it."

"I don't think so. I don't know if this is much consolation, but from the sound of it I'd have done just what you did. I'm sure I'd have had a damned good try." He grinned. "Don't think you did anything all that peculiar. Sit tight, and I'll see you in a couple of days."

Don didn't move as the other two left. The bar was still fairly full, and it was nearly an hour to closing time. It would be pleasant to sit here and have a pint—he had proved that he could leave it alone if he wanted to.

It took only a second to see through that logic, and the sight of Hamish sidling over toward the table with a glass in his hand was the extra spur he needed. He stood up, nodded quickly at Hamish and was off through the door before the conversation could begin. But the image of the drink not taken sat with Don all the way along the road back to the house.

He stood knee-deep in the familiar, lapping ooze. His smooth, muscular body caught pale light from the faint and fleeting shimmer of the cave walls, a moving phosphorescence that soothed his delicate skin. The smell that rose from the dark water was comforting. It was the Home Place, the company of the People.

Yes, Our Son. Welcome, and speak.

A ripple across the surface seemed to resonate with the mind-message. He leaned forward and placed the palms of his hands on the water for full communion. He could feel the essence within his arm, feel the flow to them like wax from a candle. The vibration that carried back along his arm lulled and soothed him as no other feeling ever could.

"*I have news to bring. I fear it is not good news.*"

Jamie MacPherson paused, waiting for reaction. Off to his side lay the Guardian, quietly encouraging and supporting him. Jamie noticed the signs of change. The Guardian should be spending most of his time here now, allowing the natural aging to proceed. Second Change was very close, no more than a few weeks away. In better times, the Guardian would have ceased his work in the world of the Others long ago.

Speak your news.

"*I have given fluid again to the new Vessel. The Seed is well within her.*"

This is good news.

"*Yes. But I also drew something from the Vessel. She reveals to me that the Others somehow have a copy of the papers written by Knowlton.*"

He felt the alarm pass like a shock along his arm. The group mass of the Elders wriggled, spasming along the connection that led to the Guardian. Liquid spilled over the edge of the Bath's gleaming lips in pearly breakers.

The papers were dealt with. You and the Guardian did this.

MacPherson bowed his head, waiting for the agitation in the water to lessen.

"*A copy was made. A machine was used to make a copy, by the American. Fortunately he did not understand. But*

276

they were given to another, the Englishman Wilson, to take to London for expert study." Jamie MacPherson felt shame, for him and for the Guardian. They should have prevented this. *"Wilson is already on his way. I drew word from the Vessel too late to prevent his leaving."*

There was a long, silent moment. The surface of the water chased itself in long ripples as the Elders made their contemplation. Resolve, strength, support—they flooded into hands and arms from the dark waters. The People must be guarded, that was important above all else. Flickers of light passed through the grouped mass of the Elders.

What is the state of the Vessel?

He thought again of Mary Willis and their couplings. The yearnings of her body for his seed, his oils, and his saliva could not be misunderstood. The Little One would be growing in her womb, needing the Fluid of Shaping for many more days. He knew it. Knew it from the way that she dragged forth his seed and absorbed his Fluid to her body.

"The Seed is growing now within her. There is full control."

When he opened her fully he could almost feel in his mind the presence of that tiny life within her smooth belly. The Cycle was beginning to close, to move on again to a new beginning. The life flowed and the tides flowed, ever to a sameness and a renewal.

The dark waters surged. *You are sure? We must be sure of this.*

"I am sure. The Vessel is carrying the Seed, and it is shaping now to a pure member of the People. But many days of nature remain. The Fluid must be given often now, when the moon is strong."

Then you must stay to give Fluid. This cannot be argued.

"I know. But what of the papers, and the Englishman Wilson?"

Wait.

The mass of the Elders was moving close together, strengthening their bonds. Jamie MacPherson bowed his head and waited patiently. In the Bath by his side, the Guardian stirred, opening deep-set eyes and moving up partially from the soothing liquid.

Jamie looked across at him in the dim light. All hair was now gone, and the skin was beginning the change. In places, the body wore horny protrusions on the flesh, and the abdomen was showing the new visceral film, allowing glimpses of the inner organs. Second Change was nearly here.

The Guardian was sitting up in his Bath. His eyes were moon-white around red-veined black irises, and his tongue showed dark red in his mouth as he spoke.

"There can be only one path to follow. It is my duty as Guardian to pursue Wilson. If I fail in that, I do not deserve a place with the Elders. I must begin preparations immediately to return to the form of the Others and leave for London."

Jamie MacPherson looked at the other for a long moment. When he finally spoke, he did it using human speech instead of the tongue of the People.

"You are very brave, but we cannot allow this—I feel sure the Elders will agree with me. Better that we abandon this Little One now, and that I set a new Seed in her later, after the Little One dies in her womb. There will be other plantings and other Vessels."

"It is my right to correct for my own negligence."

"There was no negligence. We had no way of knowing that a copy had been made."

"No." The Guardian sat higher in the Bath and moved thick-fingered hands through the pink-tinged water. Although in change-form, he mouthed the human words to make his point. "This cycle of renewal has been delayed far too long. That is my fault. I thought that it was important for me to achieve power in Other affairs. Now I know I was wrong. Today we risk more than discovery—we are accustomed to avoiding that. Today we face total extinction. What do you suppose would happen if no Son was available when you reach Second Change?"

MacPherson watched as the reverse-change continued in the Guardian. The smooth white was changing to a baby-pink skin as the soothing liquid of the Bath left his face and trunk.

"Please, lie down, Guardian." His voice was gentle. "I know our history. Without the Fluid and the Bath, Second Change would be a time of torment and disfigurement. It is better if I pursue Wilson now, and we let the Little One abort. There will be other opportunities."

"But perhaps not. You are young. You have not seen the signs as I have, the way that our People have been dwindling in new births. The Others have been growing more numerous, spreading everywhere. We must adapt, fight them with their weapons. I know those weapons, I have used them myself to—"

"But you cannot function in London, not during Second Change. You will—"

Children! The Elders cut off all human conversation. *We have agreed. There is only one course of action for us now. You must both do your Duty.*

The Guardian had lowered himself again in the Bath as the Elders spoke. He sighed as the soothing fluids eased his body. *"What is your order? Better that I should pursue the papers—"*

So we have decided. We know well the sacrifice you will be making to help the people. The Son will stay in Laxford and nourish the growth of the Little One. Together we will manage the sea-farms while you are gone.

"I could go to England for a day—" began Jamie MacPherson.

No. We understand your wish to help, but your place is with the Little One. A vibration of sympathy was resonated to him from the huddled mass of the Elders. *You do not yet know the foreign parts, inland from here. And remember, the time of Second Change brings strength and cunning as well as difficulties.*

The Guardian was beginning to struggle to his feet in the Bath. His form was subtly reshaping itself, adopting the more human contour. The skin, soothed by the wash of Fluid, had lost the uncomfortable surface mottling that had been obvious when he first arrived. MacPherson reached out a hand to him.

"You make me feel ashamed that I will be doing so little. How will you live so long without the Bath and the Fluid?"

"As the others of the People have done when they were forced to remain inland. There are methods. I can take baths in saline mixtures in a hotel room. I can carry Fluid with me, as much as I need. Son, the Change is close for me—I know that. But I can endure for a few days to do my Duty. Then I will return here for the full period of Second Change."

"Suppose that Others notice the changes in you? You know how this looks to their eyes."

"Part of that work was done long ago. I have persuaded humans I deal with that I suffer ugly and painful skin diseases. If I must I will wear bandages." He turned from the Bath and stood by MacPherson's side. "No more talk now. It has been decided. We must prepare for the rest of it."

The Guardian took his hand. They looked together on the Elders, now beginning to drift slowy apart to their separate beds. Silence hung in the air of the cavern, a rhythmic, steady whisper of the tide creeping from the outside as the only breath of noise. Peace and acceptance began to flow through the standing two figures. *We serve alone now, but when Work is done we will be one with the Elders and share the Dark Peace.*

Jamie MacPherson turned again to the Guardian. "Take care. For all our sakes, take care."

The other nodded. Fully back to human form now, Charles Petherton stood naked, eyes closed, waiting for the moment of blessing.

Go, Guardian. It was a steady murmur from all the dark water in front of them. *Remember this on your journey. Where is your Place?*

"Here, with the Elders."

When will you take it?

"After the Second Change, when work is done."

How will you earn it?

"By labor among the Others; by holding the Secret; by guarding the Place; by spreading the Seed."

What will the End be?

"Life for the people."

Who will face Death for it?

"I will." (His reply was strong and steady.)

Swear.

"I swear."

Drink.

The Fluid fountained from the center of the pattern of Elders, crimson green and radiant. Filaments of silver phosphorescence drew strange patterns within its stream. MacPherson and Petherton cupped their hands in the flow and bent to drink. The pulse of the ocean seemed to throb in the cave, louder and louder, binding Elders, Son, and Guardian together as a single heartbeat.

Guard our Secret.
"Death shall seal it."
Guard the Little One.
"My life will protect it."

"Will ye be wantin' to send any reply to that, sir? I've got the operator still on the line here."

Don looked up vacantly at Hamish Macveagh's inquisitive stare. "Uh? Oh, no, I guess not. There's no reply."

He read the telegram message again.

HAVE BUSINESS IN LONDON EIGHTH AND NINTH. WOULD LIKE TO VISIT YOU TENTH AND FIND OUT WHY MARY HOLDING OUT ON ME WITH MORE MANUSCRIPT. ASSUME I'M STILL WELCOME GUEST AND YOU HAVE BEDROOM? REPLY HERE OR LONDON OFFICE OF MCA IF ANY PROBLEMS. LOVE, ELLIE.

He looked again at the address. Sure enough, it was to both of them—Mr. and Mrs. Willis. God, Mary was scarcely willing to talk to him now—what would she be like with Ellie on the scene? What in God's name had he been thinking of when he invited Ellie to come to Scotland? It was insanity.

"Would ye like a quick dram with me, while ye're here?"

Don clenched his hands and screwed up the paper of the telegram to a tiny tight ball. He glared at Hamish's inquisitive face. Damn the man, his ears were practically flapping for more details—and he was baiting the hook with a badly needed whisky.

After a few moments Don shook his head. "No thanks." He swallowed hard, biting back the urge to change his mind. Before the offer could be repeated he strode out of the inn and over to the green Austin. He didn't welcome the prospect, but he would have to tell Mary that Ellie was planning to arrive on the doorstep in a couple of days.

As he drove through the dusk, a dark-clad figure on the coast road made him swerve violently and blow his horn. It had appeared from nowhere, heading toward the village from the north. Don was too upset with his own worries to reflect that the only house on the road north of here was the one that he and Mary were renting.

CHAPTER 18

That evening, it being then one full day since Squire Lunney's murder, men of the village were led by the barking of a sheepdog to a deserted barn. Within they found a crazed and hideous creature, bloody in the jaws. The hands and feet, and according to some the whole body, were blistered and furrowed with pustulent wounds. The man, if man it was, attacked fiercely as soon as discovered, killing two villagers and being subdued at last only by use of dogs and pitchforks.

There being no magistrate nearby, and the Squire dead, the supposed felon was locked in a cellar with food and water until the magistrate's arrival two days thence. The guards report that the creature screamed and raved without ceasing for one full day, and that at the end of this time he fell silent. On opening the cellar, they found a corpse, already rotting and of a stench indescribable. When it was moved, flesh fell from the bones as though it were a month old.

Only one thing of this being's screams was intelligible to the guards. All the night long, and all the next day, he called for "The Elders."

—TOM BRANTINGHAM,
Short History of Derbyshire, 1939

"No, I'm afraid you've missed him. He already left town." The girl's voice on the telephone was casual. "No, I don't expect him back here this trip—he'll be heading on to Scotland again."

There was a long silence on the other end. "Do you know

where he is now?" said the caller at last. The voice was heavy and husky, as though laryngitis had recently inflamed the vocal chords. "This is a business matter—connected with JosCo's Sutherland County job."

"Well, I can take a look for you." There was the sound of riffled pages. "He'll be up in Cambridge for a day—I don't have a phone number, but he gave a Professor Duncan's address at St. John's College. Can you track him from that?"

"Thank you. I'll do it through the directory."

"Here, that's not Mr. Petherton from the Ministry, is it? Your voice sounds just *terrible*. Are you—"

The phone in her hand had gone dead. She shrugged and turned to another flashing light on her switchboard.

At the railway station, Charles Petherton stepped out of the telephone box and leaned against it. He attracted no attention. The station was aswarm with its usual midday, midweek activities. Porters rumbled trolleys and trucks of luggage past him on their way to the baggage compartments, steering close enough to miss his feet by inches with the metal wheels but otherwise paying him no notice. The noise added to the bustle of many hurrying feet and the loud announcement of arriving and departing trains. The whole station seemed to be filled with a loud, blaring drone, vibrating the bones of his head.

He leaned back, tightly controlling his anxiety and discomfort. The station reeked of wet cement and diesel fumes and carbolic, a pain in his sensitive nostrils.

Something had gone badly wrong. Somehow, the information passed to Jamie had been incorrect and valuable time had been lost. Roger Wilson had come to London, true enough—but he had not stopped here, not even for a couple of hours. He was already on his way to Cambridge, widening again the gap between them . . .

It did not occur to Petherton to think that Mary had misled Jamie MacPherson. That was unthinkable, for a controlled Vessel. There must have been some simple misunderstanding, on Mary Willis's part or someone else's. But the effect of that might be totally disastrous. There could only be one reason why Roger Wilson was hurrying off to Cambridge like this. The man was visiting experts, real experts—with Knowlton's deadly package of notes as his evidence.

The thought sent a jolt of anguish through his skull. He

fought back the urge to rub at his temples, where his skin was crawling with new itches and irritations. He gritted his teeth, closed his eyes, and waited for the wave to pass. Each one lasted longer than before. This one kept him there, oblivious to passing time until the impossible burning itch was gone.

His toupee, once snug and easy, now sat like a crown of thorns on his burning scalp. He had to get away from here, move as fast as he could from King's Cross to Liverpool Street Station. But before he could begin he knew he must have Fluid. In his determination to come to London, perhaps he had been too optimistic about the extent to which Second Change had already proceeded. The salt bath in the hotel had scarcely touched the irritation. Blisters and sores were already swelling again on exposed parts of his skin. Without Fluid they would soon be unmanageable.

How bad could this get? He had no wish to find out. There was a tale, told by the Elders, of a Guardian who was trapped inland near the time of Second Change. Even with their best substitute for the Fluid, he had died. Another legend spoke of one of the People imprisoned for a crime. He broke out in terrible rashes and sores and boils, and at last decomposed before the very eyes of his guards. The stories must be exaggerated, but perhaps the truth could come close to them.

The only palliative now was the Fluid. He was still carrying a half-gallon of it, safely held in a flexible plastic container that ran like a girdle around his thick waist.

He checked his watch. There would be time enough. Drink some of the Fluid here, and then by taxi over to Liverpool Street. He would be in Cambridge by seven.

Petherton walked slowly toward the sign GENTLEMEN. Nowhere else in the station would he find the privacy needed to remove the plastic bottle from his waist and drink. Even in a stall of the men's room it would be difficult—he was swathed in bulky tweed coat, a thick scarf, low-brimmed hat, and gloves. The clothes had been chosen with care to minimize the visible skin area, but he had not counted on the need to disrobe except in a hotel room.

Only one other person was in the long, tiled room. He was washing his hands and took no notice of Petherton. In a few more seconds he was able to slip unseen inside one of the stalls and push the door to behind him. He leaned against it. In addition to physical discomfort there were unpredicted mental effects. Irrational waves of fear and rage blurred his mind and made him question his own judgment. Should he endure his pain somehow until he was on the train to Cambridge? *Could* he endure it that long, without Fluid?

He placed his light suitcase across the toilet seat. Still leaning against the door he eased open his coat, unbuttoned his shirt, and lifted the flexible bottle free from his waist. He peered through the translucent plastic. In the old times the Fluid had to be carried inland in a wineskin, toughened and tanned goat hide that quickly spoiled the Fluid's strength. Now it would last for many days in the neutral plastic.

He looked at the level anxiously. Almost half gone—and it would be days before he could get back to the supply! He carefully unscrewed the wide cap at the bottle's mouth and placed it on top of his case. Dark patches were swimming in front of his eyes as he lifted the open mouth to his lips.

Now. He drank, closing his eyes and savoring the familiar power of the Fluid. It slid comfortingly into his throat, easing the pain, calling him back to the sense of silent communion . . .

The door behind him crashed hard against his back. As he fell forward a fat man blundered into the stall behind him. The bottle fell out of his hands and slid down next to the toilet bowl.

"Oh, sorry mate. Didn't know there was somebody in 'ere." The voice behind him was genial and drunken, slurring his words. "Y'ought to lock the door, shouldn't leave it like that."

Petherton reached forward frantically. The bottle had slipped halfway under the partition toward the next lavatory stall. He watched in horror as the dark Fluid pulsed from the wide mouth like blood from a slashed artery. He groaned and dropped forward to his knees, fumbling up the emptying container.

The man behind him was still standing there, frowning in a fuddled way at the spreading liquid.

"I see, yer was 'aving a nip in 'ere, eh? Well, don't you worry, I'll buy yer anuvver. Won a little bit down at the Bettin' Shop. Come on, leave that alone."

Petherton had leaned far forward. If he could have

285

reached it he would have lapped up the precious liquid from the floor. How much was left now?

He held up the bottle. *Less than a pint!* His hands trembled as he picked up the cap and screwed it back on the bottle. Blood ran beating through his ears and red across his eyes. He turned to face the door.

The man standing there was rumpled and vacant, with fat pink cheeks and eyes that were not quite focusing. His expression was still puzzled as he looked down at the pool of red green liquid.

" 'Ere, what yer drinkin' there? Gawd, it looks awful." He leaned forward. "Look, are you all right, mate? Yer face—what's 'appened to it? An' yer belly . . ."

Charles Petherton stood with his coat and shirt still unfastened. The hairless skin of his abdomen was mottled and scabrous, a sea of rising sores and ulcers. He took a quick look around the deserted washroom, then reached forward and grasped the man by the neck and front of his jacket. The red film was still beating in front of his eyes. He lifted the man off his feet, two hundred and thirty pounds of him, and carried him backward into the stall.

His grip on the other's neck was savage. The man's eyes began to bulge out from their sockets, and his face turned a deep, congested red.

"Ahh—agh." The fat cheeks were turning purple, the tongue lolling out of the wide mouth. Petherton pulled him close and moved his left hand up from the man's jacket to the base of his neck. He twisted, with a leisurely release of power.

There was a sharp snap. Blood dribbled from the lips, bubbling up with the gasp of air past a crushed larynx. The fat man jerked and spasmed for a moment like a hooked fish, then gave a final gurgle of blood and phlegm from his slack mouth.

Petherton stared at him as he became still. There was a harsh stench as the man's sphincter loosened and his bowels released their contents. The fat face had become flaccid and expressionless.

What had he done? This would make his task impossible. He dare not go back to the Elders to tell of this. They had promised great physical strength when Second Change was close—but why had no one also spoken of that frightening

286

loss of control? The man hanging from his grip had felt weightless, no more than a fly to be crushed and disposed of.

Control. He had to regain *control* of himself. A fine sweat added to the broken sores that clustered on his forehead. Ignoring the urine that dripped as a spreading patch down the other's leg, he looked at him more closely and forced his mind to begin working again.

The man must be alone—otherwise he would have been unlikely to promise to buy Petherton a drink. So the immediate danger was that someone else would enter the washroom and see them. He pulled the man's body inside the stall, closed the door and locked it. One-handed, he tried to rebutton his shirt and coat. No good. Moving his case and the precious Fluid to the floor, he laid the limp corpse across the toilet seat while he carefully arranged his clothes over his ulcerating chest and abdomen. The Fluid would have to go in the case—already he had lost so much that the flexible bottle would not take up much space.

Outside, he heard the door open. Someone walked in to use the urinal, breathing heavily and grunting with pleasure as he emptied his bladder. Petherton froze until he heard the footsteps again, leaving the washroom.

Now came the difficult part. He dare not leave any signs that he had been here in the stall—so how could he keep the dead man upright on the seat? His belt was too short, a foot too short. Petherton slipped his gloves back on his hands and bent low to take the other's shoelaces from his heavy black leather shoes. He knotted them together to give a stronger cord, then tugged hard to make sure the coupled laces would be strong enough to bear a good weight. Holding the man upright on the toilet seat, he leaned backward against the painted iron pipe, then ran the laces behind the pipe and forward in front of the broken, bruised neck. A dribble of bright blood had stained the crumpled shirtfront, and the thickened tongue lolled obscenely from one side of the open mouth. Petherton drew in a deep breath, tightened and knotted the loop of shoelace, and carefully let go.

The body sagged back against the wall, balanced on the seat. From outside, it had the necessary components to be left alone—a pair of shoes in the right positions, and no noise from the stall.

So, now for the most dangerous part. Petherton slid his

case under the partition into the next stall. As swiftly as he could, he hoisted himself up to the top of the partition, swung his leg over, and descended to the other side. The scrape of the metal wall against his inflamed chest was worse than anything he had felt since the beginning of Second Change. He crouched on the floor of the stall, panting for several minutes before he felt strong enough to pick up his case and leave. At the mirror near the entrance he quickly checked for signs of blood on his face or his hands. He was clean. Holding his case carefully close to him, he hurried from the washroom and away along to the taxi rank. Instead of having time to spare, now it would be touch and go for catching his train to Cambridge.

Would he find the police on his track before he had gone a mile? Waiting for the taxi, he ran over his actions again and again in his mind. The bloodlust was something that could not have been predicted, but now that he knew of its danger he could carefully watch out for it. It must have arisen a long time ago, to protect the People during the dangers of Second Change. But had he done all that was needed to keep the effects of that indescribable rage a secret?

He ran again over what ought to happen.

There should be plenty of time. It might be hours before anybody thought to look in that stall, maybe not until late tonight when the attendant began to clean up. Then he would find that a man in one stall wasn't moving, wasn't leaving—was just sitting silent. The police would be called, but what would they decide? A dead man with a broken neck and no other injuries, in a public lavatory. Wouldn't the natural assumption be a homosexual relationship? Certainly, there ought to nothing at all to link the death to him, or with the People. Long before the death was ever discovered he would be in Cambridge. With luck, he would be on his way back to Scotland.

The taxi over to Liverpool Street made good time. He had almost twenty minutes before the train was due to leave for Cambridge. Time to do a more thorough check of his own position.

Petherton went to a toilet in the First Class carriage and took his case with him. This time, he was especially careful to check that the door was locked before he opened his suitcase. He looked grimly at the plastic bottle. Enough there for half

288

a day, no more. He shivered. How soon could he finish his business here and be back in the North? It had to be done quickly—already he could feel the ominous changes within his body.

The sores and boils on his chest were worsening. He could feel them, opening and spreading across him every time that he moved. The skin on his legs was beginning to become horny and brittle, splitting open as he walked, to form lines of oozing scabs and itching cracks. The smell was becoming overpoweringly strong, a stink of sloughing skin and ulcerous skin wounds. He splashed cologne against his scalp, but the pain was too much to stand as it met his sensitive forehead. He had to settle for douching his toupee in cologne, making sure that it was not in places that could touch his skin surface.

He stared at his face in the mrirror. The clusters of itching pimples were beginning to join to continuous patches of sores. Soon it would be necessary to wear bandages all the time when he was near the Others.

How long could he survive like this? He stared at his reflection, forcing himself to think and act calmly. What had he sworn to do?

. . . *labor among the Others.*
What will the End be?
Life for the People.
Who will face Death for it?

Charles Petherton stared at his distorted reflection. Yes, I will face Death—but I will *defeat* Death. I will survive this, and survive Second Change, and I will take my true place with the Elders. *Nothing* will stop me from doing this.

He picked up his case and headed forward for the restaurant car of the train. Alcohol could not slow the process of Second Change, but it could dull the pain of shredding skin and weeping sores.

And he would survive—no matter who else did not.

Most of it just made no sense at all. There was only one page that Roger found himself turning to, again and again, as the train made its final slow approach across the green and brown autumnal flats south of Cambridge.

It was a map. Not a very well-drawn one, and there were distortions from what he could remember. But there was no

289

doubt about those long, fingerlike projections. If Don had taken the time to look at this particular page—really look at it—he would have treated Knowlton's papers more seriously. It was a plan of the tidal caves that ran inland from the coast, under the village of Laxford.

That thought prompted another one. There could be a simple explanation for the one sensible document in among a heap of gibberish. Suppose that Knowlton had slipped this sheet by accident into the wrong folder? A map like this would fit very well with the other working reports sent to JosCo just before Knowlton's death.

Roger swore to himself as the train finally pulled up alongside the platform. If he were right, he had just wasted another precious half hour poring over something with no significance at all. He closed the folder, took his compact brown suitcase from the luggage rack, and opened the carriage door to step down to the platform well before the train had stopped moving. That earned him the disapproving frown of a solitary porter. He stared back until the other man lowered his eyes and ambled off toward the first-class carriage at the other end of the train.

Roger went outside the station and stood looking up and down the road. The train had arrived ten minutes late. There was still no sign of the red TR-4 that Toby Duncan had told him to watch out for.

What now? Better give Duncan another five minutes, then look for a taxi.

He leaned against the wall. Maybe it was the time of year, and maybe it was fatigue after a long trip from Scotland. All Roger knew was that he felt unreasonably depressed as he watched the undergraduates streaming past him out of the station. They all looked so absurdly young. Michaelmas term, the new university year just under way, and a fresh batch of first-year students feeling their way nervously into the life of the colleges. The tart smell of wood and dry vegetable stalks burning in a garden carried him back eighteen autumns, to his own first sight of the place . . .

Roger suddenly realized what he was doing. The thought cheered him considerably. He had been getting ready to wallow, his first good wallow in years. A few years ago this scene would have been enough to spoil his whole day. He watched a pretty undergraduate dismount from a battered bicycle, trying without much success to hold her skirt in position.

Nice legs.

She smiled at him uncertainly, wondering from his open stare if she ought to recognize him.

Nice smile, too. He smiled back.

A thought for the day: the only wound that heals quicker at thirty-six than at sixteen is a broken heart. There had to be some consolations for growing older. If Mary belonged wholly to Don, age helped to make that a situation he could accept and not try to change. Not, at least, unless Don and Ellie (he saw her as short, bouncy, and highly sexed) were about to get themselves into a hot and heavy. If that happened, it would be a case of open season, and devil taken the hindmost . . .

"There should be a law against it, don't you think?"

The man standing beside Roger had been following his look as the girl remounted her bicycle and moved off down the street with a generous display of leg. He shook his head. He was about fifty years old, with a ruddy complexion and faded ginger hair.

Roger nodded slowly. "I think there probably *is* a law against it, Professor Duncan. How did you slip by me?"

He began to turn away from the other man, then quickly swung back to face him. The thing that had caught his eye was the clerical collar. It didn't go at all well with the brightly checkered sports car. "I'm sorry, I had no idea the other day that you were in Holy Orders." Roger paused. "Why didn't you tell me?"

"Why should I?" Toby Duncan began to lead the way toward his car, parked very illegally about fifty yards away. It was being eyed now by a uniformed policeman. "You were wondering why I wasn't wearing the old dog collar last week? Don't usually bother with it in college."

"You certainly don't sound like the typical minister."

"So they say. That should help me a lot if I ever get into obscene phone calls."

Duncan opened the passenger seat for Roger, then quickly ran around to climb into the driver's seat. He nodded at the waiting policeman. "Thanks for keeping an eye on this for us."

"Not at all, sir." They were waved out into the stream of passing traffic.

Duncan nodded thoughtfully to himself as they drove off. "Always wear the clerical collar when I'm driving. I mean, I went into the church at an advanced age, relatively speaking, so I tend to be more aware of what it does. This collar, now—I get away with things that I wouldn't have thought possible. That and the military connections, they work wonders."

"Jack Gregory told me you used to be in the Army." Roger noted with approval the rapid and accurate gear changes as Duncan took them through a traffic circle. "He didn't mention where you served."

"Ah, you know old Jack, do you?" Duncan turned his head for a split second to glance at Roger. "Met him at Peterhouse. I suppose? I could tell you things he did thirty years ago that'd make your hair stand on end—like quills upon the fretful porpentine, as the old bard puts it." He did a rapid shift down to second gear and whipped them around a slow-moving bus. "Yes, yes, yes—I was in the Army for a spell. In a lot of places for a spell, before I settled down here. Army, civil service, industry, entertainment."

He looked thoughtful. "Made a complete cock-up of every one of 'em. You see, I could never get my mind much past the fifteen century. Once tried to ship supplies to Byzantium instead of Istanbul. God knows where they finished up."

"Really?" Roger's voice was noncommittal. Duncan flashed him another quick sideways look of inceased respect.

"Not really—might have, though, I was dreamy enough. And it makes a good yarn, don't you think?"

Roger breathed a silent prayer as they did a swooping blind overtake of a heavy truck. The streets of Cambridge had never seemed so narrow.

"It's a good yarn, all right. Was it in the Army that you met Walter Campbell, or was it through the Church? He was stationed in the Middle East."

"Neither one, oddly enough." Toby Duncan was finally swinging the car into the forecourt of St. John's College. "You see, we never met. He wrote to me a couple of times, and I wrote back—medieval practices, that's what he wanted to know about. He's interesting. He's a fine example of a man with much zeal and little judgment or knowledge."

292

"Most people wouldn't agree with you on that—he says he's studied church ritual for years, that and diabolism."

"He has—as a layman. But if you want to be a professional in this field, you have to be ready to read everything and forget nothing."

Duncan's manner was totally self-assured. Roger wondered what his lectures must be like—quite different from the run-of-the-mill engineering sessions that he remembered. "Count me out, then. I could never carry a list of dates. Are you saying that you think Walter Campbell has been barking up the wrong tree?"

"Can't say that until I see the evidence, but he's been wrong before."

They had parked close to the chapel. The sound of someone practicing the organ inside carried clearly to Roger's ears. He stood looking round him. Duncan carefully locked the car, then frowned at Roger.

"You've got the papers with you there, haven't you? Why don't we leave the rest of your stuff in the boot, here, then I'll run you over to Peterhouse after dinner. Pity we're not eating *there*—they feed the High Table a lot better than we do."

He led the way toward the quadrangle. "I'm right here in North Court. Let's go on up and have a sherry in my rooms. Then I suppose I'll have to steal a gown from somewhere for you at dinner."

There seemed to be at least two Toby Duncans. The one who had met Roger at the station disappeared within seconds, as soon as Roger handed over the folder of papers. Now, an hour and a half later, Toby Duncan Number One was suddenly back. He handed the folder to Roger, shook his head, and picked up his untouched glass of sherry.

"Sorry. Don't know what you've got there, but I know what you *haven't* got. Old Campbell's all wet. There's not a thing to connect all this with diabolism or any other sort of religious rites—past or present."

Roger opened the folder and stared down at the first page. "You didn't recognize any of it?"

"Nothing useful. Do you want to call Campbell from here and tell him the bad news?"

"I wish I could. He's disappeared." Roger hesitated for a

293

second. "I don't know how relevant this is, so I didn't mention it before, but Walter Campbell thought these papers might have some connection with the death of the man who wrote them."

Toby Duncan took a mouthful of sherry and shook his head before he swallowed. "Maybe there is. All I can tell you is what I could read out of them, and that's absolutely nothing. If you want detective work, the genuine sort, you ought to take all this to the police."

"And tell them what?"

Roger sipped at his own fourth glass of sherry. Duncan was terribly convincing. He had slowly gone over each sheet in the folder, studying every character on every page of the smudged and streaked copy. He had shown a mild interest at one point, when he came across a line drawing of a smooth, hairless man-figure with an odd shape to its skull. He grunted and nodded his head.

"Celtic legends, northwest Scotland. Well-known stuff. Picture like this in Rouse and Skelton, chapter seven. Copy over in the University Library if we find we need it." He went on with his painstaking examination without looking up from the page.

By the time he reached the last sheet he was still reading everything but moving faster through each line. Watching him, Roger could guess at what was coming. It was no surprise finally to discover that he had made a wasted trip up to Cambridge.

He tapped the folder on his knee. "I assume that you have no doubt about any of this? I don't want to be at all rude, but you don't think that it's worth my taking this and showing it to anybody else?"

Toby Duncan shrugged. "It's your train ticket, not mine. But I think you'd just be wasting your money and their time. Come on, why don't we go down to Hall."

"Aren't we a bit early?"

"Yes. I don't want to sit near Dempsey. He found out that I worked in a medical unit for a year when I was in Cyprus, and now he keeps wanting to talk to me about his bloody hernia. His doctor told him he ought to have it operated on, but he's scared to go to the hospital. Not only that, if we can sit near Soper we might get a good cigar out of him—he's just back from a field trip to Cuba."

Others must have had the same idea. Soper was already surrounded, and they finished in the middle of the table. Roger found himself next to a thin, bright-eyed man with a pointed nose, looking out through thick glasses at the hall full of students. Toby Duncan made perfunctory introductions to the men on either side of them, then started in on his soup while the final words of the Latin grace were still being spoken.

"Historian?" said Roger's neighbor.

Roger shook his head. "No. Engineer."

He was still clutching the Knowlton folder. It would have made more sense to leave it in Duncan's rooms, but it was too late to decide that now. He didn't want to put it on the floor, and the table top was crowded. He finally slipped it under his plate.

His neighbor was nodding knowingly. "One thing about Duncan, you never know what he'll show up with next. Thank God you're not another historian. Are you a real engineer, or a professor engineer?"

"I try to be a real one. Sometimes I wonder."

"Good. Too many engineering lecturers around here who couldn't change a blown fuse." His neighbor leaned abruptly across to address Duncan. "Here. D'you ever buy those shares I told you about?"

Toby Duncan frowned and shook his head. "Forget about it, Harry. It's my fate. I'll die poor. Did you buy a lot for yourself?"

Harry—what was his last name, thought Roger. Plummer? Something like that—leaned back again and nodded his head. He looked like an intelligent rooster. "Bought five hundred, worse luck. Bloody things went down two pounds a share. You'll die poor, Toby, but I'll die in debt." He peered at Roger. "You an investor?"

"I'm afraid so." Roger resisted the temptation to go into details. Harry Plummer wouldn't be thrilled to hear that Roger had cleared thirty thousand pounds in the past five months. Time to change the subject.

"You teach economics?" (Harry's staccato style seemed to be infectious.)

Plummer looked even more pained than he had over the shares. "There's no such subject. Economics is all jargon and sloppy thinking."

Toby swivelled in his chair. They were between courses, so now he showed more interest in conversation. "I should have told you when we sat down. He's a microbiologist. Next year's Nobel prize winner, eh, Harry?"

"Won't be next year. Maybe sometime. Probably never—it's mostly politics. Here"—he turned to Roger—"why don't you stick that in front of me?"

The waiters removing the soup plates had almost slid the Knowlton folder over into Roger's lap, and two pages slipped out on to the floor. Plummer picked up the folder and moved it to a clear spot on the table top. "Shouldn't bring work to dinner. I never do. Ruins your digestion."

"This isn't work." Roger took the two loose sheets that the waiter had retrieved from the floor behind them. "This is just something I brought to show Professor Duncan. Here, would you slip these back in with the rest—stick 'em in anywhere."

Plummer took the pages and glanced at them casually through his thick-lensed glasses. Toby leaned farther toward Roger, removing himself as far as he could from Dempsey and his conversational hernia.

"I was checking them out for devil worship." His voice was cheerful. "If you look at them cross-eyed enough you might think you can see the shape of a pentacle, but it doesn't relate to anything else—no zodiacal signs and hidden symbols."

"Pentacles? You don't mean on these sheets, do you?" Plummer was still blinking at the first page, with its linked lines and vertices marked with Hs, Rs, Xs and Ys. "You've been looking for pentacles in this?"

"Tried to for a while. It won't work at all." Duncan scowled along the table. "Here, Plummer, what's so bloody funny all of a sudden?"

Harry Plummer was waving the sheet up and down and rocking backward and forward with an odd kind of gasping laughter. "Pentacles! Toby, you beat everything. Pentacles! I'd flunk my first year students after a term if they couldn't tell me what these are."

Roger had watched the interchange in silence. Now he leaned across and grasped Plummer's arm urgently.

"Do you mean that you recognize those diagrams? Then what are they?"

"Of course I recognize them." Harry Plummer laid the

sheet back on the table in front of them. "So would any biologist. This is all genetics—simple genetics. Look, see this? That's a linkage diagram for sex-linked inheritance. It shows how sex characteristics appear depending on whether the haploid cell has an X or a Y chromosome."

He crowed with laughter. The rest of the table was looking at them to see what the joke was.

"Devil worship and *pentacles*." Plummer relished the words. "You'd have been a lot closer if you'd said testicles. Here, give me ten minutes to look at these properly. Then I'll have the biology sorted out and I'll tell you what this stuff is really all about."

The guest room at Peterhouse was very quiet. Roger was in one of the newer buildings, six floors up. No sounds of undergraduate activity reached so high. By eleven o'clock only the striking of the quarter hours on distant clocks told him there was a world outside the small living room and study.

Roger had not undressed. He knew his own system well enough to decide when sleep was impossible. Even with only half the picture, he couldn't get rid of the urge to go back north to Laxford—at once, without waiting for morning. A call to JosCo in London told him that Matson and the helicopter would be in Paris with Lord Jericho for the next twenty-four hours, putting the closing touches on a development deal with Paribas. Jericho would not be back in Laxford for nearly two days. Train and car could beat that, even if it meant driving through part of the night.

Why the feeling of urgency? Roger sat in the leather armchair before the gas fire—the evening had turned cold—and tried to set everything in perspective. Even after Plummer's interpretations, none of them knew what it all *meant*.

It wasn't history or religion—so that meant that Toby Duncan didn't care what it was. It was more than biology, and nothing to do with finance, so Plummer wasn't much excited by it. Roger was on his own. He laid out the pages of Knowlton's folder on the floor in front of him and reviewed the pieces he was sure of. Knowlton had been interested in the tidal caves near Laxford. Fair enough, it had been part of his job with JosCo. He'd been interested too in the Celtic legends of that part of the coast. But according to Toby Duncan, Knowlton hadn't come up with any new drawings or stories—the old

297

carvings of odd, manlike creatures went back at least five hundred years, more likely a thousand.

The new piece was the genetic diagrams. According to Plummer, the charts that Knowlton had drawn showed the propagation of an organism in which just one chromosome had been charged. One particular chromosome.

"Just look at the picture." After disposing of a fair amount of port in the Senior Common Room, Plummer had become a good deal more expansive. "Look at it for yourself. See, he's showing a change to just this one chromosome. The Y chromosome, the one that in humans decides if the offspring will be male or female."

Roger stared at the familiar pattern. "Can you get a change like this? Wouldn't a change to the chromosome mean a mutation?"

Plummer shrugged. "Use fancier words if you want to. Mutation *means* a change, that's all."

"And the Y chromosome makes the animal male?"

"It does in humans. It's easy enough. The father passes along either a sperm with an X chromosome or a sperm with a Y chromosome to fertilize the egg. If it's X, the result is a female. If he passes a Y, the result is a male. Mind you, that's only in humans. In birds, for example, it's the other way round—a transfer of an X from the rooster produces a male."

Toby Duncan looked up from the barely legible sheet that he was holding. "Harry, are you telling me this fellow might have been drawing chicken-breeding diagrams?"

"No—count all the chromosomes. He's drawn twenty-three for the haploid cell, that's the same as in humans. It could be some other organism, but chances are he was thinking of humans." He turned to Roger. "How much did this fellow know about genetics?"

"Knowlton?" Roger shook his head. "It's news to me that he knew anything. Look, could this happen? What would it do if you had some sort of change to just the Y chromosome in a man?". .

"Oh, it could happen all right. Chances are the modified sperm couldn't produce fertile offspring—most mutations lead to sterility. But if you *did* get a fertile result . . ." Plummer paused for a moment, head cocked to one side. "That'd be interesting. You'd have two male forms and only one female.

The modified male would have some new Y chromosome. His X chromosome wouldn't be changed. So if a modified male passed a Y chromosome to a woman she'd bear a male—another modified one. If he gave her an X—bingo, a normal female."

"You mean that you'd have a new species?" Roger found that the diagrams were beginning to make sense to him. "If this change, call it Y-prime, bred true, that would be a new species, wouldn't it? A Y-prime species."

"Not quite—that's why I said it's rather interesting. You see, you've still got the *normal* Y chromosome males around. See what that means? It's as though you have two separate species of males, the Ys and the Y-primes, but you've only got *one* species of females—the Xs."

"And that can really happen—you can have two male species and only one female?"

"Well, it *can* happen—I mean, there's nothing to say you couldn't find this in nature. But I've never heard of it. The most interesting thing it does is make you wonder how to define a species. By definition, a Y couldn't breed with a Y-prime—they're both males. But either one could breed with a normal woman and have fertile offspring. Intriguing, don't you think?"

Roger would have chosen a different word. In the pleasant urbane atmosphere of the Senior Common Room it would have been easy to make everything a neat and abstract problem—but Knowlton was dead, and Roger couldn't forget the fear and uncertainty in Walter Campbell's eyes the last time he had had seen him.

Where did Plummer's intriguing abstraction change its shape to an ugly part of reality? How did this tie to Laxford, and the tidal caves, and JosCo's power plant activities?

The clocks were striking midnight. Roger counted the slow chimes. He was still nowhere near sleeping, but he was also too tired to be thinking clearly. He looked at the pages spread out before him on the floor. They should add up to a total picture, but he couldn't bring it to focus in his mind. After a few more moments of staring at the gas fire he went across to the telephone.

"Yes, sir?" The night porter sounded as though he had been asleep.

"This is Roger Wilson in Guest Room 6-C. I'm interested

in traveling north in the morning as early as possible. Do you happen to have a train timetable handy? I'm heading for Edinburgh."

"Just hold on one moment, sir. How early are you willing to go? I see a five o'clock train here, change at Ely and Peterborough, then straight on north. I suppose that'd be too early, would it?"

Roger looked at his watch. Twelve-five. He'd have to be out of here in four and a half hours to make it, but he didn't expect to sleep much anyway. Not with that uneasy feeling circling the base of his brain.

"The five o'clock train will suit me fine. Are you going to be on duty all night?"

"Until six-thirty."

"Could you give me a call at four? I'll probably be up, but I'd like to make sure."

"Four it is, sir. In 6-C, isn't it? Good night, sir."

Roger put down the phone and walked slowly over to the window. He looked out over the Cam River, out across the empty meadow and footpath. There were no lights down there, no sign of movement. He went through to the bedroom, took off his shoes and tie, and lay down on the bed under just the top blanket.

He had not expected to sleep, but within a few minutes he was drifting off. After another quarter of an hour he came up to consciousness briefly, just long enough to feel cold and to burrow down under the sheets and the other blankets. His mind began to circle down, full of wandering images of sea caves, carved figures, and Patrick Knowlton's painstaking notes and diagrams.

By twelve-thirty he was in a deep, dreamless sleep. Cambridge was a safe and peaceful place. It had never occurred to him to lock his door.

CHAPTER 19

Sex-carrying chromosome combinations for the fertilized egg:
XX = normal human female, fertile
XY = normal human male, fertile
XXY = human male, Klinefelter's syndrome, sterile
X = human female, Turner's syndrome, sterile
XYY = "super-male" type (look up details of Speck case), fertile
XY* = Selkie male, fertile
—From the *Knowlton Papers*, footnote, page 47

He stood under the overhang of the stone staircase, waiting and watching. Nearly midnight, and still no sign. Was there any way that Duncan and Roger Wilson could have slipped past him up to Duncan's rooms?

Charles Petherton carefully adjusted his position, easing his clothing past his skin. The feeling of being flayed was still there, but now he could bear it well enough to think of other things. The urge to rush to Duncan's rooms at once, as soon as the train arrived in Cambridge, had been strong, but fortunately he had done the rational thing. First, to the chemist's shop in Trinity Street, for bandages, salts and salves, then to the bathhouse at the back of St. John's College. He would need silence and secrecy to deal with Duncan and Wilson. If he could not begin until the late evening, the best way to use the time until then was recuperation in a saline bath.

He had lain there motionless in the lukewarm water for three and a half hours, feeling the inflammation and itching

301

over his body slowly diminishing. When it became more tolerable he could think better about his next action. He had to keep the main target clearly in mind: recover the papers. Everything else was secondary. Certainly, he must also leave no clues—no evidence of strange conversations or student observation. But that was less important. Who would believe hearsay when it came from a professor of ancient history, or a visiting civil engineer? It didn't matter much what else happened so long as he could locate and destroy that copy of the Knowlton papers. He had read the originals carefully, and been appalled at the degree of detailed understanding that they displayed of the Selkie life.

The clatter of feet on the stones outside the building brought him quickly to attention. He moved farther into the shadows, waiting quietly beside his suitcase until the person had passed by the staircase. It was a student.

He relaxed again. The night was becoming colder, with clouds sliding over a bright autumn half moon. His breath misted slightly in the silvery light. The cold did not bother him at all. He still wore the heavy tweed jacket, and now he had bandaged his forehead, neck and jaw. It served a dual purpose. His shredding skin was more comfortable protected from the dry air, and there was little chance that his true appearance could be described even if he were unlucky enough to be seen.

It had been easy enough to get Duncan's room location and his personal description from the porter's lodge. They had never thought to question a cultured and authoritative voice making polite inquiry over the telephone.

"Yes, sir, in North Court. But I don't think you'll find him there now, sir. He lives in College, but he'll be over in Hall—unless he's dining out somewhere."

No hesitation or curiosity. He had been reluctant at first to make even that phone call, but he had to know how to find and recognize Duncan. There was always a chance that Roger Wilson was not yet here, that he had been delayed on the way between London and Cambridge.

More footsteps, these much slower and more leisurely. Two men, pausing outside the building. Petherton backed into the shadows. Without the Fluid available, his mind was becoming dulled, his movements automatic. But he had to remain alert.

It would be at least another day before he could hope to return home for more Fluid.

"Very odd." The voice of one of the men carried clearly in to him. "But I'm sceptical. He could have made the whole thing up."

"Ah, but why would he bother? What would he get out of it?"

There was a pause, then the first voice went on: "Not a thing, I would have thought. But people don't always behave logically—you know that better than I do. Oh, well, we can talk about it tomorrow. I'm tired now. I'll maybe give you a call in the afternoon."

"Right. I'll be in. Night, Harry."

"Good night."

Petherton heard one set of footsteps moving slowly off across the courtyard. He waited. What was the other man—was it Duncan?—doing, standing alone in the darkness? After a few more seconds he heard the scrape of a match and smelled Condor shag pipe tobacco.

Outside the building, Toby Duncan sniffed, threw aside the spent match, and came slowly inside and on up the stairs.

The light on the staircase was poor. Petherton was almost certain that this was the man he wanted, but he had to make sure. And where was Roger Wilson? The other man who had just left was certainly not Wilson, his voice was too high and too abrupt in delivery.

He moved like a shadow up the stairs, a flight and a half behind Duncan. There, the man was pausing at the right door, and selecting a key from a heavy bunch.

Duncan, but without Wilson. What now? There was really no choice.

As the key turned in the lock and the door opened, he swiftly and silently ascended the final flight of stairs. One hand went across Duncan's mouth, the other pushed the door wide open. In half a second they were inside and the door was closed again.

Before Duncan had time to struggle it was all over. He found he was sitting on the couch, his neck circled from behind by two powerful hands. He could not even turn to see his attacker, and there was no light in the room. As he drew in breath to shout, the grip tightened hard on his throat.

303

"We must have no noise, Professor Duncan. Do not try and call for assistance."

Toby Duncan lay back, his mind active and his heart beating wildly. His attacker did not have the voice of a common burglar—and he knew Duncan's name. There was nothing in these rooms of marketable value—manuscripts, some of them irreplaceable, but all of them worthless commercially. And the man who was standing behind him had lifted and manipulated him as though he were a small child. It was no use struggling until he knew better what was happening and had some chance to fight.

"What the devil do you want?" He kept his voice low and his body relaxed.

Now Petherton hesitated. If Roger Wilson had not yet met with Duncan, his move against Duncan had been a bad mistake. It introduced a new factor into the problem. Even if Duncan knew nothing about Knowlton's work, he could not be allowed to interfere with the retrieval of the papers, or with the pursuit of Roger Wilson. Almost subconsciously, Petherton noted that Duncan would have to be killed—but not yet. First it was necessary to locate Wilson. He relaxed his grip slightly on Duncan's neck, leaving him free to move a little.

"I need to know where Roger Wilson is. I was told you would be meeting with him today. If you will tell me his location I will leave at once and do you no harm. This is an emergency."

"Is it? So you have to start out by trying to strangle me?" Toby Duncan tried to squirm round to look at his attacker, but the man was only a featureless bulk in the faint moonlight that entered the window behind them.

"I was not trying to strangle you." Petherton loosened his grip a little more. "But it is important that there should be no disturbance. Where is Roger Wilson?"

His voice was less steady. The effort of grabbing Duncan and carrying him bodily into the room had lit pulses of pain all over his inflamed skin, all the way from the soles of his feet to his suppurating scalp. It was a tremendous effort to hold his control—and still he had to hurry. He took a deep breath.

"Quickly. Where is he?"

"We had dinner together here, but he's not in College

304

now." Duncan sensed an increasing impatience in the man behind him. "Look, I can find you his address, but I'll need to look it up, and we'll need some light for that. What's all this about, anyway? He didn't give any sign earlier tonight that he was in some sort of trouble."

Again Petherton hesitated. His speed and power should allow him to catch Duncan easily, whatever the other man might try. The same overwhelming strength that he had felt at King's Cross Station was flowing again in his arms and body. But was there any possible way that Duncan could sound an alarm? It was difficult to imagine one.

He felt a sudden contempt for the Others and for their weakness. They were as feeble and short-lived as the jellyfish who were swept in with the tide and melted to water on the beach. The women were necessary, now as always, for they served as Vessels for the People. Old memories suddenly surged over him, of the pleasures of coupling with the women, of accepting their bodies, their obedience, and finally their worship. Those days were past for him now. But the males of the Others were weaklings, puny and hopeless, unable even to guard their wives and daughters.

His thoughts had become dark and disconnected, flashing from this room to a vision of the moving sea, to the Vessels he had known and mastered, to all that he had learned from the Elders, to the peace and security of their Home . . .

He looked down at Duncan. Nothing that this weak being might do could harm him.

He slackened his grip.

"Turn on the light that you need, and tell me where Roger Wilson can be found. Is he in Cambridge now?"

"Yes." As Toby Duncan stood up and rubbed at his neck he at once regretted the answer. He wanted to give away no information to the intruder. He turned on the desk lamp and turned to look at Petherton. "At least, he may be in Cambridge, unless he . . ."

His voice tailed off as he caught his first good look at the other man. A white bandage covered the forehead, and another was wrapped around his neck and chin, but from lips to eyes the face was exposed. The flesh was like a flow of cooling volcanic lava, cracked and pitted. Even the eyelids and lips bore angry sores. The skin looked as though it had

305

been recently seared across every square inch with third degree burns. His eyes fell to the other's hands, but as their touch had already suggested they were hidden in soft gloves.

He turned back to the desk, fumbling at the handles on the front.

"I put the card in here before dinner, I think in this middle drawer . . ."

Could a man in such desperate physical condition be as strong as that first contact suggested? Duncan was still uncertain, even while he used his body to shield the drawer that he was opening. Surely nobody could function at all with the agony that the intruder must be feeling, that would imply inhuman control—. He froze, even as his fingers finished their search in the bottom of the desk drawer.

Inhuman. Harry Plummer's "Y-prime," and Knowlton's papers.

He turned his head again to look at Petherton, still standing close behind him. "My God. It's all *true*."

Petherton didn't even seem to hear him. He stepped closer and raised his gloved hands. "No delay, now. Give me Wilson's location—at once."

As the bulky figure moved in, Toby Duncan took two long steps backward beside the desk and lifted his own right hand.

"All right. That's close enough. Just stay right there, and don't get any clever ideas—I know how to use this very well. This has seen action before."

He was holding a knife with a wicked-looking curved blade about eight inches long. The handle was laminations of dark wood and dull black leather, held together with rusty metal studs. The blade looked newly sharpened and well-polished. Duncan held it at waist height, the palm of his hand upward and his fingers lightly around the haft.

"Now then." He stared again at Petherton. "Incredible. You know, I think Roger Wilson will be at least as keen to see you as you are to see him. Keep facing this way and walk backward—slowly—to the couch. Don't make any rapid movements at all."

Petherton took three slow paces backward. His body was slumped forward in resignation, but he watched Duncan's eyes closely. When he reversed direction and leaped forward it was done so quickly that there was time for only an instinctive reaction with the knife. As Petherton's hands stretched

306

up for his head and neck, Toby Duncan whipped the blade up in a long, slanting stab to the left part of the midriff, just below the bottom rib. The point went in about an inch. Then it seemed to meet some tough, cartilaginous wall, skidded sideways, and went upward past the side of the chest.

Duncan had only the briefest moment to feel surprise that the knife had failed to penetrate the body cavity. Then Petherton's gloved fist came up to hit him on the temple so hard that he was thrown across the room. He was unconscious before his head met the carpeted floor. The knife dropped from his hand.

Charles Petherton leaned over and took one look, then straightened and stood shuddering. The knife wound felt like a long burn of corrosive acid all along his left side. His head was throbbing, and again he felt dizzy.

And still he had no idea how to find Roger Wilson, or where the papers were.

He looked down. Dark-red blood was already oozing through the rip in his shirt. It looked bad. He would have to bandage and tape it here before he could leave to look for Wilson. A new rage at the Others began to boil inside him, rage at their stupidity and their long history of cruelty to the People. His mouth was dry with fatigue and his intense need for more Fluid.

He leaned against the desk. First things first. Duncan was showing no signs of regaining consciousness. Now was the time to tend to his wound.

He went to the door and stole quietly down the stairs, supporting himself against the banisters with his right arm. His case was still where he had left it in the shadow of the stairwell. He carried it back up, opened it, and took out bandages and tape. At some time in the next twelve hours he knew that he should replace the dressings on his neck and forehead, but this took priority. He removed his jacket and stained shirt and went to look in the mirror that hung on the wall across from the window.

The cut was a clean one. It began about an inch below his ribs, to the left of the sternum, and ran upwards and to the left for about six inches. The edges made a clean line, and when he pressed on them the bleeding stopped completely.

He wiped away blood with paper tissues, then used Duncan's knife to cut off a new ten-foot length of bandage from the roll. He folded it enough to make a thick pad of material and placed it along the deep gash. He carefully taped it into position. For some reason he now felt no pain as he worked. Even the itching and chafing of his inflamed skin could be ignored while his mind concentrated on this new emergency.

In ten minutes he had the dressing arranged as well as he could manage alone. He placed the remnants of the bandages back in his case, then as an afterthought added the blood-stained paper handkerchief. He had removed his gloves while he tended his wound. Now he put them back on and looked around the room. There was nothing here that would lead anyone to him.

He went across to where Duncan was still lying on the floor.

Had he hit him too hard for his own purpose? This man was his only lead here to Roger Wilson, but now he could not be made to speak. The whole of the right temple was dark and swollen, with ugly blue congested veins. Petherton turned the body over and began to go systematically through all Duncan's pockets. They were full of odd notes, pipe cleaners, coins, and books of matches. There was nothing that related to Roger Wilson. He carefully replaced everything, then looked at Duncan's watch.

Two forty-five. He had to move faster, even though he was feeling weaker and more disoriented, with the wound in his side finally beginning to hurt badly.

He stood up and looked around the room. Nothing on any of the bookshelves, unless Duncan had been cautious and suspicious enough to hide something in among the books themselves. He would have to chance things like that—there was not enough time to explore every possibility. He moved back to the desk.

The top was a clutter of books, notes, and papers. He switched the desk lamp to a higher setting and forced himself to begin a careful search through everything there, item by item. He began to feel despair, and anger at his own lack of control. He should have taken the knife away and kept Duncan conscious, able to answer his questions. Now that chance was gone. The breathing that came from the uncon-scious body was deeper and louder. Duncan was sinking further into insensibility, becoming less and less accessible for questioning.

Petherton grimly forced himself to carry on with the search. He had gone through almost every item on the desk when he found it.

At first he stared at it blankly, unable with his dulled mental condition to realize that this was what he had been looking for. The note was on a blue scrap of memo pad. "Call me through JosCo in London if there's anything new. I'll be off back to Laxford in the morning too early for you to reach me, but if you need to contact me tonight I'll be in guest room 6-C over at Peterhouse."

The note was unsigned and undated. But it had to be from Roger Wilson. Petherton shivered with a sudden release of tension. Guest room 6-C. He could walk over to Peterhouse in less than fifteen minutes, but how would he find that particular guest room? He would need a plan of the other college.

He went across to Duncan and looked again at his watch.

Almost three-thirty. No one would visit a college at this hour. Any attempt to question the night porter would surely be noted and remembered, even if it were only a phone call from outside. He would have to work something out as he walked over there.

Again he straightened up, and this time the wave of dizzy fatigue that swept through him was frightening. The demands of his body for Fluid during Second Change had become far greater than he had ever imagined. It felt as though there were a craving from every cell. And while his body was making its internal changes he found that he could no longer force down ordinary food and drink.

He stooped again beside Duncan's unconscious form. In the old times, if any of the People were forced to move inland and had no way of carrying the supply of the Fluid with them, a weak and temporary substitute had been found. If he had no choice, it would serve him now—but he had to make it as inconspicuous as possible.

The knife that Toby Duncan had used to stab him had been placed in his case when he finished using it on the bandages. It took only a second to find it again.

He slipped the sleeve of Duncan's shirt and checkered sports jacket up above the elbow, exposing the big vein that lay in the crook of the arm. With the point of the knife he made a short, straight incision, cutting the vein lengthwise for about half an inch. The warm venous blood at once began to trickle out onto the forearm. He leaned forward, lifted the arm, and placed his lips over the neat cut.

As he crouched there his eyes went again to the watch on Duncan's wrist.

Four o'clock. The time of silence and darkness was running out.

How long had the telephone been ringing? He could feel it now, the harsh tone jarring into his brain, but he had no idea when it had started. Roger rolled out of bed and blundered through into the other room. It was pitch-dark and much colder. Using the sound to guide him he groped his way over to the phone.

"Yes?" His voice felt rusty in his throat.

"Mr. Wilson? I'm calling to wake you up, as you asked."

"Oh." Roger groaned inside. So soon? It felt as though he had just closed his eyes ten minutes ago. He didn't feel rested at all, his head was aching and the muscles at the back of his neck felt stiff and creaky. He rubbed at his stubbly chin. "All right, I'm up now. Is it four o'clock already?"

There was a brief pause at the other end of the line. "It's getting on for twenty past, sir." The night porter's voice was apologetic. "I'm very sorry, sir. I walked round the buildings and went past your staircase about half an hour ago, but I didn't want to wake you too early. When I got back here I sat down in a chair for a minute and I just nodded off."

"Twenty past." Roger came all the way awake and groped on the wall for the light switch. "Jesus Christ, I'm supposed to be on that train at five. That's only forty minutes from now. I'll never make it."

"If you can be on your way in ten minutes, sir, you'll be all right. I've got the train timetable out on the desk here, and the train doesn't actually pull out of the station until seven minutes past. I could call a cab for you here at the front gate. Or if you think it would be faster for you there's an all-night taxi service off Newnham Road, only a few minutes walk from where you are. If you go on out though—" He paused and Roger heard a sudden noise in the background, a thumping that carried clearly over the phone line. "Hold on a second, sir, there's somebody out there banging on the front gate here. You didn't by any chance order a taxi for yourself, did you?"

"No. I thought if I got up early enough there'd be plenty of time for that." Roger looked at his own watch. It was close to twenty-five past four—he would have to run like hell to catch that train. "What do you think, is it quicker to go over to the taxi place, or to call one to come to the front gate?"

"Just a minute, sir." The porter put down the phone, and Roger heard him speaking to someone away from the mouthpiece. "What's happening out there? Don't go on banging like that. Here, hold on a minute."

Roger was left holding the phone and waiting. He heard footsteps moving away, then a loud creaking of hinges. The thumping ceased. He waited.

Nothing. Increasingly impatient, he held the receiver for another full minute.

"Hello?" He was shouting into the phone. "Here, what the devil do you think you're doing over there?" He looked at his watch again. Four twenty-six. "Do you hear me? Are you there? God *damn* it."

He slammed the receiver angrily back on the stand and rushed to the bedroom. Just his luck. A night porter who forgot to give a wake-up call, then went off in the middle of an urgent conversation to worry about something else. He didn't have the time to wait around for a half-wit.

He slipped on his shoes and his jacket and threw his toilet kit, unopened, into his case. No time now for a wash or a shower—that could be done easily enough on the train. If he caught it. He took a final look around the room, then ran down the six flights of stairs—no time to wait for that leisurely elevator.

It was still totally dark outside except for the faint light of the old quadrangle lamps. He stood for a moment to get his bearings, then hurried along the side of the quadrangle. He paused there. He ought to go out through the main gate, just to tell the porter there what he thought of his performance. But that would cost him a couple more minutes. The quickest way to Newnham Road was out through the little side gate, out past the Garden House Hotel.

Roger looked along the quadrangle in the direction of the

311

front gate. It was hard to see much there, with the broken patterns of light set up by the lamps and the columns, but he thought he saw somebody heading his way. That might be the night porter, catching up at last with his responsibilities.

He had taken two steps toward the other man and was ready to call out to him when he heard the striking of the half-hour. Four-thirty. He had run out of time. If he didn't leave this moment—and run all the way to the taxi—the chance that he would catch that train diminished to a flat zero. And if he missed this train from Cambridge, it was anybody's guess when he would make another connection up to Edinburgh.

He looked for a split second longer at the heavily built figure steadily approaching from the direction of the front gate. It was weaving, just a little.

Drunk, maybe? That would explain everything with the night porter. No time to look into it now. He turned abruptly and ran off at top speed toward the side gate, too intent to pay any more attention to the figure making its painful progress across the old flagstones behind him.

With a little luck he would still catch that train.

Some wag in the construction survey team had made signs of thick cardboard and hung them on the outside walls of the trailers: *Balmoral, Sandringham,* and, smallest and oldest, *Windsor.* They were all of the same uniform silver gray, three oblong aluminum boxes raised off the ground by massive baulks of timber.

Don sat at one of the two metal desks in *Windsor,* watching the Union Jack tied to *Balmoral's* radio aerial flutter and ripple in a brisk northwest wind. The program running on the minicomputer next to the desk was a complicated one, producing new output values to mark on the map only every couple of minutes. It was an infuriating interval—long enough to make you fidget, but too short to let you do anything else useful while you waited.

The signal beeped and another value appeared on the terminal. He read it off, pressed re-start for the next data point, and marked the most recent result on the map.

The three trailers were advertised by the markers as draftproof, but wind was coming in from somewhere. The kerosene heater behind Don was enough to make the air

312

stuffy and fume-filled without raising the temperature to a comfortable level. He sniffed, shivered, and looked out of the window again. The advertised "scratch proof" plastic that composed it had changed over the months from clear to milkily translucent. Now all the shapes outside carried a faint haziness of outline like an impressionist painting.

While Don watched, the blurry figure of a man stepped out of *Balmoral* and turned to face him. He was waving his arms, gesturing to Don and shouting something to him. The wind whipped his words away before they could even reach the thin metal of the trailer walls.

Don stood up and took two steps over to the sheet-metal door. It opened sharply outward, pulled from his grasp as a strong gust caught it.

Don leaned out. "Can't hear a word, Mike. What's all the fuss?"

"Blimey, I think you must live on the phone in there." Mike was young and red-faced and a bit too fat. "There's a call for you on the other line. I tried to buzz you but *Windsor*'s line's busy. It's always busy. Who are you talking to this time?"

"Nobody." Don grinned and jerked his head back to the interior of the trailer. "That's not me on the phone—it's the computer. I'm connected in to Dounreay—the 10/70 here is tapping their data base. It's a bit slow, but we don't have the storage capacity here to do it any other way." He looked back inside the trailer. "I'm in the middle of a bunch of calculations. There'll be more results coming through any minute now, and I have to be around to take the results off the terminal. Is it somebody I could call back later?"

"Dunno." Mike turned and Don began to follow him across the muddy strip of turf between the trailers. "I asked if I could take a message, but they wouldn't have it. It's a trunk call—London, I think—and I don't know who's calling but she sounds like she's American."

American. Don paused on the lower of the two wooden steps leading up to the trailer. Ellie. Who else could it be but Ellie? He had been half expecting a call from her, but now that it was here he couldn't say if he was pleased, excited, apprehensive, or resigned—or all of those emotions rolled up together into one amorphous mass of tension.

313

He went on inside and picked up the receiver. His pulse was racing and he felt breathless.

"Don? Is that Don Willis?" .

"Yes." It was Ellie all right. Her voice was clear and expressionless, so that he couldn't tell her mood. "Hi, Ellie." His voice gave nothing back.

"Don, I don't want you to get the wrong idea about this call. It's . . . business, a working call. OK?"

"What do you mean, business?" He wasn't ready to relax his guard, even though there had been a pleading note in her last few words.

"Look, I planned all this weeks ago. I had to find a reason to come over to London, then I thought I could take a few days off, head up to Scotland, and see Mary. I mean, *you* and Mary, but I thought that Mary and I could give her book a real going-over and be all set for a final draft. You understand?"

"Sure."

"Well, I committed to the book with Capitol, and I got Blocker's approval to do it. He's expecting me to go back with the draft tucked under my arm, just the way I told it to him. Now it's all screwed up. So give me an honest answer, Don, and I'll get off your back. What have you been telling Mary—about us?"

"What? What have I been—"

Don stared at the receiver he was holding. The conversation had done a hundred and eighty degree turn and was going in the wrong direction. Wasn't it *Ellie* who must have told Mary something, making her turn from warm to cold? Now she was asking his question, what have *you* been telling Mary . . .

"Wait a minute, Ellie. You don't think that I've—"

"Look, Don, I don't blame you for being mad. What happened in New York was my fault, I admit it, and it was dumb of me. Can you forget that for a minute, and let me say something else?"

"Ellie, just a minute." Don noticed that Mike was listening closely while he pretended to be completing an engineering drawing. "Where are you now?"

"I'm at Sidgwick. I'm using this phone until Monty gets back from a meeting. Why?"

"I'm going to call you back. What's the number?"

314

"But Don—" Her voice changed. "Don, is Mary there with you now. Is that why you can't talk?"

"Not Mary. Somebody. Give me five minutes and I'll call you."

"I'm on 01-242-0681."

"Stay right there."

Don squashed any possible questions from Mike with a glare and barged out of the door. He went across the *Windsor* and locked the door on the inside before he sat down again at the desk.

The program had completed its next calculation and was patiently waiting with the new result displayed. Even in his haste Don automatically took a moment to copy the number to the right place on the map before he disconnected the telephone's acoustic coupler and dialed the number he wanted. He waited impatiently through seven slow rings. At last a voice came on the other end of the line.

"Hamish? Is that Hamish?"

"Aye."

"This is Don Willis. Would you do me a favor? Would you call through on the line to the house and see if Mary's home?"

"This minute?"

"If you would."

"Hold on for a second."

While he waited Don stared at the map in front of him, with its neat blue outlines of cave cross sections and the red depth contours. Three days of hard work had gone into it already, and it was still not finished. The picture that he was building was increasingly confusing unless he would admit one perplexing possibility. There had to be other areas in the cave system, places that were part of the flow network but not shown on any of the official maps of the tidal region. He couldn't find any other way at all to make sense of those flows.

"Mr. Willis?"

"Yes?"

Don was snapped back to a mood of tense expectation.

"There's no reply. Miss Mary's not at home now. Is there anything that we can do for you—maybe take her a message or something?"

"No, that's all right. She'll be out on the beach or the cliffs again. Don't worry, I'll see her later on today."

He hung up before Hamish could maneuver for more information about what he wanted. When he called Ellie's number, the phone was answered before it had finished half a ring—she must have been sitting waiting with her hand on it.

"Ellie, I can talk now. Are you alone there?"

"Yes. Don, what I was saying about New York—"

"In a minute, Ellie, let me say my piece first." Don hesitated, suddenly unsure how to begin. "Don't let's get things backward. I don't blame you at all—if we're going to blame anybody, I was the one that started it. I've thought about it a lot since I got back, and I may regret it now but I'll have to be honest and say I had a great time with you. All right?"

"Don, there's no need to—"

"Let me finish. I've been worrying about your visit here. I admit it. But I haven't said one word to Mary about us, not a syllable. You see she won't talk to me—just enough words to be polite, but not *really* talk at all. So I've been wondering. Did you call her or write her and say something about us?"

There was a long pause on the other end of the line. "Me? To Mary?" Ellie's voice was incredulous. "Sweet Lily, what do you take me for? Don, you might not want to believe this, but Mary's my friend even if I don't act to show it. I've been feeling bad about her since the minute you left my apartment."

"That makes two of us."

He could feel her disbelief over the silent line. A long pause.

"Don."

"Yes?"

"Just what the hell is going on up there? If Mary's not talking, what's the problem?"

"I just don't know. When you asked me about Mary a few minutes ago I finally started to get things into focus. I should have been asking myself the same thing, days ago."

"You think she's sick?"

"No. I've never seen her looking better. But I can't get through to her. It's been the same every day since I got back from New York. She goes walking down on the beach every day, stays there hours and comes back tired out. I can't get her interested in going out anywhere, and she doesn't seem to want to fix up the house any more, when a few weeks ago she was dead set on it. Look, are you sure you didn't say something that might have let her find out—about us?"

"Don, for the last time, I haven't said a damned thing. And I sure as hell couldn't have done it over the phone—I haven't been able to get her to talk to me once since you were over. You give me an honest answer now. I believe you when you say you haven't told Mary. But did you tell *anybody* what happened—anybody at all?"

"Well . . ."

"Don! *Who?*"

"Well, I did mention it to one person. Only one. A man I work with, Roger Wilson."

He heard a groan over the phone.

"Does the guy know Mary? Has he ever met her?"

"Well, yes, he has. But I'm sure he wouldn't—"

"You great *birdbrain*. Shit, no wonder that Mary doesn't want to talk to either of us. I don't blame her. 'Walking down on the beach'—you're lucky she's not walking across the top of your head in spiked shoes. Don, Don, *Don*. You great moron, isn't it two hundred percent obvious that Roger Wilson passed it on to Mary? She didn't even get to hear it from you or me—that would have been more bearable."

"But *why* would he tell her? What possible reason—"

"Ask him. He's your friend."

"I can't. He's away down south. Ellie, I *know* he didn't tell Mary. He left here the night that I told him, and he hasn't been back here since. And she was acting cold *before* I said anything to Roger."

"Nuts. You might convince yourself, but you don't convince me." There was a slight edge of uncertainty in her voice. "I can't think of another explanation. I'll bet that your buddy blew it. Christ, no wonder I can't even get Mary to take a phone call from me. I'm on her all-time cheap-whore shit list."

A great sigh came over the phone. "Don, honey, what do we do now?"

He shook his head. Was there some other way that anybody could have found out? He couldn't think of one.

"I guess I go on home, Ellie, drag Mary back from the

317

beach and have the whole thing out with her. I'll tell her what I did, and I'll tell her it was my fault."

"She'll never believe it."

"I'll do my best to make her. She knows me."

"No." Ellie's voice was husky. "Don, I started it. I ought to talk to Mary. If I can get her to blame me for everything—"

"Jesus, Ellie, that's not right. I ought to—"

"It is right. You have to look at one other possibility, Don. You don't think your friend Roger said anything. I think he did—but all right, I'm willing to admit that I could be wrong. Suppose Mary *doesn't* know about us and what we did? You want her to know?"

"Well, I don't think that I—" Don paused for a moment. "Hell, no. Not if she doesn't have to. I mean, it's not that I want her to—"

"Save the explanations. I know what you mean. So if Mary doesn't know, we don't want to ram it down her throat. Suppose she's mad at the two of us for a couple of other reasons? You don't want to go and blurt it out to her, or she'll have a reason to hate us worse. So let's do it my way. Let me come up to Laxford. I have to talk to her anyway about that damned book, or my life won't be worth living when I get back to New York—I'll have the Contracts Department all over me. If I can get to talk to Mary, I'll bet I can find out what's eating her without saying too much myself."

"And what will I be doing while all that's going on?"

"If you've any sense you'll stay well out of the way. Hide in your office, or find a reason to leave town for a few days."

"I can't do that, not just now. Roger will be back soon, and we have to work together. I'll ask him, flat out, if he said anything to Mary or to anyone else."

"Fine. Just keep out of the way. How soon can I come up there?"

"Anytime. But shouldn't I be the one—I'm her husband. I could talk to her. Don't you think—"

"No, I don't. You have to live with Mary. If I have to, I'll make me the villain of the piece. And I'm sure of one thing, we'll never get anywhere if we try and handle this as a trio." A change, to a softer, more pleading tone. "Will you, Don? Will you keep out of the way and let me see what I can do?"

"When would you come here?" He found it hard to say yes directly.

"I'll try for a train tonight. If I can get one I'll be there to-morrow."

"There's a sleeper to Edinburgh, but you'll need to reserve a place on it."

"Just let me get a pen, and you can give me directions. Hold on a second."

Don heard the phone being put down. While he waited, Ellie's gloomy words over a near-dawn cup of coffee in New York came back into his mind. "I've been there, Don. Don't let anybody tell you that sex is one of the best things in life and it comes free. It's just on a delayed-payment plan."

CHAPTER 20

Common to almost all legends of vampirism is the
strong sexual element. The victim (invariably a woman) accepts the male vampire in a ritual that is
closely allied to sexual submission. Consider the phases
of possession: the first piercing of a vein resembles
entry and penetration; the drinking of blood is a pro-
longed, ecstatic orgasm; and the swoon that follows is
the victim's postcoital exhaustion and gratification.
  —K. MEISNER, *Vlad And His Progeny*, page 105

During the first few weeks the developing embryo must be
highly vulnerable, more so than normal. Presence of the Selkie
male and protection by the pregnant female has to be somehow
ensured. *Note*: check how Selkie achieves female cooperation.
  Suggested mechanism: In that first critical period the Selkie
fetus will have hormonal requirements that cannot be fully satisfied by human female body chemistry. Unless supplements are
provided the embryo will abort. In continued presence after fertilization, the adult male assures hormone supply to female blood
using three transfer modes: through the skin via sweat or special
fluids (check glandular system); through the semen during and
after intercourse; and through the saliva, in biting or licking the
skin of the female. All three processes can take place during pe-
riodic intercourse following initial fertilization.
  —From the *Knowlton Papers*, page 24

Osmoregulation: The process by which animals regulate the
concentration of various substances in their body fluids.
  —Ibid., footnote, page 24

... regulate the concentration of various substances ...

Roger repeated the words over and over again under his breath, trying to drive the sense into his brain. He had been reading steadily as the train rattled on through the misty November morning, and now the rhythm of the wheels was getting to him. Four hours sleep was all very well, but not two nights in a row, not any more. Ten years ago he could have taken the night in London with Angela and the broken night at Cambridge in his stride, and been ready for another evening on the town after it. Now ...

He looked out at the brown loam of plowed autumn fields as they sped in patchwork array past the window of the first class compartment. They fitted his mood, barren and enervated, settling down for their long sleep under gray Lincolnshire skies. He turned his eyes back to the page on his lap.

Selkies.

The old Scots legend, the wereseals of the North. Knowlton was trying to prove that they were real, as real as the people in the carriage with him now. He arched his back in his seat and looked across at them, an old man in a brown suit with his face turned resolutely down to his copy of the *Times*, and a middle-aged lady leaning her head on her hand and gazing off into her own private thoughts. Imagine explaining what he was reading and thinking to them, seeing what their reaction would be. He could picture it now, outright rejection and questions about his sanity. Well, that was how he would have seen it, too, a few weeks ago.

He turned to a page where Knowlton had dropped his clinical analysis and waxed briefly lyrical about his visions. "I have long believed that we go through the world with our eyes closed. When this theory is shown to be true—and it *will* be, as soon as my evidence is given to the right people—then what else will we be ready to see? What other secrets of nature will reveal themselves that have been hidden from 'civilized' man?"

Was he walking through the world with his eyes closed now? If he could open his mind to all that he had read, what would he see as the pattern?

Roger sipped at his cup of cold coffee. Had Knowlton drawn one correct set of conclusions and then failed to keep going, to realize what they implied? If secrets were to be re-

321

vealed to the world, wouldn't there be efforts made to prevent that? Suppose there was a race of variants from the human form living near Laxford, a race that existed only as males— Harry Plummer's "Y-prime" form. They perpetuated themselves by mating with the women of the area, according to Knowlton with certain preferred clans and physical types.

Accept all that, as Knowlton accepted it. Now accept that when Knowlton gathered that knowledge, he had been observed. He had died, and according to Walter Campbell his death was no accident. Campbell believed that the Knowlton papers were profoundly important—and Campbell had disappeared. Maybe he was away somewhere, doing something unrelated to this, and maybe Knowlton had simply fallen off the cliff. Maybe, but maybe not. The timing was too good to be a plausible coincidence, and the originals of Knowlton's papers were still missing.

Roger put his empty coffee cup on the arm of the seat and leaned his head back against the padded support. He needed sleep or a stimulant. It was too much of an effort to try and think things out rationally while the carriage heater dulled his mind with its hot, dry air. He closed his eyes for a few seconds.

Was there any other hint as to what was going on in Laxford? Any other unnatural event there?

He thought immediately of Jeanie Inglis. It had all come to him second hand, the agonizing death on the harrow and the bizarre behavior of the minister at the funeral. Jeanie had looked like a normal, healthy young woman, more attractive than most and perhaps a little young for her years. Roger couldn't imagine her ferreting out any secrets around Laxford.

Why would any "Y-prime" Selkie want to kill her? Any hypothetical Selkie culture would want all the young women around that they could find, not to kill them but to have them bear more Selkies. Roger had a sudden chilling memory of the exhibition that he had visited with Mary back in London. "Cuckoos of the Minch," was it? How had that inscription gone? "Taking the young ones, using the womenfolk, Man and yet not-Man, Cuckoos of the Minch, Lords of Samain's Eve, Bane of Macveagh . . ." Everything fitted frighteningly well with Knowlton's paranoid conviction. Roger felt cold all over, in spite of the stifling heat in the carriage.

He licked his lips and loosened his tie a fraction. The foul breakfast he had grabbed when he changed trains in Peterborough was sitting heavy in his stomach, and he could still taste the bitter coffee. What he would like was a drink, a pint of beer and then maybe a whisky to liven him up.

Roger closed his eyes again and steered his thoughts back to Jeanie. She wasn't the sophisticated type to be thrilled by an affair with something out of the ordinary. No warped male from the sea for her—and anyway, wasn't she the girl friend of Jamie MacPherson? He was certainly normal enough, even if he did have a reputation as the town rake. But presumably the Selkies would have to *look* human, otherwise they could never survive undetected in a human community. For all he knew, half the people in Laxford could be Selkies, though none of them looked anything like Knowlton's rough drawing.

Could they somehow change themselves, adapt the way they looked?

Even as he was thinking it, Roger's mind did a quick jump sideways. Jeanie and Jamie, lovers and maybe with Jeanie pregnant. Jeanie dying, and the embryo dying with her (a human female?). Jamie alone, working at Don's house, his ties to Jeanie broken, Mary there and Don away. Mary "acting strangely"—Don's own opinion. Jamie in the area when Knowlton died, Jamie working on the house back at that time.

The thoughts all seemed to crowd into his head in a single compressed instant, fighting for dominance. Roger jerked upright as though he had been poked in the kidneys.

"My God. Mary."

The man seated across from him raised his eyes for a moment and stared at Roger with a mixture of concern and indignation. He lifted his wire-framed glasses up onto his forehead.

"My goodness. Are you all right, sir?"

The woman was staring at him too.

"Yes. Yes, I'm fine. Just remembered something that I have to do. Excuse me."

He stood up and placed Knowlton's folder back in his case on the luggage rack, while the old man opposite rustled his papers a trifle indignantly back to reading position. Roger opened the carriage door and stepped into the corridor. It was cooler here. He began to walk along the lurching passage to the restaurant car, his mind a jumble of conflicting thoughts.

Believe Knowlton, and all the implications began to tumble in, one after the other. Jamie MacPherson could be a Selkie, Jeanie could be a past consort. Her death, by accident or design, left Jamie free to seek another victim. Mary would be a good choice, the right age for childbearing, alone for much of the day. Now that he had a reference point to work with, Roger could interpret Mary's behavior over the past week or two. "Standoffish" he had thought, but that was not precise enough. Dreamy, drifty, away in a world of her own—he could match that to an exact template. When he was in his late teens, he had fallen for a woman in her thirties and they had started a torrid affair—his first one ever. The sex had inflamed his mind, to the point where all he seemed to think about was her eyes, her body, her voice whispering its secret invitations into his ear. He had drifted around, not quite all there, for weeks. His family had no idea what was going on. He was accused of acting "stuckup," "sleepy," "half-witted." No one had recognized the sexual trance, the heavy-eyed torpor that now he thought he could detect in Mary.

Mary. He cared for her, respected her, wanted her—and now he was afraid for her. What power did the Selkies have, that they could allure women and persuade them to total secrecy about the affair? It must be a survival trait, like the ability to adopt a fully human form.

The train had slowed again, rocking steadily past a long canal flanked with lines of leafless trees. The sky was reflected in the steel-gray surface of the water. Roger paused and leaned his forehead against the window. Last night he had felt the need to get back to Laxford quickly, without knowing why. Perhaps at some unconscious level he had already begun to integrate the information and perceive a faint outline of a completed picture. Should he try and make a telephone call when they reached Doncaster, call up to Laxford and warn Don and Mary?

Of what?

If anyone had called him a week ago and talked of a new strain of humans living in the north of Scotland, he would

324

have assumed that they were ready to be taken away for psychiatric treatment. If anything, Don was more sceptical than he was. He would have to go over the papers with him, place a call to Toby Duncan and Harry Plummer, and find some real evidence of the existence of Selkies before Don or anyone else in their right mind would take him seriously. He could only do that when he was back in Laxford.

He continued on his way to the restaurant car.

Five carriages behind him, almost at the back of the train, the door of a lavatory slid open. A powerfully built man, his face heavily bandaged beneath a low-brimmed hat, stepped out. He pulled the hat lower with hands wearing thick-fingered gloves of soft kid.

The bandages were clean and white. Charles Petherton knew that he could not proceed through the inside of the train without exciting great attention unless he got rid of the old bandages, stained as they were with pus and yellowed excretions from his rotting skin. It had not mattered on the desperate drive from Cambridge to Peterborough—no one saw him for more than a second as he passed them on the road. If they remembered anything it would be the red sports car, racing over the long curved roads of Cambridgeshire and Huntingdon, through a treacherous ground fog that had gathered in the bottom of the valleys. But now he must look as presentable as possible.

He took a long look at his reflection in the lavatory mirror, adjusting the placing of the bandages that covered his neck and finally tugging the brim of his hat lower over his bloodshot eyes. His appearance was still odd—there was no way that it could be anything else—but it looked respectable, with expensive clothes and neat white dressings. The old bandages had been carefully flushed down the toilet, and his small suitcase—useless to him now—had gone out of the train window as they passed through a wooded cutting.

Petherton steadied himself against the partition. After a day of agony and a night with no sleep, he could function only if he focused totally on one thing at a time. An hour ago it had been the rendezvous with this train at Peterborough. Ten minutes ago it had been the bandages, painstakingly winding them around his face and neck. Now it was Roger Wilson. Somewhere on this train he would find Wilson, and with him he would find the papers. The papers must be destroyed. Wilson must be destroyed. The secret must be kept.

There was never a doubt in his mind that he would do these things. They were inevitable, as certain as the forces of Second Change that were still running through his weary body.

Slowly and carefully, carriage by carriage, Charles Petherton began to prowl forward along the train, passing long enough at each compartment to observe its occupants. The locomotive was picking up speed now, hurtling north across the broad flats of south Lincolnshire.

"Sorry, sir. Can't serve you a drink yet, not 'til the stock's been checked."

Roger looked at the man behind the bar. He was old, with a weather-beaten and lined face—probably been with the railways an age.

"Are you on this run regularly?"

"Yes, sir." The attendant looked pleased. "I remember this run back before they was nationalized. We thought we was doing well when we averaged sixty on this stretch of track. Now we must be going better than eighty."

"You'll be retiring in a year or two, will you?" Roger leaned casually against the bar and reached into his inside pocket for his wallet.

"Next year, sir. I've got it planned out. Move out of Dulwich and down to Fairlight Cove. My mates tell me I'm barmy, but I don't mind if I never see a train again in my life." He scratched at his chin. "Mind you, it'd be different if we still had the old steam locos. I could never get enough of them."

Roger took a ten-pound note from his wallet and placed it on the bar. "Could be a while before you get that stock check, eh? I'd like a pint of beer and a triple Scotch. Keep the change and buy something for that bungalow in Fairlight Cove. All right?"

Their eyes met for an instant and the note was gone. "Thank you, sir. If anybody comes in, now, remember I never sold you anything. This is a gift from me—I can do that if I choose. Have to be bottled, we don't carry any draft."

326

He took two cans of Double Diamond from under the counter and poured them carefully into a couple of glasses.

"No pint tankards, I'm afraid. It'll taste the same."

Roger picked up a glass and downed half of it in one gulp. It tasted like nectar, sweeping away the foul taste that had filled his mouth and throat ever since he left Cambridge. He finished one glass and picked up the other. The man behind the bar was watching him sympathetically, his small mouth turned up in a wry smile.

"Yeah, I've had mornings like that myself. You really need a drink, and with the pubs closed you can't get it. Feeling better?"

"Not too great. I didn't get much sleep last night." Roger hesitated. "We've had a death in the family."

The man lost his smile. "I'm very sorry to hear that, sir. Here, just a second."

He set a clean glass on the counter, opened a fresh bottle of Dewar's, and poured generously until the glass was brimming. "Try some of that, now. It'll do you good. I know how you feel, we lost a nephew only a month back in a car accident."

Roger lifted the glass carefully to his lips. He had asked for a triple, but this was more like a quintuple. As he sipped it the bands of fatigue that had gripped his skull loosened and disappeared. He took another drink, relishing the warmth as it went down. No doubt about it, that made him feel a whole lot better. Another couple of ounces and he would have to watch out—this was no time to get drunk.

He set the half-empty glass down on the counter and put his hand over it as the bartender lifted the bottle to add more Scotch. "It's very good, but I'd better go easy. I'll have a long drive ahead of me when we get to Edinburgh."

The steward shrugged. "It'll be a while before we're there. Here, you don't have to drink it if you don't want it." He filled the glass again to the brim. "This is better than the usual Scotch that we carry with us. In an hour or two we'll have the whole gang in here, and the boss decided they'd be a picky lot."

"Whole gang?" Roger took another small sip, mainly to keep the liquid from spilling over the edge of the glass with the motion of the train. "Who's that?"

"I thought when you first came in here that you were one

of them." The steward poured a little whisky into another glass, sniffed it, and took a cautious sip. He sighed. "First rate stuff, this. Yeah, I thought you must have something to do with the exhibition. They've been having a big exhibition in London for the past few weeks, history and art and science and everything you can think of. Now the whole thing's been packed up and is heading on back to Scotland. The luggage van is full of the exhibits, and all the bigwigs are going back north with it to set it up again in Edinburgh. You ought to take a look back there, it's supposed to be really something."

"It is. I saw it down in London. The Highland and Lowland Exhibition? I'm surprised that they could fit it into one carriage."

"It's jam-packed full there, rocks and swords and bulldozers and tartans all over the place. I saw 'em loading it all on—took hours, they were doing it most of the night."

Roger sensed that the other man was getting talkative. He didn't want to be hooked into a long conversation. The break had been something he needed, that he wouldn't deny, but now he wanted to go back to his compartment and wrap his mind again around the mysteries of Patrick Knowlton's theories. He nodded politely and took another sip of whisky.

"Interesting people, the Scottish," went on the steward. "We went—me and my old lady—up to Culloden once, when there was all that talk about Nessie. We never saw the old monster, but we saw the battlefield all right. One of the nice things about working this job, travel comes cheap if you can go by train."

"Every job has its perks," Roger took a look at his watch. He ought to get back, but the whisky glass was almost full and it was too early to be carrying it through the train—the bar was still officially awaiting stock check.

"Yeah, we go where we like." The steward poured a little Scotch into his own glass. "Anyway, we went on out to where Bonnie Prince Charlie's troops got cut up by the numbers. You know how they buried them? By clans. There were mounds with big markers. MacDonald Clan, Campbell Clan, and so on. Any they weren't sure of, they stuck them all in one big grave—Assorted Clans. I said to Edie, how'd you like that, like a bloody box of Liquorice All-Sorts, mix 'em all up anyhow. You might find yourself next to your worst enemy. Mind you, I don't think any of that matters too much once

328

you're dead and gone, they can bury me up a tree for all I care. What do you think?"

"I agree." Roger decided that he could shield his glass adequately with his hands. "Look, I have to be betting back to my carriage. I had to bring work with me, and I'm supposed to have it done before I get there. So I'll be off now, and thanks for the drink. It did what was needed."

He suddenly noticed that the other man was not looking at him. He was staring past him, down the length of the carriage. His expression was puzzled.

Roger turned round. A heavyset man was standing at the far end of the compartment, his head swathed in white gauze. He was gesturing, indicating to Roger that he should go on over to him.

"Is he a friend of yours?" asked the steward. "He must have been in one hell of an accident."

"I don't know." The man gestured again. Roger picked up his glass and walked slowly toward him. The man's posture was somehow familiar.

"Wilson." The man's voice was muffled and hoarse. Roger caught a whiff of heavy cologne and some other smell behind it, an unpleasant odor that made him think of rotting meat.

"Wilson," said the man again. "It's me, Petherton. Charles Petherton. I must see you and talk to you in private. It's urgent."

"Petherton?" Roger leaned closer. "My God, it is. What the hell's happened to you? Have you been in an accident?"

"No." The other man looked at Roger closely, seeking any bulge of documents in his clothing. "Not an accident. We have to talk in private, but let me just ask you this. Did you ever hear of anything called Selkies, or see any notes that were made about them?"

"Knowlton's papers? How did you find out about them? Yes, I have them with me, back in my carriage. But what's happened to you? Have you got yourself mixed up in all this?"

"I didn't mean to." Petherton's eyes were dark and shot with swollen red veins. "I tried to help the old minister back in Laxford—you know him, Walter Campbell. This"—he gestured at his bandages—"happened because of it. I barely got away alive. Look, we have to talk about this as soon as we can, and we need to have those papers with us. Can we go along to your carriage and look at them?"

"Follow me." Roger led the way back through the length of the train. He was still holding his glass, but he was too preoccupied to worry about anyone seeing it. Anyway, the people that they passed on the way to his carriage were much more interested in staring at Petherton's bandaged head. The dressings worked loose as he moved, and thin lines of orange-red were beginning to appear along the edges of the gauze.

"Here we are." Roger slid open the carriage door and stepped inside. The man and woman were still there, sitting silent and uncommunicative. Petherton, standing in the doorway behind Roger, drew two incredulous stares but no word of comment.

Roger turned to him as he reached up to take the folder of papers from his case on the luggage rack. "Come on in."

Petherton eyed the other two occupants and shook his cocooned head. "No. We need . . . privacy. Then I will tell you all I know." He saw Roger's hesitation. "Bring your drink if you want to, but let us find another place."

"I think I know one that might do us. Come on, it's in the rear of the train."

He considered leaving his glass of whisky on the arm of his seat, but the man sitting opposite looked disapproving enough already. Finally he carried it in one hand, with the folder tucked under his arm. Petherton was following along close behind him, easing his way along the corridor with one hand on the wall of the carriage. He seemed to find it hard work to move.

Roger paused. "Here, are you sure you're feeling all right? I'm taking us on back to the luggage van, but if you feel weak we could stop in one of these carriages."

"No." Petherton was breathing heavily. "I will be all right. These are nasty skin abrasions, but I had them tended to at a hospital in London. Please keep going and do not feel concern about my condition."

Roger took a sip of whisky before he began walking again along the train. Petherton might claim to feel fine, but there was something a little odd and strained in his manner, as though he was having to work hard at forming his words and

330

sentences. The sooner they could get to a quiet place where the two of them could sit down and talk, the better.

The carriage that housed the exhibition had been added as an extra to the usual northbound train. The fittings seemed to be slightly different, and the wind whooshed through the accordionlike pleats of the connecting tunnel that tied it to the last passenger carriage. Roger stepped cautiously across the gap and tugged at the sliding door. The latch opened easily, and the door slid to one side, giving a frightening glimpse of railway track rushing away beneath them at an impossible speed. Part of the connecting tunnel was missing here, a gap between door and carriage wall.

"Christ." Roger took a quick look and then stepped forward, appalled. "Watch your step there. One bad bump on the track, and you could fall off before you'd know what happened."

Petherton walked steadily across the gap between the carriages, pausing for a moment to look at the countryside revealed by the missing section. He seemed to be totally without nerves. When he arrived in the luggage van he looked briefly around him.

"This it it? Are you quite sure that we are completely alone here?"

Roger turned, placed the folder and glass of whisky on the floor, and took a couple of paces farther into the cluttered space. In front of him was a great heap of black rocks, and beyond that he could see masses and masses of yellow-painted agricultural equipment. The walls to the left were hung with rusting antique weapons, claymores and pikes, and strangely shaped muskets. Nowhere could he see a sign of anyone traveling with the exhibition.

"No one here that I can see." He started to turn back to Petherton. "I expect that everyone is up in the restaurant car, doing themselves well at public expense. So let's get down to it. What did they do to you, and where—"

Even though he had not been looking directly at Petherton as he spoke, he sensed the murderous blow. It was delivered with a wooden batten that had held one support for a rack of weapons. He could not avoid it, but he instinctively twisted so that, instead of his head, the point of his left shoulder took its full force.

He was thrown forward straight into the pile of black

rocks, his whole left arm numb and useless to cushion his fall. After the impact he lay there, amazed that he was still conscious. His head had smashed directly into one of the biggest rocks.

He was too shaken to move. As he lay there, his face along the rough planks of the floor, he was looking at another of the rocks just a few inches from him. He realized what had saved him from a broken skull. The "rocks" for the exhibition were shaped boulders of polystyrene foam, carefully painted to look like masses of black basalt.

His left arm had no feeling at all. As he eased his head around to face back toward Petherton, he tried to move his fingers. They responded weakly, with a feeble scrabble of nails along the wooden floor. He tensed himself for the effort to try and sit up, then saw the polished black shoes out of the corner of his eye. They looked immense, supporting the heavy columns of legs that went up out of his field of view. He could hear Petherton breathing, a hoarse gasping that carried above the noise of the train's wheels.

Roger forced himself to lie completely still, eyes slitted open.

After a few seconds he heard the clump of footsteps. He moved his head a fraction, enough to follow the sound. Petherton was back at the entrance to the carriage, bending over to pick up the folder of Knowlton's papers that Roger had laid down when he entered the luggage van. Next to the folder stood the glass of whisky, still half-full of amber liquid. As Roger watched, Petherton straightened up holding the folder and removed the pages of notes. The folder itself fluttered to the boards.

Petherton had taken off his gloves. As Roger watched, a long flame jetted out from it and ran along the length of the sheaf of papers.

A butane cigarette lighter.

Petherton's attention was all on the papers he was holding. Roger opened his eyes wider and peered at the hand that held the lighter. It was covered in a milky ooze, with streaks of blood welling out of the sores and ulcers that raddled the cracked skin.

As the papers ignited, Roger's mind was forced to accept a fact that ran adrenalin through his veins and cleared away all effects of the whisky he had drunk. Petherton was a Selkie. And now he was destroying the only evidence.

The weapons on the carriage wall were far out of reach. Roger rolled to his left and forced himself unsteadily up to his knees. With his right hand he reached forward and picked up the glass of whisky from the floor of the carriage. As Petherton turned toward him he hurled the contents straight into the bloodshot eyes.

The spirit splashed over Petherton's whole face, from his bandaged forehead to his open mouth. Alcohol entered his eyes and reddened nostrils. He gave a thin, whining scream and dropped the burning papers to tear at his bandages.

Roger leaned forward and scooped up the papers in his right hand. His whole left arm was beginning to tingle and ache with the fire of returning feeling. He transferred the papers to his weakened left hand, feeling a hard bulge in the middle of the packet. With his right hand he levered himself up from the floor and leaned weakly against the side of the carriage.

Petherton was still blocking the way back to the body of the train. He had torn the whisky-sodden bandages away from his face and was grunting in pain, a deep, chesty sob of agony. He turned slowly toward Roger.

The face was unrecognizable. Petherton's healthy, youthful skin was gone, replaced by a dark and scabrous mass that oozed a viscous fluid through a network of fine cracks. Deep pocks and ulcers covered one side of his face, and bulging eyes stared at Roger from sockets that were losing their lids. As Roger moved away from the wall the eyeballs swivelled after him like bloodshot marbles. They followed Roger's own look toward the rack of rusting claymores and dirks on the far wall of the carriage. As Roger took two quick steps toward them, Petherton lunged forward to block him. Just before the thick hands could grasp his arm, Roger pivoted and kicked up as hard as he could into Petherton's groin.

Instead of doubling over in agony, the other man grunted and closed his grip on Roger's right arm. Roger tried to pull away but he found himself thrown over against the wall, smashing into it with a force that seemed to crack his spine and shoulders. He staggered away behind a box of radio equipment, forcing himself to retain his hold on the packet of papers.

Petherton finally showed the effects of Roger's kick. He groaned and seemed to fold into himself, bending at the waist and reaching down to nurse his testicles.

Roger saw his chance. He moved back to the wall and reached up to grab the closest weapon, a pitted old knife with a thick and vicious blade. His fingers had already touched it when a grip like a power vise clamped on his right shoulder. Roger groaned and tried to struggle forward the extra few inches that he needed to get his hand on the knife.

No good. Petherton was pulling him backward, moving him effortlessly away from the wall and toward the door of the carriage. He fought against the grip, flailing and kicking. He was as helpless as a hooked fish. Petherton towed him along, steering them toward the open door and the gap between the carriages. It was a force of nature, a powerful riptide that could not be withstood. The pain in Roger's shoulder was so intense that it almost outweighed everything else in his mind.

He was being moved out to the open space near the door. The rush of wind took hold of them, and he could see the blur of colors as his home county rushed past them. The clean smell of the outside merged into the powerful, cloying odor that came from Petherton behind him. Roger looked at the hurtling countryside, knowing that this might be the last sight that would ever meet his eyes. He was being pushed out, farther and farther. Petherton only needed to release him, and he would fall onto the track from a train that was traveling at more than eighty miles an hour. The gravel bed was a blur beneath him.

This was the end.

Roger hung suspended over the track, arms striving to force him back into the carriage. He seemed to see everything with a total clarity, like a small child looking at something for the first time.

Why had Petherton held him for so long? Why had he not simply released him to fall to his death?

He tried to twist around to look at Petherton. The heavy breathing was close to his face, and one powerful arm was reaching over his shoulder, past his head, grasping at his left elbow.

The papers. Petherton had realized that Roger still held Knowlton's papers in his weakened left hand. He was reluctant to let Roger fall to his death until he had taken the packet of hand-written sheets that documented the existence of the Selkies.

Roger made a huge effort and brought his arms close enough together that he could transfer the packet from one hand to the other. He still held the hard object that he had felt through the sheets in his left hand, and he used it to reach back over his shoulder and beat at Petherton's grisly death's-head. It produced no effect at all. Petherton tightened his grip and pulled Roger in toward him, reaching out to take the papers from his hand. His fleshy paw was on the packet, pulling it irresistibly from Roger's grasp. Roger smashed at Petherton futilely with his own free hand. It had no effect.

They were locked in very close to each other, Roger's back tight against Petherton's chest. As he felt his grip on the papers being broken, Roger realized for the first time what he was holding in his left hand. It was Petherton's butane lighter, dropped to the floor of the carriage when the whisky had hit his eyes and face.

Roger used his last strength to move his arm in closer to his body. He put his thumb in position and pressed down.

The spark struck. Seconds later, to Roger's accelerated time sense, the jet of gas ignited, a foot-long torch of blue white heat. He twisted desperately and thrust it straight at Petherton's staring eyes.

There was a scream and a sudden smell of charring flesh. Roger felt himself falling, dropping outward as Petherton released his grip on his shoulder. He dropped the papers and clawed desperately at Petherton and the side of the carriage for support. The sheets went fluttering and spinning out across the hurtling landscape. Petherton, his hands to his eyes, did not even notice their departure.

Roger made a last desperate effort, yanking hard at Petherton's arm in an attempt to pull himself inward. As he moved in, the other man swung past him, trading momentum with him like a pair of balanced puppets. Roger found that he was lying on his back on the floor, head and shoulders out over the edge. He grasped the side of the doorway and kicked upward, thrusting at the other man's belly. Petherton teetered on the edge for a long moment, his hands still covering his eyes. Then he overbalanced, falling outward into the rushing wind. Roger saw the body fall to the track and cartwheel like a broken doll down the side of the cutting, rolling in a blur of rocks and gravel.

It was a few seconds before he could even find the strength to pull himself back so that all his body was supported inside the door. Finally he did it. He lay there for many seconds, clutching at the door frame with a grip so powerful that he did not know how to release it. He was still panting and shivering, trying to force himself to stand up and move into the luggage van.

At last he thought he had full bodily control. Roger raised himself to his hands and knees. And then, helpless, he vomited breakfast, whisky, and sour bile. It spattered to the floor of the carriage. He could not coax his battered body near enough to that open doorway to be sick out onto the track.

CHAPTER 21

Ellie leaned forward.

"Stop here before we drive the last bit."

The driver sighed and pulled the taxi to a halt by the side of the road. Ellie poked her head out of the window and stared hard at the inn ahead. Pretty good. It was the way she had imagined it from Mary's description in the book—a bit more drab, but that meant Mary was adding color and romance to reality. Well, that was fine for this type of novel.

She looked down briefly at the pages on her lap, then pulled her coat tighter around her. The effects of the car heater in the back were nonexistent, and the clear, sharp cold seemed to well up from the floor.

"All right to go on again, ma'am?" She could hear the resignation in his voice. They had been pausing every mile or two all the way from Inverness, allowing Ellie to test Mary's eye for description against the actual scenery. The driver had agreed to it readily enough when they started, but now she sensed that his patience was fading.

"Yes, let's go on. The place I want to be is only a mile or two past the inn, but I thought we might stop there for a sandwich and a drink." *And to check out a suspicion of my own.* "Will that be all right?"

"It sounds first-rate, ma'am." The driver was an older man, fifty to fifty-five, but the prospect of a drink ahead made his voice sound twenty years younger. "And it's very kind of you to think of it."

I like that last comment, thought Ellie. *He's making sure there's no misunderstanding about who'll be paying.*

She looked at his profile as he put the car in gear and took

337

the Morris the last quarter of a mile to the Over The Water. Mary had made an accurate observation. People here didn't seem to age in the same way as they did in America. He had no tension lines on his face, and his brown hair carried only the odd strand of gray in it. You couldn't imagine somebody like this driver deteriorating to wheezing breath and a heavy, sagging belly. The old Scot simply dried out and toughened up, husbanding strength against the battle with old age.

"If you're feeling real hungry, ma'am, mebbe they'd be able to do us a cooked dinner."

His voice was questioning. Ellie wasn't in the least hungry herself, even though her last meal had been breakfast, over five hours ago, but she nodded. "It would be nice to get some warm food and a hot drink."

A shocked silence. *He's afraid I'm going to offer him tea.* "Of course, you can have whatever you fancy."

"Thank you, ma'am."

She had better try and eat something, even if there were butterflies in her stomach. Within an hour she ought to have an answer. She could confirm the suspicion that had flown into her mind even before she had spoken with Don. Was Mary refusing to talk to them for quite a different reason—to hide her own guilty conscience? If so, someone in Laxford must know the facts.

Ellie wondered again at her own motives. She got out of the car and followed the driver into the Over The Water, pausing on the threshold to get a feel for the place. It smelled of old wood and beer and cooked meats, and behind those there was a blend of other less familiar scents that combined to a unique and pleasant aroma. Mary had tried to describe this, but it had mainly eluded her. "Entering the Over The Water," she had written, "is like stepping into a timeless place. It fills you with memories of the past and intimations of the future, but you can't separate those from the sensations of the present." Ellie hadn't understood those words when she read them in the manuscript, but now she did. Smells have a strange power to call up memories, and the smells here were that mixture of a familiar past and present and an indefinable (the future?) addition.

She had closed her eyes for a second. When she opened them she found that she was the center of attention. Everyone in the small, quiet group at the bar was staring at her, wondering what she was doing. She went across to the table, where her driver was already settled in and looking around him expectantly.

A little old lady in a flowered apron came over to serve them.

Ellie ordered a toasted cheese sandwich, tea, and a whisky. Mr. Ackroyd, the driver, ordered fish, chips, peas, and a pint of best bitter, then looked at Ellie and added a double whisky as though it were an afterthought. Ellie shrugged to herself. Capitol would be picking up the tab, and Ackroyd would find it hard to believe some of the lunch and dinner bills she had stuck them with in the past. You couldn't find anything in Laxford that would match the price of even a modest lunch at The Four Seasons.

The old lady brought them their tea and beer at once, with a teapot for Ellie that would give her at least six cups.

"Your name wouldn't be Dora, would it?" she asked, as the waitress was turning away.

"It would." She stared down at Ellie. "Now how in the name of heaven would you be knowing that?"

Ellie smiled at her. "Mary told me about you in her letters." *And you're in the book, too, but I don't know if we want to get into that.* "Mary Willis. She told me you made her a marvelous breakfast."

Dora beamed. "Why, 'twas nothin' but tea and porritch with treacle. I should have guessed it, you're a friend of Miss Mary's—we've had so many people come here these past few weeks, all on account of this power station thing. I can't keep track of them. But Miss Mary's not like that at all."

"Have you seen her recently? I'm on my way up to the house after we've eaten."

"Oh, only for a minute or two, yesterday. She seems to be awful busy these days, gettin' that old house in shape, scrapin' and paintin'. But she's doin' well with it, she looks twice as healthy now as the day she came, all rosy cheeks and bright eyes. It's a pity she's not in the village more often, Hamish says she really belongs here."

Not often in the village. So much for that bright idea. "She spends most of her time working by herself? It sounds like a big job."

"Aye, there's a fair amount of work there. Mind you, Jamie gives her a hand on the heavy stuff, he's over there

339

pretty regular these days." There was a shrill whistle from the corridor that ran out of the back of the bar. "There's your food, I'll be back presently—no good lettin' it get cold."

Ellie poured her tea and watched Mr. Ackroyd dispose of his beer in four long swallows. Jamie, eh? Maybe the idea wasn't all that wrong. She caught Ackroyd's eye and pointed at his glass. He nodded, grinning to show a poorly fitting set of dentures.

"Thank you, ma'am. Keeps out the cold. No wonder these folks on the coast drink so much, there's a real nip in the air out here." He sniffed and wiped his mouth on his jacket sleeve. "These coastal villages are mostly the same, good beer and whisky and bad food."

"You should order haggis."

Her tone was light, but he took it seriously, frowned, and shook his head. "Only at Hogmanay. Out here it's safer to go for fish or mutton."

Dora seemed to have been displaced as waitress. Their food was carried in to them on a big wooden tray, by a little, bald-headed man who was looking at Ellie with indisguised interest. He put the plates and cutlery down in front of them, then paused by the table.

"You'd be from New York, would ye?"

He was clearly only talking to Ellie. She nodded. "I would. And you'd be Hamish Macveagh, would you?"

His reaction mirrored Dora's.

"From Mary," she said before he could get out his question. "She wrote me long letters from here—I feel as though I know the people here before I've even met them."

"Well then." Hamish went over to the bar and came back carrying three filled glasses. "This one will be on the house. It'll be your first drop of Lochinver Honey, and there's no way that Miss Mary could ever tell you about that properly in any letter. Will ye be goin' on up to visit her now?"

"As soon as we've had a chance to have a meal." Ellie looked down at her untouched sandwich and cooling tea.

"Aye." Hamish caught the hint and raised his glass. "Well, *slainte*. I hope that we'll be seein' ye here sometime—an' bring Miss Mary with ye. She's not here as often as she used to be."

He hovered a few seconds longer, then reluctantly started back toward the kitchen. Ellie smiled to herself. Mary had

340

captured Hamish and Dora well in her written descriptions, even if the mysterious Jamie had not been mentioned there. She stared across at Mr. Ackroyd as he glowered at his plate and crammed great forkfuls of fish, chips, and peas into his mouth.

Somewhere in Scotland there had to be an attractive man. She hadn't met one yet, but maybe Mary had found him.

Whisky and beer seemed to serve as the time machine that carried Ackroyd back to the Second World War. Ellie allowed the whisky that she had drunk to drift her away and ignored the blow-by-blow account of Rommel and Ackroyd that came from the seat in front of her. He didn't seem to care if she was listening or not. She hoped that his head was feeling a lot clearer than hers—Hamish had poured one for the road with a lavish hand.

She snuggled down into her winter coat. Mary's typed manuscript was on the seat next to her, but she had read all that she had cared to until there was a chance to talk about it. With any luck, Don had done the sensible thing and would be out of the house when she got there.

Don. Two years ago she could have had him. All it would have needed was a word. He had been at low ebb then, his marriage falling apart and his self-confidence down to zero. She had been looking for other conquests, strokes for her ego as well as her body, and there had been the smug feeling of motherhood that she'd felt toward Mary, that it would be *wrong* to take him from Mary, *little* Mary, all alone in the big, bad city . . . That superior feeling had been the ego trip to end all ego trips, the way that Ackroyd was fighting the war to end all wars—or had that been World War One?

The tires of the car were bumping and scraping over the gravel and the chips of granite. Ackroyd had somehow leaped ahead to D-Day, and the sky ahead had covered over with dirty gray clouds. Ellie thought of the night she had spent with Don, just a couple of weeks ago. Wonderful. Through all the other aspects of her visit to Laxford, she couldn't repress the guilty thought—that the real reason for the trip, hidden so deep that she couldn't find it, was a desire to see Don and find out if the same chemistry hit them again. It had been two years since the last time they had slept together, and somewhere along the way the intensity level had gone up and up. Was that why she was so interested in seeing if Mary had found some other option? It was hard to prove otherwise.

Ackroyd was storming the Normandy beaches and the first drops of rain were falling as the car pulled up outside the house on the cliff. Ellie jerked herself out of her trance and sat up in her seat. This was the place, as Mary had written about it, "as though the carved wood and stone had been rooted in this one spot for thousands of years."

"D'ye want me to wait and see that there's somebody here to meet you?"

"No, just let me off at the door. The car's there, so somebody's home."

She took her bags and gave him the fare and enough of a tip that he insisted on getting out and carrying the bags over to the door for her. She hammered on it with the big iron door knocker and listened to the echoes through the wood. After a few seconds she tried the doorknob and leaned her weight on it until the door creaked open. As Ackroyd moved to the car and turned to drive back down the road, she waited, reluctant to invade the house without permission.

Where was Mary? Don ought to be away, but if the car was here Mary should be here too.

She stepped inside—no point in standing there in the growing downpour—and placed her two bags inside the door.

The house felt empty, even though she could hear a creaking in the wooden timbers above her head. Maybe Mary had stepped outside into the backyard. She went on, through the kitchen, and out the back door to face the cliffs. The world ended about thirty yards away, at the cliff's sheer edge. Off to the left, near the road that led back to Laxford, she saw two hurrying figures, bent over to protect their faces from the rain. They were moving to the very edge of the cliffs. One of them could be Mary—she had a coat and pants just like that. But the other one . . .

Was it Don? He looked too short, and she had never seen Don in a leather jacket.

They were disappearing, apparently heading straight off the edge of the cliff. Ellie opened her mouth to call to them, then stopped. She was full of strange feelings, mingled hope and

342

fear that her first suspicion would be proved correct. The man had placed his arm around the woman in the moment before they disappeared, and she had leaned against him, melting into his sturdy frame.

Ellie went back inside and opened her case. She slipped a plastic raincoat over her thick overcoat and pulled the hood up. The ground outside was slippery in the rain, and she walked carefully.

Why hadn't she had the sense to wear jeans? She swore at herself, at the stupidity of a business suit out here in Laxford. If she had to climb down that cliff it would be ruined. She came to the top of the path down and paused. It was steep.

A gust of wind caught her hair and blew the rain hood back. She pulled it into position again and peered over the edge. Should she try and go down there? It was fifty feet or more of steep, zigzag path, past rocks and boulders covered with lichen and hardy weeds. If it was not Mary down there after all, she would look like an absolute fool.

The smell of the sea was cold and strong, carrying up to her at the cliff top. She scanned the beach below and saw two distant figures, skirting the lapping waves and disappearing past a shelf of rocks. The woman's head was cradled on the crook of his arm, oblivious to the rain, and her hand was resting on his buttock. Ellie marked the line that they were taking. If she could just make it down the path without killing herself . . .

She took a few tentative steps. Her open-toed shoes were a more stupid choice than even her long skirt. The angles of the path varied from steep to very steep to precipitous, and in some places she didn't feel safe to move farther unless she had a good handhold. The rocks were slick with the rain, and there were places with loose dirt and gravel. She forced herself to go slowly, ignoring how long it was taking her. Even if the people she was trailing had vanished when she got there, it was no real disaster—but falling off this cliff would be, without a doubt.

Breathing heavily, she at last set foot on the pebbled and sandy beach. The footsteps of the people she was pursuing, close together and remarkably parallel, led like a weaving, dotted trail across the shore. She set out to follow them, slowly and cautiously.

The tastes and feel of the sea were fresh and insistent on her exposed face and legs. She went on down to the line of the tide, through patches of stranded kelp and greenish brown seaweed, then on past still tidal pools where the raindrops set up complex patterns of ripples. The rocks that jutted up from the sand were savage and jagged, broken and sharp like splintered grave markers.

She rounded the final shelf of rock, her steps cautious and her thoughts wild. If they were lovers, Mary and the man that she was with, how could she ever break that news to Don? It was a question that she should have asked herself long ago, when the first suspicion had come to her. There was no way that she could sit down and calmly tell Don that Mary was being unfaithful to him, not after she had encouraged him to his own unfaithfulness. No matter what Mary was doing, she couldn't be the one to tell it. Maybe it would surface by itself, if Mary was growing reckless. But she had to be around when it all came out; Don would need comfort and attention.

Ellie stood on one leg and shook a stone out of her shoe. Just ahead of her was the end of the beach, a line of white breakers where the waves met the face of the cliff. There was no sign of the couple she was following.

Where could they have gone to? She turned, and saw that the rock shelf formed the top of a series of dark openings in the cliff wall. Tidal caves. What a perfect hiding place for a lovers' tryst, even if it was a bit too cold for more than holding hands and hugging.

The footprints she had been following disappeared here, in rough pebbles and rocks, but there was a scuffled area at the mouth of the nearest cave. Ellie began to move quietly forward, then hesitated. Suppose that she was going to blunder in on the private affairs of two total strangers? It would be difficult to explain why she was there, a foreigner in unsuitable clothes. She tried to make her movements quieter yet, hoping that any small noises would be drowned by the crash of waves along the shore.

The mouth of the cave was only shoulder high, an oval opening that glistened with salt water from the ebbing tide. She stooped low, careful to avoid the jagged roof, and peered ahead.

Nothing. Ahead of her, as far as the outside light would penetrate into the gloom, she saw that the cave divided into two passages. She would go to that point, then come out again. There was an increasing feeling that she had been wrong, that Mary was not here. One quick look inside, then she would go back and wait patiently at the house.

She went on, until she could see nothing ahead of her. The cave was higher here, so she could walk upright. Ellie reached the branch point and stood silent. There were noises in the left hand branch.

Breathings and soft gaspings. A sigh, then a woman speaking in low tones. A pause, and then the woman spoke again.

Ellie was afraid to breathe. She took the shallowest of breaths and waited to hear a male voice answering the female. It did not come. Only the woman again, soft-voiced and earnest.

Ellie inched forward, wishing that her eyes would adapt more quickly to the darkness. She could see a little into the left-hand cave, but only enough to see general dim outlines there. She steadied herself against the slick cave wall.

Chilly air, a woman's voice, and a curious smell, drifting to her through the gloom.

Strong, musky perfume, like that she had given Mary.

The woman's voice had faded. Now she could hear a heavy breathing, matched to a soft slither of skin moving on skin. That sound at least could be interpreted. Ellie felt sympathetic stirrings in her own belly, an electric shock deep inside her sex organs.

Her throat was suddenly dry. They were making love, here in the damp and chilly cave. She needed to know only one thing more before she left. She needed to be sure that it was Mary.

She inched forward, straining her eyes into the darkness ahead of her.

There was strewn clothing there, thrown carelessly on the ground. Beyond it a strange swelling rose from the floor of the cave. As she stared at it, she realized that she was seeing a thick pile of blankets, supporting the coupled forms of a man and woman. The blankets gave off their own faint light, a smear of phosphorescence in the darkness.

It was Mary. She lay naked on her back, arched upwards

345

in ecstasy. Her mouth was open, and her long blond hair swirled back in wild disarray. She was reaching upward with her arms and legs, clamping the man on top tightly to her, pulling him into her hard at each stroke. She was giving little grunts of effort and encouragement, with broken words of endearment between heavy, deep breaths.

The man was completely silent. Mounted between Mary's legs, he lay against her abdomen and her hard excited breasts, moving his whole body back and forth, back and forth, over her. His head was down, nuzzling or biting at her neck and shoulders. He was . . .

All the breath seemed to be pulled out of Ellie, as though she had been thrust into a vacuum. Her eyes were adapting, and she could take a closer look at Mary's partner.

She tensed with revulsion and horror.

The creature who lay on top of Mary, penetrating her with deep, steady strokes and obviously providing her with intense pleasure, was not human. It was a squat, powerful form, with a domed, glistening skull. The white skin reflected a glossy sheen, a covering of viscous droplets that smeared into Mary's body with each long stroke. It made no sound, only the slide of skin on pale skin.

Mary was arching higher, moaning deep in her throat. She was reaching her climax, lifting up with all the strength of her long legs and muscular back. As Ellie watched, she gave a last shuddering breath and clasped the creature to her, supporting all its weight on her thrusting pelvis. They were locked in a long, quivering embrace.

The moment for Ellie to leave had passed but she stood there, gripped by horror and fascination. The bestiality of the coupling was so contrary to Mary's trembling ecstasy that Ellie had to watch for another few moments. There *must* be some way to explain what she was seeing, to resolve the contradiction that lay before her eyes on that jumbled pile of blankets.

Mary was fondling the gross head, crooning words of love while the creature continued to bite and nuzzle at the soft skin of her neck and shoulders. Her hips were still slowly pumping against him, squeezing and draining.

After a few more seconds he stirred with a different movement, lifting up to move away from Mary. She muttered a protest, still trying to hold him with her arms, but he slowly disengaged from her.

He reared back and rose to his knees. The thick penis that slid its length out of Mary was still half-erect and darker in color than the pallid torso. Mary was reaching up to him, opening her eyes dreamily, but he straightened his body and pulled restlessly away from her.

Ellie saw a hairless torso, the muscles under the skin as sharply delineated as in an anatomical drawing. The broad chest led down to a thick waist and a flat, concave abdomen. His skin was bloated and distended with blood, and yet unnaturally pale under a coating of gleaming sweat. Below the waist, the heavy genitals seemed disproportionate to the thin, muscular legs.

Now he was turning his head this way and that, sniffing at the damp air through broad, flattened nostrils. The searching eyes were invisible in their round sockets. Finally he came completely upright and stared at the rock behind which Ellie was hiding.

She held her breath. She had pulled her head back when he began to turn toward her—but did he sense her presence?

Ellie began to edge backward, as quickly as she dared and as quietly as she could. Before she had taken four steps he was rounding the corner of rock, tracking her with his head held low. She had another quick glimpse of the heavy skull and smooth white skin, covered now with a drying layer of his viscous sweat, before she spun around and ran back through the cave toward the gray outside light.

Her loose shoes hindered her speed, turning and sinking on the loose pebbles underfoot. It was too late to take them off. She was still a few paces from the cave entrance when he caught her from behind, reaching around her neck with one hand and gripping her elbow with the other. Impossibly strong. Ellie screamed and struggled, twisting to kick out at him. He ignored her. She was dragged easily across the wall of the cave and held there, one casual hand across her throat, pinning her back against the cold rock.

She was facing bright blue eyes that stared unblinkingly into her own. He was only a few inches from her face. Each time she tried to move or cry out the thick palm moved in harder on her throat, cutting off the supply of air. She wanted to look away, look anywhere rather than meet the

347

blaze of those eyes. There was a noise off to her right, and she struggled to turn her head a fraction.

"Mary!" Her voice was cut off by the pressure of the hand on her windpipe. She could only plead with her eyes, watching in silence as the other woman padded forward.

Mary was rubbing thoughtfully at her shoulder where a line of red swellings marked her fair skin. The front of her body was covered with a thin layer of drying white liquid that still gleamed wetly in her pubic hair. Her breasts and cheeks were flushed, as though the thrill of orgasm was still running strongly through her veins and arteries. She came barefoot across the sand and pebbles to stand beside the monster, one hand reaching up to rub at her tangled hair.

She was completely naked and totally unselfconscious. Ellie stared at her. Could this be Mary, the woman who was always prudish about even *talking* about her own body?

Mary was smiling, the innocent smile of pure pleasure. "Why, Ellie." She turned to the creature beside her. "This is Ellie, the friend of mine that I told you about."

"Mary—" The hand was there again, cutting off her breath.

"Ellie, this is Jamie." Mary looked fondly at the squat beast by her side. She was smiling still, with the look of someone who has a gift to offer. "Didn't I tell you about Jamie, Ellie? He's my love." She kissed the broad skull. "Isn't he gorgeous?"

She reached down and stroked the creature's drooping penis with a casual touch of easy familiarity. The intense stare into Ellie's eyes was diverted as he turned to look at Mary. She met his gaze, her eyes wide open and expressionless. After another twenty seconds she began to nod her head.

"Ellie, Jamie would really like to get to know you better, even though he knows you're not from the true clan." She sounded thrilled. "Won't that be wonderful? I'll have to go back to the house in just a little while, but there's no need for you to do that, is there?"

Ellie gave a grunt of horror, struggling against the hand that held her throat until the world began to turn dark around her and her lungs ached in her chest. It was hopeless, he was immensely strong. She turned despairing eyes to Mary, pleading and imploring.

Mary nodded.

"It's all right. You can stay here with Jamie now. He wants to know you well, to see if you can help him too."

She frowned and looked round, a sudden worry creasing her broad forehead. "Now, where do you suppose I put my shoes?"

CHAPTER 22

The song had been coming nearer, little by little, sometimes louder and sometimes fainter but gradually growing in volume. The singer had an immature, high-pitched voice, and it was always the same song and the same words. "There was I, waiting at the church, waiting at the church, waiting at the church . . ."

At last it was near enough for a rustle and whisper of dried leaves to add itself to the girl's singing. The sequence of sounds had a steady, repeated pattern. Rustle, rustle, a long pause, then a verse of song, and rustle, rustle again. The puzzle of the sounds gradually began to unlock his consciousness, percolating into the deep breathlike trance that had held him motionless for several hours.

His senses came back slowly. Hearing first, and a long time later he became aware of the brown carpet of fallen leaves beneath him. When he opened his eyes, the stabbing shafts of sunlight that broke through the trees were unbearable agony. He grunted and closed his eyes again. Hearing had surfaced enough that he could detect the faint and far-off sounds of autumn birdsong. While he was still unable to move, another sound came, a frightening roar that increased until it shattered his ears and shook the ground he lay upon. After a few seconds it passed and peace returned.

He blinked and raised his head a little. Through half-focused eyes he could see an orange-brown blur wending its way past his line of vision, back and forth, left and right, gradually coming closer. The singsong little voice went on, "And he went, and left me in the lurch, and oh, how it did upset me, rather . . ."

He tried to lift himself higher. The sudden pain in his chest was unbearable, a driving dagger of twisted and ripped ligaments. With that pain he came back all the way to complete awareness. He knew who he was, and what he was doing. He gasped. The knowledge of a task neglected, a present danger, grew in him while he lay motionless in that painful sunlight. Finally he stirred again, easing himself up a fraction of an inch at a time until his weight was partially supported against a thick elder bush.

He ran one ruined hand slowly around the base of his ribs. He was bleeding again there, the knife wound had opened. He recalled the fiery pain in his eyes, the spinning plunge from the train, and the fall down the steep slope to the soft earth of the woods at its foot. The force of impact had been tremendous. It would surely have killed any ordinary human—would have killed him six months ago. Only the increasing pliability and flexibility of bone structure that came with Second Change had permitted him to survive.

The Change was still proceeding. He could feel through his torn shirt the thickening cartilage that girdled his abdomen.

The shattering roar was growing again, beating into his head. He lay forward, his chin on his chest until the train had passed.

Where was Roger Wilson now? Was he still speeding north, or had he too fallen, to die on the steep slope next to the tracks? He had to find out.

He lifted his head again and looked painfully around him. Then he realized that he had been incredibly lucky. Less than two yards in front of him the ground ended. He leaned forward, and saw that there was a sheer drop down to a brick-lined culvert that ran back under the railway tracks. A little farther, and he would have rolled right over the edge. Not even his changing body could have withstood that fall.

He felt a sudden uneasy tension, and slowly moved his head again, wincing at the pain of strained neck tendons.

Someone was standing close to him, silently watching every move that he made. It was a little girl, eight or nine years old, wearing an orange dress and leather, ankle-length boots a couple of sizes too big for her. She carried a cloth shopping bag in one hand and was staring at him with quiet, round eyes.

"Did you fall off a train?"

351

Her voice was deeper than he would have expected from the singing. He managed to nod.

"You're all scraped and scratched."

He cleared his throat and tried to speak. At first no sound would come.

"Uh—uh—fell. Fell down there." He waved his hand a little at the slope behind him.

She looked at him seriously with bright, brown eyes.

"Will you be all right?"

He allowed his head to slump forward again to his chest. It was a huge effort to speak, even for a short sentence. He was horribly weak. Without help he was doomed, he would never find his way through these woods and reach a road. But he could not accept help—above all else, he must avoid any offer of medical assistance.

After a few seconds of weary thought he forced himself to lift his head again.

"I'll be all right."

"You look sick, I think I ought to get Granpa." She held up the cloth bag. "We're mushrooming; we do that when I come for the day. He's farther over there; he'll be able to help."

"No."

The word was a feeble croak, and already she was turning away. He watched her hopelessly as she skipped and ran off through the trees, heading down the side of the railway line. Looking after her as she disappeared from sight, Petherton realized that there must be another tunnel of some kind running under the railway, parallel to the culvert in front of him. The girl must have dipped down into it, and would now be on the other side.

He tried to struggle to a more upright position. A grown man would see at once what the little girl had not, that his wounds were not the result of a simple fall from a train. The evidence of gross differences was growing with every hour. He managed to struggle out of his tweed jacket and placed it over his head and shoulders, shadowing his face.

The wood was again completely quiet. He saw that the sun was slanting lower through the branches, and the temperature felt a fraction cooler. He must have lain here unconscious for at least six hours, oblivious even to the noise of the main-line trains that rushed past every few minutes.

352

There was a flicker of orange again through the trees. The girl was coming back, leading the way, and behind her walked a gray-haired man. When they were in sight of Petherton, the man called the girl back to him, spoke to her quietly, and handed her a bunch of keys. She nodded, turned, and went back through the scattered trees to the tunnel under the road.

The man watched her go until she was out of sight, then came on and stopped about three yards away.

"I thought Rachel was making this all up." His voice was soft, full of a West Country burr. "Can you talk, eh?"

"Yes." Petherton nodded and cleared his throat. "I had an accident. I fell off the train. Don't worry. I'll be all right."

The other man was carrying a light knapsack on his back and held a thick ash stick with a loop of heavy wire fastened to one end of it. He stepped a pace nearer and peered at Petherton. His look was alert but puzzled.

"I thought you'd turn out to be a tramp, but you certainly don't sound like one. Fell off a train, did you? Here, why don't you slip off that jacket and let me have a look at you. I'm no doctor, and I can't do anything for a serious wound, but I always carry a first-aid kit when we come out here to look for fungi. I've got antiseptics and ointment, and a couple of good bandages. Let's see what I can do for you."

"No." Petherton huddled farther under his jacket. "I need no help. Thank you, but I don't need it."

"You don't, eh?" The man was bending lower, peering at Petherton's exposed hand. "I'm sorry, but I don't believe you on that one. I don't know if you fell off a train or not, but I think you ought to be in a hospital. Look here, my Lagonda is on the other side of that cutting. In less than a quarter of an hour I could drive you up to a hospital."

He straightened up, waiting for some reply. Petherton desperately tried to decide what he ought to do. He badly needed bandages and ointments, but he could risk neither examination nor a visit to a hospital. And he had to have Fluid. It had been almost twelve hours since he left Toby Duncan's college rooms, and now that he was again conscious, the craving from his starving body was a constant call on his attention. Already he was terribly weak. Without Fluid he could only get worse.

The other man swung his ash staff impatiently.

353

"Come on, man. Look, I don't know what you've done, and I don't much care. There's better people in the jails than out of them these days. Once you get to a hospital, what you tell them and what you do afterward is none of my business. But I'll tell you this much, it's going to be cold tonight. I heard the weather forecast, and it'll be dipping down toward freezing. If the sky stays clear we'll have a ground frost. You can't afford to spend the night out here in those clothes, and from the look of you I don't think you could walk out without help."

He banged at a tree trunk with his stick. "Come on, let's get you down to the car."

He sounded confident and determined, and unlikely to listen to any suggestion that he should leave. Petherton looked across through the trees toward the cutting. There was no sign of Rachel. He felt a stab of pain from his battered chest, and a twist of hunger deep inside him. That decided it. Only one course of action was left.

He nodded his head.

"I'll come. Help me up."

He held out one hand and grasped at the elder bush with the other. The man put down his ash stick and took his arm. Together they straightened to a standing position, Petherton leaning his weight on the other man.

His plan beyond that point had been simple. One twist would break the neck cleanly and silently. After he had quickly taken the blood he needed, he would tip the body over the edge into the culvert and be strong enough to slip away through the woods before the girl Rachel returned to look for her grandfather.

It went wrong half a second before he reached out for the old man's leathery neck. At that moment, the other caught his first closeup look at Petherton's face. He gasped in horror and disgust and took a quick step backward.

Petherton's lunge forward was short by inches, but he followed it up with a painful, dragging step toward the man. The other moved backward again, out of reach, without any thought of the ground behind him. His rear foot went over the edge. There was a moment when he wavered on the brink, waving his arms violently in an attempt to regain his balance, then he slipped backward and was gone.

Petherton heard a brief cry and the slapping thump of a

body against hard brick, twenty-five feet below. He had fallen forward to his hands and knees when his lunge at the other man had missed. Now he crawled slowly to the edge and looked over.

The body lay twisted and broken below him. For a few seconds he wondered how he could climb down there, but he soon realized that he could never manage it, not in his present weakened condition.

He crawled slowly back to the elder bush and leaned against it, breathing painfully. His rib cage felt as though someone were pushing hot wires through it. The sun was sinking lower. He realized that it would be dark in little more than an hour, and already he could feel the ominous chill on his exposed skin.

Petherton thought about his failure as a Guardian, about the report that must be carried back to the Elders. His options were crowding down to nothing, reducing themselves to a single, inevitable action.

For five minutes more he was slumped there, motionless. Finally he turned his head and looked over to the left. It was here at last. A thin, young voice was singing again, "waiting at the church, waiting at the church . . . ," and again he could see the blur of orange skipping happily through the darkening wood.

He pulled himself higher against the bush, wiped his battered hands on his jacket, and waited for Rachel.

CHAPTER 23

When the wind blew from the east or the south, *Windsor* was partly shielded by the other two trailers. But a north wind, or one slightly west of north like today's, came down on the channel of the Minch with a clean run all the way from the Arctic Ocean, and the point where the trailers stood on the cliff was the first to intercept its southward swoop. *Windsor*, nearest to the edge, received the full weight of those northern blasts.

Don leaned back in his chair, tapped a pencil against his teeth and listened to the sounds around him. He could track each of them to its source. That high, shivering rattle came from the trailer roof. The aluminum sheet above his head vibrated like the top of a taut snare drum as the wind brushed across its surface. The lower, pulsing note was gusts of wind hitting in an irregular rhythm against the side and setting up a sympathetic resonance in the line of metal file cabinets that ran along that wall. And there was no doubt about it, the wind was still strengthening. It was close to noon, and for the past four hours the noises had grown steadily as the wind move round from west to north.

Don sniffed, pulled out his hankie and blew his nose hard. He had slept poorly last night, and now he was full of morning sniffles. Maybe he had a cold coming on. Whatever it was, his head felt thick, and he was having trouble concentrating on the report that he was writing. He wanted to go down to the caves, but he had to finish this and leave it for Lord Jericho before he could cut out of here. He blew his nose again, leaned back in his chair, and stared up at the plain ceiling. After a few seconds he looked at his watch, reached over to the clock radio on the shelf behind him, and switched it on.

He rubbed at his itching eyes, waiting while the announcer worked his way past the latest bad news on inflation and the declining productivity, then at last went on to the weather.

". . . north-north-west and steady until this evening. Gale warnings are in force from . . ."

Now would be the perfect time for it. There would be a long sweep of the tide around the point and into the caves from the north. With a spring tide due in forty-eight hours, the difference between the official flows in the caves and Don's recomputed ones would be as big as they would ever get.

Get the report done and out of here, that was the thing to do.

Don was not surprised when he heard a bang on the door behind him. He had jammed it shut to try and keep out the drafts, but Mike was due here any minute, bringing a jug of coffee and no doubt complaining about the impossibility of making a decent brew with an electric percolator. But at least the cup would warm his hands; they were white and chilled around the fingertips and he had trouble holding the pencil.

He took a quick look at the drawer in the desk. Maybe a few drops of whisky in with the milk and sugar? He was very aware of the flat bottle, a solid presence less than two feet from him. It was still full, and he wanted to keep it that way—but the real sign that he had it all licked would be when it could be moderation instead of all-or-nothing.

Don stood up, went to the door, and pulled the sheet of padding felt to one side. Before he could get to the handle the door was yanked open. He stared as the man standing leaning against the outside wall blundered in.

"Roger. Hey, I thought you were going to be another day in Cambridge."

"I'm here." Roger's voice was hoarse. "Don, where's Mary?"

Without waiting for an answer he walked across to Don's chair, groaned, and dropped heavily into it. He was limping slightly and favoring the left side of his body. Don saw a vivid purple bruise on the left cheek and two long parallel scratches that ran from temple to chin.

"My God, Roger, what's happened to you? Have you been in a car crash?"

"No." Roger sighed and rubbed tenderly at his left side. "Not that simple. Never mind me—where's Mary?"

"She's home, back at the house." Don glanced again at his watch. "No, by now she might be in the village—she told me she had to do grocery shopping today, but I needed the car. She'll have walked in. What is all this?"

"Mary's all right, thank God for that." Roger relaxed, slumping forward to rest his elbows and forearms across his knees. "The bloody awful phone system round here, they must have put it in when they got off the Ark. I've been trying to get through to you for nearly fourteen hours now, from Doncaster and then from Edinburgh and Inverness." He sighed. "Christ, do I feel buggered."

Don noticed the black-rimmed eye sockets and the gray pallor of his cheeks. "Look, why the questions? You look as though you've been out boozing all night long."

"No such luck." Roger laughed harshly. "No such bloody lucky. I've been driving over those God-forsaken roads from Inverness. The bastard that I hired a car from sent me off with a nearly empty tank—all I could get—and I wasted three hours waiting for a garage to open and freezing half to death—the car heater didn't work either." He rubbed at his reddened eyeballs. "Don, do you have any hot coffee? I could really use some."

"Mike should be here soon with a pot unless he's got lost on the way. Here." Don reached into the left-hand desk drawer and took out the bottle of whisky and a six-ounce glass. "This might do you more good than coffee."

He saw that Roger took a quick look at the level in the bottle before he poured. It was deep satisfaction to know that there was less than an inch of liquor gone from the top of it. He sat down in the other chair.

"So come on, tell me what's happening. You look like the town drunk—out for a night on the town and lost a fight."

"No." Roger drank down an inch of whisky, shivered, and shook his head. "I won the fight. Here, where's your car parked?"

"Round at the back of *Sandringham*. Why?"

"As soon as I've had another go at this I want you to take us over to Laxford. I'm not sure that clapped-out heap I've

358

been driving will ever start again—the dynamo's not working right and the battery's been getting lower and lower. But the sooner we get to Laxford, the better I'll feel. I want to actually see Mary, then I'll be a lot happier."

His serious tone was sending shivers up Don's spine. Surely Mary was all right? She had seemed it when he left her—still cold to him and with no sign of affection, but as fit as she'd ever been. Problems? He had to find out what *their* problem was. Maybe if Ellie arrived today they'd find out what had been eating her.

"Roger, I've had more than I can take of the funny talk. For God's sake, man, I mean to say, you keep going on about Mary—why the hell *shouldn't* she be all right? I'm just her husband, you know—I've got some interest in her too."

Roger slammed the empty glass on the desk, took a long, shuddering breath, and abruptly stood up.

"You're quite right. I'm too beat to think straight. Let's go, and I'll tell you all I know on the way in to Laxford." He stood for a moment, staring Don in the eye, then shook his head. "It's going to sound odd to you. Don't tell me I'm all wet until you've heard everything. That's something I've been worrying about all the way up here, how would I ever get anybody to listen to me. It all sounds too much like the sort of thing you hear from people before they tell you they're really Napoleon. I was thinking of old Campbell, how we listened to him and humored him, but I really thought he was as mad as a hatter and ready to be locked up. Come on, I'm too tired to hang about and wait for Mike's coffee."

Don had to move the markers, flashlights, and lines to the back seat of the car to let Roger climb into the passenger seat. He noticed that Roger sat at an angle, still keeping his left side well away from the seat back. He had closed his eyes, content to let Don take care of the drive over to Laxford.

"Remember the papers that I was going to take down to Duncan in Cambridge?" he said. His voice was low and slow, as though the physical effort of getting here had taken every element of energy from him, but his words were clear and organized. "Well, I took those papers to him. He told me what I thought he'd tell me, that they had nothing to do with devil worship. Campbell had been wrong. But that night—the night before last—at dinner . . ."

He left out no steps. By the time they reached the Over The Water, he had carried Don carefully and fully from the meeting with Duncan to his departure from Cambridge by the early train, when he had sat in the carriage and the final picture of what he had heard from Campbell and Duncan and Plummer built its logical structure in his brain.

"But why didn't you and Campbell realize all this when you looked at the papers?" Don sounded unconvinced. (Roger didn't sound insane—but he could certainly be badly overstressed.) "After all, you had what Knowlton had written down, and you say that he knew the whole thing, three years ago."

"It wasn't easy. Campbell only saw what he wanted to see—diabolism and gematria and rubbish like that. I couldn't see a pattern at all. All Knowlton's papers were one big, scrambled mess of bits and pieces. It was like being given a jigsaw puzzle: all the pieces were there but it wasn't organized. Don't forget those must have been Knowlton's rough notes."

"But you lost them?"

"Yes. They're scattered over half Lincolnshire. I wish we could find the originals. Anyway, Knowlton would never have given anybody those notes to read. He'd have redone everything into a logical order before he used it."

Roger blinked his eyes open as the car slowed and stopped. "I would never have put things together if it hadn't been for Harry Plummer. He pointed out what those diagrams were all about. And I still wouldn't have really believed it—not deep down—unless I'd had some other evidence. Direct evidence."

Don said nothing. Even if Roger's stories of creatures who lived in Laxford and preyed on human women to bear their children was no more than a fairy story, there was no doubt that Roger believed it. And Roger sincerely feared that Mary might be in some sort of danger. That was enough.

Before the car's engine had stopped turning over, Don was outside and running into the Over The Water. Roger went much more slowly. He climbed wearily out and followed Don toward the inn. Before he got there he paused and looked around. There was a familiar noise in the air, rising above the wind, a thrum-thrum-thrum of broad rotors. After a few more seconds he saw the unmistakable shape of the helicop-

360

ter drifting westward along the loch, yawing and pitching in the strong gusts.

It would land about a quarter of a mile inland, on the gentle slope that led from the church to the village. Roger frowned, rubbed the back of his hand across his aching head, and turned to go on toward the inn.

What day was it? Had he lost twenty-four hours somewhere? Lord Jericho must have made a change of plans and come back from Paris a day earlier than he had expected.

There were only five people in the bar. Dora, Don, and three silent customers who were drinking their midday beer and talking neither to Dora nor each other.

"Oh, yes, she was in here this morning," Dora was saying. She was busy wiping the bar down with a damp cloth even though it already looked quite clean. "We had a bit of a chat. But she already went back home. I told her, I said, 'Miss Mary, there's going to be heavy rain later, we always get it when we have a blow along the Minch this way, and you're out here with no coat. You ought to go on back as soon as you can,' I said."

"But she seemed to be all right?" Don looked at Roger as he spoke.

"Why, of course she did." Dora squinted up at him, her shrewd blue eyes puzzled. "Now, why would you think she might not be? You know how the air around here seems to agree with her; she was looking as well as she could ever look. I was telling Hamish"—she nodded at the landlord as he came through the door that led back to the kitchen of the inn. "I said to him just this morning, I said that I thought he was right, Miss Mary's a real Macveagh, she thrives here just like she was born to it. Didn't I say just that, Hamish?"

"Aye, that she did." Hamish nodded his greeting to Don and Roger.

"You saw Mary too?" Don was feeling a lot better, but he wanted all the confirmation he could find.

"This morning? No, I was inland buyin' a couple of carcasses of mutton, an' she was off back to the house before I arrived here. Gone back to look after your visitor, I suppose." Hamish tried to hide his curiosity with a poor show of nonchalance. "An' how's the young lady likin' Laxford, eh?"

"Mary?" Don couldn't follow Hamish's meaning. "She loves Laxford, you know that."

361

"Not Miss Mary, I meant the other lady, the one as came yesterday. What was her name, now? I don't think she ever told it, but she's the one stayin' with you, the lady from the United States."

Roger saw Don's face flush with feeling, and the hand that rested on the bar twitched slightly as Don swung to stare hard at Hamish.

"We had no visitor yesterday. I thought we might have one. Ellie Durning?" He paused, but Hamish looked blank. "She never came. I'm expecting her to get here today. Are you saying that she came *yesterday?*"

"That she did." Hamish looked around the bar for confirmation but was met with blank looks from all but Dora, who nodded her agreement at him. "You saw her, right? And served a drink to her, her and the driver."

"Aye, an' she said she was on her way up to your house." Dora frowned and stared at the polished bar counter, trying to recall any other details of the visitors. "She knew who I was, called me by name. She told me that Miss Mary had wirtten about me in letters to her. Would that be the same young lady as you were expecting?"

"Yes." Don shook his head and turned to Roger. "Ellie was supposed to come here yesterday or today, depending on what she could manage for train connections. But she never came to the house last night, and Mary didn't mention anything about her arriving during the day. What the hell could have happened to her? She couldn't disappear between here and the house—not unless she fell over the cliff on the way."

"No, sir." Hamish was polite but firm. "I know she didn't have any accident on the way. She didn't walk, see, she had a driver brought her here. And he stopped by for a drink on the way back, to see him on his way, like. And he told me he'd dropped the lady off right at the house."

Hamish rubbed thoughtfully at the top of his bald head and narrowed his eyes in concentration. "Now there's no other house on up the road from here that he could have taken her to by mistake, I'm certain sure of that. So where would she be?" He looked across at the door, and his expression brightened. "Here's the mon with the good thinkin' piece on him. Maybe the Laird can suggest what happened to her?"

Lord Jericho had stepped into the bar, breathing hard from

a quick walk up the hill. His cheeks were rosy, and the spiky strands of hair around his bald dome pointed in all directions, blown about by the boisterous wind.

"Phew. Bit brisk out there, eh?" He bustled up to the bar counter. "Roger and Don, I was hoping I'd find you both here. We tried at the trailers, and Mike there told me you must have gone off somewhere. We need to talk." As he came closer to the group around the bar counter, he saw their faces and sensed the tense atmosphere. "Now then, what's going on here? More trouble?"

Roger looked around the bar. The three regulars had finished their beer and left, irritated by the noise and the conversation. That left Hamish and Dora. Could he rely on the fact that neither of them was linked to the Selkies? Dora was a safe bet, and Hamish's job, appearance, and reputation made the idea that he might be a secret sire of local bastards seem ludicrous. It would be a calculated risk, but an acceptable one.

"We do have a problem," he said. "We don't know how big. But what are you doing back so soon? We thought you'd be there at least another day."

"I called the Ministry from Paris, trying to clear up that snag on the reporting requirements. I s'pose you heard about it too, from the look of you. No approvals for a change unless Petherton signs off on it, and nobody down in London seems to be able to reach the old bugger." Lord Jericho scowled at the memory. "Have you been in touch with him in the past couple of days, Roger? One of the girls at our offices says he was trying to reach you by phone."

"Yes, I've been in touch with him." Roger turned to Hamish. "Pour us drinks all around—yes, you too, Don. You'll need this one."

He waited for a few seconds as Hamish arranged the glasses and began to pour (doubles—Roger's voice spelled trouble), then turned back to face Jericho.

"I've seen Petherton." His voice was under tight control, but his hand was rubbing the side of his face, touching the bruise and the red line of deep scratches. "He did this to me on a train from Peterborough to Edinburgh. I had to kill him. If I hadn't he'd have killed me."

"*Killed* him. Petherton?" Lord Jericho's blunt features remained calm but his eyes bulged outward a fraction. He

363

looked at Hamish and gestured at the filled glasses. Hamish handed him one without a word. "You *killed* him? Roger, don't bugger about now, we can't do with joking."

"I'm not joking." Roger reached out for a glass and tossed back the spirit before he spoke again. "God knows, Joshua, I wish I were. This is news to Don, too, so I might as well tell all of you what happened. You said we've got problems, Joshua—"

"I bloody well did. But I was talking about Ministry reports, not killing people. Petherton was a nuisance, but he was harmless enough—"

"Petherton was a monster. We've got problems, but they're a lot worse than you think." Roger turned to Don. "I heard what Hamish said, but I think we ought to go on up to your house while we talk about this. We've heard that Mary's all right, but what about Ellie? All this has to be tied together, Petherton and Ellie and Campbell."

"Ellie? Who in hell is Ellie?" Jericho had drunk down his whisky as easy as breathing and was reaching for another full glass.

"We'll get to that." Roger sighed. "God, what a mess. Come on, we'll all fit in your car, Don, if we're willing to squeeze in with the equipment. Let's do one more thing before we go. Let's call the house from here and make sure that Mary really is all right."

"I'll do it this second." Don walked to the next room where the link from the inn to the house was located.

Roger turned to Jericho. "Joshua, I'm dead serious about all this. There's been murder in Laxford—murder and worse. And it's not over yet. I want you to talk to Toby Duncan down in Cambridge and listen carefully to what he tells you."

The call went through in a few seconds, while the others stood in total silence. After four rings the phone was picked up at the other end. Roger turned the earpiece so that everyone could listen to the reply.

"Hello? St. John's Porter's Lodge? I'd like you to put me through to Professor Duncan."

There was a pause at the other end, then a startled voice said, "Hold on a moment, sir."

The silence at the other end stretched to ten seconds. Then it was a different voice on the telephone, gruffer and stronger.

"You were calling for Professor Toby Duncan?"

364

"That's right. Would you put me through, please."

"This is Inspector Barker of the Cambridge Police Department. Would you be kind enough to identify yourself and tell me why you are calling Professor Duncan." The words carried clearly out into the room.

Roger raised his eyebrows and shrugged at the others. "My name is Wilson, Roger Wilson, and I had dinner with Professor Duncan the night before last. I want to ask him a couple of questions."

"Ah." A grunt from the harsh voice at the other end of the line. "Where are you speaking from now?"

"The Over The Water Inn, in Laxford up in Sutherland County." Roger could not sense what was coming from the neutral tones down in Cambridge. "Could I please speak to Professor Duncan?"

"I'm afraid not, sir. Professor Duncan has been killed."

"Killed?"

"Almost certainly murdered. We will need to speak to you soon, sir. I must ask you not to leave without notifying me in advance. If you had dinner with him two days ago you must have been one of the last people to see him alive."

"I'll remain here." Roger's voice was husky. "Can you tell me how Professor Duncan died?"

"No, sir. Remember to notify us of your movements should you wish to leave Laxford. We'll be in touch with you."

There was a click and the hum of an open phone line.

Roger put the receiver back on the hook and looked around at the others. He was breathing hard and rubbing nervously at the parallel scratches that ran down the muscles of his left cheek.

"Petherton killed him. I'm sure of it. Joshua, that's not the evidence I was going to provide you, but it ought to be more than we need. Come on, let's get the hell out of here and up to that house. Where the devil has Don got to?"

"I'll go and get him, sir." Hamish scuttled breathlessly back through the bar and into the other room.

"He said Duncan was murdered." Jericho dropped into a seat by the bar and scratched at the wisps of hair surrounding his bald crown. "By Gor, *murdered*. Roger, I'll be damned if I can hold all this together. You'd better give me a proper briefing. For a start, who was this fellow Duncan?"

"Somebody that Petherton suspected knew too much about what's been going on in this village." Roger was massaging his left shoulder with his hand, digging savagely into the tender muscles and wincing as he did so. "And poor old Toby Duncan didn't know half of it. That murderous bastard, he deserved worse than he got." He swung round as Don followed Hamish back from the other room. "Well?"

Don shook his head. "Mary says she never saw Ellie, yesterday or today, and everything's fine up at the house. We have to get on up there. Somebody's not telling the truth. Hamish, are you quite sure that you and Dora didn't—"

"Sure and certain as we can be, sir. It's not a thing a man could be makin' a mistake on, now is it?"

"It's not." Roger looked at Don. "I know it's hard to think that Mary could be lying, but I think that Hamish had better come on to the house with us. I want to see if Mary sticks to her side of the story with Hamish there to give his side straight to her face."

"So you think Mary's lying." Don's voice was cold and angry.

Roger shrugged. "I never said that. All I say is both stories can't be right. The sooner we get on up there, the sooner we'll have this sorted out. Let's go. I'll sit in the back with Hamish, and you and Joshua can sit up front. I'll explain what I know about this, Joshua, while we're on the way. Now, come on and let's start moving. I can't take much more of this."

Driving on the road along the cliff edge was tricky once they were piled into the car and on their way. Strong winds struck at them from the side, with odd gusts and swirls that tugged and twisted at the car's steering. Don had to attend to the simple business of driving, listening to Roger with only half an ear. Could Mary have been lying to them? And why? That made no more sense than the rest of it.

Curled up in the cramped rear seat, Roger quietly unfolded all the events of the past week, Campbell, Duncan, and finally the meeting with Petherton—with the thing that Petherton had become. He spoke in a flat, unemotional tone, but his hands were trembling on the seat back when he came to the final moments in the luggage van of the train.

Hamish was completely silent. The old stories and bogeymen of his childhood were back in concrete form, in a form

366

that wouldn't go away when daylight came. He grunted once, when Roger talked about Jeanie Inglis's death on the harrow. That was still too fresh in his memory.

Lord Jericho asked occasional questions, staring forward impassively through the windshield. At one point Roger leaned forward between the driver's and the passenger's seats.

"Joshua, you sound as if you don't believe any of this. I swear that I've not exaggerated a word."

Jericho shrugged, still noncommittal. "We'll see. I've been through a fair bit of strange stuff in my time—more than you lads might think. I'm not ready to make up my mind yet." His tone was calm, but the tough streak that had lifted him from a slum childhood was showing through. And he was lighting a strong black cigar, something that was never indulged in so early in the day.

Don's attention was still only half on the talk in the car. A new thought was in his head, and he kept stealing quick looks out to the left, to the sea. The tide was still on the ebb, defying the gale-force winds that tried to drive the water toward the shore. His mind carried on with the subconscious work of assessing the sea flows in the tidal caves. Other matters had higher priority, but conditions were as good as they would ever be for disposing of the mystery that had plagued him for the past month.

Inside the house, Mary listened to the sighing of the wind around the back door. Changes in air pressure made the old wood stove balky, reluctant to produce an even and well-balanced blaze. When she opened the doors to load more wood, thin streamers of blue smoke came curling out into the room, scenting the air with the sweet smell of apple wood. She was on her knees in front of it now, reluctant to open it again and make the kitchen even smokier.

She still wore the slacks and heavy sweater that she had put on for her trip to the village. As soon as she'd got back she had kneaded fresh dough and placed it to rise on the shelf over the back of the stove. Now she was dreamily waiting, drifting back into the pleasant thoughts that conversation with people in the village had briefly disturbed. She had enjoyed the slow walk home, admiring the sea's changing scenes. The wind didn't seem to touch her skin. She had felt warm and rosy, enjoying the easy movement of her body and welcoming the effort that her muscles provided against the long upgrade that brought her to the house.

Later today, as soon as the bread was made, she would go and see Jamie and they would slip away together into the private world that he had made for them. She could not imagine how she had once lived without him to guide her and to protect her.

Mary frowned as she stood up and dusted wood ash from her knees. Jamie would tell her when the time was right, she knew that, but she wished that it could be sooner. When would she and Jamie be able to tell everyone? Then they would all be happy for her. And Don and Ellie would be especially happy, because she knew that they loved her and would be thrilled at her happiness.

Perhaps Jamie would bring Ellie with him to the meeting today, now that they were all friends. And soon Jamie would let her meet his other friends, his beloved Elders who lived at the heart of Jamie's world.

A sudden draft blew smoke out of the dampers in the front of the stove. The front door of the house had been sharply opened and a gust of wind had rushed through the whole house. Mary rubbed at her nose, leaving a gray smudge of ash on the tip, and turned puzzled toward the door to the living room. It was too early for Don to be home, and today she was supposed to go and see Jamie instead of him coming to collect her.

But it *was* Don. He was moving quickly, his face anxious, and behind him were Roger and Hamish Macveagh. She stood still, wondering what they were doing here in the house.

"Mary. You're all right?" Don came over to where she was standing and grasped her arms hard. Too tight. He was hurting her. She pulled away, unable to understand why he would grab her with such force.

"I'm all right, Don." She pointed behind her at the ledge. "See, I'm making bread for us. I'll have it ready to put in the oven in another few minutes."

Don had turned to look back at the others, so she smiled at them over his shoulder. She was fond of both of them, especially Roger. There had been a time when she thought that she would get very close to Roger—maybe even become his lover. But that had been *before*.

Mary wondered if they would all like coffee. Of course she

368

was all right. Why *shouldn't* she be all right, when everything was so wonderful?

She saw that Roger was looking at her strangely, not smiling at all. He was bruised, he had hurt his face, but he looked somehow relieved. It was Don who still looked angry or worried; he had turned back to her and his face was still unhappy. She could see the tightness around his mouth and the little vertical lines of tension above his nose.

"Mary." He was coming close to her again and suddenly she felt afraid. He did look angry, angry and intense. "Mary, Hamish says that Ellie came here yesterday. I know you said she didn't, but he says that he saw her at the inn, and he saw the driver who dropped her off here at the house. Mary, I've got to ask again. Did you see her here?"

It came like a sudden shock through her body. Hamish said she must have seen Ellie. Ellie. Had she seen Ellie, yesterday?

You didn't see Ellie. You were not in the caves.

She felt the sudden flash, an image of warm lovemaking and building excitement, then Jamie pulling away from her. She could feel the pain and misery of his withdrawal. Don's face looked huge in front of her, staring intently into her eyes.

"Ellie? Did I see . . ."

You did not see Ellie. You did not leave Ellie with me.

But Hamish was here, and he said that Ellie had been at the house. And Don's face was still there, still looking straight at her.

You must act normally. You must protect our Secret. Whatever you do, you must not speak to anyone about us.

"Ellie . . . I didn't see Ellie here. I didn't see her here."

Roger's face was next to Don's now, and instead of relief she could read questioning there. She backed away from them, retreating across the kitchen. Hamish was coming forward too, his thin face red and perplexed.

"Now, Miss Mary, she must have been here—even if you didn't see her. The driver told me that he dropped her off at the door. When he turned the car and looked back she had the door open and was comin' in here. Miss, did she come in and leave again?"

She had made a mistake, she realized that now. Instead of saying that Ellie was not here she should have said that she

369

had been and then left, gone back, gone somewhere. The faces were still crowding in, still forcing her backward.

Don't give away our secret. Don't tell them anything about us.

The voice beat firmly inside her head.

Mary had backed up as far as she could go, with the wood stove and the range above it right behind her. She could feel the heat through her thick slacks.

"I—I don't know what happened. I didn't see Ellie here." She clung to that thought, it at least was the truth. "I never saw her *here* at all."

There was a battle going on inside her now. Jamie's order was fighting the need to explain, the need to make Don and Roger understand. She had to make them understand, or that would fail Jamie too.

Behind them she saw Lord Jericho appear in the kitchen doorway. He was smoking a cigar, his head hunched forward on his shoulders and his chin jutting out. He walked into the kitchen, moved in front of Don and Roger and shook his head.

"It's no good, lass." His voice was gentle. "I've no idea why you're doin' this, but it'd be better for all of us if you'd tell us the truth. Here, this was over by the front door. See the name on it?"

He was holding a blue and white slip of cardboard in his hand. Mary realized it was an airline luggage tag, the sort they put on your baggage when you checked it in at the airport. Ellie must have put her name on it.

She felt dizzy.

Don't let anyone know Ellie was in the house. Hide anything she left there. Hide it, hide it, hide it.

Ellie's two cases, standing by the front door.

Hide them, hide them.

But she had failed. They knew that Ellie had been here, they would learn about Jamie and their secret place. They would take it all away.

Mary gave a low cry of anguish and looked at the faces looming in front of her. They were accusing and cold, forcing her deeper into trouble with Jamie, making her betray him. She could not face them. Mary spun around, staring about the kitchen for an escape from that insistent and frightening inquisition.

370

"Look out!"

It was Roger, moving suddenly forward and trying to reach her. He was thwarted by the sudden pain in his left arm and shoulder, still aching and refusing to move fast enough.

He had seen the iron pan behind her, standing steaming gently on top of the stove. Mary kept it there as a useful source of water hotter than the old gas heater could produce. Roger realized that Mary's elbow would catch the long handle as she turned.

He was too late. The pan tilted and boiling water cascaded out and onto the floor of the kitchen. Mary's slacks shielded her from most of it, but her right foot and ankle were in the path of the scalding steam. A full pint of water splashed over them.

Mary had never felt any pain like it. She screamed, high and faint, then began to fall forward toward the stove. If Roger had not reached out again and yanked her back she would have gone face-first onto the dull black surface, a five hundred degree heat that would strip flesh in a second. He gripped her firmly, holding her upright.

Mary didn't hear the noise behind her. There was a storm inside her head that masked external events. She felt as though she had been yanked from a warm and comfortable bed and plunged into a snow-fed waterfall. The pain could not be resisted. It dragged her brutally up from the pleasant lotus land where she had been drowsing away the days. She surfaced reluctantly, coming back to the unpleasant reality of the moment. Someone was carrying her through to the living room and placing her on the couch there. She opened her eyes and saw that Don was taking off her shoes and gently turning up the leg of her slacks.

She reached out for his hand. "Don. What happened?"

"You'll be all right. It's a nasty scald, but it could be a lot worse. Lie quiet now." His voice was tender.

"Don, I didn't mean the water. I mean what *happened*—to me." She was shuddering inside, recalling the way she had been torn apart by the opposing commands. "Don, it's true. Ellie was here. She was here yesterday."

He paused in his examination of her foot, frowning up at her. "I thought she must have been. But Mary, where did she go?"

371

Suddenly a voice inside her was back, screaming again, *Say nothing, say nothing, say nothing.* She didn't want to talk of Jamie, of the pleasant hours they had spent, talking together and laughing about the village and the people. But she had to help Ellie, Ellie had never been in the caves before. She might be in danger there.

Say nothing. Keep the secret.

"No." Mary gasped the word aloud. "She went . . . she went to . . ."

It was impossible to force the words out, they were blocked in her throat. But she had to say them. "The caves. Down in the caves." Her voice was a gurgling sob. "Ellie's in the caves."

She groaned and closed her eyes. She had said it, but now there was a tearing pain behind her eyes, the twisting grip of a brutal hand stripping her mind out of her body.

"The caves." Don stood up suddenly. "Christ, they're a death trap for anybody who doesn't know them. Ellie must have been there all night. *Mary.*" He shook her. "Mary, why did she go there? Was somebody with her, or did she go alone?"

Mary couldn't answer. The hand was still there, squeezing down, pressing her to silence. Her eyes were wide open but the living room was dim, black bordered and swimming with dark clouds and smoky shapes.

Don was shaking her urgently, squeezing her arms. "Mary. Can you hear me? Was she alone?"

Mary managed to shake her head, a weak little movement against the cushion. "No." It was the faintest of whispers. "Not—not alone."

Roger had stepped closer and was now bending low over her, his face only inches from hers. "Mary, don't faint now. Answer me if you can. Was it Jamie MacPherson who took Ellie down to the caves? Can you hear me, Mary? Was it Jamie?"

Jamie, Jamie.

Mary felt tears welling into her eyes. She would have to answer, even if her brain burst within her head. But it would be another betrayal, another loss. She still had to speak. Jamie should not have taken Ellie there, that was wrong. She lifted her head a fraction of an inch and nodded weakly.

Then she had to close her eyes again as the pressing hand rushed her away into the terrifying darkness.

"I was wrong." Roger looked down at Mary's unconscious face, then turned to Don and Lord Jericho. "Damn it, I thought all along that it was just Mary who was in danger. I was wrong—it's Ellie, too."

Don was still crouched by Mary, his eyes blank and shocked. He cleared his throat and swallowed twice before he could speak. "She's in terrible danger. Jamie took her down to the caves. To the caves." He stood up slowly. "When we were driving over here I still thought it might all be some kind of misunderstanding—even when you told me that Duncan had died in Cambridge I couldn't accept most of it. But what do we do now? That—that *thing* you told us about has got Ellie."

"She's down there, but she's probably still alive." Jericho had shouldered his way past Roger and was looking thoughtfully down at Mary, still lying with her eyes closed. "They don't usually kill women—not if Roger's right. She'll be down there now. Don, how well do you know those caves?"

Don was pulling himself together, concentrating to give a logical reply. "I think I know them pretty well. They're a labyrinth, but I've been studying them for months. I don't think the official plans that you gave me are any good—the caves have extra chambers up under the cliffs. But I've made my own plans, and I really think I can find my way through there better than anybody."

He took a long breath and straightened up. "I agree, we have to do it. If none of this had come up I wanted to go down there anyway and check out my ideas for flow rates. I've got the kit in the car. If you'll stay here and look after Mary I'll go—this minute. The sooner I leave, the better the conditions down there to look for her."

"Not alone." Roger was shaking his head, rubbing at the back of his hand where a few splashes of boiling water had caught him. "Jamie's a Selkie, same as Petherton. You can't believe how strong he'll be—far stronger than you or me. You'll need help, all the help you can get, and you'll need something to protect yourself with."

"Don't suggest it, Roger." Don was looking him over. "You've been battered by Petherton and you were up all night. You couldn't protect me any better than a day-old kitten could. I should go."

"I'm a damn sight better than nothing—give me something to hit with and I'll produce a pretty good bash with it. Don, you have to have help. We don't know how many of those things there might be down there. We've only heard of Petherton and Jamie, but there could be a lot more of them. Knowlton talked about other forms, things that they change into later on in their lives. We don't know what they might be like, or where we'd find them."

Don had paused, turning indecisively from Mary to Roger and back. He had the sudden memory of Jeanie's funeral, of the coffin slipping and Jamie stepping in and holding up the load of three men. Then of the caves with Petherton, watching him carry a fifty-pound set of markers easily in one hand—why hadn't he suspected something back then? Petherton said he'd looked for Don, but when they got out on the shore Petherton still had the set of markers. How hard could you look for somebody if you were willing to carry a fifty-pound burden along when you did it?

Don nodded reluctantly. "I guess you're right. I could use some help. But what about Mary? Doesn't she need a doctor?"

"I think not." Now Lord Jericho had stepped forward and bent to look at Mary's scalded foot. "It's not too bad. I can take care of it for now—I saw plenty of burn cases during the war. This one's superficial. And it's more important for you to go down there with reinforcements than it is for us to stay up here and worry about Mary's leg. That'll keep. I think we should *all* go, if these Selkies are as strong as Roger says."

"I agree." Roger turned to Hamish. "Can't you get somebody up here from the Over The Water to tend to Mary—that phone line runs through there, doesn't it?"

"Aye, it's a direct line."

"Then if you'll get Dora or Lizzie here we can all go with Don."

Hamish drew in his breath. The old fears and bogeys were crowding back in on him. After a few seconds he made up his mind. He nodded.

"I'll get one of them to walk on up here, and I'll come with ye. But what if we have to fight them? I'm no coward,

374

and I've fought as a fair welterweight in my time"—he doubled his small fist and jabbed vigorously at the air—"but I'm not one to take on Jamie MacPherson. He's a big lad, monster or no monster."

Don shrugged. "There's no weapons in the house, no guns or anything like that, I suppose that we could use the car jack, that's about all."

"We can do better than that. Hamish, you go ahead and make your call to the Over The Water." Lord Jericho was automatically falling back into the habit of organizing people and giving instructions. "Don, we don't need rockets and flamethrowers—I hope to hell we don't, or we're all in deep trouble. You can get a fair way with this stuff here, though."

He walked over to the fireplace and bent by the massive andirons. They were old and solid. Lord Jericho picked up a heavy iron poker with a polished brass handle and swung it hard against the paneled wall. There was a hollow thud and a deep dent in the solid oak.

"I wouldn't like a whack from that. Here, Roger, you have a go with this poker, and I'll take the rake. Hamish can have the tongs. Bloody hell." Jericho was looking down at the iron tongs with their wicked clawed ends. "Where did you find these, in a torture chamber? I'd not like to be the Selkie who cops that lot across his chops."

"What about me?" Don was still standing empty-handed.

"You travel light—we might want somebody who's a bit more mobile. Stick a middle-sized kitchen knife in your pocket; that's as good as anythin'." Jericho looked down at the rake he was holding. "God knows I hope we won't have to use these, but if we do you all remember one thing. Hit hard first time, and don't bugger about with these Selkies, whatever they look like. I've not liked the sound of what Roger's been tellin' us, not liked that at all." He turned to Hamish. "Did yer get through to Dora and Lizzie?"

Hamish nodded. He was swinging the tongs experimentally, the breath quick and nervous in his throat. "Aye. They'll be up presently. I told 'em we'd had a bit of an accident to Miss Mary, but nothin' more than that."

"Good. That's it, then. Let's go to it. All right?" Jericho looked at the other three. Roger was pale and perspiring, the bruise on his face showing vivid against his pallor. Don and

375

Hamish were both fidgety, full of nervous tension and eager to get the thing over with.

"Let's get the flashlights out of the car."

The four men filed silently out of the living room. Don gave a quick look back at Mary, to make sure she was all right on the couch. A couple of minutes after they had left she stirred restlessly. She was slipping back toward sleep, but all she could think of was the way that she had betrayed Jamie. Betrayed him, and now maybe she would lose him forever.

She thought of his handsomeness and kindness, of the pleasure that she felt just looking at him. That was all she asked, just to be allowed to look at him.

The pain in her scalded foot was lessening, sinking to a dull throb, but she did not feel that she could move from the couch. A tremendous drowsiness was coming over her, draining away all her energy. She would have liked to leave the couch and run down the cliff to warn Jamie, but the shock of the burn had left her weighted down with fatigue. Never mind. When she woke again she could put things right with Jamie.

Mary turned her head on the soft velvet cover. The clouds were sweeping past inside her head, and there was no point in trying to fight them. It was better to go to sleep now. Sleep, and escape from her new worries. She closed her eyes.

When Dora arrived she found Mary quietly asleep, smiling to herself. She was holding the soft cushion of the couch close against her breast. Dora did not wake her. Instead she made herself a pot of tea and sat in the living room, watching Mary and listening to the noises of the wind. It was still growing stronger, and the rain that she had forecast was arriving. Wind-driven sheets of water drove in at the house from the northwest, drumming on the door of the kitchen. Beyond the cliff, half a mile away, the tide had turned at last. Instead of the beach increasing in size it had begun to shrink, moving inward with the wind-blown breakers imperceptibly inching forward along the strand.

CHAPTER 24

So long. It should not take so long.

Jamie stood thigh-deep in the quiet water and waited, head bent. The only sound was the faint murmur of an ebbing tide. He ignored it, forcing his attention inward, sensing and seeking through his outstretched hands.

It must be his own mental condition that hindered the link. Usually the union came within a few seconds, even when he was not in the true Selkie form. Today he had waited minutes, unable to still the turmoil and worry within his mind.

He exhaled heavily. The dark water rippled like oil away from his body, spreading a soft phosphorescence across the cave. Even though it was no colder here than usual, he shivered. The bond with the Family had never felt so weak. If he had to take the full burden, even if the Guardian did not return—he felt a sad certainty that he would not return—the work could not be done without counsel and support from the Elders. He had to set his worries to one side and attempt a persuasion that he had never before needed.

I am here. The message resonated through his hands to the waiting water. *I am here.*

The surface broke into swirls and cross-ripples. A pattern of bubbles rose to make a moving hexagonal pattern around him. Jamie sensed that he had become the center of a white star of arms, each reaching to him and to each other. The bubbles and the small whirlpool died away. There was completion.

You are not at peace here. There are more problems?

The familiar soothing hold was disturbed today by something else. He was not the only one feeling tension.

The Guardian has not returned. It has been too long with Second Change so near. I fear for him. And I must know what to do with the woman.

If the Guardian can return, he will. The other woman must be destroyed and evidence of her arrival must vanish.

The answer had come without hesitation. Jamie paused, not sure how to begin his plea. Never before had he thought to argue with the Elders.

I have a problem. The new woman left signs of her coming at the house. I have sent the first Vessel to take the travel bags and hide them. I do not think they will be found.

Good. There was a warmth and approval in the message that comforted Jamie, but the question hid an edge of urgency. *When will the woman be destroyed?*

Again Jamie hesitated, not sure how to present his idea.

I am the Bearer of the Seed. He paused.

Yes.

And without a Young One the People will die. The thought struck him like a new blow as the message went out to the Elders. He was the only hope for the People—they realized that more than he did. *We are so few now, where once we were many, with many new Young Ones each year. Where I alone bear the Seed, once scores of the People bore the Seed.*

Yes. The assent carried a core of melancholy. *You alone bear the Seed.*

I could use the new woman as a Vessel. She is healthy; she is of the age to bear young. I ask permission to use her.

The surface came awake again with ripples and clusters of rising bubbles. The reply was swift.

The woman is not of the Clan.

No. She is not a Macveagh—but she could be a Vessel, a bearer of young ones. Jamie trembled as the message burst from him. This was the key point, the place where he could not guess the answer.

That is not the way of the People. The reply was cold.

But these are new times. The Guardian has gone; the People are few now. We have heard nothing of the other clans for many years. Even if they live, their ways are not our ways. We must find a way for the People to grow again.

We are few. It was the first concession. *Wait.*

378

There was a movement of pale bodies and limbs beneath the dark surface, spreading steadily away from him. The Union was broken, and he felt desolate and alone. Even though he could invoke his right of choice and do whatever he chose to do, the punishment might be terrible. Exile, the loss of the Place forever.

He waited. The darkness in the cave was broken only by the soft underwater glow, the blue-white, cold light that came from beneath the shelf of rock at the side of the cave. The minutes stretched on until he felt that he could stand the delay no longer, but at the same time he understood the reason for it. What he was asking went against all their traditions. Finally the water began to move again around him, and the formation of white bodies took shape beneath its surface.

We believe that the Guardian will return; he will not fail. He has never failed.

Jamie cringed. It was not said, but he knew the implication. He had failed, failed with Jeanie, was failing now unless Mary bore the young one.

And yet we cannot ignore your message. (Jamie felt the warmth of feeling that came from them.) *You are right; we are too few now. We must try new things if that is all that is left. Even women who are not of the Clan must not be ignored.*

Jamie jerked upright in his relief, almost losing the Union.

I may use the other woman?

Perhaps. If not this woman, then perhaps some other. We are worried about this one. Before you do anything else, bring her here for our inspection. Do this now, and we will give you our answer at once.

Usually when Jamie broke off from the Union he felt a sense of loss and rejection. But now he was too filled with his new purpose to be aware of anything else. He took a deep breath, raised his head high, and started purposely for the upper levels of the caves.

Ellie lay there without moving for a long time. Her head ached, and her throat felt swollen and painful. She opened her eyes reluctantly, then closed them again. Still dark, it must be the middle of the night. She was cold and clammy, her stomach was grumbling and sour, and somewhere the sound of dripping water tolled louder inside her head with each new liquid impact. She had no idea where she was.

Hangover, said the voice inside her. *Bad hangover. But . . .*

She tried to remember when and where she had been drinking. There was no recollection, no muddy thoughts of a party or a business dinner. Let's see, last night she had been—where? Where was she *now*?

Ellie took a deep breath through her nose, and a smell of seaweed and heavy musk brought the nightmare rushing back. She had dreamed she was in Laxford, to see Don and Mary. The big house on the cliff. Following dream figures down the cliffs, along the shore. Into the caves.

The sounds. The gross parody of lovemaking, with Mary fondling and fawning on the monster. And after that . . .

The sound that came from her bruised throat was something between a gasp and a sob. She brought her knees up close to her chest in an old reflex and lay there on her side, unwilling to open her eyes again and look about her. That musky smell enveloped her. If it was here beside her, Mary's monster, she could not face it now. She lay there, listening for any sound in the tomblike dark. There was nothing, only the steady rhythm of the water drops.

After a few minutes a new thought took hold of her. If she was alone, who knew how long that would last? She had to escape from this place, wherever she was. And she had to do it fast. There was no time for self-pity or looking back. As her survival mechanism engaged and took hold, she rolled over and raised herself to a crouched position. She had been lying partly in a puddle of water, and now she dragged herself clear of it and stood up. Her skirt clung cold against her thighs.

Something clicked, a metallic sound in the darkness. Ellie tensed all over.

Perhaps it was coming back. The memory of the squat body and powerful smell rushed back and filled her consciousness. Mary had left, and then those eyes had come closing in on her, boring through her while one hand held her throat. She had been unable to look away—it was incongruous, those bright blue eyes in the devil's mask, forcing her down toward unconsciousness. That was her last memory before she awoke here. The thing must have carried her away from the shore.

As the memory of Mary and the creature came more strongly to her, Ellie shuddered and reached down to her belly. Her clothing was damp but otherwise undisturbed. Thank God. That at least she had been spared.

The thought brought a need to act. The darkness around her was not total. There was a gleam of light coming from one side, through an arched opening like a narrow tunnel. She went toward it, looking for the source of light. It seemed to come from the side of the tunnel itself, a faint gleam of green. The other side of the room where she had awakened offered nothing but silence and Stygian darkness. Ellie began to move as quietly as possible along the tunnel.

The floor was hard and level rock. After thirty paces she came to a broader area, where a long shelf had been carved from the tunnel's face. A line of globes stood there, each one alive with the same soft green. They were of various sizes, from grapefruit to football. Ellie touched one and felt a cool smoothness like blown glass. When she saw that the tunnel past this point was totally dark, she picked up a globe and followed its gleam as the path before her spiraled downward.

The light was too feeble to show more than the tunnel's sides. She clung close to the left, stealing along with every sense high strung and alert. Shadows seemed to move along ahead of her, drifting off past the globe's soft light. Each drop of water that fell on her from the roof made her shiver with the shock. Ellie felt a sudden wave of claustrophobia.

She had to get out.

She would have liked to lie down and curl up into a little ball somewhere in a corner, but the knowledge of what she had seen in the caves drove her along as fast as she could go.

It still felt like a nightmare. Mary and the creature, locked in strenuous copulation. She heard again Mary's ecstatic grunts and moans, then felt the creature pursue her and pin her against the cave wall while Mary watched approvingly. It was the stuff that nightmares were made of—but here she was, struggling on through the cold reality of this endless cave. She *had* to get out. Nothing else mattered at all.

She visualized the shore. She could see the waves streaming in, taste the salt wind, feel the sand slip and yield under her

381

feet as she ran wildly for freedom. Then she would go back along the cliff road, back to the village and the safety of the old inn, back to where she could tell people . . .

Blindly following the tunnel, Ellie had not paid much attention to the walls. Now her hand, sliding along it, had met something soft and mushy, like an opened, overripe melon.

A wet, filled sack fell toward her, knocking her to one side and landing heavily across her legs. She reached down to push it away at the same moment as the stench hit her. She gagged, pushed hard, and saw it fall limply to the rock floor with a soggy thump. Ellie stood up quickly, picking up the globe as she did so. Almost unwillingly, she leaned forward to see what she had dislodged from its position by the tunnel wall. The smell was overpowering.

It lay there, just visible in the soft light.

The eyes had fallen in, dark open pits in the bony face. Gray hair was pasted in an uneven line against the forehead, and a purple black tongue showed like a thick slug in the half-open mouth.

It was clear that the body had been decomposing for a good while. The black suit bulged with the gases that had bloated the abdomen beneath. As Ellie looked, a gas bubble found a way up the gullet and released itself with an obscene gurgle, while the Adam's apple above the clerical collar moved with a travesty of life. The shirt was dark and mildewed, neatly buttoned and intact.

Ellie had jerked back so hard that she banged her head and shoulder against the cavern wall. She did not notice. With no control of her body she was running hard, blindly along the tunnel. The globe dropped from her hands. Not even the danger of headlong collision with a rock wall could slow her mad dash forward.

Nausea slowed her before fatigue did. She stood and leaned against the wall, while hard dry heaves shook her whole body. When she was at last under control she began to move forward again, feeling her way along the cold wall. In less than a dozen paces her hands encountered a new structure, a gate of wood and metal that stood across the whole tunnel. Only her sickness had saved her from running headlong into it.

Ellie felt along the sides. There had to be some way of

382

opening it, a latch or lock. Please God, a latch on this side, and a path that would lead back to the open air.

The bolt that she felt at last under her bruised fingertips was massive, a couple of inches of thick metal than ran deep into the cavern wall. She placed her palms against the handle, focused all her strength, and tugged.

Moments later, her breath raw in her sore throat, she paused to mark her progress.

The bolt had not moved at all.

Ellie changed her hold and heaved with all her weight.

The bolt jerked back a half inch. Her moment of victory went as quickly as it had come, driven away by a new sound along the tunnel behind her.

Someone was coming. She could hear heavy footsteps. The movement of the bolt would make a noise, but it was her only hope. She renewed her efforts, gritting her teeth and ignoring the pain as the metal dug into her hands. The bolt moved again, another half inch. Two or three more, and it would be open. Thick fingers gripped her shoulders.

Even though she had nerved herself for its appearance, the Selkie's final approach behind her had been completely noiseless and surprising. As feeling drained from her legs, Ellie dropped to the floor and slipped out of the closing grasp. She rolled to the left and scrambled into an upright position to make a run back along the tunnel. The creature behind her grunted its irritation and followed her.

She knew that she would soon come to the glow of the strange globes, and that would be the place where she had to decide in which direction to flee. Which way to go, back to the place where she awoke, or onto the shelf of rock?

Ellie had forgotten about the minister's sprawled body. Her left foot caught on the shrivelled neck; she took one more unbalanced step, then fell hard to the ground. The impact was enough to drive the breath right out of her. As she tried to force air back into her pained lungs she was lifted, one arm around her shoulders and another under her knees. The creature did not seem to notice her weight at all. As Ellie recovered her breath she began to squirm in its grasp, reaching up to claw at the round eye sockets. The Selkie took no notice, except to tighten the grip on her shoulders until she could not move her arms.

She felt the tears brimming out of her eyes as she was carried steadily down a long, turning corridor. Even if he had dropped her to the floor and left her there, she no longer had the strength left to run for freedom. Ellie's nostrils were filled with the frightening musky smell, and she was weeping with fear and frustration.

Farther along the twisting corridor the light steadily increased. The dark shape of the tunnel walls took on form and definition, so that Ellie was able to see that this was far more than a rough surface of natural rock. There were murals here, detailed paintings of Selkies at work, spinning fine nets and rope, shaping delicately colored bowls of some natural clear substance—not glass, for they were molding it easily in their thick hands. And moving through odd underwater gardens, they were harvesting swollen bladders that leaked a richly colored liquid like fine claret. Everywhere, in work or play, the sea appeared, running its endless patterns through the cavern scenes.

After a few seconds she realized what was strangest of all about the paintings. There were no females here, human or Selkie. Some of the older creatures seemed neuter, or at least with hidden sex organs, but no woman was portrayed anywhere—even though there were drawings of young ones, smaller and more human-looking than the rest.

If there were no women, what would her fate be here?

Ellie was so drained of energy that when the Selkie stopped and placed her gently on the ground she did not move. She looked dully around her. They were now in a large open cave, on a shelf of rock that ran beside a broad and calm pool. Occasional ripples spread across the quiet surface.

The next shock came when he stooped beside her and methodically began to remove her clothes.

"No." Ellie tried to crawl away across the hard rock. "Oh, God, no. Don't touch me."

Her voice was high-pitched, close to hysteria. The Selkie ignored her completely. Her clothes were coming off with wet ripping sounds. She shivered with cold as he calmly removed her blouse and bra, seemingly indifferent to the shivering blue-white skin and tender breasts beneath his touch.

384

She was suddenly naked. Ellie tried to curl up, to cover herself with her hands. Before she could do it, he had picked her up again and stepped forward to the edge of the pool, wading slowly into it until he was covered to mid-thigh. While she shivered and groaned, he lowered her gently into the water.

She had expected more freezing cold on her unprotected body. Instead, the pool was quite warm. Its touch was viscous on her skin, lapping first over her legs, then up to hips and torso. She was left with her head above water and everything else immersed in the blood-warm pool. Her heels touched the smooth rocky bottom, and the Selkie held her—quite gently—by the shoulders. She could move only her lower body.

The pool was alive now, transmitting the pulse of pressure waves through its depths. Ellie felt a wash of moving water drifting past her legs. Then came the first touch, soft and tentative, on the outer part of her left thigh. She screamed and kicked out violently. The touch disappeared.

Peering down into the clear water she saw a shadow of long arms around her body. The torso was a ripple of flaky muscles, ending in thin, spidery legs, white and frail. The water ahead of her was stirring as more bodies moved underneath. There was another gentle touch on Ellie's bare leg.

She kicked again, but this time the touch remained. Another joined it on her other leg. She jerked her whole body, enough to drive her head for a moment beneath the water. The Selkie lifted her clear again as she choked on the warm brine.

Now the questing arms beneath held her too firmly for the grip to be broken by a kick. They were inching higher, exploring her body with patient and unhurried care. As they probed her most tender parts, Ellie began to scream. Her voice went past hysteria, up to a thin thread of demented torment. Her head was lolling to the side. Without support it would have slipped beneath the surface.

Eventually the Elders were finished. They withdrew from Ellie's unheeding body, and Jamie placed one hand on the surface of the pool. Union came quickly.

Is she suitable? He held his breath while he waited for the answer.

The Elders had conferred briefly.

We cannot be sure. Perhaps. You may proceed with your plan. The timing is fortunate, she has just ovulated. Good fortune in your effort. When will it be done?

Jamie lifted Ellie clear of the water. *Soon. When she is warm and dry.*

He broke the Union and waded to the shelf. Ellie was shivering now, muttering softly to herself. That was not good. He wanted control, but she was close to the edge of madness. Cradling her to his chest, he began to walk back up the sloping path. There were blankets and heavy shawls in one of the store-places, enough to warm her.

The Vessel was a precious object, a possible bearer of another Young One. It must not take cold or come to harm. This must be done with care.

Warming against his chest, Ellie was no longer shivering her heart out. She was muttering quietly, soft and broken words of complaint.

"Don," she said. "Oh, Don. Keep me warm."

She nuzzled closer. Jamie paused, his blue eyes thoughtful.

The second waking was easier, a slow ascent into warmth and soft light. She had been asleep, tormented by dreams, and now she was safe inside the rough caress of blankets. Ellie opened her eyes.

"Thank God you're awake. I didn't want to move you until you were rested."

The gentle Scots voice came from her left. Ellie blinked and turned her head to look at him. Her pulse had started a faster beat; now it slowed and she relaxed. The young man kneeling by her side held an oil lantern in one hand and was peering at her, a worried expression on his blunt-featured and good-humored face. He smiled when he saw that she was looking at him.

"Ye've had a nasty fever—an' ye've been dreamin'. Tossin' an turnin', I had a job keepin' the blankets on ye. Aye, that's better."

He reached out his free hand and touched her gently on the forehead, testing its warmth. In spite of his reassuring tone, Ellie flinched at the touch. He pulled his hand back at once.

"Now, then, don't be upset."

386

"Where am I? And where are the—the—" Ellie's voice was trembling, unable to find words.

"Why, we're in the old storeroom, see?" He swung the lantern, so that Ellie could see around her. The rough walls were shelved and full of tools, bottles, and old casks, dark and dusty in the uncertain light. "Ye see, ye had a fall comin' down the cliff. I saw it, but I couldn't do a thing to stop it—a right bad bang on the head, ye took."

"I—I" Ellie paused. Her head was spinning, and she felt sick and confused. She lifted her arm. It was covered now, clad in the same dress that she had worn to come to Laxford. A fall? "I fell down the cliff?"

"Ye did. I'd have carried ye back on up, and we'd be back now in Laxford, but the way's too steep there. An' I didn't dare to leave ye, not the way ye were moanin'." He smiled again. "So I carried ye back in here—it's none too fancy, I'll admit, but at least we're warm an' dry. Are ye well enough now to try that cliff? I'll help ye, but I'll not try it if ye feel dizzy still."

Ellie sat up slowly. He reached out his arm to give her support and pulled back the thick blanket that covered her. His shoulder was strong and muscular, and she leaned against it gratefully as she remained for a few moments in a sitting position. Her clothes were dry, her blouse neatly buttoned, although there were grains of sand clinging to the cloth along her left side and on her bare calves.

He had followed her look. "I took your shoes off and put them over there." He shrugged apologetically. "I'll get them now, but I thought ye might sleep a bit easier without them. Here."

He released her, stepped a couple of paces across to the wall, and returned with her impractically high-heeled shoes. Ellie looked at them as she took them. Had she climbed down a cliff in these? They were made for slipping and tripping. As she bent to put them on she felt another sweep of nausea and a throbbing ache in the back of her head.

"Easy now." He had reached over and held her as she swayed forward. "Don't be rushin' things, we've lots of time. Tell me when ye're ready, an' don't push yerself. Ye hear me? Take yer time."

She leaned against him and slowly levered herself to her feet. The rough walls seemed to weave about her for a second, then steadied. He stood beside her, silent and sympathetic, until she could straighten.

"God, I feel weak." Ellie waited for a few seconds, her head against his solid arm. "Can you help me along? I've got to get some feeling in my legs."

"Of course I can. Trust me now, I'll not be droppin' ye."

His voice was deep and soothing. As they began to move slowly forward, Ellie suddenly realized how fortunate she had been. If she had fallen alone, and no one had seen her, by now she might be dead, drowned by the rising ride. She felt a quick twinge of alarm. Where was the tide now?

After a moment she relaxed again. The man she was with knew these parts; he'd obviously know tide times and the safe way back to the village. Unconsciously she allowed him to support a little more of her weight. He seemed to ease her along without noticing it, without any effort.

"Ye see, we're doin' fine now." His voice was comforting, a light breath across the top of her head as she let it lie against his chest. "We'll be out of here, an' ten minutes after that ye'll be back up on the top, an' in Laxford afore ye know it. Come on, lassie, ye can lean on me."

Ellie allowed him to steer her along while she closed her tired eyes for a moment. It was so easy to let him do all the work, to listen to his soft voice and relax in the pleasant aroma that seemed to flow from his thick shirt and soft skin. She would keep her eyes closed a few moments longer, and he would guide them both—he felt so solid and comforting, it was easiest to relax and lean her weight on his muscular arm. *Relax, trust him, let him take care of her.* Silly to worry when he would look after her. *Relax, trust him, let him take care of her . . .*

There was a last instant before she surrendered completely. She opened her eyes. She wanted to look up and smile her gratitude, then she would relax again.

Jamie, impatient beyond bearing and confident that she was quite ready, had made a mistake. He had allowed the change to begin. Beads of viscous liquid were already growing on his pale cheeks and upon the forehead that shielded the deep-set eyes. It was too late to stop.

Ellie looked up at him for one long, frozen second. He held her tightly, too strong for her to break away. This time, the screams that came from her throat climbed past the bounds of sanity and on to a new world where she could escape from the new nightmare. She did not feel the hands that moved her again to the soft pile of blankets and methodically stripped off her clothes.

CHAPTER 25

One look at the path down to the shore was enough to force a change of plans. The rain driving in on the cliff had eased a little, but it had converted a descent of moderate difficulty to a slalom of glistening rock faces and slick clay. Lord Jericho inched a little closer to the edge and wiped the cold drops from his nose and forehead with his sleeve.

"What do you think, Roger? You're the climber."

Roger had been moving cautiously along the cliff, estimating the holds and the angle of descent.

"No way. Not in this weather, even with ropes. One stiff gust and you'd be done for. Hamish, isn't there some easier way down?"

"Aye. Not too far, back mebbe half a mile toward the village, an' it's like regular steps there. I've been on it in weather a sight worse than this. We'll not be bad off if we tak' it slow."

Jericho shrugged. "I hate to waste more time, but I see nowt else for it. Come on, back to the car an' let's be off. How's that tide running, Don?"

"Ready to turn any time now." Don lingered for a second looking outward, trying to confirm his estimate from the far-off line of breakers, then hurried after the others to the car. Lord Jericho seemed quite calm, and Roger looked too tired to care. Only Hamish, with his tight mouth and jumpy movements, seemed to echo Don's own dread about what might have happened to Ellie.

Even the easy path that Hamish had promised seemed determined to slow their progress. Both hands were needed to climb down safely in the rain and gusty wind, and before they could begin there was time wasted lowering their weapons on a length of rope, then cautiously following them down to the beach, single file. Hamish went first, holding hard to the supporting line of rope, followed closely by Don and Roger. Lord Jericho brought up the rear, grunting and breathing heavily through his mouth. No one spoke, even when they were down on the damp shingle looking around them in the gray afternoon and shielding their faces against the persistent rain. Don led the way north to the caves, hugging close to the cliff face for the shelter it offered from the cold buffets of the wind. The water had already soaked through his shoes, and now a trickle was evading his collar and sending its cold fingers down his back and left shoulder.

He paused at last at the southernmost cave opening. The others moved alongside him as he swung the beam of his flashlight to illuminate the first few yards of the entrance.

"We could take this one, but I'd rather not."

Jericho wiped at his face again and leaned forward. The caught droplets in his bushy eyebrows sparkled in the uncertain light. "Why? I'd like to get in out o' this rain, sharpish."

"I think we ought to start in the place where the flow patterns have looked wrong. That's two entrances north of here."

Jericho looked briefly at the two others and shrugged. "You're the boss when it comes to caves, Don, not me or Hamish an' Roger. We'll be followin' your lead."

"Right." Don nodded, turned, and led the way again along the pebbled beach. He looked to their left, seeking out the lines of foam that would mark the edge of the water. The wind was driving in from the northwest—the tide would rise sooner than the tables predicted.

Hurry up.

No matter how calm Lord Jericho might be, Don couldn't stem the tide of his own thoughts. The Selkies might have done something to Ellie in the caves, but that wasn't the worst of it. There were dangers more final than seduction or rape, even by a Selkie. His memory kept surfacing the reports that he had read when he first examined the written background on the Laxford caverns; simple, factual accounts of people who entered the caves and were never seen again alive; sometimes the bodies drifted ashore days or weeks later, scarcely recognizable, and sometimes the disappearance was total and permanent.

391

Don tried to suppress unwanted memories, concentrating on the mental picture that he had formed of the interior of the tidal caverns; but instead he found himself thinking of Ellie herself, Ellie as he had last seen her, with a red headscarf around her dark hair, waving him a smiling but wistful good-bye in the gray dawn of East Side Manhattan. Was that going to be his final memory of her?

Again he tried to think of logical planning and the paths ahead. For the next hour there was no place for anything but determination and a clear head.

When they came to it, the cave was lower and broader than Don remembered. He had to crouch forward at first and move in an efficient but ungainly shuffle until, after fifteen yards, the roof height increased enough to provide adequate headroom. He waited for the other three, then shone his flashlight ahead and looked carefully at the walls, floor, and ceiling. After a few seconds he turned back the way they had come and stood for a moment motionless.

"What's wrong?" Lord Jericho was breathing hard, but his eyes were bright and alert.

"Nothing." Don began to move slowly deeper into the cave. "I wanted to check the flow of air in here. It's all right now, but if you feel a breeze coming from behind us let me know. When the tide gets to the caves we ought to feel it if air is pushed in some caves and out of others. Half an hour after you feel a breeze in here, it will be full of water. See?" He shone his flashlight up to the roof, where the rock surface was still glistening damp. "This one floods all the way, right to the top. Get caught in here and you'd be dead."

Hamish had turned his face upward. His mouth was gaping open, and he gave a little groan. Once inside the cave they had all pushed back the rain hoods that Don had improvised from plastic sheet, and now Hamish's bald head was gleaming ruddily in the reflected light. His clothes had begun to steam gently in the clammy interior of the caverns. The discomfort they were all beginning to feel was another reason to hurry. Don led the way forward again.

It was an awkward, scrambling progress over shells, sand, and sharp rocks. Don had disturbing memories of the last time he was here, following Petherton's casual lope over slippery surfaces strewn with lank seaweed. Despite the worry that told him to run, he forced himself to slow a fraction. It would be foolish to tire them out or risk a turned ankle—foolish and worse. Jamie would be as at home down here as Petherton had been, in his own element while they staggered and floundered.

He paused for a second. The cave had narrowed to a tunnel five or six feet across. Now the floor had begun to slant gently upward, reversing its previous trend. Sand and pebbles were patches between ledges of solid, slate-gray rock.

Don inched forward again, his attention on the roof and walls. So it was Hamish, creeping along second in line with his eyes nervously lowered, who saw it first.

"Hol' on a minute, Mister Willis." He bent down. "What's this here?"

He was scrabbling at a patch of sand between two rocks. After a few seconds he stood up holding a sodden bluish object.

"What is it?" Lord Jericho, who had again been walking last, came up to him and shone his flashlight. "A book?"

"Aye—or it was. It's had its day." Hamish carefully opened the soaked and battered cover and shone a light on the inside page. "*The Quest for the Historical Jesus*, by Albert Schweitzer. There was a name written inside here once, but I canna' read it. It's just a blur."

"Walter Campbell." Roger leaned against the wall, his face livid in the torchlight. He looked worn out. "He used to carry that book around with him—I saw it in his car. And Schweitzer was one of his heroes."

"Ye think mebbe the Minister was doon here an' dropped it, then?"

Roger shook his head. "I'd hate to say just what I think. If Campbell had this in his jacket pocket, I don't see it falling out unless he was being carried through here."

"Then ye mean he—"

"Yes." Roger abruptly rubbed a grimy hand across his forehead to cover his eyes. "Let's get a move on. We can't do a thing to help, whatever happened down here. Let's look for Ellie."

Don was already moving, shining his light along the widening tunnel. It was opening again, higher and broader, to form an extended cavern, but it was also dipping deeper into the hillside. Soon they were splashing along through shallow pools of dark, still water. It grew deeper, inch by inch, until in a few minutes they were shivering as it lapped to their chilled calves.

"This is one of the tricky places if we're at all late getting out of here," said Don. "The current runs fast through this part, especially where it narrows. If the water were waist-high in here I doubt if you'd ever push through it. We have to be back here and out in less than an hour—at the most. But we don't need to worry yet."

Lord Jericho, plowing along right behind Don, snorted. "I'm worryin', even if we don't need to. I hope to hell you know what you're about, Don, because I'm totally lost down here. Are you looking for something special, or do we have to walk ten miles in this bloody place? We could be down here for a week."

"If we didn't drown or starve." Don didn't sound as though he was joking. "I'm doing my best. I know we can't look everywhere for Ellie, so I'm assuming that the best starting place is one where the calculations we did on the flow rates went to hell. It's just ahead of us now. There has to be something there, a thing we can't find on any of the charts you gave me. Keep your eyes open here."

"The Department of Environment charts?" Roger, trailing along at the rear, laughed harshly. "Don't place too much trust in them. You know where we got them from?—Petherton gave 'em to us."

Don had paused, knee deep in water, and was frowning at a narrow side passage that ran off to their right. It was no more than shoulder-high, and appeared to terminate in a blank wall or rock.

"I know he gave them to us—that's one reason I'm willing to believe they're not right. Am I imagining it, or is there an echo down that passage when I talk? It's a blind end according to the maps. Wait here a minute."

He ducked his head and waded away along the low passage. After a few seconds his voice came echoing back, hollow-sounding and muffled. "We're on to something, I think. There's another cave opening up here, a narrow one. I'm going to take a look."

"Not by yourself, you're not." Lord Jericho had lowered his head and was shuffling rapidly after Don. "Remember, we came with you because Jamie's too much for one man to handle. You hold on there, an' we'll all have a go at it together."

Don waited impatiently until they appeared in sight, then forged ahead. The new tunnel narrowed to less than three feet across, but they were emerging steadily from the tidal ponds. In twenty more paces they were moving up a steady incline that curved slowly to the north and led to a series of flat ledges of bare rock. Roger called a halt for a moment to remove a pebble from his shoe. The rest of them waited uncomfortably, trying to wring some of the water from their wet trousers. Before they moved on again, Don once more turned his flashlight to the ceiling. He whistled softly.

"Well now—see that?"

The others stared up at the unmarked rock face.

"See what?" asked Hamish after a few moments. He was breathing hard and gripping the heavy iron tongs in both hands. "Mr. Willis, I can't see a thing up there."

"Look at the roof. It's *dry*. That means we've climbed above high tide—the caves aren't supposed to do that. Look, you can see how high the last tide got by looking at the walls."

Lord Jericho stepped over and placed his hand on the dark tide mark. He nodded. "That's good news. If we stay here, we won't drown. And if Ellie was up here, she'd be safe."

Don shook his head grimly. "Safe from the tides, you mean. She'd never have found this place unless she was brought here. This part of the caves will be safe, even at spring tide. If we get trapped in here it won't be a disaster. Come on, though—I'd rather not be down here all night."

He was leading the way again along the curved tunnel. In a few more minutes they were faced with another decision. The structure of the cave system became more complex, with a three-way branch in front of them. The left-hand path continued a slow upward turn, spiraling as far as the torches would show to the right. The middle and right-hand paths dipped back downward and turned slowly toward the left. The lights picked out again the gleam of black water.

"Up or down?" Don waited for the others. "None of this on any charts."

Roger shone his flashlight along each branch in turn. "I don't know as it makes much difference. It looks as though the two right-hand paths curve back and run *under* the left-hand one, but that doesn't make much sense. Maybe they will merge again. Will the lower ones be full at high tide?"

"I'm not sure, but I expect they will."

"So let's take the left path. We're here to find Ellie *alive*. That means the higher parts of the cave."

He started forward without waiting for discussion from the others, moving slowly along the left branch and hugging close to the wall. Lord Jericho ignored his own warning to stick together and took a few steps along the middle branch, trying to see what lay beyond the curve. Roger's echoing shout brought him hurrying back to follow the others.

"What is it?" He was puffing and grunting from the exertion as he came up to them.

"Dunno." Roger turned to him. "What do you make of these, Joshua? It's not easy to see what they have to do with Jamie and Selkies, but what are they doing down here at all?"

The upper level had opened out to form a broad chamber with a roof about ten feet high. The floor was smooth and level, as though the hard rock surface had been ground flat by generations of patient masons. To the left, past the point where Roger was shining his flashlight, four coffin-like cases stood on the floor. Each was made of dull gray metal, over six feet long and a couple of feet wide and deep.

Jericho walked over to them and looked at their close-fitting lids. He banged the sides, one after another, and grunted. "Nothing in here, from the sound of it. They're just—hold on, though, there's something in this 'un. Give us a hand wi' this lid."

Don had stepped forward, and together they slid back the heavy covering. He played the beam of his flashlight along the interior.

"Water. Just water." Jericho leaned forward, took a cupped handful, and raised it to his mouth. He sipped, and grimaced. "Sea water, I'd say. Well, thank God for that. I don't mind tellin' you, I was having some right funny ideas about what we'd find when we were pullin' back that cover. Coffins full of water? Don't make any sense."

"It does if you believe Knowlton." Roger was peering closely at the side of one of the cases. "These look old—they've been here ages. The Selkies can't stand to be away from the sea for long, and when they're old they need to be

396

near it or in it all the time. They'd need something like this if they had to travel inland for a few days. I think there's more than just water involved; there's some sort of special liquids they need as well."

"D'yer mean Petherton had one of these things with him? How'd he ever carry it?" Lord Jericho was sliding the lid closed.

"No—but he looked as though he wished he had one. I told you, he was falling apart. His skin was peeling off him just as though he'd been scalded. I'd have had no chance with him if he'd been fit and at full strength."

Hamish had come forward too, and was peering into the half-closed coffin. There was no fat on his body, and he was shivering violently in the damp chill.

"Mister Wilson, d'ye mean they'd lie doon in that, an' close it up, an' it all full of water? Did ye know, there's old talk round this part of the coast, about coaches travelin' at night, an' nothin' inside but a coffin." He shivered again. "An' I've laughed at Dora when she told it, an' said she was an auld gas-bag."

They had started to move again through the cave, Hamish bringing up the rear and looking back occasionally at the silent set of coffins. The right-hand wall of the cave suddenly ended. They found themselves walking along a broad ledge like the step of a giant staircase. The sheer rock face on their left was featureless, and on the right there was a vertical drop of eight or ten feet. Turning the flashlight in that direction, Don saw another, narrower ledge of rock below and the dull glint of water beyond it. He ran the light over the surface of the lower pool. The patterns of ripples and eddies threw back gleams of red and green and the surface was in constant, perplexing motion.

Don swung his light along the whole length of the chamber. "That must be where those other branches lead—follow the right-hand path, and you'd finish below on that ledge. I don't understand why the ledge isn't covered by now. There has to be something that's changing the whole flow in here. Hey, what's that?"

He turned suddenly to the left, following a big rippling wave along the surface. The tidal pool was partly hidden behind a shelf of rock, making it impossible to follow more than a part of the pattern of cross-ripples. Close to where they were

397

standing, the broken flow smoothed out to regular streamlines parallel to the ledges of rock.

"There's nothing there." Roger was leaning farther over the ledge. "It's just the flow of water—maybe the tide's rising fast now."

"It is, but that's not the answer." Don paced along their ledge and looked down from another angle. "Something seems to be breaking the flow from underneath, and there's eddies coming from behind that jutting point of rock. See the way that you get broken flows there, and they even out over here."

"That's well an' good, Don." Lord Jericho shrugged. "There'll be time to worry that another day—but we'll not be findin' Ellie down there. Come on."

As he moved out along the edge, Hamish followed a pace behind, playing his flashlight beam off the angled rocks of the lower cave. He could imagine monstrous shapes in every moving patch of shadow.

"Keep moving, Hamish," said Roger from behind. Hamish had stopped suddenly.

"There's somethin' down there." His voice was high-pitched and excited, and the hand holding his flashlight was unsteady. "Doon there, off at the end."

"Where?"

Roger was following the line that Hamish marked out, tracking it with his own flashlight. The cavern stretched away to the right, yard after yard of evenly flowing water. The light shone weaker and weaker as its cone broadened across the darkness.

"There's nothing there, Hamish." Roger turned his light back to the ledge.

"I tell ye, there was. I saw it, doon at the waterline—like a big white seal, right in the water."

He shone his light again across the cavern. Don had come up beside him and was peering out over the dark drop in front of them.

"Come on, you two." Lord Jericho's voice was impatient.

"One minute more." Don's tone of voice made the others turn back toward him.

"You see something too?" asked Roger. All four men were standing in line, grim and bedraggled, straining their eyes to see something at the farthest reach of Hamish's flashlight.

398

"I'm not sure . . ." Don blinked his eyes. "I thought at first I could see something—some sort of structure there. But now I can't see it, the light's too faint. I thought . . ."

"Point your torch to where you think you saw it, and hold the beam steady." Roger took his own flashlight and aimed its beam to follow and merge with Don's. "Joshua, shine yours the same way—we've got spare batteries if we need 'em. You too, Hamish, let's have some light out there."

It showed plainly in the multiple flashlight beams. A wall of heavy timbers had been built at the far end of the cavern. They could see the thick metal pins and solid chains that held the wooden oblong firmly in position against the dark wall of rock. The lower ledge of rock below them ran around the cavern in a great semicircle to end at the wooden barrier.

"Swing your beam down a bit." Lord Jericho had moved his light down a fraction to concentrate it on the lower part of the timbers. "It looks like a bloody *gate*, right down to the waterline and below it. Who'd ever want to build a thing like that down here?"

"It's not an ordinary gate." Don was frowning along the merging beams of light. "Look at the pattern of cross-battens on it. Each one of those timbers can slide out of the way independently, or if you wanted to you could swing the whole thing open in one piece. It's a sluice gate."

"But who'd be regulating the flow through here? Roger, was there anything in Knowlton's papers to say the Selkies would need to do that?"

"Not that I saw." Roger shrugged. "But Knowlton didn't know everything—we know things now about the Selkies that he had no idea of. No wonder Don's been having trouble computing flows through the caves—controlled flow through here would change everything."

"Mebbe it would—but why build it?" Lord Jericho turned to Don. "Wouldn't this be a giveaway that there's something down here?"

"Who to?" Don was feeling a minor satisfaction to counter his worry and fatigue. He had predicted where the flows didn't look right, and now he was being proved correct. "I don't think anybody ever had any interest in flows here until we started looking. Petherton had worked himself into the job that had control of this part of the coast—he'd have fixed any inquiries."

"But why build this at all? It must have taken months to do it."

"I think I can answer that. The Selkies needed to have the flows here evened out. With a wind and tide like the one we've got tonight, you'd expect a real tidal race through here—twenty-five or thirty knots. If there's things down there"—he nodded to the water below—"the way Hamish says he saw them, they'd be in trouble without a way to control the flow. Without the gate there'd be a monstrous current ripping through here as the tide rises and falls. I think there's another big cave on the other side of that barrier."

"Aye, an' the tide's rising now." Jericho's voice was grim. "We'll worry about dealin' wi' what's down there on the way back. How much more of this cave is there to search, Don?"

"I wish I knew. It's not on the maps. But we'll have to start back soon, or be stuck here until the tide goes down again."

They were moving again as he spoke, walking along their ledge and keeping well away from the sheer drop on the right. When the path split again, Lord Jericho took the upward turn without pausing to discuss it. The other way spiraled down to the lower rock ledge and the rippling pool.

"There's been more work done here." He pointed his flashlight at the rising path in front of them. "That's not the work of nature, if you ask me."

The upward path was a regular series of steplike ledges of rock. It led up and up, twenty and then thirty feet of vertical ascent. Roger, bringing up the rear of the party, felt himself becoming light-headed with fatigue as he struggled along after the others, his head down. The bruise on his temple was throbbing painfully, and he had to stop and lean against the wall. For a moment he thought that he had imagined the breath of cool air that touched his aching temple. He waited. It came again, the lightest of zephyrs on his bruised and sensitive skin.

"Joshua!" The others were fifteen feet ahead of him. "Stop for a minute. Can you feel it? There's some sort of current of fresh air coming through here. There. I felt it again."

Lord Jericho was standing motionless, trying to control his heavy breathing. He turned to Don. "He's right, I can feel it too. But how the blazes can there be . . ."

"I don't know—tides wouldn't make that variable air flow.

400

We're feeling the effects of gusts of wind somewhere. Hamish, do any of these caves lead all the way up to the surface? I know that the maps don't show it, but is it possible?"

"I never heard tell of anythin' like it, sir. Course, ye'll find them in the village as'll tell ye the whole underground 'tween the sea and the loch is riddled wi' caves. But that's nothin' but talk, an' ye'll never find a man who says he can show you it himsel'."

"I think Roger's right, though." Jericho was scowling upward along the rising tunnel. "There's a definite draft through here, an' we can't be all that far below the surface now. Hello then, what's this?"

His flashlight beam played over the tunnel walls above them. Twenty feet ahead it revealed a wooden structure set into the side of the tunnel. He moved up to it cautiously. It was a heavy wooden door, closed on each side by three metal bolts that fitted into niches carved into the face of the rock.

Don stepped forward, lifted his hand to the bolts, then hesitated.

"Go on, lad." Lord Jericho had dropped his voice to a gruff whisper. "I don't know what's behind there, but it's our best chance yet to find her."

"What about Jamie MacPherson?"

"That door was bolted from this side. We'll not find him in there."

One by one, Don carefully and quietly drew the bolts. Roger and Lord Jericho stood on each side, supporting the weight of the heavy door. As the last bolt slid free, they gasped with the unexpected load. Don was reminded again of Roger's comments and his own observation—Jamie was far stronger than an ordinary human. Working together, they gently lowered the massive timber frame to the floor. Hamish shone his light through the opening.

The rock chamber beyond was at least thirty feet long and eight feet high, but the first impression was one of chaos rather than size. The interior was divided into three main sections by tall wooden partitions. It was a general storage area, but the arrangement within defied logic. Along one entire wall, and strewn at random through all three sections, the flashlights showed lines of squat containers. Each one was made of wood, glass, or plastic, and would hold a few gallons of liquid. The glass reflected a dark gleam of red inside it.

401

Beyond the barrels and bottles, and in places mixed in with them, random heaps of brown objects had been assembled. They were fist-sized, knotted and shriveled like clumps of some dried fungus. Farther back in the chamber the light shone off delicate glass flagons, full of cloudy green liquid.

The four men stared at white carved statuettes, human figures of ivory-like bone; at a great collection of chisels, adzes, and hammers, all carefully oiled and sharpened; at blown-glass spheres of rainbow colors, with stylized paintings on their sides; and at neatly piled squares of leathery fabric, skin-colored and etched with abstract patterns. Everything was illuminated in a green light that gleamed faintly from mottled globes on walls and ceilings.

It was too much for the eye to take in at one glance. They stood and peered about the chamber, their attention moving from one mystery to the next. It was a minute or two before Don caught sight of the piles of woolen blankets and shawls, partly hidden by another wooden partition at the rear of the chamber. It seemed to him that they did not fit the rest of the chamber's varied contents.

He stepped forward so that he could see what lay behind the screen. Even as he was moving, a sense of sick anticipation was in his throat, making it hard to breathe normally.

The blankets were arranged in crude heaps. The left-hand one was thicker than the others. Lying on it, facedown and with her lower legs covered by a rough tartan shawl, Don saw a woman's body. She was naked, silent, and still.

CHAPTER 26

Don was the first to reach her. He bent by her side and touched his hand to her shoulder.

She was warm.

As he leaned closer, he could see the gentle rise and fall of the unmarked skin of her back. He straightened and leaned back on his haunches.

"Thank God." His eyes were closed. *"Alive.* Roger, she's alive."

Lord Jericho had bent down beside him and taken hold of one of Ellie's shoulders. "Here, give me a hand to turn her over." His voice was gruff and matter-of-fact. "She feels warm enough, and I don't see any obvious injuries, but she's lying odd. See how slack this arm hangs? Let's get a good look at her. Roger, you take that arm and leg, and turn her this way. Hamish, get that flashlight in here on her face."

They carefully turned her so that she was lying on her back. The arms and legs were loose and relaxed, slack-jointed as a doll's limbs. Lord Jericho felt for her pulse, nodded, and rolled back an eyelid to peer at the white that showed behind it.

He shrugged. "I dunno. Wish I knew a bit more first aid. She seems normal enough, but why doesn't she wake up? Looks like we'll have to carry her."

"Like this? Is it safe?" Don had picked up a shawl and was pulling it over Ellie's body.

"No. We'll have to get some clothes on her. If we take her through the caves like this she'll catch her death." Lord Jericho turned to Hamish. "See if you can find the clothes she

403

was wearing when she came. They ought to be some place in here."

Hamish nodded. After one startled look at Ellie's naked breasts, he had averted his eyes. He put down the iron tongs he was carrying and began a search through the clutter of objects that filled the chamber. Without the protection of the weapon he was doubly nervous, peering around him every few seconds.

The section they were in yielded nothing but blankets and loose scarves and shawls. He began to rummage among the assorted objects in the left-hand part of the chamber, one wary eye on the open doorway. When he found the heap, he thought for a moment that it was more of the shriveled lumps of brown fungus. Only the bright reflection from a buckle brought his eye back to the dusty pile.

"Mr. Willis! There's something strange here. Can you come an' tak' a look?"

Don was still on his knees next to Ellie. He didn't move at Hamish's nervous call, and after a few moments Roger went through to the next partition. Hamish was crouched over a jumble of objects holding a wallet in one hand and a shoe in the other.

"I don't like this, sir. See these? Clothes, they are, an' mostly leather an' metal. An' this is all explorin' kit, the same as people bring in when they're wantin' to explore the caves."

Roger picked up a black camera case that had been thrown carelessly onto the pile. "You said people disappeared into the caves, and never came out?"

"Aye." Hamish swallowed. "But where are they, then? I mean, if these were their clothes an' explorin' stuff." He glanced again at the open doorway leading back to the caves. "I mean, wi' this here . . ."

"See if you can find anything that might fit Ellie, and bring it back to us. Maybe we can find who these things all belonged to when we're out of this place."

He went back to the other section, still carrying the camera case. Don was crouched by Ellie, unmoving. He did not even seem to be looking at her, just sitting and staring straight ahead.

The conversation between Roger and Hamish had drifted past the periphery of his attention. He knew they had fresh evidence that the Selkies were dangerous to humans, but that

404

was not the true reality. True reality was Ellie's pale body, in a coma from which she would not waken.

The sight of her naked body had forced into his mind a memory of the last time he had seen her unclothed. She had been all energy and excitement and urgent life. What had the Selkies done to her?

"Ellie." He bent close, chafing one of her hands between his. "Ellie, can you hear? You'll be all right now."

The old trite words—how true were they?

"Ellie, do you hear? We're taking you out of here. You're safe now."

He looked at the silent face. Had he imagined it, or had there been a tiny movement of her dark head on the thick blanket?

"Ellie. It's Don. Can you hear?"

Lord Jericho had taken another shawl and was tucking it snugly about her slight body. He nodded sympathetically.

"Keep talking to her. She's got some sort of shock by the look of it. Wonder what happened to her? We've got to keep her warm now, even if we have to move her in a minute. Roger, get a couple more of those blankets. Roger?" He stood up and shone the torch around. "He was here a couple of seconds ago. Where the devil has he got to?"

Roger was nowhere to be seen, but Hamish was coming over, his arms full of a strange assortment of items of clothing. He was looking at them doubtfully.

"It's no' what she was wearin', there's not a sign o' them. But mebbe it'll do to get her oot o' here. Is she awake now?"

Don shook his head. He had seen Ellie's eyelashes flutter a moment before, and now her eyes were open a slit, the dark irises coming into view, but she was not conscious.

He patted her gently on the cheek. "Come on, Ellie, wake up. We have to get you dressed and out of this place. Do you hear me?"

Lord Jericho looked down at her and shook his head gloomily. "She's still a long way under. If she doesn't come out of it in a minute more, we'll have to change plans. She'll have to be carried back through the caves, and that's goin' to be a real devil of a job. She's not that big, but unconscious people always weigh heavy."

He straightened up. "And now then, where the blazes have you been? We need all the help we can get here."

"I know." Roger had reappeared in the doorway, startling all of them. "I was out there." He jerked his head back at the tunnel. "I wondered if we really had a way to the surface up there—that would make everything a lot easier; we'd go there instead of through the caves."

"Aye. So what's the position?" Lord Jericho had read the tension in Roger's calm tone. "No way out?"

"Worse than that. About twenty feet farther up, the tunnel levels off to a long flat stretch, and I'm sure there's a way out at the end of it. But there's somebody up there now, getting ready to come down here."

"Jamie?"

"I'm afraid that has to be my guess. I heard rocks being moved—it must be a well-concealed entrance up there, but I've no idea how much time it will take before he's inside and coming down here. We have to go back through the caves. Don, can she walk?"

Don had raised Ellie to a sitting position and was supporting her there with his arms across her back. He shook his head.

"She's come out of it a little way, but she's still too far gone to walk. We'll have to dress her and carry her."

"No time for that now." Jericho's voice was firm. "We'll have to take her as she is, wrapped in blankets. It'll be none too easy, but we have to be out of here before Jamie's down this way. Come on, lift her."

As Don and Roger raised her to her feet Ellie gave a weak mutter of protest. Roger stared at her half-open eyes. "Don, she's awake—her eyes are opening."

"I know. She acts like she's half-awake, but I can't get her to respond to anything. It's like she's aware but not able to control her body. She's been like this for the past few minutes. We can't afford to wait until she's better."

"Maybe you're right. But if we're carrying Ellie, that only leaves Hamish and Joshua to handle Jamie. I don't like those odds."

"Nor me," said Lord Jericho gruffly. "An' I doubt if Hamish is any too thrilled at the idea. So let's get the hell out of here now, and hope we can be away before he shows up. You two get goin'. Hamish, give me a hand to get the door upright, then off you go after them. They'll need somebody to

406

point out the way with a flashlight—I can't see either of you having a hand free for that."

"You're staying here, Joshua?" Roger's voice was baffled.

"Stayin' here? Bloody hell, no. All I'm going to do is try and get the bolts back in that door. With any luck Jamie'll think she's still in there an' be in no hurry to open it. Now, bugger off, and don't stand there gassing."

The tunnel outside was still deserted. Don listened hard as they started downward, but there was no sign of Jamie. He tried to look at his watch. Fifteen minutes more and the lower caves would be flooded too deep for them to get through.

He heard the bolts going into position as they reached the flat part of the ledge. The noise was frighteningly loud, but as soon as they were on the ledge a new sound caught his attention. The tide was in full flow. He could hear the chuckling, racing water all around, carried through the rock faces and streaming through the network of caves. The pool on their left was still and quiet, protected by the sluice gate, but even there some extra flow was finding its way in. The surface was a rippling web of criss-crossed wave patterns.

Hamish had moved in front of them and was directing the way, the flashlight creating a bobbing pool of brightness. Don turned his head for a moment to look back. Lord Jericho had appeared on the ledge, hurrying quietly after them. He was weaving a little as he moved—the effort of lifting that door must have taken its toll. Don slipped, almost stumbled, and turned his attention back to the job of carrying Ellie. He and Roger were managing fairly well, with Ellie's arms supported across their shoulders and a spare blanket holding the main weight of her body. Roger's face looked gray in the reflected light. He was almost ready to collapse. The fight with Petherton and the all-night journey had drained him of energy. Don thought of the narrow passages ahead and wondered how they could get through them carrying Ellie.

With half his attention on her, he was taken by surprise when Hamish stopped with a sudden groan of dismay and fear.

"For God's sake, Hamish, don't do that." Don had almost gone off the ledge in the attempt to avoid walking into him. "What are you stopping for?"

"Ahh—it's uh, uhh—" Hamish stood petrified, staring

along the ledge. Fifteen yards in front of him a white form had slipped into the flashlight's beam and was standing motionless on the broad ledge. The deep-set eyes gleamed catlike in the darkness.

Beside Don, Roger grunted in disbelief.

"Petherton!"

The creature was changed but not yet unrecognizable. It was naked, and the white legs had begun to atrophy and lose muscle like the limbs of a bedridden ancient. But the midsection and chest were powerful and well-fleshed, a match for the thick, smooth-muscled arms and strong neck.

Roger stooped to lower Ellie gently to the floor, then took a step forward. It took a positive effort of will to make his legs obey him, even though Petherton showed no signs of attacking. He was thoughtfully rubbing with clublike fingertips the red line of a recent knife wound below his heavy rib cage. The skin of his head and torso was covered with droplets of salt water, as though he had emerged from the pool only seconds before. Roger saw with horror that the lower belly wore only shrivelled remnants of genitals. The scrotum was empty and the penis shrunken and insignificant.

"Get out of the way." Roger lifted the poker he was holding to make sure the creature in front of them saw it. "We're coming through. Don't try and stop us; we have weapons and we'll use them."

Beside him, Hamish had backed up a couple of paces and nervously raised the iron tongs to shoulder height. Petherton shook his head. The sound that came from the wide mouth was thick and garbled, a sneering grunt of dismissal.

"Come on, Hamish. We can handle him—he's unarmed." Roger looked around for a moment to Don and Lord Jericho. "You're the rear guard—come on in if we need you. Ellie'll be all right there for a couple of minutes. Ready, Hamish?"

"Wait, we canna go there." His voice was quavering. "We can't go agin yon—yon—"

"We have to," said Roger. He began to move forward, the ledge close to his right hand. In the confined space he hoped that there would be room enough for a free swing with the poker. Hamish was inching along, half a pace behind. As they came closer Roger could see that Petherton's skin was still scarred and mottled, peeling away from babylike pink skin beneath.

Roger judged the distance carefully, and as soon as he was within reach he flailed forward with the poker. It caught Petherton square across the right shoulder, cutting into the skin and crushing the bone. Petherton gave a high-pitched whimper of pain and tried to grab at the poker with his left hand. Roger danced back out of reach, raising the poker again for another blow.

As he did so, Hamish moved forward. He had the tongs high above his head for a killing blow on the domed center of Petherton's hairless skull. The tongs weighed at least ten pounds, solid iron bars with sharp metal claws. He was already bringing them forward with all his strength behind them when two things happened. Petherton lifted his hand as though asking for mercy, and the wide mouth opened to speak.

"Hamish Macveagh."

The words were slurred and twisted, as though the throat was losing the power of speech. Hamish hesitated for a second, amazed to hear his own name.

It was long enough. Petherton took a rapid step forward, wrested the tongs easily from Hamish's grasp, and with the same movement smashed him away over the edge with a sweep of his arm. Hamish managed to convert the fall to a jump and land on his feet ten feet below, but his momentum was enough to carry him off the lower ledge and into the water beside it.

At the same moment as he met the surface, the watchers on the ledge heard a shout of rage from behind them. Jamie MacPherson, fully human in dress and appearance, stood at their rear, moving smoothly toward them while Petherton, tongs gripped in one strong hand, stood to block the other direction.

Hamish had found his feet and was standing chest-deep in the water. The chill had him shivering and spluttering, but he could see clearly what was happening on the ledge above. He waved his arms.

"Laird Jericho! Mr. Willis! Jump for it, this way. It's not too far to drop."

Don turned to look at Petherton and Jamie. The latter had no weapon, but he had stripped off his jacket and wrapped it around his arm to muffle blows. He looked light on his feet and completely confident.

"Jump!" Hamish was hopping up and down in the dark water. "It's your only chance. Ye have t' do it."

"We can't leave Ellie," Don called back to him.

"Ye'll have to. Hurry, noo, while there's time. Here, I'll catch her if ye want to throw her doon here."

As he spoke he began to wade back toward the lower ledge. The current was slow, and he was making good progress. Suddenly, when he was only ten feet from the edge, the water near him swirled with a swift pattern of spreading ripples.

Hamish stopped, stumbled, and looked uncertainly down into the water. All at once he began to scream and writhe. He seemed to be trying desperately to force himself forward, but he was making no progress. After a few seconds something thick and white slipped up from under the water, attached itself to his chest, and dragged him under.

The surface of the pool splashed and shivered with the desperate struggle going on below. Hamish broke to the surface again, screaming and gasping for air. He was beating frantically at the surface with a hand from which blood was pouring, and his other arm was spouting crimson from a ragged stump. In spite of the gaping wounds on his face and neck he made another effort to force his way to the safety of the ledge. He progressed a few feet, almost close enough to grasp at the edge, then the white arms curled smoothly around his body and inexorably pulled him down. Within a few more seconds the surface of the pool was calm.

The action on the upper ledge was frozen. Lord Jericho, Don, and Roger stood in a tight circle around Ellie's unconscious body, facing outward. Don had taken out the knife from his jacket, and Jericho and Roger were gripping the rake and poker, ready to jab or swing with them. For a moment Petherton and Jamie seemed in no hurry to attack.

"What was that?" Don had turned to Roger in disbelief. "What lives down in that pool?"

Roger was shuddering. "Selkies," he said softly. "The Elders—the form Petherton is changing to now. I knew they had to spend more time in water after Second Change, but I never dreamed it went this far. Poor Hamish, we couldn't do a thing to help him."

"They live down there?" Don was looking down at the

410

quiet pool, suddenly alert. "You think the Elders are in the pool?"

"Never mind the Elders." That was Lord Jericho from behind them. "Worry about us. What do we do now? It's a standoff; they've got both ways blocked, and we can't stay here forever."

"I know." Don stepped forward. "You hold them off here and look after Ellie—I know one way to break a deadlock."

Before Roger or Jericho could restrain him he moved to the edge of the ledge, went to a sitting position, and pushed off to drop heavily to the lower shelf of rock. Then he was up and running along it toward the sluice gate at the far side of the cave, keeping always well away from the rippling surface of the pool.

For a few seconds the others watched him in bewilderment. Then, as his objective became clear, Jamie gave a bellow of rage and moved to the edge of the rocky platform. By that time Don was at the gate, heaving with all his force on the side chains. The heavy timbers were secured by iron pins, with one massive master cross-pin that would release the whole structure. Don strained to raise it, feeling the pressure of water on the other side of the gate working against him. The sluice was massive, five feet high and built of baulks at least eight inches thick, but fortunately the pins had been kept clean and free to move. The master pin suddenly slid up a couple of inches under his desperate jerks.

By then, Jamie was jumping down to the lower rock shelf and Petherton had begun to move forward to follow him. Looking down at the surface of the water, Don saw pale shapes moving toward the gate. He forced himself to ignore them and to focus all his strength on the metal bar in his hands. Another heave, and the pin was slipping up again, inch by reluctant inch. And now the force of the water was working for him, squeezing the tapered pin and helping it move upward against the clamp.

Jamie was only feet away. Don saw that the pin was buckling under the weight of the gate and the pressing tide behind it. He jumped to one side, grabbed the knife from his jacket and prepared to fight for his life. But Jamie must have realized that he could gain little advantage by attacking Don: the sluice was slowly creaking open, the metal fastening screeching as the thin end was sheared through. Instead,

Jamie jumped to the gate, put his shoulder against it, and made a terrific effort to push it back far enough to let the pin slide home again into its holder. He was a second too late. The ends had sheared off. Under the weight of many tons of water, the massive gate was opening.

Jamie dropped into the waist-deep water, put his great arms against the sluice, and pushed with all his strength on the baulks of timber. It was useless. The force of the rising tide eased him back, slowly and effortlessly, inch by inch, until he was between the sluice gate and the chest-high ledge of rock.

By the time he realized the danger it was too late.

Don watched as the racing tide pushed the gate open farther, pressing in on Jamie's pinioned body. It was slow—many seconds from the moment when Jamie's back met the immovable rock to the beginning of the groan of agony. The murderous compression continued, inch by inch. It ended with the collapse of Jamie's rib cage, with a spout of blood from ears, nose, and open mouth that cut off his final terrible scream. His eyes started from their sockets in the last moment of intolerable pressure, then his head lolled forward onto the top of the sluice gate.

Don heard a horrified groaning by his side. The Guardian had failed in his duty, and Petherton, arriving too late, had been forced to watch Jamie's final moments while he stood on the ledge, impotent to help. Now he came forward and reached for Jamie's crushed body. As he passed Don brandished his knife. Petherton gave him one contemptuous backhand blow that flung Don back and smashed his head brutally against the rock wall; then the Selkie slipped into the water to try to free Jamie's body.

As he stood there waist-deep, the full tidal race arrived. It poured in tumultuous flood through the open sluice, a foaming torrent of turbulent water, and rushed on along the length of the pool. Petherton was seized in its grip, his heavy body lifted and carried helplessly through the cave. He reached for a snag of rock, clung there one-handed for a few seconds until a crossing wave crest hit him, then was borne on in the middle of the torrent. Roger and Lord Jericho, watching from above, saw the thick torso sucked under in the vortex that had formed at the end of the cave.

The tidal wave bore was scouring deep under the shelf of

rock and flushing out the secret depths. Scores of struggling white shapes appeared, to flail helplessly as they were battered and crushed against the rock ledges. They were legless and neuter, ovoid bodies with serpentine arms and bulging heads. One by one they vanished into the foaming whirlpool, until the pool beneath was empty of life.

Don lay unconscious where Petherton's blow had left him. The tide was tugging at his body, lapping higher on the ledge. Already his head was partly under water.

"Stay here," shouted Roger above the noise of the rushing tide. "I'll have to get him—he'll be gone in another minute."

Lord Jericho nodded his assent. As Roger ran unsteadily along the upper ledge, Ellie's eyes opened, and she began trying to sit up. Lord Jericho, his attention split between her and Roger, wrapped the blanket around her and directed the beam of his flashlight down to the lower cave.

It was going to be close. Don's head was now completely immersed, and his body was beginning to lift and move in the tug of the rising current. Roger was staggering dizzily along the path to the lower ledge, skidding and veering along the uneven surface. Then he was splashing along the narrow shelf, hugging the wall until he could at last reach down and drag Don's body away from the edge.

He started on the upward path and used his remaining strength to pull Don a few feet along the rising incline, then paused and leaned against the rock wall. The white foaming waters seemed to be running their pattern inside his head. There were streaks and burst of light there, dazzling and confusing.

Roger tightened his grip on Don's unconscious body and waited for the dizziness to pass. It was another precious thirty seconds before he could summon the strength to haul Don the rest of the way up to where Lord Jericho was waiting.

"You go back and look after Ellie," Lord Jericho shouted. "She's coming round now. I'll see to Don."

Roger nodded. "I don't think he's breathing—he was a long time with his head under."

Jericho did not reply. He had turned Don over and was pumping his chest, leaning low and forcing air in and out of his lungs. After a few seconds Don coughed twice and began to vomit seawater from his mouth and nose. Lord Jericho

413

groaned with relief and went on with the forced respiration. For the first time he could pay attention to the ugly wound on the back of Don's scalp. It was three inches long and deep enough to show the bone. He touched it gently, feeling around the gash.

"How is he?"

Roger was standing in front of him, supporting Ellie.

"Breathing—but I think he may have a fractured skull. It doesn't look good." Lord Jericho nodded at Ellie. "She's awake, eh? Can she help us get Don out of here? He'll have to be carried, and you look as though you're ready to pass out."

Roger was shaking his head. "Look at her, Joshua. Look at her eyes."

Jericho straightened up and followed the beam of Roger's flashlight. Ellie's pupils were contracting in the glare, but the eyes were as blank and mindless as a pair of brown buttons.

"Can she walk?"

Roger shrugged. "If you lead her. Watch."

He took a couple of steps along the ledge. Ellie followed him docilely, her hand flaccid in his grip. The blanket draped around her was hanging loose, but she made no attempt to cover herself.

"We'll have to manage them between us," said Lord Jericho. "It's not safe to leave either one down here. How are you feeling?"

"Not good. Pretty near done in."

"Right. You give me a hand to hoist Don up on my back, then lead the way—we'll have to try to get out the way Jamie came in, it'll be all flooded down there. If Ellie will keep walking, tow her along behind you."

They hoisted Don onto Lord Jericho's back, his arms and head hanging down. Roger took Ellie by the hand, wrapped the blanket closer around her, and led the way up. As they passed the chamber where she had been imprisoned, he looked at his watch and shook his head.

"Do you realize we've been down here less than an hour?"

"Aye. Keep moving, Roger, fast as you can. Don't stop for anything."

He bit back the next words. It would do Roger no good to know that Don's breathing was becoming faint and irregular.

414

This was no way to handle somebody with a head injury, but what options did they have?

Lord Jericho tried to ignore his aching legs and plodded single-minded after Roger. For the first time in thirty years, he regretted that JosCo had won a contract.

CHAPTER 27

Snatches of phrases at first:

". . . easy once we're this far . . . have to get the door open ahead of time . . ."

". . . everythin' set in the 'copter 'fore we go . . ."

". . . better by car . . ."

". . . see how them second opinions look . . ."

The words had been brushing past for minutes, hushed tones that lingered just beyond comprehension. Drifting in and out of sleep, Roger caught them through a narrow, shifting window of consciousness.

Finally, a deep growl. A mention of his own name. A pleasant and pungent smell. The combination woke him fully, and the voices focused into clarity.

". . . all afternoon," said Mary's voice—a long way off.

"No harm in that. He looks all right." Lord Jericho. Close. "Needs the rest. Didn't want to drag him back down there wi' me, not in his condition. Eh, now, speak of the devil. I think he's awake." Jericho raised his voice. "Roger? How do you feel, then?"

Roger squinted up at the overhead light. He turned his head toward the voice. Sitting a few feet away in a well-stuffed armchair, Lord Jericho held a steaming and aromatic cup of coffee. He was watching Roger closely.

The armchair was flanked by two enormous dogs. One of them, a well-mixed mongrel, lay quiet with head on paws. The other was a straight cross of Border Collie and Alsatian. It was muttering to itself and moodily licking its back leg.

Slowly, Roger sat up. His legs felt like logs.

Where the hell was he?

A rumpled blanket covered his body. He had no recollection of its arrival—or of his own arrival. He looked across at the window and saw that it was already late afternoon, gray light fading to early dusk.

By the fireplace, Mary squatted on her knees, sweeping ash from the hearth and then reaching up to straighten the ornate clock on the mantelpiece. The fire irons were back. Mary placed them by the brass fender; tongs, poker, rake.

Roger rubbed a hand across his eyes. His mouth felt dry and wretched, his voice unwilling to produce sound. "How did I get here?"

Mary stood up and moved closer. She smiled down at him, her blond hair hanging loose past her shoulders. The long green housecoat showed her full body to its best advantage tho thought rose irresistibly in Roger's drowsy mind, she looked beautiful.

"You've been here since this morning," she said. "After breakfast you just passed out. Nobody wanted to wake you."

"You were done for," added Lord Jericho. He was wearing a borrowed overcoat that hung on him like a wrinkled sack, its lower part splattered with mud and water. "You shovelled in enough food for two, then yer passed out. Comin' back to you?"

"I s'pose so." Roger yawned, and the tender skin on his left cheek tightened painfully. "I didn't *want* to go back to sleep, I remember that much."

"Aye. You wanted to be off back to the caves. I reckoned we'd manage well enough wi'out wakin' yer. Me an' these two"—he nodded his head at the dogs—"an' a couple of bobbies from Golspie, we decided we'd manage. Went down at one o'clock, after lunch, an' only got back half an hour ago."

Roger tried to stand up.

Dizziness, whirling in his head.

The caves, the sluice, the last meeting with Petherton.

It rushed back all at once. He dropped to the couch.

"Roger." Mary moved to his side.

"I'm all right."

"Can I get you anything?" She was alert, her eyes bright and troubled.

"No." Roger looked around the room. "Don, and Ellie . . ."

"Still upstairs. Don't worry, there's a nurse with them.

417

They'll be off in a few minutes, as soon as JosCo's helicopter gets here."

"Off? Where to?"

After a moment's silence, Lord Jericho stood up and moved over to look down at him. "Hospital. I'm havin' 'em flown down to Edinburgh. Friend of mine, Billy Westcott, he says he'll have a look at 'em."

"Sir William Westcott?"

"Aye, I reckon that's the one. Still Billy to me—I knew him when he'd no backside to his breeches. He'll take good care of 'em." He paused. "Did yer hear the diagnosis?"

Roger shook his head. He glanced over to Mary. He could not read her expression, but on the surface she was calm and unworried.

"Nothing definite yet," Lord Jericho continued. "So mebbe we should wait an' see what Billy says. Ellie's awake all right, but there's something wrong with her. Acts like she's not all there—you know, the way she was down in the caves. They want to run tests on her. No sign of injury, I've seen nothin' like it before."

"What about Don?"

"Aye. We-e-ell." A shrug, and a rub at the bald head. Even before he asked, Roger had sensed that Lord Jericho would rather avoid that subject. "Don, that's another matter. The doc won't give us a real answer. It's a bugger. Don was under water an' not breathin' for quite a time. An' he's got a hairline fracture on the back of his skull. Concussion for sure. If he didn't get enough oxygen after he was knocked out . . ."

"Brain damage?" Roger found it hard to say the words. "They think Don might have brain damage?"

"Can't rule it out," said Lord Jericho unhappily. "But you know how doctors go on, they won't give anythin' definite. Might be some brain damage from anoxia, an' nobody'll be sure until the concussion's gone." He shrugged. "I want to hear what Bill Westcott says before I go any further."

Roger had kept his eyes on Mary. Now she sat down beside him and folded her hands on her lap. He reached out to touch them.

"Mary, I'm sorry. I wish I could do something. I've been lying here, while you—"

"Hush now." She patted his hand. "You've done so much

418

already, it if wasn't for you . . . I'm sorry, I don't want to think about it."

But her voice was calm and matter-of-fact. Roger marveled at her control. Was she preventing a breakdown by walling herself off with rigid self-discipline? God knew what she'd been through recently. Roger couldn't bear to think what could have happened to her, what had happened now to Ellie and Don, her closest friend and her husband. He turned to Lord Jericho.

"Joshua, what did you find down there? It's hard to believe that those creatures exist at all, but if there's more of them we've got to get them."

"Aye, I knew you'd be askin' me that." Jericho sighed. "I've not got as good an answer as I'd like. It looked like they were killed off last night. Every one of 'em. The whole cave is washed clean. Where the water took 'em it would smash 'em on the rocks, then out to sea. I can't see anything livin' in last night's gale, not wi' the way the waves was crashing on those cliff walls."

"But what about the places above high tide? Did you look there?"

"Aye, course we did. Not a sign. Ginnie and Monty here"—he gestured at the two dogs, who pricked up their ears at their names—"they weren't happy down there, growlin' an carryin' on all the time, but they didn't find anythin'. Not a smell, not a sign. The Selkies are gone."

Roger leaned forward to rest his head in his hands. "Joshua, we have to find them—if they're all dead, we have to get at least *traces* of them. We've so many questions left unanswered. If human women bore their children, why didn't we hear about it ages ago?" He straightened his back, and winced at the stiffness there. "This thing isn't over until we know how they could make a woman keep their secret. And how does a young Selkie get passed off as a normal human baby?—the mother must help it for a while, at least until the First Change that Knowlton talked about. God knows how many children, now . . ."

"Don't worry, Roger. We'll keep on lookin'. But it's not top priority for us. Don an' Ellie come first. Everythin' else is farther down on the list. Y'know, I'm havin' trouble getting the police to take any of this seriously. They look at me as though I'm going daft when I tell them how Hamish was killed. I can see their point. No body to show them. We go down there an' all we find is junk—old bottles, an' bundles of old clothes. So I tell 'em the caves was full of monsters, an' they killed Hamish an' bashed Don on the head. Imagine how that lot sounds to somebody who spends their life worryin' about wife-beatin' an' maybe a bit of burglary."

He stood up wearily. "I'm tellin' you, we've a long haul ahead of us before people believe us. Unless we find somethin' more definite, it's just us, our word. And Don's, when he recovers."

If he recovers. The unspoken thought flashed between the two men.

"You keep Mary company for a minute while I look upstairs," said Lord Jericho. "I want to see if we're ready to leave there."

His heavy tread on the stairs seemed to leave an uneasy silence separating them.

Roger started to speak, suppressed his real question, and nodded instead at Mary's foot. "How's that burn feeling?"

She shrugged. "Not important. Roger?" Her voice was low and hesitant. "Roger, I don't know how to talk to Lord Jericho about this, but I talked to the doctor, too. He says Don may never be normal—may have been in the water too long. We won't know until he recovers consciousness. Days, maybe weeks. I have to prepare for the worst."

Roger nodded. He struggled against the feelings that her closeness aroused in him. The faint, pleasant perfume she wore called him back to more cheerful days, when they first met in London. He wanted to comfort her, to carry her back to that happy time.

Guilt filtered through desire. What made him think this way, with Don still unconscious upstairs?

He coughed. "Prepare for the worst and hope for the best. I'm sorry, platitudes won't help, will they? Take that one back."

It was hard to face her steady gray eyes.

"Look, you have to give time a chance. You know, Mary, Don has to get better at his own speed. Even if it does take months, there's no harm in that. Just don't rush to a wrong conclusion. Suppose it does take months—"

"I'm prepared for that." Her quiet voice cut off his words.

Another long silence. Roger could hear Lord Jericho

420

clumping about upstairs, exchanging occasional gruff words with the nurse.

"Did Joshua say anything else about Don?" asked Roger at last.

"Only that I shouldn't worry about money. There's all we need for treatment and convalescence, no matter how long it takes."

"That's Joshua. He means it, too."

The heavy footsteps overhead moved to the stairs. Suddenly aware of how close he had moved to Mary, Roger leaned self-consciously away as Lord Jericho came down into the room. The two dogs thumped a greeting as he walked over to the couch.

"Well, all ready up there," he said. "Mary, I have to go back with the 'copter and talk to Westcott, tell him how Don got hurt. He wants every detail. We'll have Don and Ellie in there, too, an' the nurse an' the stretchers as well. It'll be full up. I've got a car on the way here, an' I think we'd do better if you follow us down by road. It'll be here in a few minutes. You come, too, Roger, if you want to."

Lord Jericho was rubbing his hands together uncomfortably. If there was really bad news, he was looking for some way to cushion it for Mary.

Roger knew him well enough to help out. "I'd like that. Mary and I could drive down together, maybe."

Lord Jericho looked at him gratefully. "Think you're fit enough to give us a hand movin' the two of 'em down? Stairs are awkward at that turn."

"I'm feeling a lot better. I'll be glad to help."

As Roger followed Lord Jericho up the old stairs, he took a quick look back at Mary sitting on the couch. She seemed deep in thought, her hair fallen forward to shroud her face.

Upstairs, Ellie was sitting in an upright chair, staring straight ahead with her hands on her knees. She did not move as they came into the room.

"Come on, Ellie," said Lord Jericho gently. "Time to go." He reached out and took her hand. She rose without speaking. Even though he stood in front of her she did not acknowledge Roger's presence. As Lord Jericho led the way to the door she followed quietly.

Roger watched them leave. Ellie's movements were strangely tight and mannered, as though every step required a

421

conscious command to be carried from brain to limbs. It was painful to watch. Roger stepped through into the other bedroom and found the nurse sitting by Don's bedside. A dark-haired woman in her early thirties, she was red-cheeked and heavily built.

"Has she been like that all day?" Roger jerked his head back to the other room.

"Aye. There's been no change. She's had a bad shock, she has." The nurse shook her head. "I've seen it like that afore. No way of knowing when she'll come out of it." She reached forward and turned back Don's blanket. "He's all dressed. I wanted to keep him nice and warm 'til we were all ready to go."

"How is he?"

She shook her head. "Best if I don't guess. He's stable, that's as far as I'm qualified to judge. Terrible shame, and him with such a nice, pleasant wife."

Don lay on his back, arms and legs straight and loose-jointed. A spotless dressing covered his entire scalp, extending down to just above his eyes. Roger leaned close. He fancied he could see a dullness, an emptiness that already lay across Don's features. Was it imagination?

"Don?"

The nurse shook her head. "No good trying that, sir. It's too soon. The doctor did a couple of things, just try-and-see, like, but he said even if everything comes back to normal it will take a few days before we see him waking up."

She moved to the bottom of the bed, carefully lifted Don's legs, and swung them to one side. "Give me a hand with that end, and we'll manage easy. He's big, but there's a knack to it. You lift as I tell you. We'll have him downstairs before you know it."

Roger slipped his hands under Don's arms, leaning forward to take the weight. He found himself staring at the closed eyes and wondering what lay behind them. Was it the Don Willis he knew?

They moved slowly and carefully down the curving staircase. The nurse directed Roger's movements tersely and competently. Mary had opened the front door and they were able to carry Don straight outside.

Last night's wind had dropped away to nothing. The helicopter waited now under a low cover of flat, sullen clouds.

Ellie was already comfortably tucked into a folding bunk inside the cabin. Lord Jericho and the nurse made sure that Don was safely housed in a second bunk, then Lord Jericho came back to the cabin door. He gazed down at Mary and Roger standing together a few feet away.

"Car ought to be here for you any minute. Matson saw it when he was flyin' in here. Are you comin' down to Edinburgh, Roger?"

"I don't know. I wouldn't mind staying here for tonight."

"Aye, that might be best. You still look a bit battered. All right for him to make himself at home, isn't it, Mary? No point rushin' around 'til you're better."

Lord Jericho pulled his old hat lower on his head. He looked about him uncertainly, delaying the moment of departure. The rotors were beginning to turn. He stepped reluctantly back into the cabin.

"Well. We'll be off, then. See you soon."

A final wave from the cabin. Roger and Mary stepped well clear for the take-off as the helicopter revved its engines and lifted away into the dusk. One minute more and it was gone, swallowed up by a low cloud bank. The air became strangely quiet, with no wind or sound of breakers from the sea.

They walked side-by-side to the house. Mary led the way in, and they sat quietly down on the couch in the same position as before. Now that the other people and the two dogs had gone, the old building was silent and depressing.

"We've used the last of the milk," said Mary suddenly. "If you stay here . . ."

"Oh, I dare say I'll manage without for one night." Roger kept his voice light and cheerful. "Mary, do you have any real plans made? You'll need something to do while Don's getting better, but you may not want to stay here. It's a long way from hospitals and good doctors."

"I won't stay here." Preparing for the drive down to Edinburgh, Mary began to braid her hair. Her voice was calm. "I like Laxford, but I won't stay here."

"I suppose that's natural." Roger hid his own disappointment. "You want to be back in the States with your relatives, eh?"

"The States?" Mary showed her surprise in the quick movement of her head. "No, I wasn't thinking of going there, not for a while. We've nobody to rush back to. It's nice in

423

this country. I just meant we won't stay *here*, in Laxford. We need a peaceful place. We'll not find that here, not with Hamish dead and—and everything else that happened."

"So. Where to, then?" Roger picked at nonexistent lint on his trousers, then continued in a low voice. "If you've no special place in mind, I've got a suggestion. I have a cottage down in Sussex, quiet and a few miles from the coast. If you'd like it, it's yours. For as long as you like."

"No." Tiny frown lines appeared on Mary's forehead. "I said I don't want to stay here. But I love the sea." Her eyes stared off into the distance. "I want to be somewhere on the coast. Maybe Wales, or Cornwall, or somewhere in western Ireland. Somewhere peaceful, a place where I can look after Don without people poking their noses in on us all the time. A place for Ellie, too—she has nobody in New York, and she'll need to be looked after. I want her to stay with us, as long as she needs to."

"You'll try and look after her yourself—look after both of them? You'll need help."

"I'll manage." She smiled at him. "You see, Roger, I've never been in a position before where I've actually been *needed*. It makes me feel—you know—worthwhile, in a strange sort of way. I have something to do now, and it's important, really important." She rested her hands lightly on her lower abdomen. "I've never had that before, Roger. Never."

Roger looked at her rosy cheeks and smiling eyes.

"Mary." He seemed to lurch into speech. "Mary, you're a wonderful woman. I've thought that since I first met you. You'll do a good job, I know it. But who'll take care of you, and keep you company?" He reached forward and took her hand. "Who will you talk to, and who'll worry about you? Mary, we all need somebody. Somebody to help."

"No, Roger." She drew her hand away, and her voice sounded suddenly childlike. "Thank you. I understand, but I need to be alone for a time, to understand myself. Get to know myself again. I'll be fine, don't you worry." She cocked her head slightly as though listening hard. "Is that the car arriving?"

She stood up and went to the window. Her packed bag already stood by the door, and she took her heavy top coat and scarf from the stand in the entrance hall.

Roger walked hesitantly to her and stood behind her.

"Mary?"

She turned and they stood eye-to-eye. He tried to read her expression and her emotions, but it was like looking into two gray clouds, soft and deep and enigmatic.

"Mary. Remember we're here. Joshua—he likes you, and he likes Don. He'll do anything you need. And I'm here, too." He put his hands lightly on her shoulders. "I care about you, Mary. A lot. If you ever give me a call, I'll come running. Don't forget that."

He was staring at her intently, willing her to understand. Under his direct gaze she suddenly shivered and looked down.

"Roger, please." Her voice was husky. "Not now, I can't handle it. I feel too vulnerable."

He sighed and let his hands fall to his sides. Not looking at him, Mary slowly wound her scarf around her neck.

"You don't have to worry about me, Roger. I'll promise you this. If things don't work out . . . as I hope, I'll ask you for help. I truly will. And I know we'll see each other again." She smiled. "Maybe we can write to each other. I don't know many people over here, do I? Just the ones in Laxford." She pulled open the door, jerking it to free the sticking jamb. "You stay here as long as you want to. It's yours to use."

She stared out, then turned to face him again. "Some other time it might have worked out differently. But now . . ." An odd expression of mixed determination and recollection crossed her face. "Now I have obligations. Promises to keep."

The waiting car had already turned round to face back toward Laxford and the road south. Roger watched as she moved gracefully across the flagstones and opened the rear passenger door. She hoisted her suitcase easily inside. The driver made no move to get out to help her. Roger could see a bulky shape, well wrapped in a thick overcoat and with black gloves and a black cap pulled low over his eyes.

Roger's hair seemed to prickle at the nape of his neck. That heavy body, and the shape of the head . . .

"Mary!" He found himself running fast toward the car. "Mary, for Christ's sake stay *out* of there."

She turned to him in astonishment as he came up to the car door. The driver turned his head. Roger saw a fat-faced young man with pink cheeks and a long and straggly moustache. He was looking very confused as he rolled down the window.

"Something wrong, sir?" said a surprised Lancashire voice. "I mean, do yer want to come along with us? Lord Jericho said you might. There's lots of room back there."

"No, no." Roger stepped back and waved his hand. "That's all right. I got a silly thought there for a moment. I thought you . . . well, never mind that. Off you go, Mary. Maybe I'll see you in Edinburgh tomorrow?"

"Maybe." She smiled, and he leaned inside to help arrange a thick tartan traveling rug across her lower body. "Maybe. Don't worry about me any more. It will turn out all right, I know it inside. It will be all right, I promise you."

When she waved good-bye she was still smiling, leaning back in her seat. Roger watched until the car's lights were out of sight, then took a long look around him. The hills were swathed in fog. They seemed to be asleep, settling in for the long Highland winter. The evening tasted of bracken and salt dampness, and his exhaled breath rose to join the mist around him.

Roger felt suddenly cold and weary. The power plant project would go on, but there was nothing here for him now, no pleasure in the work ahead. He sighed and walked back to the quiet house.

The watcher on the hill stood leaning against a tall rock. He listened to the last growl of the departing car, and watched as its lights were swallowed up in the fog. Then he turned his head slowly to watch the new lights come on in the house on the cliff.

His breathing was hoarse and ragged, an unsteady rise and fall of the heavy chest. After a while he stood upright. Leaning on a thick stick, he moved slowly and painfully through the heather, fighting back the agony of recent wounds.

On a fork in the rough path, he paused.

The fog had folded in tighter on the house. Faint yellow light shone from two of the windows, and a figure stood for a moment there, closing a curtain. Soon it was gone.

The Guardian's grip tightened on his stick. He paused for a minute, considering.

Then he set out on the path that led to the cliff edge and the quiet sea.